I0615928

# Acknowledgements

I have to acknowledge the valued contributions of these beautiful people, who gave me constructive support to put my imagination onto paper.

These are but a few!

My wife Kaye, who although totally confined to her nursing bed, was always there when one of my radical ideas needed airing. Then there were her nurses, Michelle, Donna, and Joyce, who had to suffer the endless readings of the previous day's writings. Still they never lost faith and laughed and cried, in the right parts.

Then there was No.3 Daughter Karin, she unselfishly contributed many hours from her busy days to attend to those administration matters and to correct the many times I stuffed up the computer.

I must not overlook Charmaine, the ever-patient illustrator who spent long hours trying to interpret my imagination, and Anne for her mighty effort to edit my manuscript. A great team.

1

# THE MINER

**A MINE** – an excavation dug in the earth for the extraction of most minerals.

**A MINER** – a person who works in a mine.

# Chapter 1

11 January 1988

.

*The office of an Advisory Company in Perth Western Australia*

Chris stood before the desk of his supervisor, Archibald Graystone. How many times was it this week this had happened? Four? Five? He had lost count.

"Mr Kennedy," Graystone addressed him formally. "I have been reading the copies of the letters you have sent out to the various clients within the last week. How many times do I have to repeat myself? I want to see every piece of correspondence you send out." The supervisor threw a copy of one of Chris's letters onto the desk in front of him. The copy bore many red lines and comments. "Look at this," the supervisor all but screamed. "It is pitiful. Fancy thinking a letter like that would induce the client to invest with us. Well? Answer me!"

"Sir," Christopher answered, "that letter was sent out Monday; this morning I received a call from the company's accountant. The board of his company had reviewed my letter and had agreed to lodge $100,000 with us this afternoon. He has also requested we arrange a meeting to discuss transfer of many of their other holdings. I had only just finished my conversation with him when you called me."

"For an investment by a company of that importance you should have transferred the call to me," the supervisor blasted. "Make sure you do not have any further contact with them without my consent."

Chris was struggling to contain a sharp retort but managed to control his true feelings and *quietly* said, "Sir, if I am to adhere to your wishes, I have to tell you I did accept the accountant's invitation to join them in their private box at the football on Saturday." He was thinking to himself, *"This jerk will stuff up the whole deal, exactly like he did when he stuck his nose into the Smithson Resources deal. I wonder if Mr Jamerson the CEO is free, I had better let him know what is going on. The opportunity to do business with Enterprise Manufacturing is too good to miss."*

"Just go, Kennedy," the supervisor was yelling. "I'll take your place at the football Saturday."

Helen, Jamie Jamerson's PA smiled as Chris walked up to her desk. "Hello Chris, social visit I hope," she warmly greeted him.

"No, Helen. Is the man in?" he quickly asked.

"Yes, Chris," she replied. "Do you want to see him? He does not have another appointment till lunchtime. Hold a moment while I buzz him."

Minutes later, He stood in the CEO's lavish office. "Good morning, Chris. What can I do for you?" the CEO asked. "It is a little unusual for a clerk to call on me without their supervisor. Is it important?"

Chris squared his shoulders and stood straight and tall and answered confidently. "Sir," I recently wrote to a very successful manufacturing company—Enterprise Manufacturing Company—outlining what we could do for them."

"Yes, Chris," the CEO interrupted, "I saw the copy of your letter; it was very good. Any bites?"

Chris did not hesitate and quickly outlined the details of the call from the company's accountant and what had occurred with his supervisor, adding, "I do dislike 'white-anting' him like this, but the transaction must be treated with great care."

"I see that," the CEO replied. He appeared to be speaking his thoughts, and quickly said, "Chris, I want you to take up that football invite. I will sort out your supervisor."

"Thank you, sir," Chris gratefully said, then as an afterthought added, "I am sure I can secure the business."

He turned and was about to leave, but the CEO delayed him by saying, "There appears to be bad blood between you and Mr Graystone, your supervisor; I would like to see it resolved quickly."

That comment made Chris prickle, and he quickly replied, "Sir, I always endeavour to do my part."

He turned and quickly left the CEO's office, but not before he heard him buzz to Helen, "Helen please have Mr Graystone come down here immediately."

Chris was about to resume his seat at his desk; he was just in time to see Graystone rush from his office. He saw him return about ten minutes later. As Graystone was about to enter his office he turned and stared hard at Chris. That look was loaded with malice and hatred. "Looks like I am in for a rough time," Chris thought. "Oh well. I suppose while he is blasting off at me he is leaving others alone.

The afternoon at the football was a great success, and as they were all departing the managing director of Enterprise Manufacturing—the company whose business Chris was targeting—placed a friendly arm over Chris's shoulder and exclaimed, "I see our investments will be in good hands! Well met, young man. Please call just as soon as all the details are available.

Chris worked on the details at home over what remained of that weekend and placed the complete file in his typist Mary's inbox first thing Monday morning. Mary looked at the file and commented, "Had a busy weekend I see, Chris."

"Sure did, Mary. I didn't get a lot of sleep. Please do an extra copy and send one straight down to the CEO's office. The other copy goes direct to Graystone."

"For you, Mr Kennedy, it will be a pleasure. I will have this lot ready by lunchtime—it looks like a good one," she softly said.

The proposal was typed, proof-read, and signed and on the way to the supervisor and the CEO by twelve o'clock. At one o'clock, Graystone literally crashed from his office, shouting, "Has that letter gone, Kennedy? I told you on Friday I want to see everything you write before it leaves the office. Once again this letter is rubbish."

At that moment, Helen walked up. "This is for you, Chris. The CEO is impressed."

The copy Chris had sent to the CEO was marked with numerous notations, each one said either "agree" or "excellent." The handwritten note at the bottom of the letter simply said, "Well done, young man."

Graystone took one brief look at the CEO's copy. He screwed his copy into a tight ball and viciously flung it hard into Chris's face and stormed off.

"How do you put up with him?" Helen commented.

"Easily," Chris laughed. "I just treat his outbursts with the contempt they deserve."

Never-the-less, he had a hard day and as he walked to his bus stop that evening, daydreaming a little, he was thinking, "The sooner I finish my studies the better."

For the previous three years—four nights per week without fail—he had attended the University where he was studying mining engineering. He always had a *bent* for anything geological and would often spend his weekends collecting rocks. Each and every one of his semesters were completed with flying colours. His lecturers and tutors had all agreed he was a natural and all his assignments received high marks. His last paper on geotechnical engineering, had contained some rather radical suggestions and thoughts that he had acquired from those conversations with those advanced mining company people in America. He had modified those conversations to suit Australian conditions. The lecturer had run the suggestions through a lecture group during one of the evening classes. The whole group of students had agreed with the bulk of Chris's suggestions.

It was one of those rather empty nights in his week. "No lecture tonight, so I might duck over and see my sister," he thought. "I haven't seen her for over a month and I do not feel like sitting in my small apartment by myself again tonight."

His apartment was small, cold, sparsely furnished and impersonal. It had served him for two years only as a place to sleep. Most of his meals were eaten at one of the numerous cafes that dotted the suburb nearby. He had long dreamed of something better. "That sister of mine will hammer me again about getting a permanent girlfriend. I would, if I could afford one," he laughed to himself. He changed from his one suit and drove his very old car very carefully to his sister's house, hoping all the time it will make it.

His sister smiled as she opened the door and after giving him a warm hug of welcome laughingly said, "I have a large roast leg of lamb for dinner; would you stay and eat with us?"

His big sister was an excellent cook, so he had no hesitation in accepting the invitation.

After a pleasant evening with his sister and her husband he returned to his depressing apartment. As he showered and crawled into his cold bed he rather bitterly thought, "Things must surely get better."

About that time, things did not get any better; in fact, they seemed to deteriorate. His car broke down on the way to his lectures, the landlord put up his rent, two of the best men in his department left. They confidently told Chris, they had had a "gut full" of Graystone, and although it was not over those men leaving, Chris had an intense argument with Graystone, culminating in the supervisor blasting at him, "If you don't like the way I do things just get out! Just leave!"

Chris was most distressed over the whole incident; he felt all his efforts over all those years to be appreciated had been wasted. His attention to his studies waned, and his health deteriorated.

Rex, his elder brother, was an economics graduate and was the senior partner in Kennedy and Dixon—a very successful accounting firm, of high repute. Being a particularly observant person, Rex had become increasingly aware and concerned with what was happening to his little brother, and after work one evening approach him to try and ascertain what was happening in his life that was causing him so much worry.

Rather reluctantly, Chris tried to tell Rex of his disenchantment with his work environment. Rex was silently astounded with what he was hearing and he admired his sibling for putting up with it for so long. That admiration for "the kid" was further reinforced when Chris had told him he only had eight months to go before he completed his mining engineering studies. However, after that, he still had twelve months of hands-on time with an operating miner before he could graduate and look for a job as a mining engineer.

Rex had not hesitated and quickly said, "You cannot go on as you are; I will help you out of your present predicament. Firstly, you must quit that rotten job, and go to university full-time to complete your studies. I will look after all your expenses while you are at university, and as soon as you are working, doing your final year with the mining company, you can pay me back. Mining engineers get good money, so you should be alright from then on."

Chris breathed a long sigh. At last he could see an end to all his despair. "Thank you for that offer, bro. It is most generous. I will possibly need a few thousand dollars; is that still alright?"

Rex only smiled and place a hand on Chris's shoulder and said, "Little brother of mine, what sort of a brother would I be if I didn't help you in your time of need. Be assured, that amount is no trouble."

Chris was almost emotionally overcome, and stuttered, "Thanks Rex; since it is all right with you, I will take up that offer and will start making arrangements to quit the investment company right away. The thought of not having to put up with Graystone's crap had already made me feel better."


He made a point of being an hour early at the Investment Company office the next day, and by the time the rest of the department staff had arrived, he had cleaned out his personal gear from both his desk and computer files and had hand drafted his letter of resignation. He dropped the draft into his secretary's inbox; it was marked "For your eyes only, Mary. Please type as soon as possible. Thank you."

About ten seconds after she arrived, Mary stood in front of his desk, softly and rather emotionally saying, "Thank you, Chris, I have won the bet, but I'm not really happy to see you're going. You are the best boss I ever had." Her eyes were brimming, and Chris felt the sincerity of her comment.

"Bet? Bet? What's this bet business?" Chris questioned.

Mary was a little hesitant then answered, "Your number two, Alan, has been running a 'book 'on how long you would last—the whole department is in it. After Graystone's outburst last week, I change my bet, from three months, to one week. I knew you had had enough of the rubbish that dickhead handed out to you. The letter will be with you in five minutes. I would love to see Graystone's face when you give it to him."

"Do two copies, please Mary. I will let the CEO have one immediately," Chris quietly added.

Mary took a deep breath and fled. Chris thought he saw a small tear drop from her eyes. The typed letter was on his desk in less than the prescribed five minutes. He signed all copies, marked one CEO, and handed it to his typist, saying "Would you be good enough to look after this for me, Mary." He picked up the original and walked boldly uninvited or summonsed into Graystone's office.

"What do you want, Kennedy? I did not call you," Graystone snapped at him. "Go away—I will call you if I want you."

Chris had difficulty in containing a laugh which was bubbling up inside him, and very loudly said, "You can call until you hopefully choke! I will not be there. Read this you poor excuse for a man and GO TO HELL! I AM SURE THERE IS A SPOT THERE FOR PEOPLE LIKE YOU!"

Graystone's face went through a multitude of colours and expressions and finally resolved itself to settle on a florid red with a gaping mouth. Chris very correctly turned and walked out of that office. He spent half an hour saying goodbye to his work colleagues, picked up his battered briefcase and headed for the lifts. "That's the first bridge crossed," he thought as he waited for the lift. The lift arrived, and he stepped in for the final time. It felt good!

Frederick Riley, his lecturer at the evening classes, expressed his disappointment when Chris advised him he was quitting the night-time class and would complete his course by enrolling in a full-time day class. He was hopeful he could do this.

"It may be a little bit difficult. I will see what I can do to fix it for you, Chris," Riley offered. Lecturer Fred Riley had followed Chris's progress from the very first day he had enrolled for the course to diligently attend those night classes. Riley was impressed by Chris's dedication and obvious intelligence. "I'll see if I can get you into Professor Raymond Strahan's group—he is the best," Riley told Chris. "He has actually worked in several mines, so his experience will be invaluable to you."

Professor Strahan greeted Chris with a warm handshake, and assured Chris his enrolment in the daytime class would be processed "post-haste." "My quota of students is at a maximum," he laughed. "This might tread on a few toes, but I cannot ignore Fred Riley's recommendation. I will squeeze you in somehow."

Chris immediately warmed to Strahan, and quickly said, "I believe I shall enjoy being instructed by you, Professor Strahan."

"You are not here for your enjoyment," Strahan snapped. "You will be coming here to learn. You have chosen a good time to start: the new semester commences next Monday, 830 am sharp, room 76 A."

"Thank you, sir," Chris quietly said. "I will be there." As he walked away from Strahan's office, he was thinking, "That's bridge number two crossed."

Strahan was a hard taskmaster: unless it was perfect it was not good enough. He repeated several times over the course of the semester, "You are responsible for the lives of many men so there is no room for compromise." He hammered this into his students' thinking regularly. By mid-term half the original class had requested transfers to other tutors. Not so Chris: he revelled in Strahan's criticism of his shortcomings and only strived harder for perfection.

They were at the completion of the final term when Strahan called Chris to his office. He addressed Chris in a rather patronising voice—Strahan had come to like this student. "Chris, I have taken the liberty of speaking to a couple of senior engineers I know, from a few of the better mining companies. You will most probably get a call from them with offers for you to spend your practical time with them. Choose carefully, bearing in mind all the theory and exercises of the past four years have only prepared you for what is out there—experience! experience, sir, is what you must acquire and, frankly speaking, I believe that should you continue to apply yourself to obtain this experience you will become a very good engineer."

"Thank you, Professor," Chris humbly replied. "It has been a great pleasure studying under you."

Strahan was smiling broadly, and quickly replied, "You have been a good student, Kennedy. Now go and strut your stuff. By the way, you will graduate with honours."

He did get the offers and chose to go with one large Multinational Group with mines all over the world. Consequently, for the next twelve months he was required to travel with the chief engineer to many parts of the world. Chris matured in both mind and body in that time. He was now a fine specimen of a man, standing about – six feet four; and with strict adherence to a gym routine, he was very fit.

The "Chief" was a very mature fellow, on the verge of retiring. He often shared with Chris much from his mining years and all that had occurred to him. His one major regret was that he had never gone out on his own; he would have liked to have spent some time exploring, discovering, and setting up his own mine.

This "regret" stuck in Chris's mind for some time and became so strong he decided he would not go through life bearing the same regret. He knew full well it would not happen unless he made it happen. To do this he must prepare.

Chris had enjoyed the year with the multinational company. As the year drew to its end, the manager—Herbert Mason—called Chris into his office. "You have shown us you are a very talented young man Chris," he said. "As you are about to complete your studies for you mining degree, we would like to offer you a permanent position on our team. You need not give us an answer immediately, but it would be good if we had your decision by the end of the month."

Chris did spend much time considering that offer; however, the old chief engineer's comment about getting "out" and doing his own thing weighed heavily in his thoughts, until he finally decided that was what he wanted to do. Mason was disappointed with his decision and warned Chris that he had seen many young dreamers embark on the same voyage only to end up bankrupt and often physically broken. Chris thanked him for his advice but stuck to his decision.

He had managed to save a good portion of his earnings and felt a high degree of satisfaction when he found he was able to repay Rex and have a bit left over. Rex had little enthusiasm for his decision, and only said, "I do not like it; but it is your life, and I know you will do with it exactly that what you want to do.

Chris spent many hours prowling through used-car yards and pouring through the used vehicle pages of the newspaper. He finally purchased a twelve-year-old "tray top" Land Rover from a farmer who swore, the "Landy" was in good nick.

He sat by the river for a whole afternoon trying to convince himself to take the next step. With a great deal of trepidation, he finally decided, he would do it! After all what else was there that he wanted to do.

Decision made, he set to, to "equip his expedition." He was no rank amateur when it came to managing money, and within the confines of his budget he managed to reasonably cover the cost of most of his needs. After paying two months rental in advance for the apartment, his bank balance was looking pretty sick. "I think I have kept enough back to cover my fuel costs," he consoled himself.

He had spent considerable time in the Mines Department offices, studying as many maps as he could get his hands on, and resolved that, that area marked as the Outback, looked to have some promise. Full of hope and apprehension he set off.

It took two days for the Landy to lumber the 400-plus kilometres to the first hop on his itinerary: that regional city with a very colourful history, way out there!

He had stopped at the service station about five kilometres short of the city centre to fill up all his fuel tanks, including those two forty-four-gallon drums on the tray. The service attendant was a typical outback sort of bloke, salt of the earth, chatty type of fellow; and more than able to fill him in with much of the local news and gave him a few worthwhile directions.

"There is a turnoff on the right-hand side about 110 k, down the main road," he said. "Not many people use it; it is a dirt road that goes for about twenty kilometres. After that, you will need four-wheel drive. Take care, many people get lost out there."

By nightfall the next night he was many kilometres, "out there." He lay on a bed roll looking up at the night sky. As he looked into that black sky he thought to himself, "There must be one million stars up there—it is so peaceful; I think I am really going to like this." Brimming with contentment, he lay there recalling the recent telephone conversation he had had with his parents.

Chris's parents lived on the East Coast. He spoke with them at least once a month. You could lay money on it that his mother's first question was always, "Have you found a girl yet?" He had called his parents the day before he left the city and was reminiscing over the telephone conversation. Out of context, his mother's first comment was, "Your sisters tell us you have quit your job at the Investment Company and are off working in mines all over the world. Why on earth did you do that? I understood you're well settled and going well. Your father wants to talk to you about this mining business; your great grandfather and his brothers pushed wheel-borrows across the whole country in search of gold."

His father cut across her conversation, his strong voice saying, "Good on you Christopher—that's a good decision, son. My great granddad and his brothers always said there was a fortune out there somewhere waiting to be found. Some of his tales were very vivid. As a boy I sat and listened to them for hours."

"So that's where I got the gene from," Chris laughed. "It has been passed down to me from those old Kennedys."

It was his mother's turn to cut in. "You always were my greatest worry, Christopher. Now you are only going to add to it."

"Please do not worry, Mum," Chris quickly answered. "I have prepared myself. You would be pleased to hear I have completed my university course and am now a graduate mining engineer."

His father was a perspective type, and softly said, "Good luck, son; your great grandfather will be smiling. Take care!"

His mother's agitated voice came again. "Get away you wicked old man; get off the phone. Don't encourage him; I want him where I know he is safe and well," Mum continued, loudly saying, "We have some news for you too: we have sold the farm and have moved to town. The farm was a bit much for your dad to run by himself."

That was a bit of a pointed dig at me," Chris thought as his mother continued, "We have bought the hardware shop in town. Your father has been elected to the Council, so between that and the shop, and with his golf and bowls he is very active."

"What about you, Mum?" Chris had asked.

"Oh, I am all right," she answered. "I am still involved with the CWA (Country Women's Association) and the Red Cross. Church does also take up any spare time. Are you still going to church?"

"No Mum," Chris honestly answered. "I have been very busy."

"That's one more thing to worry about," she cried, then almost as an afterthought very firmly asked, "Are you coming over here for Christmas this year? Your brother and his wife and children and your sisters and their families are, so I am demanding you come to."

"I will try, Mum, I promise," answering with as much conviction as he could muster.

His father had cut in again, saying, "Chris, my boy, I am going to send you five diaries your great granduncle Troy kept while they were prospecting. I am sure you will find them very interesting."

Another week had passed, and now the beaten track was only a vague memory. Never in his whole life had he felt so at peace. This evening he had set up camp adjacent to a patch of gum trees. An inquisitive possum dropped down from out of the gum trees and sat nearby. He tossed it the remnant of an apple he had eaten for dessert, and thought to himself ,*the sailors of old used to say ; when the apple barrel is near empty it is time to turn back; I am not ready to turn back yet, I saw a fairly prominent escarpment on the horizon about sunset; there may be some interesting minerals in the face; I'll have a look at it tomorrow*

Sunrise found him packed up and heading towards that escarpment. As he got closer he could see it appeared to run for a very long distance. "It looks to be at least 200 metres high and bare of vegetation. Obviously, there is a non-fertile surface on top," he thought. He could see that, although nothing grew on the sharp cut-off face of the escarpment, a short area around the base was covered with thick vegetation, even a few trees that were over thirty-metres high. "There must be a bit of water seeping from the base of those cliffs for them to be growing so well." His miner's knowledge was flowing freely. "This whole escarpment is out of character for the region; there are signs of periods of folding and much of the structure is granite and greenstone. Could be some iron ore, dolomite and jaspilite. What a conglomeration. The area must be so old—may even date back to the Devonian era," he thought. His mind had been stimulated, "I'm going to prop here about for a while and look around. I wonder how this was formed? I am thinking it must have been some sort of massive upheaval resulting in the whole escarpment being forced upwards."

In an endeavour to get some protection from the unforgiving sun and wind of the Outback, Chris set up a more comprehensive "camp" in close to the base of the escarpment. He dragged out the second-hand four-man tent he had managed to acquire and set it up. He stood back and looked critically at his handiwork. "Not Buckingham Palace," he laughed to himself, "but it will suffice if I get any weather."

The day was still young. "I have time to explore a little," he decided. He meandered along the base of that monster rock, stopping often to examine an interesting outcrop or deposit. He did not get far. He found the whole face was, too high, too smooth, and no hand or foot holds he could use made it impossible to scale.

After about three hours of this meandering he decided, "It's nearly time to turn back, "it would not be good to be caught out here after sunset; maybe I will keep going for half an hour or so."

No sooner had he made that decision that the escarpment suddenly ceased. Instead of a high cliff face, a drop-off yawned before him. With the greatest of care and more than a little trepidation he crawled to the edge of the drop-off. He could see that the floor of the canyon appeared to be a little over 200 meters below him. It was a verdant green and a reasonable-sized river ran lazily through it. He could barely make out the opposite side of the geological anomaly—it looked to be some fifteen kilometres away. "This is most interesting," he thought. "Tomorrow I will bring some equipment and see if I can climb down into it."

The point where the escarpment ended and the drop-off began was only half a kilometre from where he had stopped and set up his camp. He unpacked the old well-used binoculars he had bought and focused them along the sheer face of the escarpment. The cliffs ran the complete perimeter of the canyon. As he swung his search back he focused a little lower down that sheer face and was looking, about 100 metres along that sheer cliff face, when he stopped in surprise. The river he had seen burst from the cliff face and amidst a cloud of spray, flung itself down into the canyon. "My goodness! How beautiful," he thought. "I must get down there and take a better look."

He walked quickly back to his camp and collected a long rope and returned to the cliff top. He stood for a long moment, looking apprehensively down the cliff face. "I must be mad to think of doing this, tonight, I will come back in the morning; before the day gets too hot," he thought to himself. With the rope slung over his shoulders, he walked slowly along the cliff top, hoping to find a place that would possibly present a climbable route. Before long he found where a section of the cliff top had broken away to create a precarious looking downward access. He watched a wallaby negotiate the jumble of rock and scattered scrub. "I'm no wallaby, but that doesn't look too difficult. I wonder if I should look along a bit further."

He searched further along the cliff top. There were a few places that were perhaps possibilities, however none offered a better way than that first route he had discovered. As he was walking back he took time to look out over the canyon. The scene that opened before him was mind boggling. The floor of the canyon was carpeted in a lush green by the vegetation, growing in profusion protected from the searing Outback winds by the cliffs; green patches of grass dotted the area. All this vegetation thrived on the abundant supply of water from the river. Now he could see it clearly: that river was a little larger than he first thought. It flowed lazily for approximately one hundred metres, in some places forming good-sized pools, before pushing on to flow into a lake, further down the canyon. The lake looked to be about three kilometres long and two kilometres wide. The water in that river and the lake were clear: perfectly crystal clear. "I bet there are fish in there," Chris thought to himself. Using the binoculars once again he could see all the way across the lake to the far side. Water that had escaped from the clutches of the lake emptied out to form another river that flowed towards the far side of the canyon. He could not define what happened to it after that; it appeared to disappear into the cliff face.

He left the rope there and returned to his camp, intending to have a quick meal and have a good night's sleep before attempting that precarious decent. In his excited frame of mind sleep eluded him and he groggily arose before sunrise. The sun had just poked its nose over the horizon when he again stood at *that* cliff-face, looking out over the sinkhole. "This is so beautiful;" he once again thought, and with butterflies in his stomach; and the  rope over his shoulders; he took the first tentative step onto that breakaway section. The rock he stood on slid and slipped a little then stabilised. "I'm going to have to watch my step," he thought and proceeded to cautiously continue his downward climb. After three hours, he had attained a firm ledge, and found he could go no further. He was hot and dust-covered, perspiration was running down his back. "Now what?" he questioned. The ledge he stood on was about 100 feet from the floor of the canyon. "I think my rope is just about long enough to allow me to climb down the rest of the way using it," he decided, "but first I must find a secure anchor point." A large tree root, apparently dragged down when the section of cliff top cliff top collapsed, protruded from the jumble of rock. After testing it for stability, he decided it was suitably secure, and very carefully tied off the rope to it. Next, he stepped to the edge of the ledge, lifted the remainder of the rope from his shoulder and hurled it with all his strength out into the canyon. He stood there watching the rope as it unravelled cleanly and breathed a sigh of relief when he saw that the rope had comfortably reached the bottom. "This is going to be a bit different," he was thinking." I am pretty fit; but I have little experience with rope climbing; this will be a test of my endurance and prove just how fit I really am. I guess if I take my time it will be okay. I see there are a couple of smaller ledges further down; they may afford me an opportunity to take a rest now and again."

Going down that rope for him was not easy. The 100-foot climb took him two and a half hours before an exhausted man had accomplished the descent and had found a seat on a large boulder. After sitting there awhile he once again pulled the binoculars from the small back pack he had carried down the precarious climb and swung them along the cliff face. "It is a good thing that I did apply myself in the geological lectures," he thought. "This area is remarkable. By my guess, over a long time, maybe even millions of years, the river that in those days did flow underground, had eroded out some softer material in the base of the escarpment to form a massive underground cavern, and that some underground phenomenon—maybe an intense earthquake; perhaps it was about the time the escarpment was forced up—had caused the eroded area to collapse in on itself and form this virtual massive sinkhole. That's a wild guess, but for the moment I cannot see any other explanation. What a geological find; I reckon Professor Strahan would give his back teeth to see all this. I bet he would have a better explanation."

He sat for a while as he recovered, threw his small backpack aside, then flopped fully clothed into the clear river. The cold water revived and invigorated him, and he commenced to amble along the riverbank, drank a few mouthfuls of that beautiful water, and chucked a few pebbles at nothing in particular.

He was reaching into the shallow edge of the pool when something caught his eye. "What's that?" he said aloud in his surprise and stooped to pick up an acorn-sized stone. It gleamed yellow and was quite heavy. "This is a gold nugget," his mind registered. He examined that small stone for a few minutes, then dropped it into his pocket and quickly looked about the shallows. There were many more small nuggets sitting there seemingly awaiting his collection. After about ten minutes he had a fine pile of nuggets sitting on the riverbank. "Well! I came out here to look for gold; now that I have found it, what do I do now." His training came to his mind, and he looked to where the river burst from the cliff face. "There must be a deposit in there somewhere; there is a lot of quartz rock in the riverbed, so it will possibly be a quartz reef with a pretty substantial vein of gold in," he excitedly thought. Then, taking a deep breath, tried to rationalise the situation. "This will have to be handled carefully," he thought. "I wonder if a lease or even a license to mine has ever been issued to cover this area. I will have to return to the city and search the records. I wonder if the Mines Department in the regional city has any record covering this area.

After collecting a few more nuggets, he restrained his collecting to "just enough to have them melted into a small bar, and have it analysed for purity, then just go on from what I find there."

With that decision firmly in his mind he packed the nuggets into his backpack and headed back to where the rope lay on the cliff face. The thought of climbing back up that rope, to say the least, did not appeal to him. Despite having those few short rests, he was aching from head to toe from the earlier effort of climbing down. "I do not think I will try to climb back today," he thought. "I will rest tonight and climb back in the morning; hopefully I'll be more up to it then."

He made himself as comfortable as possible and attempted to sleep. Sleep came slowly; however, his weary body did succumb and he slept.

The next morning when he tried to move, every muscle in his body complained. "I cannot just stay down here," he admonished himself. "I must get back up." Getting back up was no easy task. As he attained each of those smaller ledges, he had to sit for some time to recover. It was close to midday when he slowly crawled—totally exhausted—onto that first ledge. "Made it!" his befuddled mind rejoiced. "I'll rest awhile then to continue on. Thankfully, since I do not have need to use the rope, the rest of the way should be much easier." Easier? That was not so. His weakened legs all but refused to push him upwards and by the time he was within reach of the cliff edge he was down on his hands and knees crawling. Five feet to go, he slipped and fell backward, fortunately, only about ten feet, landing heavily on his right shoulder. The pain was unbearable! "I think I have broken it," he lamented. Fortunately, the damage was not that severe, and after twenty minutes of crawling he finally managed to drag himself over the cliff edge. He could only lay there, managing to gather a small amount of strength, then stagger back to his camp. He forced himself to make a meal; he found it difficult to even open a can of mixed vegetables but did manage to heat a cup of water and using a teabag made himself a cup of tea. Feeling a little revived, but still hurting all over he flopped—still fully clothed—onto his bedroll and fell into a deep sleep, waking only once during the night, when he rolled onto the damaged shoulder.

As the pain subsided he tried to look out into the darkness. It was a moonless night and the darkness was absolute. He lay there contemplating his situation for only a few minutes before his exhausted body demanded rest and he fell back into a deep sleep.

The dawn light flooding into Chris's tent wakened him. The dirty be-whiskered man stretched and winced as his damaged shoulder reminded him it was still there. It took a couple of minutes before the pain subsided, and he angrily thought, "I was a blasted idiot to climb down that cliff." Then remembering much of the previous day, he thought, "Still, it was interesting, and I did find those nuggets. Suddenly, it hit him, "Where is my backpack?" He recalled that moment when he had reached the first ledge and had gratefully removed that heavy pack to place it to one side, and in his condition of exhaustion he had not given it another thought. "It's still down there," he cried in anguish. "There is no way I can possibly gather together enough strength to climb back down there to retrieve it. It can just stay there." He very bitterly thought, and growled, "That whole day was wasted; all I have to show for it is this one small nugget I had put in my pocket."

Now completely disillusioned, the very dismal man packed up his camp and decided to head back. "Where am I?" he asked himself. He realised he had no idea—he had meandered, North, South, East, and West, in his travels. "If I follow my tracks that should take me back," he decided, and set off down the track he had come.

The Landy had travelled for just over an hour along those tracks, when it went down. It had happened before so Chris angrily and very resolutely dragged the shovel from the tray and started to dig. This time the vehicle was well and truly dug in; bogged so that both axles sat on the ground. "What next?" the angry man shouted, as he attempted to scrape the loose dirt from underneath the vehicle. It was useless! Several times he stopped digging and attempted to drive the vehicle out of the bog, each time only succeeding in having the vehicle sink further into the loose scree. After digging for a further two hours, now totally exhausted, desperately tried again to drive the recalcitrant Landy free. The motor was screaming, and the clutch burning when he heard a loud thump. Now very concerned, Chris crawled as best he could under the vehicle to try and establish what had caused that noise, and why the Landy now totally refused to move. "Oh struth!" he exclaimed, "I think I've broken an axle. Now what? It looks like I'll have to walk the rest of the way. I wonder how far it is." Panic welled up within him, and he collapsed down, and lay propped against the front wheel.

He roused himself as the sun was setting, made himself a small fire, heated a can of stew, made himself a cup of tea, and tried to rationalise the extent of his predicament. "I could stay here with the Landy, and hope somebody spots me. There is fat chance of that! I haven't seen anybody for weeks, so walk I must."

Without further ado he packed a small sack and set off. After two days, despite his careful rationing, he had consumed his meagre supply of water, and dehydration was setting in. The unrelenting searing Outback heat exacerbated his discomfort. He staggered on, diligently following the Landy tracks. "I know this place," his confused mind recorded, then in a moment of recognition he realised he was following those tracks all right but in the wrong direction—he was back at his campsite at the escarpment. He threw down his now almost empty sack, weekly raised both hands and screamed to the heaven's, only to collapse in the meagre shade of a large boulder. Almost immediately his mind was assailed by a tirade of whispers that increased in volume to a roar. The roaring was now accompanied by a vision of a multitude of screaming, writhing ghostly apparitions that screamed into his mind, demanding he return their treasure and seemed to draw his mind to the edge of the cliff and further demanded he cast his body over. Something in his being rebelled and he screamed with all his might; *"NO! THAT IS NOT FOR ME,"* and struck out at those apparitions, that fled from his mind.

He had no idea how long he lay there before a cool wet cloth was placed over his face, and a few drops of water were being squeezed into his parched mouth. Dark faces, full of concern looked down on him. A deep voice whispered, "The Eulooway have not taken him, he is not dead; see, he is waking up.

Chris tried to sit up but flopped back as he was just too week. Several pairs of strong arms helped him sit. "See! He has beaten the Eulooway," the deep voice came again. "He will survive."

A further small amount of water was placed on his lips. Chris lapped at it, his tongue searching for more.

"No more for the moment, gifted one; you must take it easy," another voice said.

Chris's befuddled mind was trying to take all this in; all he could think was, these dark men had saved him.

A receptacle of some description that contained a further small amount of water was placed in his hand which was guided gently but firmly to his mouth. He tried to pour the water into his mouth, but was restrained, and the deep voice softly came and said, "Steady Abdiel, not yet."

Chris had no idea how long he sat there; from time to time he was being fed increasing amounts of water and then a soft mash of something. He dozed much.

The morning sun woke him. As he stirred, that deep voice he could now ascertain emanated from a smiling black face said, "Good, you are awake. Are you feeling any better?"

Chris's tongue would not work and he simply nodded.

The voice was continuing: "We must go, this is not a good place. It is too close to the home of the Eulooway. We will take you with us. See if you can stand."

By now he was surrounded by six or seven smiling black faces. As he stood he was hit by a spasm of vertigo and staggered forward into the midst of those faces. Strong arms steadied him, giving him time to take a deep breath and allow the spasm to pass. A skin containing water was handed to him, and he drank deeply. The water revived him and he was able to stand by himself.

Another voice laughed, and said, "He is strong; did you see how he pushed the Eulooway from him. He will be able to walk with us."

A little more of that mash and more water and Chris was feeling better. He looked to the nearest face and managed to say, "Thank you."

There were many grunts of approval, and the group dispensed to retrieve their gear, mainly spears, clubs and carry bags. That deep voice firmly said, "We go now; follow us if you want to." The group moved off, with Chris in their midst, being assisted from time to time when he stumbled.

For Chris it was a torturous day. Towards its end, more and more often he fell heavily before those strong arms caught him; each time he fell he was lifted gently back onto his feet, handed a little water, which the group paused to watch him drink, then turned and continued on.

As the sun was setting they stopped; a fire was built and a small skinned marsupial was thrown on it.

One of the dark faces came to where Chris sat, slumped in exhaustion. "We'll be home tomorrow. The women will look after you. I am Marlee; we are of the . . ." he rattled off a name, Chris had no hope of remembering let alone pronouncing. "We had followed your tracks and saw where you entered the home of the Eulooway. We did not expect to see you ever again. No man who had ever entered their home had ever returned, and we were surprised and frightened when you climbed back. You have a very powerful spirit, and it must watch over you and protect you, so that you were able to escape from those dreadful spirits. You are strong, and we have admired the way you fought. Now you must spend time with us and get better. Your name is given; it is ABDIEL. To us that means, HE WHO IS THE FAITHFULL SERVANT OF HIS GOD. Your God must be the most powerful of all to overcome those evil spirits.

Chris was rather overcome with this discourse and softly said, "Once again, I can only say thank you, Marlee. I am not so special; I am only a young man out seeking to find gold. Chris remembered the small stone in his pocket and quickly rummaged in his tattered trousers in search of it. He found it and showed it to Marlee, who instantly asked, with a voice full of horror, "Did you find that in the home of the Eulooway?"

"If you mean, did I find it when I climbed down the cliff? YES! This and many more. I lost the others."

Marlee jumped up shouting, "HE HAS NOT ONLY DEFEATED THE EVIL ONES, HE HAS STOLEN SOME OF THEIR

TREASURE! HE IS EVEN MORE POWERFUL THAN WE FIRST THOUGHT!"

This was all beyond Chris at that time, and exhaustion once again took over and he lay down and fell into a deep sleep, not knowing a runner had been sent ahead to the village to tell the people of him.

Chris was awakened by the arrival of the village people who sat patiently watching him.

"Good morning all," Chris said for want of something to say.

Marlee stepped up and quickly said, "The people have all agreed we must care for you. Our medicine man tells us you will bring us good fortune."

The young miner was becoming more and more confused with all this, and managed to humbly say, "I can only thank you all; I am most grateful to be here and I will do whatever I can to help you."

There were nods of approval all around. The whole community then rose and commenced to walk to what Chris assumed was home.

It was near midday when they arrived at a shaded waterhole. Numerous Mia-Mia (lean-to bark huts.) dotted the banks. "We will live here for a while, Abdiel," Marlee advised him. "The hunting is good, and there is much water."

For the first weeks Chris did very little; he explored the area about camp, then eventually went out with a hunting party. In that time, he had learned much about the Outback and came to believe that it was a wonderful place with many deep secrets. The tribe— they preferred to be called that; Chris was happier, to call them, the People—were astounded when Chris brought down a large kangaroo with a bow and arrow he had made. From then on, he was often invited to join a hunting party. Those hunting parties were always successful.

"See! He does bring us good fortune," one of the elders commented.

Chris lived with the people for almost six months. He learned that many of them had attended the mission school. "Now I understand why you can understand me when I speak," Chris commented. Marlee and the elders of the people would often sit with Chris and tell him of "history" of the tribe. The tribe had existed innumerable years, and once roamed over a greater portion of the Outback, in great numbers. Even before the arrival of the white explorers, sickness had claimed many, and only what Chris could see remained; another small pocket of the people existed. They lived out there, Marlee said; indicating exactly where by waving an arm in the direction of the distant horizon.

Marlee advised Chris that, the terrible white man grog had entered into the lives of most of those people and they barely existed now. In his time with the people, Chris had regained his health, and now was a strapping powerful looking man. He had questioned Marlee of the whereabouts of the "sinkhole."

All Marlee would say was, "It is a place of evil," and would discuss the matter no further. Chris resolved in his mind, that perhaps he had been dreaming, but that small acorn nugget put paid to that line of thinking. He now wore it, hanging on his chest by a strong ligament from some unknown animal.

Chris had become very good friends with the men, women and children of the people—even the camp dogs wagged their tails as he walked by. Marlee advised him the tribe were about to move on. "We do not like to stay too long in the one place; we like to move on before we use up the hunt too much. We will return here later on."

Chris thought about the move for half a day and finally decided it was time to return to his own people. He had given them little thought, and now guilt plagued him. After explaining it to the people, there were reluctant nods of approval all around; they did understand his need to seek his own tribe.

Clad only in a loin cloth of animal skin and carrying his bow and arrows and a water bag he set off to return to *civilization. He* had no fear of getting lost or not surviving—the Outback now shared many of its secrets with him.

It took many weeks to walk the distance back to civilisation. It was only because of his quick reflexes he avoided getting "skittled" when he first walked along the main road he had found that morning. The good hearted truckie offered him a lift which he readily accepted.

After five minutes, the truckie was most surprised to find he had not picked up a native, but a highly-educated white person.

As they travelled, Chris told the truckie his story.

"Holy cow, Kennedy!" the truckie exclaimed after Chris had told him his name and his story. "I had better drop you off the cop shop; they will be very surprised to see you."

The police officer manning the front desk was completely gobsmacked as Chris repeated his story to him. The policeman leaned back in his chair, looking long and hard at Chris, and somewhat hesitantly said, "Kennedy, Kennedy, let's see if we have anything on file. He then thumbed through a rather tattered file for a few minutes, then shouted in triumph, "Here you are: Christopher John Kennedy, mining engineer, missing since . . . GOOD GRIEF MAN!" he shouted, "you were written off as lost over six months ago; not many come back after that amount of time. There are a few numbers here for us to ring, to let them know should you ever turn up."

Rex was quite forthright when he spoke to Chris, even though his voice was full of relief, he very forcibly said, "It's about time you bloody well turned up. I was starting to get a bit worried about you." True to form Rex soon had him organised, and two days later a very smartly dressed, very good-looking man, walked from the arrival tunnel into the city air terminal. Rex was waiting; he did not recognise Chris at first, and when he did he flung his arms about Chris, rather enthusiastically saying, "What have you done to yourself, 'man'? I see your holiday has done you the world of good.

"Some holiday," Chris laughed as he grabbed his brother and returned his hug, all but crushing Rex's ribs. His sisters were there to greet him too. It felt strange to hold a female; he had forgotten just how pleasant it was.

Rex had kept up the rental on his apartment, but Rex's wife very firmly said, "You are to stay with us for a while until you get settled."

It took but a short time for him to fit back into civilisation and living the "white-fella" way. Chris had thought more than once, "I think the people of the Outback have a better lifestyle than this mob. Eventually he returned to his apartment and started searching for a job.

Herbert Mason, the manager of the International Mining Company where he had previously worked was most pleased to see Chris. Mason regretfully advised Chris his Mining Engineering team was full. Chris was about to leave when Mason quickly said,

"Hold a minute, Chris. We do have a vacancy in our research lab. Would that interest you?"

Chris didn't hesitate and replied, "That would be very good, Mr Mason, but you will not forget me if a vacancy occurs in the Engineering team, will you? I am sure I would gain much from a time in the Research Lab learning what they do, and at the same time catching up with anything new." The salary was very good and he was able to save a regular amount.

He made a point of visiting the university to talk with the mining lecturer, Fred Riley, who was most pleased to see him fit and well. "I was quite upset when I heard you were missing," he said. "Was it worthwhile? Did you find anything interesting?"

Chris produced the nugget pendant from around his neck, and showed it to Riley, and related the story to him of how he found it. The bit about the sinkhole and the cliffs did interest the lecturer who asked, "Do you think you could find it again?" to which Chris replied, "I have tried, sir; I spent many days searching for it. The people I befriended would not even think of helping; their fear of the place prevented them from even discussing it. Every time I mentioned it they became most upset. There is so much about their culture that is difficult for us to understand. Maybe one day I will go back and search again."

Chris did enrol for another post-graduate course, to ensure he kept up with what was new in the industry.

The diaries his father had sent him provided him with much evening diversion. Chris was able to fully understand much of the difficulty his great granduncle Troy, and his friends, had had to face. Philosophically he thought, "I know well that man may change, but that place was aptly named, the Outback—it will never change; it will always be harsh and demanding, even to those who love it.

Some of those pages listed the emotions and despair and times of joy of any success's, be they large or small. Many were written daily; others would have a hiatus of days, or even weeks. As Chris read those pages he came to understand those men were tough and uncompromising. They carried their camp in heavy wheelbarrows and relied on instinct and experience to try to establish a hopefully potentially successful mine. Many of their "mines" ended up being nothing but a hole in the ground. Those diaries often recorded the meals of "tinned dog." After a little research Chris found that was tins of bully beef, an emulsion not unlike the modern-day salami sausage. Many meals consisted of what the Golden Outback provided. Roasted lyre bird was a special delicacy.

The last diary related the sad story of how two of his companions died. The cause was not noted; however, there was an implication they had to be dug out. "So, it could have been a cave in," Chris had surmised. He read how his great granduncle Troy had wheeled the dead men for many days, back to civilisation so their families could give them a decent burial.

The pages of those diaries, and what they had shown Chris, weighed heavily on his mind, and he started thinking, "I must be mad to even think about going back there." But that bauble hanging from his neck was so very real, and something kept calling him. Great granduncle Troy's dream of that fortune out there just waiting to be found was no dream. He had seen it.

The work in the research laboratory was rewarding and he learned much and could now identify many minerals by look, or touch. "All this is very good but it is not providing me with the satisfaction I seek," he was thinking one evening as he walked to his bus-stop. The bus stop was adjacent to a news-agency. During his time working at the Investment Company, and of late at the Research Laboratory, each and every day he had called in to that newsagency to purchase the daily newspaper and had a standing order for the monthly issue of the Miners Journal.

Mrs Mac who ran the newsagency was a jovial lady; she liked Chris and was most pleased when he returned. Chris had noticed the large sign in the front window of the news agency that boldly announced the Lotto draw that coming weekend was an estimated $30 million—a record. "Why not," he thought. "To win that would be great." So, he set to and filled out a coupon. He filled in the whole six panels with random numbers.

Mrs Mac smiled as he handed her the coupon and said, "Be a nice one to win, eh Chris? It would buy a year or two's subscription to your journal."

Chris nonchalantly stuck the ticket she had handed him into his wallet and thought little further about it.

He had repaid Rex all the money Rex had paid out during his absence and to support him while he was looking for a job. Now his savings were approaching a figure with which he could buy a small new car. He did not have a girlfriend, and often thought about Helen from the Investment Company, and wondered if she was still unmarried. "Daydreaming again he admonished himself."

The weekend was spent with a group from the post-graduate mining class on the weekend camp out. As usual Monday was work at the laboratory. It had been a slow day and he was walking slowly back to his bus stop.

As he passed the newsagency, Mrs Mac rushed out crying loudly, "Chris! Chris! Somebody from here has won first prize. I think it is you!"

This didn't register with Chris for a minute, then the realisation hit him. "The 30 million you mean?" he stammered.

"Yes! Yes!" Mrs Mac shouted. "Do you have your ticket on you?" Chris produced the ticket in question. "This is it," Mrs Mac shouted with great agitation. "Come on in; I'll put it through the checking machine."

It was the winner. The enormity of the situation eluded Chris for a few minutes then it struck. "Are you telling me I have won $30 million, Mrs Mac.? How do I get paid?" he whispered.

"I can collect it for you, or you can take it to the Lotto office yourself. That will possibly be quicker. I have never had to collect an amount that large before. To date, this is one of the biggest payouts that Lotto has ever made; they may want to make a bit of a fuss about it. Tell them very little Chris," she counselled, "otherwise your name will be in all the newspapers and you will be plagued by many people pestering you to give them some." She gave him a big hug and gently said, "It could not have happened to a nicer person; what are you going to do with all that money Chris? I know you will not waste it, but do not let it change you." Can I give you a share?" Chris generously offered.

"No lad, the commission pay me a good bonus for selling the winner," Mrs Mac laughingly answered. "But that is most kind of you."

Chris sat in his bus in a cloud, trying to rationalise. "What first?" he thought.

He told nobody of his good fortune. In due course the funds were in his bank account. He immediately had a call from the bank's investment advisor.

"Thank you for your interest," Chris counselled him. "I am well experienced with investing," and hung up.

Chris's mind ran rampant. "What to do with all that money. A new apartment? No, that does not appeal at the moment. I will get a new car, something small, just for me."

The dismal apartment finally got to him. One of his ex-clients was a property developer. Chris called on him to "just see" if he had anything which could be of interest to him. He got a very warm reception from the developer, Claude Jacobson, who Chris had given some advice a year or two ago.

"That advice you gave me, Christopher, actually saved me a good pile of dollars," the developer effused. "I heard you had left your job. Want a job with me?" he enquired, seemingly hopeful.

"No job," Chris replied. "I only wanted to find out if you had any apartments for sale."

"Always have apartments ready, Chris. What are you looking for?"

Chris ran through the features he would like. The developer thought for a moment and called to his secretary: "Jackie! Has that apartment in the Blue Waters estate been resold?"

His secretary's voice came back: "No, Sir. We have an offer but it is not attractive."

"Thank you, girl," the developer called through the open door to her. "Chris this is a four-bedroom apartment, three with ensuites and has a separate bathroom with spa and a large living area;" the developer said using his typical sales jargon. "It is on a bus route, in the parklands out near the University."

"Sounds ideal," Chris replied. "How much?"

"Jackie," the developer again shouted, "please bring me the file on that unit," and turned to Chris and quickly said: "I'd like to do a deal with you for this unit. The fellow who was to buy it put down a $350,000 deposit but has since disappeared, and the time to take possession and settle has long passed. The court has given us clearance to resume and on-sell it."

Jackie placed the file on the desk before the developer and turned to leave, hesitating at the door for a moment, and softly said, "Hello Mr. Kennedy, let me know if you need to see anything else. There are several other apartments you may be interested in." She returned to her desk and started to type a letter but gave up in exasperation. "What's the matter with me? I don't usually make mistakes," she thought to herself, then mused a little longer. "So that's Mr Kennedy. He is nice, very well mannered, even stood up when I entered the room, appears to be quite tall—hard to tell exactly. That unruly mop of hair makes his height a little deceptive. I wish I had had a better look at those eyes. They were so soft and brown and very intense—suits his face. That face is why I cannot concentrate on my typing; it was so strong, a powerful jaw, clean-shaven, strong white teeth that showed when he smiled at me. His shoulders were wide too, he's slim, really good looking well-mannered and smart. What he did for Jacobson's was very clever. I only saw him for a moment or two. I wonder if he has a girlfriend. His type does not last long out there without somebody hooking into them. Now I'm just going to push him out of my mind and get back to work." Jackie paused in her thoughts then tried to get back to her work but gave up in frustration and went out to buy a sandwich and coffee. That face would not leave her mind.

The developer had flicked through the file then firmly said: "Chris, I owe you 'big time', so think on this. Original price of that apartment was $650,000. At that price I made a good cop, so I would like to offer it to you for what is outstanding. You can have it for $300,000 clear purple title. Let me buy you lunch and we can go and have a look at it."

"That's most generous," Chris quickly answered. "That lunch bit sounds good."

After a most pleasant lunch, Jacobson and Chris viewed the apartment. It took only twenty minutes before Chris decided the apartment was perfect for his needs; what's more, the price was very good.

"I would like to accept your offer, Mr Jacobson," Chris quietly said, as he shook the developer's hand.

"Good," Jacobson quickly said. "Call at the office tomorrow morning, Chris. I will not be in—I have to go south for a few days as I have another big one on the go down there. Jackie will have a key for you."

"Can I give her a bank account for her to draw the payment from?" Chris quickly asked.

"No hurry to settle," the developer replied. "Settle when you are ready."

Chris arrived at the developer's office early the next morning. Jackie had been warned he would be in to sign up and collect a key. She had made that bit extra effort to make sure she looked her best. Dressed in a very chic business suit that accented her best attributes and being close to six-feet tall with long, luxuriant straight blonde hair, that shone with all that extra brushing, the peaches and cream complexion with those blue, blue eyes, she had drawn many a wistful look from both male and female co-travellers on the train on the way in that morning. The female passengers wishing they could look like that, the male passengers—well enough said!

"You look very nice this morning, Miss Jackie; in fact, very, very nice," Chris complimented her.

"Thank you, Mr Kennedy," Jackie softly responded to his compliment, and to hide her confusion said, "All the papers are here for your signature and here is the key. Mr Jacobson did say you may want to settle immediately, and he did give me strict instructions not to accept any money until you have inspected the apartment more fully. With Mr. Jacobson away, the office will be very quiet and if you give me a moment I will come with you. It is a beautiful apartment; do you have someone who can help you with your decorating?"

Chris responded to her offer quite enthusiastically: Thank you, Jackie; after we have seen the apartment perhaps you will allow me to buy you a coffee."

The "coffee" extended into a most enjoyable three hours, which included lunch.

"That was painless," Chris mused that evening. "I did enjoy her company. What next? I will have to tell the building supervisor here I will not be renewing my lease. I think it is due for renewal on the first of next month, so the timing is good."

He was still trying to resolve the priorities. Jackie did ask me about decorating the new apartment. I wonder if that decorator lady who came to the Investment Company before I left last year is available. I heard she is very good."

Four weeks later, Chris sat on the kitchen bench of his new apartment. There were plenty of chairs; he sat up here as the view of the apartment was a little better. The lady decorator had done a marvellous job. He was deriving much pleasure from sitting there sipping the first cup of tea, brewed in the brand-new pot from water boiled in his brand-new kettle. He had bought very little from his old apartment. The building supervisor had told him a young couple were going to move in as soon as he vacated.

The supervisor confidentially whispered, "I think they have very little to move in with."

Chris did not hesitate: "Offer them everything. I mean everything I leave, the lot. Fridges, washers, bed linen everything. What they don't want please just junk."

Now all his old ties had been gradually severed. He sat at the lounge rooms very wide window, reflecting, "Now what? I have graduated with honours nonetheless," he proudly thought, "got a new car and apartment. No engineering job, although I have three good offers to reply to. No! I'm not interested in a job at a moment. I have learned so much, time to start using all that knowledge. Go prospecting—that idea does really appeal to me. Firstly, I must get a good vehicle, not just a regular four by four, something I have designed and built to my specifications. The Yanks have a pretty good unit—they use it in the Middle East; it looks to handle most conditions well. That manufacturing firm I was dealing with just before I quit the Investment Company may build it for me."

The manufacturing company's Managing Director was pleased to see him and listened intently as he outlined his needs. "It is a bit away from our normal activities, Christopher," the Managing Director commented. "I can put you onto a small firm who does play with those sorts of things. They are very good. We often load some of our tricky problems onto them."

For the next two weeks, Chris worked on the design of his desired vehicle. He had converted the third bedroom of his apartment into a studio. He found working at home most pleasant. His mentors from the University—Prof Strahan and Fred Riley—looked over his final design and made a few minor suggestions. They did make one comment that amused Chris immensely.

"There is one major comment I must make," the professor said with an obvious twinkle in his eye. "It is a shame I am not twenty years younger, I would come with you."

Chris had followed up the recommendation the Managing Director had made and had telephoned the recommended small engineering firm to make an appointment to visit.

"Come over tomorrow morning, Buddy," the very Aussie voice invited. "I'll have a look at what you have in mind."

As he walked through the cluttered front area of that engineering firm, Chris was a little apprehensive with engaging this fellow's services. "If his work is anything like this junkyard I do not think he will suit my purposes," Chris thought. The proprietor's features were a reflection of his front area. Untidy hair, once-clean clothes which were coated in various layers of grease and oil. His hands were stained, and the nails definitely required some urgent attention. Nevertheless, Chris handed him the folder which contained his designed vehicle.

After about ten minutes of completely ignoring Chris while he studied the contents of the folder, the untidy bloke simply said: "Looks a challenge. Leave all this with me and come back tomorrow after lunch."

The following day they sat in his cluttered office. Chris's drawings were spread out over his large desk. The first thing Ed (his full name was Edward Tristan Black) said was, "Don't like your idea to modify the Yank machine; it will be better to build it from the ground up. *Gonna* cost you a buck or two or three."

"Give me a ballpark figure," Chris quickly said. "We can just go on from there. I will put $100,000 up front for a start to get this thing underway."

"You are talking my language, mate. We are a bit quiet at the moment so we can get stuck into it right away. Armoured tyres? Hell, lad! What war are you going to?"

"No war, Ed," Chris laughed. "Only a bit of bush bashing."

Ed grunted a reply of sorts then firmly added, "I reckon it'll be close to quarter of a million, some of that gear you specify will be pretty pricey. Does that change things?"

"Not in the least," Chris snapped, "so long as the quality of the fittings are as I have specified. I know some are a bit costly, but I want nothing but the best."

"I may make a few suggestions as we go," Ed said. "I can already see where I can fit some bits that are better than those you picked. I will talk with you before I change much. I hope you will spend a fair bit of time here with us—there will be much to explain."

"It's a deal," Chris enthusiastically replied and offered his hand to cement the transaction.

"See you in three days' time, my fine friend. I'll have a fair bit for you to see by then."

Chris collected his mail from his box in the foyer of his apartment building. Lots of junk, one envelope with the Investment Company's logo prominent, took his eye. He ripped the envelope open. It contained three pages advising him of his resignation entitlement. "This is unexpected," he thought. "Because I virtually walked out I did not expect anything."

The bottom line simply read an amount of $76,000 will be deposited to any bank account you care to nominate. The third sheet was a letter of recommendation signed by the CEO. A handwritten note had been added: "Call and say 'hello' any time, Chris," and was signed Jamie Jackson.

He had been back into his apartment less than fifteen minutes, and had only just finished opening his mail and was pouring himself a cup of tea when the buzzer made him aware there was somebody downstairs wanting in.

"Yes," he spoke into the intercom.

"Good, you are in," came the reply. "It's Jackie. Can I come up?"

"Sure," Chris replied. "I am always happy to let a very pretty girl in," and he flicked the appropriate switch that enabled her to enter the building. He walked briskly to the door, and stepped out into the foyer, intending to meet her at the lift. He was halfway across the foyer when the lift stopped and Jackie stepped swiftly out.

"Hi, Chris. It's nice to see you again; have you got a minute or two? Mr Jacobson has asked me to get the name of your decorator. All the tradies who worked in your apartment raved about what you had done. May I see it?"

"No problem Jackie," he replied. "Come on in."

Jackie was most impressed with the decorator's work. "It's beautiful," she commented. "Jacobson's have a forty-three-apartment building that is ready for decoration. My boss is a bit peeved with our regular guy. He will definitely contact your lass. Was she expensive?"

"A bit," Chris replied, "but I thought the apartment was so good it deserved a bit of special attention."

"Talking about special attention," Jackie laughed, "your king-size bed looks like it needs some *special attention*! Shall we try it?"

"Oh Jackie, you luscious bundle of femininity, you do me a great honour with your thought, but I am due at a university dinner in about one hour. Can I give you a call and we can arrange another day to fix that darn bed?"

"You are a beast Christopher Kennedy, but please call me soon." she did sound a little disappointed.

"Gentleman" that he was, Chris walked her to the lift.

Before it arrived, she wrapped her arms around his shoulders and kissed him very deeply. "Bye" she whispered and stepped quickly into the lift. The door hissed closed and she was gone. "What's the matter with me," Chris admonished himself. "She's a real honey, and I lied to her. I do not have a university appointment."

. Ed had told him of a special CAT V 12 diesel motor, which would be just the ticket for his SUV, that was for sale. A friend of Ed's had a mechanical workshop in GERALDTON. That regional city was about five hundred kilometres up the coast. Ed's friend had especially bought that motor for a client; unfortunately, they have found it was not exactly what they had envisaged. It was just sitting in the workshop, still in the shipping crate. Ed's friend's client would be happy to get rid of it and try and redeem a bit of the money he has spent and would probably grab a fair offer. Chris was to pick Ed up at 6 AM and they were to drive up there. They chatted as they travelled.

Ed laughed as he told Chris the boys in the workshop had named Chris's SUV "Goliath". "I thought it funny at first but it is appropriate. He is a monster."

Chris told Ed of his intention to do a bit of prospecting. He had no idea where: "I'm going to head out into the Outback and go where my nose points."

"All a bit vague," Ed commented. "I do envy you because you are able to do it. Your bus—Goliath," he corrected himself, "will be perfect for what you're going to do."

Fortune smiled on him and he was able to pick up the motor for about half the money it cost. Chris had offered to take it off their hands at the full cost they had paid.

The client would not hear of it: "Half is more than enough. I can just write the difference off against this year's Tax," he said.

For the next six months, Chris worked with Ed and his boys on Goliath. The SUV was starting to take shape.

.

Both his university lecturers, Riley and Professor Strahan had asked to be allowed to see the legendary Goliath. It was all but finished and stood proudly amongst the clutter on Ed's workshop floor. Both men spent two hours going over Goliath with a fine-tooth comb. Their final consensus was that there was one major deficiency.

Chris was immediately alarmed. "What have I missed?" he cried and both of the lecturers burst out laughing.

"Where are the dancing girls?" Strahan chuckled through his subdued laughter. "He really is something special, Chris, as I would expect from you. May I use the design to give my classes a vision of the perfect prospecting vehicle?"

"When are we leaving?" quipped Riley, with the emphasis on the "we."

"Sorry, Mr Riley," Chris contained his laughter. "By the time I fit all the dancing girls in there will be no room for you."

"Ah, theme's the breaks," Riley laughed, then quizzically asked: "Why the computer, we could not get it up?"

"It's mainly for information, although it can be used on some of the new communication sites" Chris answered. "It assesses the operation of almost everything, individual tyre pressures, and sends a warning if one is down. The tyres are loaded with a goo that instantly seals any puncture, so any loss of pressure has to be severe. It also measures the weight on individual springs and has the ability to equalise that weight. It also measures tension on all transmission components—you know, all differentials and torque shafts, lots and lots of other bits and pieces. All the best. If a problem occurs, a warning icon highlights on the computer screen."

"It's like the cockpit of a 747 in there," Riley commented. "It's almost idiot proof. He's a credit to you, Mister. Did Ed call it "Goliath?" Better watch out for kids with slings, especially any kids named David."

The professors thought that was very funny. The lecturers did delay the departure and sat on boxes in the workshop chatting about exploration and sharing a companionable moment or two quaffing a "coldie." Before they left, both insisted on obtaining business cards from Ed, just in case they were ever asked to recommend a good engineering firm, they would have his name readily available.

Chris drove carefully to his apartment: "There is no reason to delay my departure." The thought ran through his mind as he drove. Goliath is ready and fully fuelled, the post-studies all complete. I enjoyed them, lots of new stuff, all my bills are paid. I think I'll leave tomorrow."

But there was an unforeseen delay. Jackie sat in the foyer, she looked beautiful. "I was passing by and thought I would drop in and say hello," she softly said.

"Hello Jackie! Bye, Jackie," Chris lightly laughed.

"You are not going to dodge me this time, you rotten thing," Jackie snapped. "If I do not fix that bed of yours soon I will bust! Or probably just chicken out!" Chris had let that last comment slip by.

"Better come up," Chris very seriously answered. "We cannot have you 'bursting' here in the foyer."

It was two days later when Chris and Jackie finally decided they had made a fair attempt at fixing that bed. Those two days had delayed his intended departure; however, it was a very contented man who walked into Ed's workshop with a stuffed pack over his shoulders. Ed had simply said, "Off are we, Chris? Good luck, mate. Don't forget it is most important to have him back before he goes over 10,000 k."

"Okay" Chris replied. "Here is the bank and code you can use to cover any bread you may need." He firmly shook Ed's hand, slipped into Goliath's driving seat, hit the button marked motor, and listened while Goliath purred into life. They had run that CAT motor many times, but this time a delicious thrill ran through Chris. "This is it, I am finally off. OH, HELL! I feel like a kid with a new toy—it feels so good."

Goliath eased from the workshop into the street and onto the freeway. A motor-cycle traffic officer ran alongside him, flashed his lights and indicated he wanted Chris to pull over. Chris reached over into what was Ed's idea of a glovebox and retrieved the registration papers. It had taken half a day to get Goliath registered, the inspecting guys had wanted to know everything, their notes attached to the application form covered two pages. Nevertheless, Goliath was passed as being completely roadworthy.

The traffic officer was needlessly abrupt, he tapped on the driver's window. "Get out! What the hell is this, it better be legal or I will throw the book at you," the officer blasted at Chris. Chris didn't say a word but thrust the registration documents into the officer's outstretched hands. The officer perused the form minutely and was about to hand them back to Chris when a squad car pulled up in front of Goliath.

A burly sergeant stepped out. "What's up, Michaels? What's he done?"

"Nothing, Sergeant," the officer answered quickly. "I was only doing a registration and license check."

On the freeway, during peak hour? You must be mad." The sergeant took a quick look at the paperwork. "It's perfect," he snapped. "This was not necessary, Sir. Please be on your way. Your vehicle looks to be something special. Going bush, eh?"

"Yes," Chris quietly replied, "just as soon as I can get myself out of the presence of this bloke," indicating the traffic officer with a shrug of his shoulder.

The episode had taken the gloss off his mood. It soon returned when he hit the open road. Later in that day, he topped up his fuel tanks at the same service station just short of the regional city. Once again, he got to talking with the owner who remembered him and was happy to chat. "Going out again are we; you are a devil for punishment. You look better set up this time. Do all twelve of those wheels drive?" the Service Station owner rather respectfully asked.

"They sure do," Chris replied.

"You will be okay, then. Best let the Boys in Blue know this time, you caused a bit of strife last time, they did not even know you were out there, I was the only one who had seen you. They are pretty good and will keep a watch for you. You got a two-way?"

"I do have," Chris answered. His two-way was interconnected to Ed's workshop and had a range of over 1000k.

He did call at the police station. The police officer thanked him for telling them of his plans; shook his hand; wished him good luck and bid him goodbye.

By nightfall he was "out there." Goliath had revelled in the tough going and setting up camp was accomplished in moments. Defrosted steak and pre-packed veggies never tasted so good. "It has not changed; those one million stars are still up there," he sighed for the twenty-fifth time as he looked into the black sky. "It is so peaceful. I do like this."

As he lay there a sudden thought struck him, "it's all very good to appreciate all this but I must have a better plan in mind.

What first – find the escarpment.

Secondly – locate the sinkhole.

Next – get back down into it. This time I must make sure I can get back easily, there is no way I want to go through the trials of having to climb up that cliff again. That winch we had fitted to Goliath with the idea it could be used to alleviate that; it has only been given a bit of a trial run in the workshop. It should be okay.

After that what? – I think once I have established exactly what I want to mine, I will have to pinpoint the exact location of all this and try and establish what permits, if any, have been issued to cover it. Until I have established whether or not I can mine that area there is little point in planning further. That's enough planning time for sleep."

Sleep did not come quickly; his mind kept running through his plans and memories of what had happened last time he had ventured into the sinkhole; and of that river and the gold nuggets he had found in it.

It was a weary young man who reluctantly rose from his sleeping bag; but after 2 cups of tea and a bowl of cereal softened with powdered milk; he packed his overnight camp back into Goliath and re-commenced his search. Nowadays, thanks to the knowledge he had acquired in his time, with the people, not once did he worry about getting lost.

This was the pattern for the next ten days. Drive all day, set up a temporary camp, eat and evening meal, sleep, arise as the sun rose and continue on.

Toward the end of the tenth day he started thinking; "I know I am heading in the right direction, but it seems to be further than I thought. I must be getting nearer the escarpment now. Hell's-Bells!" he cried out loud; "that escarpment is so big it should be easy to spot." In a moment of realisation, it struck him; "I must be going mad, I'm talking to myself."

It was mid-morning the next day; when he sighted, what he thought were those wonderful cliffs on the horizon. "THERE IT IS!" He shouted jubilantly; and accelerated Goliath toward it; unfortunately, in his excitement he bogged the SUV. "Good one!" he exclaimed; in admonishment; "serves me right for being stupid." It took him the remainder of the morning to dig the huge vehicle out of the bog. As a precaution, and to ensure did not happen again, he fitted the caterpillar tracks.

The day was ending as he carefully approached the cliffs of the sinkhole.

Bursting with excitement; he bounded from the SUV and stood looking out over the sinkhole. In the light of the setting sun it was a beautiful sight. "Just to see this makes any hassle about getting here makes the effort seemed insignificant; and so very worthwhile; he thought.

In the fading evening light, he set up camp, made a meal – which he found difficult to eat he was so excited; set out his sleeping bag. He kept thinking all the time of all that, that had to be done tomorrow. Consequently, he only achieved a little sleep and rolled very wearily from his sleeping bag in the "piccaninny dawn" (that light just before sunrise.) After forcing a tasteless breakfast down, he again stood on the cliff edge looking down into the sinkhole. As he stood there, he made a firm decision, to stop rushing headlong into this and take much more care; nevertheless, he was once again overwhelmed with the beauty of the sinkhole and the Outback. He had fortuitously stopped in what he considered was the ideal spot to embark on his assault on the cliff. It was about 100 meters along from where the river burst forth from the face. Here the cliff was sheer, with nothing of any significance protruding. "Ideal;" he thought and drove Goliath very carefully to within ten feet of the cliff edge. He uncovered the winch which had been built securely affixed to the front end of the chassis of the SUV and rolled out enough of that 10 mm stainless steel cable to reach the edge of the cliff. The adjustable harness he had made especially made, took a few minutes to be adjusted to fit him securely. That harness had been built to be used in conjunction with the remote-control device that not only control the winch but included control of Goliath's ignition system and motor speed. He hooked the cable to the harness and stepped to the edge of the cliff, thinking to himself, "I know my sanity is open to question; fancy even thinking of doing this." Regardless of that thought, and holding his breath, with his stomach now somewhere up near his epiglottis; he stepped over the edge of the cliff and hung there, suspended over the abyss spinning slowly. He hung there for around 30 seconds then firmly pressed the down control button on the remote. Instantly he plummeted down. Panic stricken he hit the stop button and jerked to a bone wrenching stop; to once again hang there while he gathered his shattered wits. "That wasn't what I had planned to do," he thought as he again pressed that down button, this time rather than press it firmly he gently caressed it and was lowered sedately down. It took about 12 minutes to descend the remaining 250 m before his feet touched the ground. Not satisfied with this, he pressed the up button carefully; and was instantly swung off his feet to commence the upward journey. Although his stomach was still churning with all this down and up; after being lifted about 10 feet he reversed the direction of the winch and was again placed on the ground.

"It works perfectly;" he elatedly thought as he removed the harness, which he left attached to the winch and placed it on a nearby boulder.

A quick swim in that cold river helped him revive immensely and he contentedly sat in the morning sunshine drying and planning.

For the next three weeks he explored and surveyed the sinkhole, each day becoming a little more confident with being hauled up and down the cliff face by Goliath. He had collected a large bucket full of those nuggets from the river and sat in the evening light examining his almost completely filled notebooks. He sat back and thought deeply. This is of little use to me, unless I can establish whether or not this area has been pegged; and if it has been, can I gain possession of it. This can only be done if I returned to the city and search the records.

Next morning; he packed up his camp and commenced the trek home. It took him almost two weeks to get back to the main road that led to the regional city. A police car out on patrol on the main road slowed and an officer leaned from the window and waved him down. The officer stepped briskly from the patrol car; saying "Young Kennedy, isn't it?" he asked. "That unit of yours is easy to identify. It's good to see you young fellow. We were starting to worry about you. You are about ten days overdue," the officer admonished him, then quietly asked "Have any luck?"

"A bit," Chris replied. "Sorry to cause you any concern. It is a big country out there."

"You have done well, sunshine," the officer complimented him. "We have records of some folk who are still missing—some date back a year or two. People come up here with their heads in the clouds. They do not realise how dangerous it is out there. The biggest danger is our own ignorance. In fact, there is a fresh report in last week: a girl, an artist, is about four weeks overdue. We have a chopper out there looking for her at the moment. Silly bitch! Going out there by herself. Don't like her chances! Are you going out again? Let's know if you are?"

"Sure will," Chris answered.

He made the two police officers a cup of tea and sat on the roadside with them sipping the tea.

As he passed them their cups of hot tea, one officer laughed, "You are surely well set up Chris. We should get some of the stuff you have fitted to our car."

They were interesting fellows. They had been stationed here for some years and were well informed and related several interesting stories and a couple of humorous anecdotes of the many times they had been called upon to rescue people lost out there.

Their stories often included a few brief references to the difficulties of having to drag people who had gotten themselves lost out in the National Park. Keep out of that," they warned. "The ecological people are pretty touchy. They even have a couple of people located in town and they keep a close watch on the park. It would serve you well to get to know them."

"That's a fine idea," Chris softly said. "I will do that; they may even be able to give me a *'rundown'* on the park boundaries."

"That they will," laughed one of the policemen, "right down to the last millimetre."

With that they climbed back into the patrol car and roared off. Chris packed up the impromptu morning tea and headed for town.

He booked into a motel and began to explore the *"regional city."* It was not so large; really, it was nothing more than a big country town. It had an interesting history. He located the government crusher and smelter. There was a fairly substantial mining operation somewhere nearby, he had been told—its operations provided employment for many of the locals. The crusher and the smelter operation were operated under the watchful eyes of one Bill Bailey. Chris located him in his tin shed office and introduced himself. Bill was a jovial chap, nothing seemed to distract him and he ran a tight ship. They chatted amiably for a couple of hours.

Bill insisted on being able to inspect Goliath, his only comment was: "Best bloody rig I have ever seen."

Chris produced the nuggets he had collected. "Could you process these for me, Bill?" he asked.

"Come over to the office," Bill mumbled. "You have to fill in a couple of forms. You have a prospecting license I hope? These look pretty good. I'll run them through tomorrow morning first thing. The machines are clean then; so, there will be no chance of contamination. Do you want to sell the out-product to us? Gold is being bought by the state at $190.00 per ounce today; it may be a little different tomorrow. If it is worth over $10,000 I have to collect 2.5% royalty."

"Bloody bushrangers," Chris laughed. "Yes, but nice bushrangers," Bill laughed with him. By the end of the visit the pair were good friends.

The local Mines Department; had good records of permits that had been issued, and a comprehensive library of the areas those leases covered. There was very little that was not already encompassed by some permit or another. The National Park boundaries dominated the maps.

"No licenses are issued for exploration of that area by this office," the clerk explained. "They have to be issued by the Minister for Mines. The clerk had taken a closer look at the records Chris was showing interest in and commented; "a lot of these permits are very old; in fact, some are close to the final renewal date. Many have not been developed in any way so it would be easy for you to do some illegal digging ignorant that you are actually committed a crime." The clerk appeared to be enjoying handing out this graphic warning.

"I'm getting nowhere," Chris cried to himself. "I have no idea where the sinkhole is and whether or not it is already tied up. I really think I need an aerial survey."

He returned to the crusher office to find out what had happened with those nuggets, and to also discuss the problem with his new-found friend, Bill.

Bill agreed: "An aerial 'look and see', was a good idea. I think you had better get a move on to register your claim Chris," he strongly advised. "Those nuggets you bought in yielded just on twelve kilograms of 0.9999% pure gold. We owe you $13,520. I have deducted the royalty tax and processing charge—you can claim that as a tax deduction. I cannot buy any more from you without submitting a formal application to register you as a gazetted miner."

"Bloody Hell, Bill," Chris cried. All this administration rubbish is harder than actual gold mining."

"It's only a 'one off' thing," Bill sincerely commented. "Once you have waded through all the crap, it's fairly plain sailing. There is a tourist set up about five kilometres out on the North Road; they hire out helicopters. They may be able to help you with the aerial survey."

"Thanks for all the advice, mate," Chris humbly said. "I will go out to that tourist set up immediately. Want to join me for dinner."

"I will take a free dinner any time," Bill laughed.

The Tourist facility was a very professional looking set-up, operated by a large burly ex-air force officer called Hector Kennelly. "You want to hire a chopper for a couple of days to have a look at some of the outback. I won't ask why, but will ask when and where?" Hector asked.

"I want to run over the boundaries of the National Park for a start and maybe go on from there," Chris advised.

"Don't have a machine that can go that far, sorry mate," Kennelly loudly replied.

Chris was not deterred: "You have a big helicopter parked out there; could you not load it up with extra fuel drums or something?"

"You mean the Boeing CH 47 Chinook? Yes, that could be done, but that bloke will not fly. I bought it last year to set it up as a 22-passenger wagon for group ventures. I got ripped off! It only just managed to make the flight from Perth to here. I do not have the 'ready' to repair him."

"A job for Ed," Chris thought. Speaking quite softly but emphatically he asked: "Hector, would you consider this. I would like to repair the machine for you. I would cover all the costs. In return, you would take my job to fly me around for a few days."

Hector's reply was full of enthusiasm and sincerity: "You get him fixed up and you can have him free for a month. I'll even fly you myself."

"Done!" Chris snapped loudly. "In the next couple of days, I will bring a guy up from the *"big smoke"* to have a look at him to see if he is fixable. Is that okay with you?"

"Sure is," Hector quickly answered. Do you want me to fly your guy up? I have a daily mail run to the city. I usually have plenty of space on the return trip. I would include the costs of his fare in our deal."

The mail plane and Ed arrived at about 1.00 pm, the next day. By mid-afternoon, after Ed had spent hours going over the Chinook, he reported. "It can be fixed; He's not that old, and spares will not be a problem. Bit pricey though."

"When can you start?" Chris abruptly asked.

"I need the work," Ed replied. "Can you get him down to the workshop? It will be better to work on him there than to try and fix him here."

Chris organised for the helicopter to be trucked to Perth. Ed offered to ride down on the truck with him, to ensure the helicopter received a minimum of damage.

"It will be about a month," Ed called, as the large transport departed.

Hector stood hands on hips, watching the departing truck. "You sure do not muck about, Chris," he commented. "When that Chinook comes into service, I will have plenty for him to do. I did advertise group flights—I have two bookings already!"

"What next?" Chris asked himself, "Gazetted Miner. What the hell is that?"

He once again, sought Bill's advice, and regardless of the fact they were sitting at the dinner table in a very nice restaurant, Bill happily explained what was needed.

"More darn paperwork." Chris grumbled, but didn't hesitate, and telephoned Rex at his home. "Brother, dear," Chris crooned.

He was immediately cut off by Rex: "When I hear that voice, I know my peaceful life is about to be stuffed up. It is about time something new happened to brighten my days. What is it this time, mate?" Rex quipped.

"Here, talk to this guy," Chris said. "His name is Bill. He will tell you what I need. Can I see you Friday?"

Rex and Bill chatted for about half an hour, before Bill handed the telephone back to Chris. Rex was still waiting.

"Can you help?" Chris asked hopefully.

"Piece of cake for us, really," Rex answered. "What do you want to call the company?"

Chris thought for a moment—the thought flashed into his mind. "Call it Quo-Vadis Holdings Proprietary Limited."

"Okay", Rex replied. "See you Friday. Twelve o'clock. You owe me a lunch!"


He didn't wait until morning. Overnight he drove Goliath back to the *"big smoke,"* left him at Ed's workshop for the 10,000-kilometre service, grabbed his town car and headed for his apartment. Although his mailbox was quite full, the contents had been sorted into neat piles, priority on top. All the junk gone.

Despite it still being early morning, the apartment building supervisor appeared from his office. "Hello Chris," he cordially said. "The young lady said you were due back. I do think she conned me out of your mail box key, but she's such a doll I couldn't refuse. I hope it was okay?"

"No worries, Jeff, thank you. What was her name?" Chris, whose curiosity had been aroused asked.

The Super; looked quizzically at Chris. "It was Jackie. She said you had asked her to attend to the mail."

"Again, thanks Jeff," Chris softly said as he turned and walked to the lifts, his mind drifting over that very *"foxy"* girl from the developer's office and the pleasant luncheon and those two days he had shared with her *fixing that big bed*.

He had only dumped his pack on the lounge chair and was putting the kettle on for a cup of tea, when the phone rang. No hello, no greeting, just: "It's about time you surfaced. Jeff your Building Super has only just this minute let me know you are back, I'll be there in thirty-five minutes. Now don't give me any B.S. about not being '*on*'. There are a few important things to talk about."

"Okay, sweetie," Chris all but helplessly replied. "Just allow me time to have a shower."

"Don't rush. I'll be quicker than thirty-five minutes just to catch you in the shower," she sniggered.

"Wanton woman," Chris laughed into the telephone and hung up.

Jackie was there in less than thirty minutes. He had managed to unpack his soiled clothes and complete his shower and sat at a coffee table intending to open his mail, before Jackie arrived. The top pile marked *"important"*, although not large, received his first attention. On top of the pile was a handwritten note: "If you're reading this, you're obviously back. Please phone me immediately. I need your help. It is not to fix that bed, but that would be a good idea, but I need your help for something else. Love you XXX. J."

"WOW, this is a nice development," Chris thought. "I wonder what her problem is."

At that moment, his door buzzer snapped him from his thinking. Jackie's image flashed across the screen, and without answering, he flicked the "allow entry" switch. This time he was quick enough to meet her at the lift.

She flung herself into his arms and held him close: "Chris! Chris! I need you so badly."

"First things first; we will attend to the important things later," Chris lightly said, then quickly added, "Are you in trouble?"

"In a way, yes!" She whispered.

"OK," he responded, "we will sit quietly, have a cup of tea; and you can tell me all."

Cups in hand they sat together on the soft lounge.

"It's like this," she commenced and went on to explain what her problem was. "Claude Jacobson Proprietary Limited is being sued by a number of creditors. I have been subpoenaed to appear in court and one of the plaintiff's solicitors had told her she is being joined in the action, on the grounds she fraudulently conveyed to his client that Jacobson's were trading very profitably. I had no idea Claude had any problems—I was never privy to any of his trading figures. Claude apparently had a problem with drugs, and his problems got the better of him. He went off the deep end and had 'OFF-ed' himself."

"You mean, he took his own life," Chris hastily asked.

"Yes!" Jackie cried. "He shot himself. Now I do not know what to do. The office has been closed and I am due in court on the sixteenth. That's ten days from now." She was close to panic. "Chris! Chris! I have nobody, you are all I have to turn to."

"You poor kid," Chris sympathetically replied. "We cannot have this. You look dreadful," Chris attempted to say this in a consoling way.

"Thanks for nothing," she cried. "If I look half as bad as I feel you are not wrong."

"Jackie, girl," Chris very firmly said, "go and have a long hot shower, slip into one of my T-shirts. When you have finished come back here and together we will sort this out."

"I feel better already," she whispered and headed to one of the ensuite bathrooms.

In his years with the Investment Company Chris had made a multitude of contacts. "Time to call in a couple of favours." Chris thought. The senior counsellor from one of those contacts, a very prominent law firm, personally took Chris's call, and was genuinely warm as Chris outlined the problem.

"I cannot see any real problem, Chris," he advised, "so long as she has not signed any statement implicating herself or has said anything incorrect to the plaintive at any time; I believe she has no case to answer to. Send her up to see me tomorrow—be here at 9 am. She will not need to make an appointment."

"Thank you, sir," Chris gratefully replied. "She will be there."

"Now, Chris," the lawyer asked, "what are you up to these days?"

Chris related his story to him.

"Well, young man, I wish you luck and good fortune. Really, I envy you that you have the guts to go back; and the energy and drive to strike out as you have. Do not hesitate to call again, if you ever need any assistance."

The lawyer's good wishes were well received by Chris who thanked him for everything and hung up.

Jackie returned to the lounge room, clad rather obviously only in the T-shirt—one of his largest. The T-shirt did little to enhance her figure; however, it did have a couple of *good points.* He related his conversation with the lawyer to her and took good care in advising the lawyer's name and the address of the law firm. "I hope 9 am is okay for you," Chris asked. "It is important you are there on time. Now that we have got that under control, let's get down to the important stuff. I was about to make myself a snack. Would you like a bite to eat, or do you need something more substantial? I have not eaten yet."

"Yes, to the snack!" and with a glint in her eyes, "and yes; to the something, else" she cheekily answered.

She stayed overnight. They arose early in the morning to attend to his letters. She was a very professional PA and they quickly had his affairs "*ship shape*".

"I would really like to give you a job," Chris told her, "but when you realistically look at it I do have little need for a full-time PA."

She extracted herself from his arms, where she had snuggled herself, and sat up in front of him. "Christopher," she softly said, "I have always known there never was a long-term future for us. I do love you very deeply, but I ask nothing of you, other than to be near you for a while from time to time."

"Oh, hell, Jackie," he cried. "You make it hard for me. I have a great affection for you but for the present I only want to be me. I would really be very poor partner material."

After she left, to keep her 900 o'clock appointment; he endeavoured to catch up with a few things. He rang Rex, who was pleased to hear from him.

"Glad you rang, bro, I have some forms for you to sign. The name you choose for your company has been accepted by the Companies Office," Rex informed him.

"Is that another government office I have to deal with?" Chris wailed. "The list never seems to end."

"Be warned my erstwhile brother," Rex laughed, "by the time you are set up and running; there will be many, many more. Tell me, what have you done with your accounts? Better bring them to us so I can keep an eye on you and ensure you don't get yourself into strife; and please remember you have an appointment here at twelve—you owe me lunch," Rex reminded him.

Conversation over lunch was very intense. Chris did tell Rex of his lotto windfall.

Ever the accountant, Rex had enthusiastically absorbed that information. "We can use that to capitalise your new company. I will set it up so you are the Managing Director. I had think it best to nominate myself as Company Secretary. The way it will be set up your company will have an initial issue of one-hundred shares, issued at one dollar per share. All those shares will be registered in your name. I will also issue one-hundred B-class non-voting shares. I hope you will not object if I take the liberty of issuing five of those B-class shares to myself and Jazzy, my wife. The remaining ninety-five shares will remain registered in your name.

"That's very good," Chris answered. "While you're about it, I would like you to issue some B-class shares to a few people. I will send you a list. Give each of those people on the list one share each. Each share is to be issued with a premium of $200, deferred payment." The list included, Riley one share, Strahan one share, Bill Bailey, Jackie, Ed, Hector and Chris's sisters, all got a mention.

Jackie was waiting for him in the foyer, when he returned to his apartment. She was almost glowing; obviously, she had had time to go home, and to a 'girlie' salon, and slip into a new very nice outfit.

"I owe you dinner, my hero," she excitedly exclaimed. "Your lawyer friend rang the plaintiff's solicitor while I was there in his office. Your lawyer gave him a real serve! The consequence of all this is they have withdrawn all action against me. Now I can breathe again." She then firmly added. "I have decided I am going to come back with you to your regional town, help you set up an office, and find myself a nice job. Don't argue; after dinner I intend to pay you back big time."

"That all sounds very good," Chris enthusiastically replied, "especially that payback bit. There is one thing we should get quite clear here and now; we must have a firm understanding, like you said: No Commitment!"

"It's a deal," she laughed. "No more serious stuff tonight. I am so happy. Let's go out and just have some fun."

It was after 9.30 the next morning when he extracted himself from her arms and after much wrestling managed to answer the ringing telephone.

Ed's voice boomed out: "It's about time you answered your bloody phone. This is the fifth call to you I have made this morning."

"Sorry mate," Chris apologised, "we had a big night. What's up?"

"I got the helicopter into town last night. The boys have looked over him. We reckon we can have it up and about in ten to twelve days. None of us have a pilot's license so you will have to arrange somebody to work with us for the last three days. Most of the spares were available here, but I have had to order a few smaller bits from the States."

"That's all good news," Chris complimented him. "I will be able to organise your pilot." He stuttered the last bit, as the wanton woman lying beside him took advantage of him. It was sometime later that morning before he could eventually crawl into the shower by himself. He had had to kick Jackie out so he could get a proper wash.

"This must stop," he reflected. "I'm getting nowhere. Not that I'm not enjoying it, but there is a limit to having fun. I have things to do upstate. I will go back tomorrow."

"Please Chris," she pleaded over brunch, "Take me with you. I am not ready to be left alone just yet. I do understand our deal but you are so good I cannot get you out of my mind."

"Okay, one month at a maximum; after that, I'll send you packing," he growled.

"Not if I give you the flick beforehand," she giggled.

Jackie loved travelling in Goliath as next morning they drove to the regional city. She was obviously very happy, laughing and chatting almost continually: "He turns me on almost as much as you do," she laughed, as she snuggled a little more deeply into the passenger's seat. She had very quickly ascertained the complexities of Goliath's on-board computer and searched a list of office space available in the regional city.

After searching for only a short time, she found a four room office with a good-sized reception area, and with an attached nice bathroom, all in a very good location and laughed with Chris; a few days later as he affixed a shiny new brass plaque, declaring: "Office of Quo-Vadis Holdings Proprietary Limited," adjacent to the door surround of the front door. New PC, and printer, filing and telephone cabinets, the works were soon installed.

"I do not expect to spend much time here," Chris said, "but it will be good to have a nice set up."

Jackie most efficiently took over and set up a very comprehensive and efficient filing system. They had agreed, on a base salary for her to look after his office while she looked for a full-time job. Looking after his office would be a good fill in.

Hector had called in to the Quo-Vadis Office. Ed had contacted him to let him know the chopper was ready for a test flight. It had taken the twelve days he had prescribed to have him ready.

"I am going to have to close my office for a couple of days while I'm away, "Hector grumbled. Jackie didn't hesitate, "I could look after your office for you until to you get back, Hector," she said.

"That would be a big help, even if you just answered the telephone and took messages for me. I did have a girl—she left a month ago. I've been looking for somebody since then," Hector said, as he looked appreciatively at Jackie.

"If it is okay with Chris, I will come out tomorrow morning at 7 am. Is that too early?" she said. "You can show me the ropes then."

"It's okay with me Jackie," Chris replied. "The sooner we have that big helicopter here the better, and as I am going to spend some time at the maps office, there will be nothing much for you to do here."

Hector took a commercial flight the next morning—Jackie ran him out to the airport. They chatted on the way.

"Been with Chris long," he brazenly asked her.

"Oh, yes, a fair while," Jackie replied, not specifying exactly how long a fair while was. Hector was a bit quiet after that.

It was not much of a "test" flight; instead, it was more of a "full on" flight. As soon as Hector had that Chinook in the air he headed north.

"I see he has full tanks," Hector laughingly said; he was apparently very happy, and called loudly; "next stop home;"

Ed who had joined Hector in the so-called test flight, to see how the helicopter would perform, became most concerned and cried; "What happened to the test flight? don't you have to submit a flight plan?"

"I'll fix all that up later," Hector laughed. "I will record it as a delayed memorandum of a tourist's flight plan. I have to do this sort of thing all the time."

The test flight (*call it what you like,*) took slightly over three hours. As the big machine touched down in the tourist park of the provincial city, Jackie had stood at the office door watching as they closed "Donald" down—that was the Chinook's nickname that Ed's mechanics had given him. After all, that cumbersome machine did, with some stretch of one's imagination, have the appearance of a duck.

Hector had his large arm over Ed's shoulder as they walked to the office. "He flies like new Ed. You are a bloody marvel."

Ed had laughed at that and quickly replied. "Cut out the bloody bit mate; but when you see Chris tell him I'm putting a return air ticket, business class, of course, on his bill."

"What did it all come to?" Hector demanded.

"None of your concern," Ed had laughed. "Chris had told me to tell nobody of the cost only to send him the account. He tells me you're going to use Donald to do some survey work in the bush. I think I will hang around for a bit and come out with you and Chris for a couple of days."

"Give me five, Hector responded. I will just duck into the office and see how Jackie went, and then I'll run you both into town."

Hector burst into the office. "I am home, honey," he jokingly shouted, then stopped in his tracks. The confusion he had called his office was now a very professional tour's office. He had always maintained the park grounds to a very high standard; however; his office had always been left to be attended to "*later*".

"What have you done, girl?" he shouted.

"Just tidied up a little, sir. I will come out tomorrow and explain where everything is now. Chris came in earlier, he had heard from Ed's mechanics that you and Donald were on the way back. I am to tell you that you are all to come to dinner tonight. He said to bring your wife."

"That would be a bit difficult Jackie girl," Hector laughed as he replied. "My wife split with a real estate guy years ago. I have not heard from her since then."

"Did you divorce her?" Jackie very quietly asked.

"Never got around to it; never gave it a thought really. I must do something one day." Hector softly replied.

The dinner turned out to be a riotous affair. Ed and Hector were great company and with a couple of drinks under their belts became a couple of clowns. Chris did not try to compete with them. He and Jackie could only hold their sides laughing.

It was close to 2 am when Chris finally put the pair in a taxi. Ed was going to "kip" (*sleep*) at Hector's.

"The girls will not mind." Hector had said. They had learned Hector had two teenage daughters and from the way he talked, he adored them.

Chris and Jackie lay together talking over the events of the evening. "He is a very interesting man is our Hector," Jackie said. "While I was tidying up I found a drawer full of awards; one was for valour under fire, and there were many others. Did he tell you he was a Major when he resigned to set up the park? She had rolled over and now lay half over him; and whispered; I hear you are going out exploring again tomorrow. Can I come out with you? Please sir! I will pay my fare now if you say yes." Her whisper had become most seductive!

The fare was paid, with interest.

The next morning Donald lifted off with three passengers: Chris, Ed, and Jackie; and of course, the pilot. Hector was well versed with the location of various points of interest and knew well where the southern boundary of the National Park could be found. "This is from where we'll start your survey, as you have seen; even this boundary is a long way out. I will have to turn back now as we are down to half a tank of fuel."

"I did fit a 500-litre reserve tank to him," Ed shouted from the rear of the large craft. "It will give you a bit extra flying time. That switch near your left knee brings it on."

"That was a good move, Ed," Hector complimented him, "and by what 'Mr *I want to see the whole of the Outback* wants! I will need every drop of juice he will carry."

"I have some special gear on the way up," Chris advised them. "As soon as it arrives we can get to work."

The gear arrived the next day. It was quickly unpacked and the special survey equipment and cameras were quickly installed in Donald. Ed's expertise contributed considerably. Even with Ed's help it took a week to get the gear installed and tuned.

Jackie now ran both offices. They had the telephone line of the Quo-Vadis office redirected to the tourist park. Having to answer two telephones was no problem for her. The two companies shared her rather generous salary cost.

Chris had purchased a nice apartment in town. Uninvited Jackie moved in and had a wonderful time furnishing it.

For two weeks Donald flew along the boundaries of the National Park. Chris had organised fuel dumps along the track which he had taken to get to the sinkhole. The fuel merchant who serviced the three 5000-litre tanks soon learned the best way to get fuel to the tanks was to hook a large flat top trailer carrying a 15,000-litre tank, behind a Caterpillar bulldozer, and spend three to four days coming and going. He didn't mind, he found it was quite pleasant to drive out there, and what's more the money was very good.

With the availability of this extra fuel, the numbers of times they had to return to town was much less. Jackie complained bitterly with this development but soon found a way to overcome her problem of Chris's absence. When she was aware of the imminent departure of the searching survey team, she would arrive at the tourist park a bit earlier and would simply be sitting in Donald awaiting the arrival of the men and would absolutely refuse to be left behind. Consequently, she got to spend a very pleasant day or two out there with them.

Every night, be they in the bush or in town, Chris went over the survey sheets and photographs, in some places looking two or three times through a magnifying glass. They had attempted to fly along the length of the escarpment or to follow Chris's tracks, but had to turn back when once again the fuel tanks got too low.

Chris was getting desperate—he could not find that sinkhole. Surely the lake could be seen from the air, but NO! —he could not find it. In desperation, they loaded Donald with a maximum number of drums of fuel and set out to create a small fuel dump as far out as possible.

"Please take care," Jackie whispered as they lay together one night. "You are taking so much time flying everywhere and accidents do happen. I would die if anything happened to you."

Operating from that small fuel dump worked well. On the second day out, Chris, who was sitting beside Hector, was the only other person on this flight. Ed had returned to his workshop and Jackie had missed out this time.

"We have found it," he cried excitedly, "There it is! At last! It's a bit further out from the Park boundary than I thought, but I wasn't dreaming. It really does exist."

The green, verdant sinkhole was there below them. "Can you set him down on that flat spot please Hector, I want to do some surveying?"

"So, this is where the legendary Quo-Vadis mine will be," Hector quipped. "Looks like a beautiful spot to bring tourists too, he added with a laugh;" as he set Donald down on that flat spot.

"Any blasted tourist poking his nose around here will be welcomed with a load of buckshot," Chris snarled. "Anyway, it is far too far for even Donald without that refuelling dump." Donald was fully provisioned for a proposed tour group; and after a brief static ridden radio call to Jackie at the tourist office; she simply told Chris, "they were clear for a week," and grumbled a little about missing out on being there when they had found the sinkhole.

Chris's surveying skills were put to the test for the next couple of days. Hector wandered exploring throughout the sinkhole.

He chucked a small nugget to Chris. "Found it down by the creek. Is this what you're here for?" he quietly said.

"Sure thing," Chris replied. "I know I can trust you to keep your mouth shut. If word gets out because of that big mouth, I will modify your love life, '*big time.*'"

"Ouch! Better keep quiet then," Hector replied, and added very lightly, as if hiding something, "I have plans for my love life."

While Chris worked, Hector fossicked. It took a further three days before Chris had accumulated all the information he needed. "I will have to assume that distant corner of the National Park. The mines Department maps will record that accurately. All I will have to do now is to relate my survey findings to that information. Oh, happy day!" He started to sing loudly, "and off key."

In the meantime, Hector had accumulated a good heap of those yellow nuggets. Two were half the size of his not-so-small fists.

Chris looked at the heap and laughed. "I'll go you halves in that lot."

"HELL MAN," Hector blurted, "This is your gold, and you are giving it away?!" He stopped in mid-sentence: "What you reckon this lot is worth?"

"I had only picked up about quarter of the amount you have," Chris replied, "but at a rough guess I would say there is at least, one-hundred in that heap."

"One-hundred what?" Hector shouted.

"One-hundred big ones; maybe closer to two hundred thousand dollars," Chris laughed.

Hector was struck for words, until he finally managed to stutter, "I cannot just take 100,000 dollars from you. I know you are not short of the green stuff, but 100,000 thousand? Hell, man—that's a fortune," he cried.

"Please cut out all this rubbish and know there is plenty more where that came from," Chris laughed at him. "Let's get back to town—I have some work to do."

In their haste to get away, they nearly forgot to pick up the pile of nuggets.

Once they were in the air, Hector became very quiet.

"Off in dreamland are you, Mister?" Chris interrupted his daydreams. "Come back to reality for a moment please. There are things to be done, some of those things involve you."

Things to be done was an understatement.

Bill had hefted the sack containing the nuggets: "Seventy to eighty kilograms in here. Is it as good as the last lot?"

"Cannot answer that, mate," Chris replied with a laugh. "Some confounded amateur picked them up. It is probably half full of wallaby droppings. I am off to the office now. Call we if you want anything further," then added, "Want to meet me at the pub later?"

Jackie was waiting at his office when he got back. "Hail the hero comes," she cried joyously and kissed him very passionately. "I've missed you. How did it go?"

"Perfectly," Chris replied. "Hector's back too. Can you come in here tomorrow? I have much to do and you can help?"

"Yes," Jackie quickly answered. "Hector can run his own ship for a few days so I will come in here and do my best to distract you. Did you see the new furniture? I have even purchased a very large settee. It definitely needs some attention," she giggled.

"Save your 'attention' needs for tonight, you wicked girl. I will give them my full attention then," he whispered.

That made them both smile broadly in anticipation. Chris produced all his notes and proceeded to set them out in various relative piles on his desk.

"What is all this?" Jackie inquisitively asked.

"This is the Quo-Vadis mine," Chris proudly replied. "Now start being helpful and duck down to the mines office and get me a copy of the survey map of the southern boundary of the National Park. Ask them to make sure all the datum lines and their readings are noted."

"I have already done that. When you said you were heading for the National Park before you left the other day I guessed you would need this. I have the maps of the whole park and the survey numbers," Jackie said with pride.

"Hector said you were a blinking marvel. Now I can see why he said that," Chris said with a smile.

"He said that, did he?" Jackie asked. She appeared to be a little distracted.

They worked on the maps until well after midnight. Jackie proved to be more than just a pretty face, and her concise method of recording information was immeasurably helpful. Chris only had to ask what the numbers were on such-and-such point and in a minute, she would rifle through the files she had created, and the numbers were in front of him.

She greatly admired his professionalism and expertise. "You know exactly how to go about creating a very precise picture of that sinkhole, Mister," she said, her voice full of awe. "You make it very easy for me to admire you and love you."

Near 1 am, Chris straightened up, stretched, and shouted jubilantly: "That's it! I now know exactly where the sinkhole is. I have superimposed the figures on the Lands Department map and can just about tell you the answer to anything about that area you may ask."

"I do have a question," Jackie asked without hesitation. "Are you going to find me some dinner? — I'm starving!"

"Sorry Superwoman," Chris replied, "but there is not much open at this time of night. Would one of Joe's Best in town fill up the hole in your tummy?"

"A double burger with the lot and a double serve of fries has my mouth watering already," Jackie hungrily replied. "I do love Joe's-Burgers, can we just pick them up and go home and wash them down with a glass of red and two hours of passionate lovemaking?"

"Ring the order through now—it will save having to waste time waiting for the burgers," Chris quickly offered.

"Brilliant suggestion," she squeaked as he playfully pinched her bum.

They did not get to the mines office until after 11 am the next morning. Somebody was just too comfortable to get out of bed. The mines office was empty of clients and Chris soon had the whole staff locating and bringing to him details of all the leases that had been issued over the coordinates he had recorded. He could not believe it when he found the permits did not cover the sinkhole but did cover most of the escarpment. The sinkhole area had never been pegged and no leases had ever been issued over a fair bit of the adjacent land.

The head of the Mines Office looked over Chris's figures. "I would like to use these figures to fill in the gaps in our own maps. How much would you want for them?" he asked. "These are very professional and it would be quite costly for us to initiate a survey to this degree of accuracy. I believe leases were never sought for the area, or surveys done, because nobody could get into that sinkhole."

"It is okay by me, Mr Mines Office Chief. You can have them for nothing. In return, I would like all the information you have on leases........"

Jackie quickly handed him his maps and he instantly continued. "Here, here, and here," he almost growled as he stabbed his map with a long finger. In the time he had been in the Mines Office he and Jackie had found that licenses to mine had been granted that covered that section of the escarpment which had aroused his interest, particularly the area, but did not include the nearby drop off. Leases that had been issued did not cover the face of the drop-off from where the river that ran through the sinkhole exited. The lease ceased fifteen kilometres back from that cliff face. The remainder of the whole escarpment was covered by four different permits; they were all held by one man.

The Office Chief, watching over Chris's shoulder, commented, "These licenses are very old and are due for renewal in a month or two. We have not yet heard from the leaseholder. If he does not renew we will have to get a court order to resume them. That is a confounded nuisance really. If you are interested in them why don't you buy them off him now and renew them yourself; in that way it would save us resuming them, going to court and waiting for somebody to reapply for them. You will be doing yourself and us a favour if you approach the leaseholder and buy them. You could then renew the leases and in truth save us a lot of hassle. I would personally see that the sale was recorded quickly without any hiccups. It is a bit irregular to just hand out names—we usually require a formal letter—but in these circumstances and because you have been most helpful to us I will overlook the need for a formal application and supply you with the present leaseholder's name."

He turned and addressed a clerk sitting nearby. "Langley, please immediately bring me the files," and rattled off a series of numbers. The clerk jumped up and within five minutes returned with the four files. They contained very little.

"You can see Mr Kennedy," the Office Chief firmly said, "nothing has been done on any of them; there is only the initial application, the approval, and a copy of a receipt, in the file." He again turned to Langley and snapped, "Copy all four applications quickly now, and give them to Mr Kennedy; we have held him and his is very lovely assistant up long enough."

"Rotten old pervert," Chris protectively thought to himself; but said nothing.

Langley darted up and handed all copies of the lease applications to the senior who perused them for a moment then handed them to Chris. "If you are ever asked, I never gave these to you, just say you found them," he whispered in a most conspiratorial way.

"I do not think I have ever met you, sir," Chris answered softly. "It is amazing what one finds just lying about these days."

The survey figures on the application were very amateurish and not in Chris's league. "These were obviously done from a ground survey using very old-fashioned equipment. I will have to renew the markers quickly," he thought.

The leases had been applied for and granted to one Henry Augustus Morris; the address given was in the old dignified section of town.

It took Jackie little time to find a phone number for Mr Morris. "He is very old, Chris," she said. "Look at the birthdate on those lease applications—its way back in the 1900s.

The telephone was answered by a sharp speaking young female. Chris introduced himself.

"Grandfather is sleeping, Mr Kennedy. I will have him return your call when he awakens. Can I tell him what it is about?"

"I would like to talk to him about some of the leases he holds that are about to require renewal." Chris quickly answered her.

"You are not from that big mining company are you Mr Kennedy? If you are he will not even reply—he hates them," she rather aggressively said.

"No," Chris replied, "I am a brand-new prospector. I would like to talk to a man of his knowledge and experience."

"He would like that," she softly said. "He loves to reminisce about the old days."

She would have chatted on further, but a voice called, "Who is it, Steph?"

"It is a Mr Kennedy, Grandpa. He wants you to tell him about the old days. He is just starting out."

"Tell him to drop by tomorrow after breakfast."

Chris heard the reply.

"Did you hear that Mr Kennedy? If you came about 10 am it would be good—he is usually settled down by then," conveying the message most efficiently, then added, "Be prepared for quite an earbashing," she laughed and hung up.

Grandpa Morris must have had a good night as he was quite congenial and welcomed Chris and Jackie, especially after Jackie presented him with a bottle of Grandfather Port.

"You surely know the way to handle an old bloke, young lady," he laughed, as he examined the label. "I do like a drop of good port after dinner. Steph tells me you are interested in a couple of my leases; not the big one next to those big bastards I hope. But come to think on it, I would do well to get rid of it; just to snot them on the nose. That lease has caused me so much strife; even took me to court to try and make me sell it to them. The judge tossed them out."

Chris and Jackie sat entranced with the old tales of his many mining adventures. They were not in the least ear-bashed.

Grandfather Morris paused in his discourse and appeared to recall he had been talking about that confounded lease. "After the court case, they offered me $100,000 for it. I don't need the money and told them to stick it. You want to buy it son? You look to be a decent type and your sister is nice." The old fellow was looking at Jackie with a twinkle in his eye, and his whisper could be heard at the other end of the house.

Chris felt a sharp pain in his shin—Jackie had given him a swift kick. He looked questionably at her, she mouthed back, "Sister?" and kicked him again. Chris manipulated the discussion to the leases on the escarpment.

"Waste of time that lot," the old fellow grumbled. "Darn near killed me out there. Lost both pack horses—stupid beggars, fell over the edge. I only just made it back. Don't waste too much time on that lot, lad; it will be better for you to take the good lease. He spoke as if it was a done deal. "I'll let you have it for the $100,000 I've been offered."

"That is a lot of money," Chris strongly replied. "It will take a lot of my capital. If it is a dummy I will be hurt. I think I should have some sort of back up."

"You appear to be interested in those leases on the escarpment," old Morris slowly said. "I tell you what, the old man spoke as if he was bargaining in a Chinese market, "take the big lease for $100,000 and I will throw in those four leases that cover most of the escarpment for $2,000 each."

"What do you think, Jackie?" Chris asked. "Can I afford $108,000? She keeps my books, Mr Morris," Chris explained.

"Yes, I think that money in the bank will cover it Mr Kennedy." Jackie had joined in on the charade.

"Okay, Mr Morris, done deal," Chris strongly said. "Do you want a cheque now? I can get the agreements drawn up fairly quickly."

"Just get those agreements drawn up as soon as you like, Morris gleefully replied. "Give Steph the cheque—she can bank it this arvo. I would love to see the Mine Manager's face when he learns I have sold that lease."

"He is a vindictive old bugger," Chris thought. "He would never forget it if one did him a bad turn, and, even though they don't need it, these old blokes cannot wait to get their hands on the money. Things are working out perfectly." And leaning close to Jackie's ear whispered he softly said, "You owe me 'big time' young lady—my shin is still sore."

He quickly stood, shook hands with Morris, thanked him for his time and waited while Jackie collected her bits and pieces, then strode to the door.

As they stepped into the entry, he heard Morris, in his whispering bellow, say to Steph, "Now, girl, that is the stamp of a young fellow you should be trying to hook onto."

Chris did hear Steph say, "She is not his sister, Grandpa; no girl looks at her brother in the way she looks at him."

Chris smiled to himself. Jackie abruptly said, "What is so funny, Mister? Are you still laughing at that *sister* bit?"

"Perhaps," Chris deceptively replied, "but let's get back to the office. Are you free for the rest of the day? There is much to do."

"I will have to tell Hector," Jackie replied. "He can watch the shop—I am sure it will be okay. Can I tell him what has happened?"

"No!" Chris all but snapped. "Until I have this signed, sealed and delivered, we keep it quiet."

A long telephone conversation with the lawyer friend, a comprehensive letter dictated by Jackie to the lawyer's shorthand typist that contained all the details, a call to Rex to let him know what was going on, a cursory call to Ed, and a follow-up call to the Chief at the Mines Office were all completed quickly. Jackie amazed him with her efficiency.

He sat back in his office chair and tried to focus his racing mind. "All done and it is not even lunchtime. I will order in some lunch and just go over all the details with Jackie," he thought. "Just in case I have missed something."

He picked up the copies of the letter Jackie had dictated to the lawyer's secretary and started to read. He looked up at Jackie. "You have even included all the dimensions of every lease; where did you get them from?" he asked.

"It is easy," she smiled. "All you have to do is to know where to look for things and how to dig them out. Most government records are all stored electronically you know. Claude, my old boss, knew all the keys. He told me of them."

"Thank you, girl," Chris said, his voice filled with wonder. "You make it harder for me every day to keep my side of the bargain."

"Don't try too hard, my man. I am yours for the asking." With that she stood from her desk and came to him, enveloped him tightly in her arms and kissed him extraordinarily passionately.

Chris surfaced and held her back a little and whispered, "We must celebrate a little. How about dinner tonight? That new restaurant—you know, the floating one—has just opened. Would you like to try it? I hear it is very good. Full formal dresses required even to get in," he added.

"Just my style," Jackie laughed. "I'll knock off a little bit early and get my hair done."

They worked together for most of the afternoon. About 3 pm the telephone demanded their attention. She reached to it; it was the lawyer. She raised her eyebrows a little and whispered, "Lawyer; he was quick!" and handed the telephone to Chris, "Chris;" the lawyer said; "My girl has just taken the letter to the Post Office, it is coming to you priority post, you should get it in the morning. I have covered everything; the agreements will never leak. The details you supplied were right on, my compliments."

The letter did arrive on the returning mail plane the next late morning.

Chris carefully read the documents, all twenty-six pages of them, and smiled to himself. "He must have had the whole of his office staff working on this," Chris gratefully thought. "For what I can see, there is absolutely no way old Morris can ever come back at me for anything."

Jackie printed off four copies of each document, assembled them in separate files, and within an hour and a half of the letter having been received, read and copied, the complete files were placed in front of Chris on his desk. "I am off now," she said. "I have told Hector you need me tomorrow. He's okay with that."

Chris telephoned Morris—Steph answered the call. "Oh, it's you Mr Kennedy. May I call you Chris? I hope we can be good friends," she spoke most seductively.

"That would be very nice Steph," Chris replied equally softly. "Would your grandfather be available tomorrow at 10 am? I have some documents for his signature. He may want his solicitor to see them before he signs."

Steph did not hesitate and quickly said, "He will not have a bar of legal people after the run-around they gave him with that court case. I am sure so long as the documents are all straightforward he will sign them. He is quite excited with the whole thing. Will you stay for lunch?"

"I am terribly sorry, Steph, but I already have a commitment for lunch," Chris replied. "Perhaps we may have dinner one night?" he asked, tongue in cheek.

"I would like that, Chris. Just the two of us?" Her reply was loaded with barely hidden implications.

Dinner with Jackie the previous night had been one out of a fairy-tale. All *tarted up,* the couple attracted many admiring glances. Jackie's appearance was the main reason. She looked superb. The weather was perfect, the venue magnificent, and the meal was prepared and presented with obvious expertise. They danced closely and talked easily.

"You may bring me here as often as you wish," Jackie cheekily told him.

"I will see that happens," Chris more or less committed himself to the "task."

They decided not to go home that night but to book into the Five Star resort hotel that overlooked the river. Their loving that night assumed a hitherto unknown level and consequently they eventually fell asleep locked in each other's arms.

A loud knocking on the door woke them. "Breakfast, sir," called the porter.

"Hell!" Chris suddenly thought, "What's the time? Surely it is not eight already."

The porter wheeled the breakfast trolley in, took one look at the contented couple, and thought silently to himself, "Huh, honeymooners."

Chris thanked him, gave him a good tip, and escorted him out. Jackie was very slow to rise. Chris simply lifted her and carried her into the bathroom. They showered together.

"Just to save water," he gleefully exclaimed as he soaped her all over.

It was 9.30 am before they rushed home, changed from the finery they had been forced to put back on, which was all they had to wear. That drew a few questioning glances as they stood at the reception counter checking out. They had rushed to the apartment changed quickly, dived into the office to collect the files, and had managed to arrive on the Morris doorstep at 10.02 am. Steph opened the door; a look of disappointment crossed her face when she saw Jackie was with him. She had obviously taken great care with her appearance that morning.

"Good morning Christopher and Miss. Right on time," Steph said. "Grandfather is waiting."

Morris only ran a cursory glance over the documents, referred a couple of times to his own files then added, "A JP. friend of mine will be here in a minute to witness everything. He leaned closer to Chris and in his normal booming whisper said, "Steph has spent half the morning preparing morning tea so you better say something nice about it."

"No beg your pardons with this guy," Chris thought. "Still, it is good to do business with him."

All was signed sealed, and morning tea, which was delightful, was over, and at 12.30 Chris and Jackie left bearing documents that said that Christopher John Kennedy was now the legal leaseholder of five registered mining leases.

Rather than carry those precious documents around with them, they headed back to the office. As they walked in the office door, Chris gently took Jackie in his arms and very sincerely said, "Thank you, Jackie. I could not have accomplished all this without your help. I will never be able to repay you."

"I do know a way," she slowly replied, "but it is well that I keep it to myself and let time run its course." Then lightly she said, "Feel like a picnic down by the river just to switch off? You can register these documents at the Mines Office tomorrow." Then she pensively added, "Christopher Kennedy! You beautiful man, no matter what happens, never forget I love you with my very being. Now before I change my mind about that picnic and race you off here and now let's go. That settee has never got the attention it needs and it looks so very inviting."

That quiet secluded spot by the river got all the attention it needed that afternoon.

The next morning at 9 am they arrived at the Mines Office, documents in hand.

The Mines Office Chief was rather nonplussed and raved on a bit. "I bet you had her with you," he said as he winked at Jackie. "Coercion I call it. She could make Old Nick himself sign the pledge." He ran a quick glance over the documents, paused at the signatures for a moment then said, "All legal. Come back in three days. I have to send these documents down to head office for assessment and costing. Do you want to include renewal fees? If you do, you have to give me the appropriate renewal applications. You can do that now if you wish."

"Yes please," Chris did not hesitate with his reply.

"Hope you have your cheque-book with you," the Office Manager growled.

"No, I haven't," Chris quickly replied. "Give me the forms, tell me the cost, and we will have everything back to you by lunchtime tomorrow."

"That will be in time to buy me lunch," the manager rudely replied.

"I am terribly sorry," Chris half-heartedly replied, "but I will have to defer the lunch bit. I have already made plans for most of tomorrow."

Back in the office together they completed the four-page application for renewal forms. "Darn Government loves paperwork," Chris grumbled. "Still, I suppose it is necessary."

Everything was done, cheque made out and they were about to leave when Hector pushed into the office crying out! "Can I have my girl back; my office is getting into a mess without her."

Chris only laughed. "I know how you feel mate—she really makes things sing. We have finished up here and if it is okay with Jackie it is okay with me. But be warned," he told Hector firmly, "for a while I'll need her much more often."

"That will be fine," Hector replied. "I have managed to employ a junior girl to help and knowing Jackie I'm sure she and the new girl will easily be able to handle both companies."

"Pair of slave drivers," Jackie sarcastically commented. "Well I can get all the excitement I need working with Chris, and I get some peace and quiet in the tourist park."

"That's what you think," Hector interrupted her. "The office is a mess. With all the bookings for Donald and all the other tours, things have gone haywire."

"I will soon sort that out," Jackie confidently replied. "What's the new girl like?"

"She's good," Hector answered. "She has some brains and uses them."

Chris pushed into the conversation. "I will need a chopper for four days, Hector old man. When can you fit me in?"

"It will have to be after the school holidays," Hector answered. "Things get a bit quieter then."

Chris turned to Jackie, saying, "Book me in a slot when you get a chance, sweetie. It does not need to be Donald—just a bird that can get me there and back. If it was not important I would use Goliath and just drive up."

Jackie left with Hector and Chris delivered the completed renewal applications and cheque to the Mines Office himself. "Since I have over two weeks to wait for the helicopter to be available I think I will have a *bo-peep* at that big lease Morris and the big Mines Manager had squabbled over," Chris thought to himself.

The surface of the lease was rather innocuous. Chris picked up a few stones, looked closely at them, and tossed them aside. He strode to the boundary of the lease, looked out over the adjacent mining activity. He quickly recognised the Green Stone Reef the mining activity had uncovered. That reef of Green Stone headed directly towards his block. For a matter of interest, he engaged a drilling contractor to poke a few test holes down for him. He marked out where he wanted the holes by placing a small pile of loose stones on the position. The next day the drilling contractor had his rig in position *doing its thing*.

Chris was in his office when the Mine Manager burst in. No hello or attempt to introduce himself, just an angry, "Morris tells me you have bought the lease from him, and you are going to develop it. The old sneaky bastard only laughed in my face. He appeared to be enjoying himself. What do you want for it?" No polite, "Would you sell it to us?", only what appeared to be an outright rude demand.

"Not for sale," Chris equally rudely snarled. "I have just started drilling so I have no idea what the lease is worth."

"You know where to find me if you would change your mind," the Mine Manager almost shouted as he crashed from the office equally as rudely as he had entered.

"He knows something," Chris mused. "I will go out to the lease now to see if there is some evidence of illegal drilling."

Even with his training, Chris could not locate any illegal activity.

Tom, the drill operator, saw him wandering about and came over. "Hi Chris," he said.

"Any news?" Chris asked.

"Not yet," Tom replied. "We are down 180 metres and have hit Greenstone, it looks quite good."

"Call me at any time if you want me," Chris told him. "Use this number—it is my direct number so I will get any message quickly."

"Good idea," Tom agreed and headed back to the drilling rig that was chugging merrily on its way.

Chris wandered about for a while. "I feel I am being watched," he fantasised. His fantasy was confirmed when he saw a flash of somebody re-focusing binoculars. "They are keeping a close watch," he thought to himself. "Well, to hell with them. I will do my own thing in my own time. The more they hassle me the more they will have to pay for the lease if ever I want to sell it. Anyway, I'm not really too tied up with this here. I believe the sinkhole has much better potential and I just love it out there. Can't wait to get back."

Jackie was waiting at their apartment when he "knocked off" and went home. They comfortably shared their experiences of the day. She was astounded at the Mine Manager's behaviour.

She told him about the new girl. "She is really very good and had picked up the ropes very quickly," Jackie said, adding, "She had only recently completed a basic secretarial course at TAFE and was very happy to have found the position at the tourist park."

Chris heard how Hector's business had gone "gangbusters."

"Hector had found some extra capital from somewhere," Jackie had said with a hint of curiosity in her voice.

Chris didn't tell her about the nuggets they had found during their recent visit to the sinkhole. With that extra capital, Hector had purchased two new tour buses and employed extra men to drive them, so both girls were comfortably busy. The new girl really appreciated Jackie's training.

"There are a couple of letters I need you to type," he told her as they crawled into bed. "Can you come in for an hour in the morning?"

"It's going to cost you, sir," she laughed.

"How much?" Chris asked.

"At least two hours right now," she brazenly answered and proceeded to collect payment.

They were in the office by 7.30 am. Jackie was happy to rise early and share breakfast with him. Letters done, they sat to have a cup of tea before she left for the tourist park when his telephone buzzed.

"It's Tom, your rig man," came an excited voice. "Chris, you had better get out here quickly. We have hit it."

"Hit it? Hit what?" the very bemused miner asked.

"Just get out here and see for yourself," the rig man appeared to be laughing.

"I don't know what this is about. Want to come out with me and see?" he asked Jackie. "I can run you out to the park later."

"Hector will probably grumble about you pinching his girl again," she said with a laugh. "He is getting used to me missing. Vanessa can handle things herself for a while."

Goliath rode over the rough surface of the lease.

"I do love the way he pushes through any rough spots, just like his owner," Jackie quipped.

As they drove up, Tom rushed from the rig. "You sure can pick them," he shouted. "Only a top engineer could spot the exact place to drill. You really nailed it. Come over to the shed. I have something to show you."

As the drilling rig bored down, every five or ten meters or whatever it suited the operator to do, the drill was withdrawn and the "core" sample with it. The core samples were all about fifty millimetres in diameter and three-hundred millimetres long. They were accurately placed in a core case in such a position that it revealed the progress of the drill. There were six fresh samples.

"Look at this," Tom shouted as he picked up a sample marked 210 m. At first glance, the sample looked to be an inconclusive sample of Greenstone, but as Tom twisted it around, wide streaks of gold could be seen.

"The drill must have cut right into the middle of the reef," Tom quietly said. "The boys are bringing up the next core in a minute. I set the bit to 250 metres, Ah, here it is. How does it look Mike?" he said to his number two.

"See for yourself," Mike laughed. "We are going down again to 255 metres right now to try and find how thick this reef is."

"Thanks, mate—255 sounds okay," he instructed his number two, and he impatiently seized the core sample and gasped. "Just look at this Chris—it's a bonanza."

"Very good, Tom," Chris laughed as he showed the sample to Jackie. "Look, you can see the vein of gold even in this sample," he told her.

"Oh, how exciting," Jackie responded. "How did you know it was there?"

"Went to university," was all Chris replied.

The 255-meter sample was even better. "Pull up now, Tom," Chris instructed the drill man. "I will mark out five new drill points for you, please go to a maximum of 270 metres and let me know the outcome."

He drove Jackie out to the tourist park. As she started to climb down from Goliath she reached across and kissed him gently. "Bye for now my wonderful man, not only wonderful but filthy rich. What more could a girl want? No, come to think on it, I want a bright red Porsche convertible. Pick me up at 4.30, take me to dinner and after dinner I will make a down payment on the Porsche," she brazenly laughed.

"Wanton woman," Chris laughed with her and playfully slapped her backside as she crawled out.

A week later a bright red convertible was driven slowly up to the tourist park office. "I'm looking for Jackie," the driver said.

"That's me," Jackie replied.

The driver tossed her a key: "That's yours," he said, turned and said, "I have a driver waiting to take me back." He halted for a moment as Jackie giggled, "I have not finished paying for it, but I will make one or two payments tonight." The bemused driver only threw his arms up as if in surrender and continued on his way. She enthusiastically made those payments that night. Chris was in the office early the next morning, albeit looking a little tired. Tom the drilling rig operator was waiting.

"Hi, Tom," Chris greeted him. "Been here long?"

"Only about five minutes," Tom replied. "I have the results from those five holes you asked for. Boy, you can sure pick them.

The fifth hole is about 100 metres from your eastern boundary. The reef took a dive about then. I did put down another hole about 20 metres further along, went down nearly 1000 metres and only found traces. That is about as deep as I can go with my rig."

"Thanks, Tom. You have done very well. When you put in your account, add 1000 bucks for each of your boys and put in an extra 10,000 for yourself," Chris quietly said.

"That's most generous of you, mate," Tom gratefully answered. "I am going straight away to tell the men, pack up the rig, and take everybody down to The Royal. That's the pub at the end of Main Street. Please join us if you can, but bring your wading boots," he laughed.

Chris avoided The Royal that night—he had no wish to get rotten drunk. Jackie had taken the day off from the tourist park. Vanessa was now quite capable of handling things. Jackie consoled her guilty conscience by saying to herself, "Anyhow things are a little bit quiet out there, the weather is not conducive for people to go out on tour."

They were working through an unanswered pile of correspondence, when the Mine Manager politely knocked. "Come in," Chris called.

Jackie lifted an eyebrow at him and softly said, "This will be interesting."

"Good morning, Mr Kennedy," the manager said, no aggression in his voice this time. "I am Jacques Piermont, the Chief engineer and manager for the mine next to your lease. Do you have a minute?"

"Always have time for a fellow engineer," Chris cordiality responded. "What can I do for you?"

"My number two was down at The Royal last night."

"Here it comes," Chris thought.

The mine manager was continuing. "He was speaking to a couple of the men who had been working on that rig you had drilling for you. They were most enthusiastic in their description of the results of the drilling."

"Drunk as skunks." Chris thought to himself.

"Mr Kennedy, you previously indicated you may entertain an offer for your lease. I know you're drill results changes things considerably. Would you now consider an offer of five million dollars? Chris heard Jackie's sharp intake of breath.

"No Mr Piermont, that is nowhere near the value of that lease," Chris quickly replied.

"What would you take," the Mine Manager asked.

"I really have not considered selling now, sir. I would need to do some more analysis before I would strike a sale price." Chris was playing a game of bluff.

"Spoken like a true engineer, sir. Could I have a quick look at your analytic compilations of the drill results?" Piermont asked.

"That's fair," Chris said and turning to the bemused Jackie he said, "May I have the file please?"

"Certainly, Sir," Jackie replied and passed him the folder. Piermont now calling Chris, Sir, amused her.

Chris's findings were set out in comprehensive detail. Piermont studied the pages for about five minutes, asked a couple of questions, raised his head and strongly said, "It is a valuable lead I see, please consider a sale price and call me. Do not worry about the hour." He rose and left mumbling something to himself as he walked out.

Piermont had only walked a few steps outside the closed door before Jackie burst out with, "Did I just hear you knock back five million dollars for that patch of dirt?"

"You sure did," Chris laughed. "He will come back with twenty million tomorrow now, he has seen the figures. He has the equipment and the men on site; it would cost me a fortune setting up; so, it makes sense to sell it. For how much is the question. I will hit him with twenty-five million and see his reaction."

"Twenty-five million dollars!" Jackie cried as she rolled her eyes around her forehead. "That is a disgusting amount of money. Can I have another Porsche and book a world cruise for us, if it comes off," she softly asked as she cuddled him closely. "You have a plan in mind to use all that money, sir?" she enquired.

"I sure do," he replied. "I will develop the sinkhole site. I feel obliged to offer old Morris a bit."

"You are a nice man," Jackie said. "Not many would even think of doing that."

He called on old Morris the next morning. Steph welcomed him with an unexpected kiss on the lips when she saw who it was as she opened the door.

"Chris!" she exclaimed. "And you are by yourself," peering over his shoulder. "No girlfriend this time," she wickedly thought, and kissed him again, this time long and deep.

"That's a nice welcome," Chris laughed. "Can I step back and knock again?"

"Don't waste time stepping back," Steph laughed and kissed him soundly again, and said, "Now you can come in."

Morris was genuinely pleased to see him. Chris related all that had happened and the two men sat and discussed the technicalities of setting up a mine. After half an hour of what Chris found to be a most informative discussion, Chris surprised the old fellow by saying, "I do not want to mine that lease; I have other plans but if he comes up with twenty-five million I would like to give you five million of it. I will need the rest to meet capital expenditure should my plans come to fruition."

Morris quickly replied, "I do not want any money. I did expect you to sell the lease right from the start. I was surprised when I heard you were drilling." Morris thought for a moment then continued, "Perhaps you can give me a few shares in whatever company you set up."

"I already have a registered company," Chris advised him. "Would one B-class non-voting share interest you?"

"Five million is a lot to pay for one B-class share, Mister," Morris laughed. "You must be confident."

"I am," Chris quietly replied and rather sharply added, "but if you would rather take the cash, that's fine."

"Keep your shirt on, sunshine," Morris heartily laughed. "I did not expect another cent from you so I am risking nothing. Give the share to Steph—she will get most of my stuff anyhow. She is an angel you know," Morris said rather pointedly.

"I can see that. "A very beautiful angel, I must say," Chris sincerely replied.

Steph walked him to the door holding onto his arm and before he could open the door she turned into him saying. "You still owe me dinner," she whispered.

"I do not remember committing to that obligation, young lady," he whispered rather loudly. "I see you are a very desirable woman, you know that, but I am with somebody. Jackie and I have been together for some time. I would never hurt her."

"I do know that, Chris," she said as she pressed in close, "but please remember I am here. You excite me so much."

"Stephanie Morris, you are not making this easy," Chris softly said, then very sternly added, "I see you as a very special person. You grant me a great honour and I would dearly like to be your friend, a friend only mind, you. Can we leave it at that?"

"I will just have to start from there," she giggled. "I will be your special friend for the time being only, emphasis on the only."

Chris made a hasty exit and headed back to his office. Piermont the Mine Manager was waiting.

"He came in about an hour ago," Jackie whispered to Chris. "He has waited all this time. What he has to say must be important? Piermont balked a little when Chris told him the selling price was twenty-five million, cash in hand within seven days. "I believe that price is more than generous, and you are getting a bargain," Chris said.

Piermont left rather quickly now he had a price, and was back three days later, banker's draft in one hand, sale documents in the other.

"The board took very little convincing," he said. "Four out of the five directors had at some stage of their lives been gold miners; in fact, when they looked over your drilling charts they didn't hesitate. Your discovery that the reef nosed down to over 1000 meters did cause some consternation; however, when they were reminded we are presently chasing a much smaller reef at near 2000 m they shut up." He then added. "You are a hard man," he said with a touch of admiration in his voice. "Hard, but very clever and best of all honest. You did not have to tell us the reef nosedived. What are you going to do now?"

"I still have four leases way out back. I will spend time out there and see if they are worthwhile developing," Chris answered.

"Good luck," Piermont sincerely said. "The outback can get to you, I know." He then quickly picked up all the completed forms and left.

"I am off to the bank," Chris quickly told Jackie. "If you are here when I get back, I'll buy you a cup of coffee and a cake—I can afford it now."

"Don't be too long, I feel a bit down and being with you always cheers me up," she answered.

They sat at the window of their favourite coffee shop chatting. "You know why I am feeling down?" she confessed, "You are going away. Are you really going out to your sinkhole? I have never seen it, and if you say I can come with you I will feel much better."

"I have to warn you, you beautiful person, it is a hard life out there. You would have to be prepared to put up with a very, and I mean a very primitive lifestyle. Goliath makes things a bit better but it is still hard." Chris told her these things with a very forceful voice. "On the other hand, when I think on it, it would be wonderful and I would love to have you with me. I intend to leave in a day or two. Hector will have a fit when you tell him."

"It is very quiet in the tourist bit at the moment," Jackie very quickly replied. "Vanessa can handle things easily. Hector may grump a bit but he knows that if I want to go, I will go."

Chris found it was most pleasing to have her along with him. He derived much pleasure from sharing the magnificent primitive beauty of the Outback, and the joy of her exuberance made each day so wonderful. She did contribute to his surveying activity in a most helpful way, recording all his figures in the precise manner he well knew. Jackie was intrigued as she watched Chris work, mapping out and surveying a possible better route to the sinkhole. He now had access to many satellite and Mines Department maps.

Because they stopped to do this mapping from time to time it took over twenty-two days to reach the drop-off. Jackie had stood on the edge of the drop-off, open mouthed and totally in awe.

"Chris, she cried, "it is truly beautiful. How do we get down?"

She giggled like a schoolgirl as she was strapped closely to Chris and lowered down the cliff face. "Don't you dare get frisky, Mister," she laughed. "If I am to be tied to you, suspended hundreds," she exaggerated, "of feet in the air, it will do you no good."

She was still giggling as he unstrapped her, not an easy task as she kept making improper advances. "I am here to work," he reminded her.

"You are an old killjoy, sir. I will get out of the way and go for a swim in the river, it looks beautiful and cool. It may dampen my ardour a little."

"I wonder how long it will take," Chris mused. "One minute at the most I would say," he lightly thought to himself.

He had only started to unpack his gear when she screamed.

"Forty-two seconds," he laughed.

"Chris! Chris! I have found a gold nugget. Come and look," she yelled. She held the small nugget about two inches from Chris's nose. "It is gold, isn't it?" she cried.

"Yes, Jackie that is your first golden discovery," he softly told her.

"I will have it mounted on a chain and wear it always, so I can remember all that has happened this day," she cried and burst into tears.

It was the first time Chris had ever known her to cry and it disturbed him in a very deep way. According to Jackie, Chris then spent the next hours chipping at rocks and measuring things. She did record his notes for him and after a while came to realise there was a pattern to what he was doing.

"You are pretty smart to be able to see that, Jackie girl," he complimented her. "In fact, I'm mapping this part of the sinkhole. I did do some survey work when Hector and I were first here. All this new information will add greatly to my knowledge of the sinkhole. I have established that the sinkhole was formed about the Jurassic period. We may even find some dinosaur fossils from dinosaurs that had fallen over the cliff."

"Oh, how exciting," she whispered. "It is just wonderful how you know these things," she exclaimed.

"It took me over four years of hard work just to learn a little bit," he confessed. "Being out here excites me also. Let's go exploring for a bit. I have enough notes to keep me busy for a day or two."

They wandered along the river's edge, found a good pool, had a swim and returned to the hoist and harness.

"Can you strap me in so I can see out?" she asked.

"Sure can," Chris rather dubiously answered, "but you will not panic as we get up higher; will you?"

"I will try not to," she replied. "If I get scared, I'll just close my eyes and hope."

Chris laughed and strapped them together as she had requested. She did not panic and shouted with the exuberance as the outlook expanded before her.

"You must show me how to use the winch and harness," she bravely said, "so I can spend each day going up and down."

"Mad woman," Chris laughed.

They had set up their sleeping quarters in the rear compartment of Goliath. Some nights that SUV rocked with the wrestling match being conducted in the confines of that compartment.

The sunrises in that part of the Golden Outback were truly spectacular, and the next morning, as they ate their bush man's breakfast, toast, eggs and bacon, they sat appreciating this wonderful display of nature.

"What a beautiful morning," Chris lightly said, and added, "It does make one feel sorry for all those people stuck in the city. I saw something as we drove up the other day which merits some investigation. After breakfast, I will have a look at it."

Camp chores attended to, they prepared for the day's activities. Jackie was rummaging through her clothing for her work boots. She had learned the hard way not to walk about out here without wearing strong boots.

"I bet I look a sight," she laughed. "I don't care, I am very happy. In fact; the happiest I have ever been in my life."

They walked along the escarpment base for about one-hundred metres.

"What I saw would have been about here," Chris said.

"What was it she asked? She wanted to know everything about this mysterious land."

Chris had made a point of telling her about the different rocks they found and how and when they were formed. "There!" he cried very excitedly, "do you see that Jackie? All those animal tracks are leading under that thick bush."

He pushed into the bush following the tracks. Several small animals darted out of his way. As he pushed aside a large branch of the bush. He could now see they had reached the wall of the actual escarpment. A large cave yawned before them, all the animal tracks disappeared into the cave.

"There will be water in there," Chris exclaimed. "I'm going back to grab a torch. Please don't wander off. You will get lost in ten seconds if you do."

"I will stay right here, I promise," she answered and added, "Would you bring me back a chocolate bar, please sir? Despite having breakfast, a short while ago I'm already starving."

"You will be as fat as mud by the time we get back," Chris ribbed her.

"The way you keep me on the go, day and night," emphasis on the night, "I will get back as skinny as a rake handle," Jackie replied.

"A very nice rake handle," Chris laughed.

He trotted all the way to their camp and came straight back to the cave entrance. He carried two powerful torches and four chocolate bars. "We may need them just in case we get lost in there," he said, wickedly trying to scare her.

"I will not get lost," Jackie very confidently answered. "I will let the animals show me the way out. I have a friend now. This is Pierre." A small possum sat sleeping contentedly in her lap.

Very carefully they walked into the cave. They had travelled about three hundred meters when they found their way blocked and were prevented from pushing forward for a moment by what they thought was a small pool. That small pool turned out to be a small lake approximately sixty meters in diameter.

Chris shone his torch to the head of the lake. "A river flows into this lake," he said, half whispering, and shining his torch to the opposite end of the lake. "I wonder how that inflow escapes." He then shouted excitedly, "Yes, there's the outlet. The lake empties out there. By my reckoning, this is the source of the river that flows from that waterfall in the face of the escarpment. This is remarkable," he whispered. "This lake and the river will be loaded with nuggets brought down from a very big vein upstream somewhere."

He flashed his torch along the walls of the cavern they had recently entered. "Holy Mackerel!" he exclaimed. "Look at that Jackie." The beam of his torch had stopped on a wide quartz reef.

"What is it," Jackie asked.

"That my love, is a beautiful quartz reef. Gold is often found in quartz."

The reef was about ten feet up the wall of the cavern. There had been a substantial rock fall in that area. A pile of quartz lay haphazardly on the floor. Chris hurriedly walked to the pile.

By the time Jackie caught up to him he was sitting on the floor in what appeared to be a daze. "What is wrong," she asked in alarm.

"Nothing is wrong," he answered in a rather strange voice. "Look at this." He held up a fist sized piece of quartz.

Even to her untrained eyes she recognised a wide streak of gold running through that quartz. She shone her torch over that substantial pile of rock fall, and with a most emotional outburst cried, "There must be a fortune just lying here. Oh Chris, you knew something like this was up here. What do you do now?" She was so emotionally overwhelmed, she had begun to stutter a little.

Chris very softly replied, "Until I get my brain back in the right place we do nothing. This has been here for a long time—

another day or two will make little difference. Let's go back to camp and make a cup of tea and talk this over."

"Mr Supercool," Jackie thought. "How can he do it? All of a sudden he is a multi-millionaire and all he wants is a cuppa tea."

Chris had climbed to his feet, saying, "I have a small generator in one of the side carriers on Goliath. Tomorrow we will bring it up to this big cave and set up a couple of lights. I want to be able to see a little better what is here. What is that you are holding?" Chris asked in a bemused voice.

"It's a special souvenir," Jackie laughed. "It's that first small piece of quartz you picked up, you know the one you showed me that had the gold in it. I will keep it as a memento. One day, somewhere in the future I will put all my mementos on display."

When they arrived back at their camp she immediately retrieved and opened up a battered cardboard carton. Inside, there was a conglomeration of bits and pieces that defied identification, which she had collected on their way to the sinkhole and since they had been there. "I'll just add this bit of quartz to my collection," she almost humbly said.

Chris woke early and moved Goliath closer to the newly found cave. He set up the generator in the cave and strung out several lights. Jackie had not arisen from their bed in the back of Goliath and had grumbled profusely as she rocked and rolled about when he moved Goliath. "You are no gentleman, Mr Kennedy. It would have been proper to wait until a lady arose."

"What?" Chris replied, "And lose half the day."

It was not long before her good humour returned and she cooked him a fine breakfast as a means of repenting for her outburst.

The lights from that generator made investigation of the cave a lot easier. Chris had attached a long extension cord to a powerful handheld adjustable LED lamp. The small generator could not handle this additional load when he used the portable lamp and he had to disconnect the other four lights. The portable lamp was proving most useful: he could adjust the lens to be a floodlight which lit up a good area, or wind it back to be a powerful beam.

Jackie was curiously searching for more treasures in a dark area about 100 metres from the entrance of the cave. She suddenly screamed and disappeared into the darkness. Chris immediately ran quickly to that dark area. A silent ugly hole, about twenty metres in diameter, yawned before him. The hole disappeared downward into blackness. "Oh hell! She has fallen into this!" He panicked, and without regard his own safety he rushed to the edge of the hole. He shone the strong beam down into the hole. By its light, he could see from about twenty feet down Jackie's face, contorted with fear, looking back at him. She held onto a thin tree root; it was all that existed between her living or perishing somewhere down further in that abyss.

"Hold still!" Chris shouted. "Just hang on. Are you hurt?"

"Not hurt," she cried, "but I am very scared. Get me up, quickly please." Her voice was strained and full of the fear she felt. She was about twenty feet down, too far to reach, and the sides of the hole were sheer. It was by pure providence the root had been there.

"What can I do?" The question flashed through his mind. "I need a rope. There is some in Goliath," his spinning thoughts remembered. "I am going to leave the light here and race back to Goliath to get some rope. Keep as still as possible. I will be back in a flash," he called down to her.

"Please hurry, Chris," the very frightened girl cried.

Race back! That does not adequately describe it. He practically flew and returned carrying a length of climber's rope. He formed one end into a large loop, tying a second loop in the other end.

Jackie had heard him return and cried plaintively "Please get me out."

"Jackie," Chris called down to her. "Just listen carefully and, if you do exactly as I say, you will be alright. I am going to lower two ropes to you, both have large loops. You have one hand free, loop one rope under that free arm; make sure the rope sits all the way to be under your shoulder."

She very carefully did as he had instructed. "Good girl," he encouraged her. "Now take the second rope, just try and put your right foot in the loop. Your right foot is standing on nothing, so you may have to fish about a little. I will help from here." It took about three attempts but between them they succeeded. Now she had a loop under her right foot and another under her left shoulder. "You will not fall now," he called down to her. "You are safe now; this next bit will be a bit scary. Try and straighten your right leg, as you do that you may find your body pull away from the wall; don't worry, I will take your weight and draw you up. As you feel me lift you, let go of the root and grab the rope that is under your shoulder; grab it above your head if you can and quickly grab the same rope with the other hand. Got all that? Hang tight I am going to step back out of your sight and start pulling both ropes. You may spin around a bit—that cannot be helped. Don't worry, you will be up in a jiffy.

Jackie felt the ropes tighten and reluctantly let go of the root. She spun suspended over the gaping blackness and screamed a little. "Please hurry, Chris. I am so scared."

Three minutes later she was in his arms crying; she held him so tightly it was as if she was trying to melt into him. After a few minutes, he gently pushed her away. "I am going to take you back to Goliath now and make you a strong hot drink with lots of sugar, then tuck you into bed. I'm going to put something in the drink to knock you out so your rest will not be full of bad dreams."

"Oh Chris, I think I will have nightmares for the rest of my life, I was so scared." She had a superficial wash, downed the drink, and within ten minutes she was sound asleep.

Chris ventured back to that hole. His training as a miner came into play. "This is a bit of a conundrum," he thought, "but now I am looking carefully I can see this cave was the original exit for the river, a long time ago, maybe even before the sinkhole formed, but it looks like the river diverted to eventually excavate that whole area beneath the adjacent Outback, that by some geological phenomenon collapsed in on itself; to form the sinkhole. My guess is when that huge excavation collapsed, the river took the easier way out, eventually forcing an opening in the cliff face. Hence the waterfall out there. I hope God made a movie of all this," he chuckled to himself. "It will be one of the first things I will ask for when I get up there. The hole Jackie slipped into is interesting; the sides are smooth as if they had been ground. Perhaps there had been a pipe of soft rock there, and over millions of years hard granite rocks had been swirled around and around in that soft rock to grind it down to make this hole. Animals have come in here for water for an untold number of years. I will wager there are some interesting fossils down there."

He shone the strong beam down into the depths. "There is a bottom to it, looks to be about two hundred meters down. "Hey!" That would make it about level with the floor of the sinkhole. To confirm my thoughts will be something to work on sometime in the future."

He pushed his musings aside and continued his examination of his theory, but not before stringing that rope across the entry to the darkened area. "Just to warn us," he thought, "but I cannot see Jackie venturing into here again. She will even be a little hesitant to come into the cave itself. She is a gutsy one; she will come back to explore but will be very careful about dark spots. I must ensure she always has a good torch. That pill really did do the trick, I don't think she will wake up for a few hours yet. I wonder where the river flowed to way back then. While she is sleeping I will try and establish the route the river took in those days."

For an amateur it would have been impossible but being able to recognise rocks that had wear marks and were in the wrong place, or having been moved along by the river, he was able to walk and at times crawl along that ancient river bed. After three hours of this exploring he was about twelve kilometres out into the Outback.

He came upon a substantial basin like undulation. "Where to now," he asked in his mind. Any sign of the ancient riverbed had petered out. "What I am seeing, I believe, could have been a lake," he enthused. "It would have been very beautiful here. When she wakes up, I will bring Jackie here to see what she thinks about this. She may not be interested in my geological explanations but I think this whole riverbed and this ancient lake site is worthy of some investigation. The river would have been a good size, and there is a strong chance it would have possibly washed nuggets all along its bed and into the lake. I can just imagine what it looked like. What a shame the river does not flow into here like it used to." In his mind, he was imagining how it would have been. The river, bubbling its way onto the lake. There would have been much verdant bush along its edges and wildlife would have abounded. "Come to think about it, it would take very little to divert some of that river in the cave to flow here." His miner's mind instantly remembered the dried riverbed he had followed here. "The levels are gentle except for that one spot where there was obviously a six-foot drop, probably a very pretty waterfall. I would love to see it happen again. Perhaps later I can think further on it." He glanced at his watch, "Oh hell! Look at the time. I had better get back to her quickly. She's going to need a bit of TLC for a couple of days."

He admonished himself as he ran back, "When I get carried away with exploring I forget everything else."

By taking a direct line and just crashing through the sparse Outback scrub it was only about ten kilometres to the camp. Jackie was on the verge of waking. "Made it," he gasped in relief and proceeded to heat water for a hot drink to be ready for her when she woke fully. As he worked he thought lightly, "All these little extra things like that solar panel Ed had fitted so we would have power to be able to do things like this, are just wonderful. He looked quickly at Jackie. "I think I have time for a swim in that little lake in the cave, I must stink a bit from my run."

Half an hour, later bathed and freshly clothed, he sat quietly making notes of the day's activities, when Jackie softly called, "Chris, Chris, are you near?"

Responding instantly, he jumped up and crawled to her side. He eased her into a sitting position.

"Thank you, sir," she drowsily said, and added, "What did you put in my tea? I have a rotten headache."

"Here! Drink this," Chris whispered as he handed her what remained of the tea he had been drinking. She tentatively sipped the drink, and appreciatively whispered, "Good. I have been trying to remember what happened. I know I fell into a black hole. I remember falling and grabbing on to something, but I cannot remember much that happened after that. Oh yes, I can recall it now, there was a rope."

"I think your mind is still in shock, Jackie girl," Chris said. "The level of fear you have experienced may have blanked out much of what had happened. You may be lucky enough to never remember. Your memories may return. Hells Bells! You will be a rotten drunk, if one day you ever drink too much and in an inebriated condition the protection may go; you will be a raving maniac!"

"Then I will just never have to get drunk," Jackie laughed. "Is there any warm water in the shower drum, I feel I need a good wash. You look fresh and clean."

"Had a swim in the lake," Chris confessed. "It was very cold."

"I'll settle for a warm shower. Can you set it up for me?" Jackie quickly replied.

Later in the evening they sat before a crackling fire, sipping a soft red wine and counting stars. Chris told her of the ancient riverbed and his thoughts about the old lake.

"Would you show it to me tomorrow?" she enthusiastically asked. "At the moment I would much prefer to walk outside. I am not ready to go back into the cave just yet."

"I will be happy to share what I have found, with you," Chris replied.

Next morning; before they left the camp; Chris drove Goliath into the cave and loaded him up with quartz blocks. "I want to take some to Bill and have him ascertain the gold yield," he told her.

"It must be marvellous to have a brain like yours, my lover. You know all these things about rocks and things," Jackie most proudly said.

"It just so happens, Jackie, I was fortunate to have some very good lecturers. They taught me much," Chris humbly replied.

"That does not matter," Jackie laughed. "You have your ideas about your brain, I will keep mine. By the sound of things, I will be sleeping on a load of rocks that are full of gold for a few nights; not many girls have done that," she laughed. After "putting up"; with the discomfort of hard sharp rocks sticking into her for only half the first night; Jackie unceremoniously pushed Chris to one side and crawled into his sleeping bag with him. It was a very tight fit, and purely in an attempt to get some sleep, Chris had abandoned his sleeping bag, and for the remainder of the night, slept on the front seat of Goliath. The weather was kind to them and at night for the remaining 10 days as they drove back to the provincial city. Chris made sure the two sleeping bags that could be joined together were laid out each evening.

Bill was pleased to see them as they drove into the crusher yard.

He looked at the load of quartz; and picked up a block the size of his hand to examine it.

"This is good stuff, Chris," he softly said. "I can even see value in it without a glass. Do you have much?"

Chris simply answered, "Yes."

Jackie stuck her nose into their conversation. "There is lots and lots Bill. Mr Supercool here tells nobody nothing."

"I know that Jackie," Bill laughed deeply. "This is reef quartz, very fine and very pure. Chris could tell you, you generally only find quartz of this quality down very, very deep. Quite often it would be very rich in vein gold like you see here in these blocks. Give me a hand to unload your wagon Chris, I will grab a trolley and we can run this lot through the crusher and smelter now. The machines have not operated today. The big mine is busy just ripping the overburden off a new lease they have got their hands on. I heard they finally got hold of the Morris lease. Buy me dinner tonight at the Continental and I will bring you the results of the crusher run."

"We like the new floating restaurant, mate. Do you have some formal clobber? Wear it and we will meet you there at seven."

"Sounds good to me," Bill laughed. "Getting a bit classy these days, eh Mister?"

There was much to do in the office. "It can wait," Chris laughed. So, they dallied in preparing for the evening. As usual, Jackie looked stunning. She had recovered completely from her adventure and the time in the Outback had apparently suited her. She was nothing short of beautiful.

Bill whistled in appreciation and commented, "You are far too good for the likes of him Jackie," he said as he indicated who he meant with quite a rude gesture. "But when you are as rich as he is, you can have the best. Chris old chap," he continued without taking a breath, "that little load of rock you bought in yielded 432.94 ounces per tonne—an almighty yield. You had 5.361 tonnes in that load. You will not need your calculator—I will tell you that represents 2321 ounces or at today's price of $210 per once I owe you about half a million dollars. Do you want to sell it to us or put it on the open market? The people who buy into India are paying about twenty-five percent above our price."

"No, Bill the gold is yours. When you have time, I would like to take you out to Quo-Vadis. I need some good advice. No more mining talk tonight. Poor Jackie is up to her ears with mines and miners," Chris considerately said. "I want to spoil her a bit tonight."

Jackie interrupted. "And just who are you to tell people I'm up to my ears with miners! There is one particular miner who I cannot get enough of and if he is thinking he is going back to Quo-Vadis without me he will just have to think again."

That made them all laugh and they proceeded to have a very pleasant evening.

Bill told them much of his life. He had never married, never graduated, had only a minimum of education beyond high school, but he would defy anybody to disagree with what he knew about rocks, even the ones in Chris's head! "You know that thing that contains what Chris calls a brain." He laughed and added; that pressure from the higher-ups and the continual snipping by those bloody smart-arse clerks working in the office in town, was making him disenchanted with his job.

This comment registered with Chris, who quickly asked "Want to help me set up my mine and run the processing, Bill? I will pay you good money."

Bill thought for a bit and replied, "I'm not knocking you, mate, it sounds a good deal to me, but can I tell you my answer after I have seen your mine site. I have a yearning for a quiet life, just growing veggies and flowers and wetting a line now and again."

"Wetting a line?" Jackie quizzically asked.

"He means go fishing," Chris laughed to her she laughed with him and leaning over the table whispered loud  enough for Chris to hear, "Bill! Once you see the place you will never want to leave."

"That good is it, Jackie girl? Now I have an even greater reason   to go out and see it." Bill responded with enthusiasm.

# Chapter 2

With all the administration problems out of the way and a new high-tech communication device installed in Goliath, a week later, Chris, Bill and a very happy Jackie set out to go back to Quo-Vadis. Hector was nowhere in sight to bid them farewell.

"Strange," Chris thought. "Just another conundrum to sit in the back of my mind awaiting resolution. I'm going to go a different way," Chris advised them. "I have spent some time with the regional administration people and spoke at length with a few of the planners. They have said, if I wanted to push a track out to the mine, at my own cost, they would not object. I did show them the route Jackie and I surveyed last time we went out. The regional people did suggest I check my plans with the Mines Department and the Environmental people. Apparently, they all like to have a say in these sorts of things. Blasted red tape!" Chris grumbled. "A man could hang himself with it if he's not careful. After all these people learned of my qualifications and found that I was not some amateur with a big dream, and as it was not going to cost them anything, they had all agreed it was OK, to cut a new track. The Environmental people were most interested in the sinkhole and had said they would like to look at what we are doing from time to time. They knew the sinkhole existed but had never investigated it as any endeavours had been thwarted by their inability to gain access into it. We will try that route Jackie and I surveyed; we may encounter a few problems with some of the soft spots. Did you notice there are two extra shovels in the back?" he laughed.

"You bog us, you dig us out yourself. Bill and I will sit back and watch an expert at work," Jackie wickedly laughed.

The proposed track was not perfect. It some features in its favour and a few sections that presented problems relatively few. The major problem being; at least twice a day they had to spend a couple of hours in the blazing Outback sun digging Goliath out. Chris had every conceivable piece of equipment to be used in the event of getting bogged, but it usually boiled down to having to dig the SUV out.

"This is fun," Jackie sarcastically cried, as she wrung out the bandanna she had wrapped around her beautiful neck to catch the perspiration. With her hair tucked under the broad Akubra hat, ex-army shirt and trousers, long thick socks jammed into thick heavy leather boots, she had no resemblance to that chic company secretary people knew her as. Still she thrived. Chris could look past all the "adornment" and could still see the very beautiful person she was.

"Woah," he admonished himself, "remember our deal. No getting in too deep, but damn it all, it is getting more and more difficult to keep to my part of the deal."

Bill didn't complain once; in fact, he appeared to be enjoying himself. Chris heard him say, "I love this feeling of freedom."

The plusses were a different thing. Chris had to amend his proposed survey route a few times as they came across large sweeping valleys and spectacular rocky outcrops. "The Environmental boys would have my nuts if I touch them and drove a track through the middle of them," he thought with a touch of humour. In fact, the plusses outnumbered the things which were against by about ten to one. "There are quite a few bog holes; they will have to be filled. There is plenty of dolomite deposits and other suitable stone in the nearby escarpment. In time, we could drag a portable crusher in here. Something to be done some time in the future," the miner thought to himself.

Had they taken the original track they would have been at Quo-Vadis in just over a week. With having to dig Goliath out so regularly and rerouting the original survey while Chris found an alternative, it took them nearly two weeks.

Upon arrival, they set up their camp not far from the cave entrance.

Bill looked into the dark cave and gasped: "You drove your rig into there? This I *gotta* see."

As the day was still young, Chris presented his cohorts with a torch each and set the generator going. With him carrying the variable focus lamp, he led the way. It was Jackie who very quickly warned Bill, "of that awful hole," she called it. She was a little apprehensive about the cave at first; however, Chris's enthusiasm soon overcame her fears and she moved confidently with them.

The piles of quartz rock fall containing the thick lines of gold, the quartz reef ten or so feet up, and the cave wall that glistened in the light of the strong beam of Chris's lamp, left Bill speechless. He quickly recovered his voice and cried, "My God, Chris, there is an absolute fortune just lying about here on the floor of the cave notwithstanding just how much is up there on the cave wall waiting to be mined. I have seen deposits before but nothing to the equal of this. Have you plotted the reef?" he demanded.

"Give me a break, Mister. I have only been here a week or two. You see now why I need a hand," Chris growled.

"Count me in, Chris," Bill enthusiastically replied. "Even if all this was not here, this place has already got to me. My first thought is, we have to make a way down the face."

"That's only one of the first thing's I want to do," Chris replied. "There is much more to be done. I have some ideas mapped out. Jackie '*my love*,'" Chris looked at Jackie with a smile, and said "for the next hour you are elected '*Tea Lady*.'"

"My love!" Bill chuckled to himself. "Can't blame him; with a girl as beautiful as her it is little wonder he has found no time to map that reef."

"That cup of tea sounds good, I need it," Bill said. "My brain is still reeling from what I have just seen."

"Tea ladies come at a cost," Jackie laughed.

"I will pay up later," Chris wickedly smiled to her.

"By the sound of things, I will be well served to move my sleeping gear into the cave, away from the night time activities of this pair," Bill solemnly thought to himself.

Chris and Bill talked for hours discussing the plans Chris had made. Bill made a few suggestions, Jackie took notes.

"The way I see it," Chris said, "power supply is a priority. I have given strong thoughts to installing Hydro generators. There is more than enough flow from that river, before it forces its way out of the cliff face. We will need much power to operate a crusher and the smelter." Dump trucks, accommodation and a multitude of other things were all discussed.

"All of this is going to cost a pretty penny," Bill commented. "Can you handle it?"

"It will depend on the costs of some of the big pieces and the costs of getting them here," Chris answered. But I think at this stage I know I can cover a lot of it."

"You are in a good position, Chris," Jackie softly said. "I'll let you know when to slow down. Are you taking Bill down the face tomorrow? I don't think he would like to piggyback like we do."

Chris explained to Bill what Jackie meant.

Bill laughed a lot with the thought of being strapped to Chris, and promptly said, "You are right, Jackie girl, I would not like that. We still have a bit of time; could we have a look at, 'Jackie's Big Bad Black Hole'?"

"Her what!" Chris exclaimed.

"That hole she fell into, you dill," Bill nonchalantly answered not realising just what he had said.

The two men walked quickly back into the cave. Chris removed the protective rope, and set his lantern on narrow beam, and shone it down that hole. The light revealed the bottom of the hole some two hundred meters down. It was littered with animal skeletons.

"Poor buggers," Bill softly said. "They just did a Jackie and took a dive. She was lucky you got her out."

"Don't remind her, Bill. She is not really over her experience yet," Chris whispered protectively.

"I noticed she was a bit hesitant about coming into the cave. I understand now," Bill replied.

Chris continued to shine the strong beam around the lower section of the hole. "Can you see that dark brown patch about five feet up from the bottom, Bill?" he asked. "It looks like iron ore. In that form it is basically granular. I am guessing that is why those granite stones were able to grind it away. Another thing I am guessing is that a lot of this escarpment is in fact this granulated iron ore. We may find many other instances where that ore has been eroded. This particular formation was a pipe of that ore that had been forced up between granite blocks. The river must have flowed down here as well as out the cave entrance, and over tens of thousands of years some granite stones had been spun around and around in that pipe to grind it as deeply as it has."

"How far do you reckon we are from the face?" Bill questioned him.

"I do not know, at the moment," Chris replied. "I can measure that tomorrow. What are you thinking, Mister?"

"It may be nothing," Bill answered, "but if it is not too far to the face we may be able to break through from this hole and gain access to the sinkhole that way. We could set up a hoist of sorts over this hole to facilitate getting up and down."

"Bill! You are brilliant," Chris cried as he punched Bill lightly on the shoulder in apparent gratitude." He then excitedly exclaimed, "A good lift here, set up a hydro generator down there somewhere, and set up the crusher and smelter nearby. In my dreams, I can believe this would all be possible. Tomorrow I will endeavour to locate a start point where we should commence to mine our way from the face to this hole."

"That would be a fine move," Bill said and added apprehensively, "Can you do that?"

"Went to Uni to be taught that sort of thing. Let's see if I did really learn anything. I think it is most appropriate to crack a bottle of red and drink to your idea."

Jackie was caught up in their enthusiasm as they explained what they had decided to do. "You men never cease to amaze me with your wonderful ideas. Can I help?"

"You sure can, Jackie girl," Chris quickly said. "Tomorrow I will need a lot of assistance from both you and Bill to locate that start point. You can work from the outside; Bill can work from inside, probably down the bottom of that hole."

To find the start point on the sinkhole face in relation to the black hole was not that difficult for Chris. He had taken a lot of attention to his surveying studies, and by next evening, after much in and out of the cave setting up instruments everywhere, and after numerous trips by either Chris and/or Jackie, who was now able to operate Goliath's hoist independently, making many ups and downs of the sinkhole face, Chris placed a diagram before Bill and Jackie. The diagram was marked with many geometrical symbols and measurements.

"What's all this?" Bill questioned. "Please explain to the uneducated what all this means."

"Yes!" Jackie very seriously pushed her nose in. "You, my man, are just too smart for your own boots."

Chris pointed onto the diagram and gleefully explained, "This is where we dig."

"I'm none the wiser," Bill snapped. "Just show me the spot tomorrow, hand me a pick and shovel, and I will start. Do you think we will need to blast? I know a good powder monkey if we do."

"I do not think so Bill," Chris replied. "Look at this sample of stone I picked up from the point we will start the digging. I think it is the same stone we could see from the top of the hole. You said it was iron of some sort. Not ironstone I hope—that's damnably hard. If it is ironstone, then, yes, we will have to blast."

At dawn the next day, Chris and Bill, (individually mind you) picks and shovels in hand lowered themselves to the floor of the sinkhole. Chris strode to the cliff face. A large X had been drawn on that face.

"Is this the spot?" Bill needlessly asked.

"Yep," Chris replied.

Bill stuck his face close to the spot and breathed in deeply. He was obviously smelling something. He lifted his head and smiled. "We are lucky, this is granulated iron."

"They did not teach us that at Uni. Fancy identifying ore type by smell. You are having me on, Mister," Chris reacted.

"You have your fancy instruments; I have my nose," Bill snapped. "I know which one I trust. If you behave yourself, I might teach you how to do it one day."

"Good Grief," Chris thought to himself. "Years of study and this old bloke tells me all I need is a good nose. But I cannot dispute what he has said: that is granulated iron ore; I must investigate how the ore became granulated. Possibly it got partial heated at some stage. That's enough lecturing my old friend. Let's get to work."

It was hard, physical work. "We need a Barra," (wheelbarrow) Bill complained as he shovelled a pile of loose stones out of the tunnel they had dug. All they had to show for a morning of hard work was a ten-foot deep hole.

"How far do you reckon we have to dig," Bill asked with a very weary voice.

"About one-hundred metres, mate," Chris had to swallow before he could reply. His throat was very dry. Then, as if in an attempt to maintain a degree of enthusiasm, possibly for himself as much as Bill, he added, "If it is as soft as this all the way through, it will not take all that long."

It was two very weary men who were lifted up that cliff face later on that day. Chris examined his blistered hands and exclaimed, "This is silly, Bill. We need some proper gear and a couple of young blokes to help us. I will go back to town tomorrow and see what can be organised."

"Why don't you use that new satellite phone Ed fitted for you?" Jackie asked. "You could get Hector to fly all you need out. He won't mind collecting it for you."

"I forgot about the new phone," Chris whispered. "Once again, you beautiful creature, you have proven your worth."

The phone worked a treat.

Vanessa answered the call saying, "Hector is not here at the moment but I can ring the hardware store and have them deliver all you require to here. Just give me a list and a day or two. You say you need some young men. A boyfriend of mine, Jackie will remember, I told her about him—he's the one with wandering hands—he is looking for a job, and I know at least four others who would jump at a chance to work for a couple of weeks."

"Thank you, Vanessa. All that would be a great help," Chris gratefully said, then to himself thought, "a very efficient young lady, 'another Jackie'. Just go for it, Vanessa," Chris croaked, his throat still dry, despite having been lubricated with a coldie (*a*

120

*small cold bottle of beer*). "Tell those young men, and Mr Wandering Hands, the money will be extraordinarily good, but they must be prepared to work hard and live rough. Please ask Hector to call me as soon as he gets in, he will need to use these numbers." Chris rattled off the satellite phone numbers.

Hector did call about two hours later, Vanessa having told him what was required. "You picked a good time Chris," he said. "All the fuel dumps and been topped up and I can come out just as soon as Vanessa can organise all the material you require and recruit those boys. Five lads?" he questioned, "are you starting to mine? Do you want some extra tucker? How's Jackie?" he added.

Jackie had followed the conversation. "Never thought you would ask," she pushed in. "I have never been better. This life in the Outback suits me fine," she answered quickly, then as if as an afterthought continued on asking, "When will we see you?"

"Just as soon as possible," Hector replied. "Tell Chris I will add a few extra things to his list. I can see he needs much more than a few blokes with wheelbarrows, picks, and shovels. Bye, babe!" and rang off.

Three days later, Donald set down not far from their camp. The new recruits bumbled noisily out, shouting and excitedly pointing to various features as they spied them. They had no fear of the cliff edge and stood looking out over the sinkhole, exclaiming in wonder that something like this did exist in the Outback. The few extra things Hector had added included a fully fitted out ten-man tent and large annex. Being experienced with organising the needs of group tours Hector had used his experience to include the works! He had even included an 8kW generator and fuel for it.

They set the five young men to work immediately, erecting their tent and organising the accommodation.

"I'll look after the cooking," one announced. "I love to cook."

"I will bet he will poison us," one of the others grumbled, with a touch of humour in his voice.

Bill took them back to the cliff edge. "See that spot down there, right next to the pile of dirt? Can you see the hole? That is where you will be working," he advised them.

They had a million and one questions: "Are we looking for Gold? Will we have time to fish? How many hours a day do we work? What's the pay?" Then, as an afterthought one of the lads asked, "How the hell do we get down there?"

Some eyebrows shot up to the tops of their foreheads when Bill explained: "You will be lowered down individually by hoist."

"Struth!" one perplexed lad exclaimed. "I hate heights!"

All their questions were answered to their satisfaction and the next morning after a restless night's sleep, and many moments of trepidation at being lowered down the cliff face, they all stood outside the short tunnel Chris and Bill had dug. Bill organised the procedure to be adopted, and the tunnel progressed quite rapidly.

Hector had wanted to leave almost as soon as Donald was unloaded, Chris, nonchalantly mentioned the ancient river bed and what he thought could have been a lake. "Where is it? Hector asked.

"It's a fair hike, mate, but if we hurry we can be back in time for tea."

Hector had cast a professional eye over the ancient river bed and the old lake site. "I think I can see what you saw Chris, put some water back in that river; refill the lake and we would have the perfect spot for a resort" he enthusiastically said. "I could bring people out here by chopper. We could stock the lake with fish, and those hills over to the North would be great for a few horse treks. There is a cattle station out there a bit further, but only a short hop for a chopper. I have three just the right size. I do not think it would be difficult to get the station owner to cooperate, especially if we offered him a few dollars for himself."

"When did this 'We' business come into it?" Chris laughed.

"Hell, mate, who did you think is going to fund all this?" Hector blatantly replied.

"I have more than enough on my plate at the moment," Chris rather regretfully said. "This resort business will have to go on the back burner for a while. Come to think of it, I have been worried that our activity is causing problems for the animals who used to come to the cave for water. I will make time to run a diversion from the river in the cave and feed the old river bed. That will serve to provide water for the animals and hopefully start to fill the lake. I will buy a front-end loader; Bill can use the loader to scrape the floor of the old lake and stockpile the overburden. It is possible for a fair bit of gold to have been washed into the lake bed. When I get my crusher up and running I will run those scrapings through the crusher. I do believe it will be well worthwhile."

"Don't you ever switch off from being a miner, Chris?" Hector quizzically asked.

"Why should I?" Chris replied. "That's what I am."

Chris and Hector headed back to the camp.

Hector had left a couple of the lads to unload the chopper and walked along the cliff face with Jackie. "It is really most beautiful out here. I can see why you want to come out so often. When you get back you must come and meet my girls," he hopefully said.

"I would like that," Jackie replied.

In the period that they had waited for Hector to arrive, Chris moved Goliath into position in the cave and lowered himself down the hole. Jackie had watched apprehensively as he disappeared into the blackness, illuminated now by his lantern. She would not venture any closer than four metres from the edge.

Chris had spent a couple of hours in the pit scratching out the seam of granulated iron ore. It was only a bedraggled semblance of humanity that was later hauled up.

"There are heaps of bones down there," he very seriously said. "We will have to be very careful of them. I think it would be best if we continued to mine only from the other side. The air is okay, I will definitely let the University know about those bones; they may or may not be interested."

Jackie had ascertained that she could use the satellite telephone to send messages and was able to advise the Uni. of the presence of all those fossils.

It only took a couple of days before Jackie received a telephone call from Vanessa. "I hope there is a bit of space in your tents," Vanessa said. "Three guys from the University have arrived looking for a lift out to the Quo-Vadis mine. They said they are palaeontologists and that the heads of their department had been told by you, that you had found an interesting deposit of bones. Hector said to tell Jackie to have lunch ready for us on Friday."

"We will be ready," Jackie replied and quickly relayed the information to Chris.

"It will be good to have that deposit of bones checked out," Chris thought. "The University could stop our work if they found we had failed to advise them of those bones. It is better to know now than later."

The deposit of bones did promote a good level of excitement as each identifiable layer revealed the different time spans and the nature of the animals that lived thereabouts at the time. Jackie's excitement reached a new level as they bought a well-preserved almost completely intact Tyrannosaurus Rex's skeleton to the surface.

"It is only a very young one," the scientists explained. "An adult would never have fitted into that hole." They were rather surprised with many of the fossils. "We did not think they existed in this area."

After three weeks, the Palaeontologists were satisfied there was nothing further in the hole worth investigating. Before they left they requested that they be allowed to delay their departure awhile while they poked around the adjacent area. They were firmly of the opinion that the whole of this escarpment was not only a geological phenomenon but had many interesting environmental aspects which required further study. They did assure Chris they would in no way interfere with his wish to mine.

In that three weeks, the tunnel had progressed about eighty metres into the cliff face. At times, progress was delayed when they struck patches of Greenstone.

Bill examined the tailings closely; there were signs of gold. "Nearly enough to merit crushing and smelting," he told Chris.

"Perhaps later," Chris replied. "I am more focused on getting this tunnel through."

The crew were a jovial lot and did work well together. Today they had struck a different problem. The seam of granulated iron ore had shrunk to about 600 millimetres in diameter, surrounded, this time, by dark foreboding granite.

"Ah well," Chris grumbled. "Looks like hard digging for a few days, fellas."

"Oh! My aching back," one of the crew laughed.

Chris had picked up a pick and gave that granite barrier a hearty wack. "BLOODY NUISANCE!" he shouted.

There was a loud crash, and the granite obstacle fell back.

"What the hell?" Chris exclaimed and shone his miner's lamp into the aperture left by the fallen rock. Blackness yawned at him. He shone his light deeper into the space. The light only penetrated a short distance.

"Get some more light up here," Chris excitedly called. It took a moment before a large floodlight was passed to him.

"Hold a sec. Boss," a voice yelled. "Alan is just hooking it up to the jenny (*generator*)."

While he waited, Chris and two of the other crew carefully enlarged the hole still barely sufficiently large enough to enable Chris to crawl into that black space. His training had told him better: *do not venture into dark unknown holes.* Unconcerned for his own safety, the very excited graduate 'with honours' mining engineer crawled into that new discovery. He pushed a large floodlight ahead of him.

"She's on," he heard Alan shout and the floodlight burst into brilliance. Before him was revealed a huge cavity. After considerable struggling he managed to worm his way into the cavity and stood looking around in amazement.

Bill pushed in alongside exclaiming, "Holy Jumping Moses, what have we here?"

A vast cavern opened up before them; it was all of 280 meters wide and at least 300 meters long. It stretched upwards to what looked like at least 80 to 90 meters. The rest of the crew now pushed in.

They stood alongside Chris and Bill in absolute silence, which was broken by Chris almost whispering, "Well gents, it looks like we do not have to dig a whole lot more. At a guess, I reckon that pipe we are trying to reach is only `10 or 20 meters further on from that far wall. Let's get a few more lights in here so we can see exactly what it is we have found. Be very careful where you walk, there may be more of those big holes about."

With a number of additional lights, Chris could get a better idea of the cavern and how it was formed. "This is truly amazing," Chris told Bill and the crew. "I think this is another of the mind-blowing things that happened over millions of years, about the time when the escarpment was formed. I am thinking that when the escarpment was pushed up it blocked a very big underground river. That blockage would have created great pressure and did find release by eroding any softer material. This cavern, the pipe, and our cave, would have been composed of the softer granulated iron ore, which the river, over all those years, just carved out. I do believe that river went on to wash away all that material from underneath the sinkhole, which eventually collapsed. In my mind, I can envisage all this; mind you, I have no actual proof of what I say is correct—I am only guessing—but I do not think I am far from the facts."

"You guess whatever you like, Bill nonchalantly said. "All I can see is a readymade spot for my crusher and smelters. How far do you think we are from the river?"

Chris contemplated the question for a minute. "I think about 50 metres at the most from the outlet," Chris replied. "We could even divert a portion of the river down to here to drive a couple of hydro generators. The river that we see now running through the sinkhole is, in my opinion, only a portion of a mighty river. The major portion must have found another outlet. He took a deep breath, then firmly said; "let's calm down a bit mate; I thought I was the ragtag drip in this deal but believe me; my excitement at the moment knows no bounds. I am even more excited than you." He then let forth a long exuberant shout.

The whole crew joined in.

"Back to camp," Chris called. "We have done enough today, and we are all so excited it will be impossible to work."

Jackie had to be restrained from hitching herself to the hoist, to rush down to see what they had found.

"I think it would be better if you came down with us tomorrow morning, when we have all settled down a bit," Chris sternly told her.

"Try and leave without me in the morning and I will do more than kick your shin; in fact, I will cut off your supply."

"Can't have that!" Chris laughed.

Jackie was equally excited as the men were, when the next morning she viewed the discovery. Torch in hand and at Chris's insistence always accompanied by one of the crew, she poked about the cavern. Chris and Bill had applied themselves to locating where they should continue to dig. It was not difficult and was easily identified by the continuation of the granulated ore seam.

Jackie rushed excitedly to Chris and grabbed his arm; "I have found something." She exclaimed.

"Easy, sweetie," Chris chuckled. "You may wet your pants you are so excited.

"Chris! Chris!" She dragged on his arm. "Come with me. I have found another cavern," she blurted out through her excitement. "It's up the other end."

Her discovery was worth getting excited about. The cavern was smaller than the one discovered earlier, but it ran crosswise to the larger cavern. A hastily installed floodlight had allowed Chris to measure it. The cavern was about 60 metres wide and 95 metres long, with a ceiling 40 metres up.

Chris walked to the far end. He paused there briefly. "It looks like a rock fall has sealed this end." Then thinking deeply, suddenly whispered to himself, "That isn't rock sealing this end; that is debris that has fallen from the cliff face. Jackie, you wonderful creature, you have found a much better entrance to these caverns," he jubilantly cried as he gave her an almighty hug. "And look up there, there is even a small stream of water flowing from that wall and into here."

The crew were a little nonplussed as they removed the debris to reveal a six-metre clear entrance.

"All that bloody digging, while all the while all we had to do was to find this hole," one of the crew very lightly grumbled. The whole crew were as happy with the find as were Chris and Bill.

"I don't know how I missed this," Chris told Bill. "We have been going up and down the face only ten metres from here. You and I have a lot of thinking to do as to how we best use all this we have discovered. We do not have any way of getting down here yet. I think we should continue with your idea to set up a hoist and in time an elevator in that black hole."

The tunnel from the large cavern to the black hole was completed without mishap. It was only twelve metres of relatively easy digging. The palaeontologists had removed most of the fossils, so it was not necessary to warn the boys to tread carefully. The crew stood at the base of the hole and looked up. All they could see was blackness.

"We are down so deep you get no illumination," Chris explained. "If we were outside, you would even see stars, although it is about midday."

"Another 'pearl' of wisdom," Bill laughed.

"Well chaps, we are all but finished here, we have achieved that which we set out to accomplish. We will tidy up for a few days, then call it quits."

The crew appeared a little disappointed with this. "We would all like to hang about to see the finished product," they all said.

"It will be some time before that happens," Chris told them. "You have done a mighty job, and you have my sincere thanks. From time to time I will need some help again. May I call on you?"

"Yes, please, Boss," they all replied practically in unison. "It is great working here."

In later years the young men all become permanent employees of Quo-Vadis Mines. In fact, two of them became Senior Shift Bosses. Alan became a mine manager in his own right.

"What to do next?" Chris tried to reason out. "I need some help here." He deeply thought, "It is alright to play the miner, but to be a construction man is beyond me. Bill has some thoughts, Jackie can always be relied upon for a good suggestion or two, but I need something concrete. I think a yarn with Professor Strahan and my old lecturer Fred Riley is required."

With that resolved firmly in his mind, he announced to Jackie, that as soon as Hector could pick them up they would be heading back to the regional city.

A few days later they all, including his young crew, stood in the regional city office of Quo-Vadis. The lads had pocketed their rather generous pay packets.

Chris was attempting to counsel them. "Don't waste that hard-earned money," he was saying. "I am only a few years older than you but you have seen what can be achieved if you take your future into your own hands and work hard. You all have good minds, put them to good use. Please keep in touch."

Each one of them shook Chris's hand and received a kiss on the cheek from Jackie. "I will miss you people," she told them. "It was fun having you with us."

The five boys rather resolutely filed out, each deep in thought.

"Good kids," Chris softly said to Jackie and Bill. "I would have liked to have kept them on, but for the present there is little for them to be gainfully employed doing."

Bill stood and quietly said, "If you pair will excuse me, I will take off. I see you have a heap of paperwork to attend to. I am going back to the crusher. I had best inform them that I will be leaving. I did tell them I would be absent two months. The miserable B's knocked it off my accumulated holiday leave. Chris my good mate, you have some decisions to make. Call me if you want to talk about anything. I know rocks and what to do with them, but when it comes to actual mining and all this engineering stuff I am of little help to you. Make sure he looks after himself, Jackie girl," he called as he walked out the door.

Jackie came around his desk and pushed his chair back so she could sit on his lap. "What are you going to do next, Christopher John," she seriously asked.

"I have a couple of things in mind," he replied. "The first thing is to clean up this heap of paperwork."

It took three days before they had finally attended to the last letter "Thank goodness Jackie is here;" Chris had thought; "without her efficiency I would have been stuck with this lot for a month."

"It feels strange to be back after over a month out at Quo-Vadis, with all that excitement it is taking me some time to settle back to my old routine," Jackie commented. "I have spoken with Vanessa, bless her soul. She has everything well under control. Hector really does not need me. He did tell Vanessa to tell me, do not even think about leaving. He had also told her to say if Chris wanted me working for Quo-Vadis every day, it was okay, so long as he saw me sometimes. He is a darling man."

That last bit was said rather wistfully. Chris had listened intently to all this and had slid his hand under her loose top and had fixed it onto her right breast.

She slapped his hand away. "Behave yourself," she growled. "I am trying to be serious and you do not make it easy."

"Okay! Miss Killjoy," Chris laughed. "I will tell you what I have decided. First thing is, I have to arrange to travel east for Christmas. Because I've missed the last two Christmases, Mum is a bit mad at me. If you would come with me, when she meets you she may forgive me. When we get back I am going to invite my lecturers to come out to Quo-Vadis and see if they can tell me what to do. Would you come east with me, then upon our return, come out to Quo-Vadis, or do you have plans for Christmas?"

"No, I have no plans for Christmas, Chris," she huskily replied. "I would really like to meet your parents."

"Great!" Chris most enthusiastically cried. "I will ring them and tell them now. Can you see what flights we can get as early as possible? Front end of the plane if possible please."

"I have never travelled first class," she whispered excitedly. "Do you want payment for my share right now?"

"You have just belted me and told me to behave. Have you changed your mind?" He very intently whispered.

"Oh, shut up and get on with it you great lummox," she giggled.

All went well. Despite the airlines being heavily booked for the Christmas period, Jackie had managed to arrange their flight. "Six am on Wednesday is the earliest I could get;" then quickly added; "the return flight was a little more difficult. The first available was not until mid-January. Is all that okay?" she asked.

"Three weeks with the folks may make up for the last missed Christmases! What is the exact date we are due back? I will take the University people back to Quo-Vadis immediately we return, if they are available."

Both lecturers made themselves available. "We would not miss an opportunity to see exactly what our prize student is up to," Riley laughed.

"It looks like we have some very pleasant five weeks ahead of us Jackie, my love."

"Keep talking like that and I may make sure it lasts much longer than five weeks," Jackie very softly and with the meaning full of seduction, whispered.

His parents waited for them in the lounge of the airport. His mother watched them walk in, hand in hand. "She looks good," his mother thought. "Very pretty. My grandchildren will be beautiful."

Mothers! Who can stop them conniving or planning the future for their children?

"We have booked you into the golf resort where your father is a member," his mother told them. "Two deluxe rooms. Is that alright?"

"No, Mum!" Chris replied. "We only need one room."

"Oh, you naughty children," his mother laughed. "Rex and his family will be happy to grab your spare one. I had to put their children in with them; now they can take two suites and spread out a little. We can drop you off there and pick you up later. You are coming home for dinner tonight?"

"No point in arguing that order," Chris smiled inwardly. Jackie had met Rex but had never met his family.

Rex's wife, Jasmine, took an immediate liking to Jackie. "Rex had told me of you. Now I see what he meant when he said you are a most attractive person. I hope we can be very good friends."

Chris's two other sisters, Carol and Nanette, were most warm and simply said, "Welcome to the mad mob, Jackie."

"Is this the *one*?" Carol surreptitiously asked Chris.

Rather than go into the details of their relationship Chris simply replied, "That is to be seen."

"Well from what I am seeing you cannot do much better," Carol very firmly said. "She is really nice."

Three weeks with Chris's family was very enjoyable. One small incident occurred when one of the girls asked Jackie about her parents. "They are about," was all Jackie answered.

"That is something to follow-up," Chris thought, but thinking a bit deeper said to himself, "Why do I want to know? It is none of my business. She'll tell me if she wants to know. She did say more than once something about a sister."

As they walked to the boarding area for the return trip, Chris's mother was most insistent that they, pointedly including Jackie, visit more regularly, and do not leave it for another year.

"Yes Mum," Chris said. "We will try to come over more often, but I do have a very busy year ahead of me.

They had been back in the regional city for two days and were finding it difficult to settle back to work. Chris constantly perused mining magazines and journals and had Jackie search out as much detail of this or that of a particular machine. The lecturers were due tomorrow and Chris had arranged with Hector to fly them all out to Quo-Vadis.

"Bill is already out there, Chris," Hector told him. "I flew him out a week ago. He said he could not stand the city life anymore and had quit his job. Grumbled something about 'blasted kids' in head office who thought they knew everything. Are you taking Jackie?" he blatantly asked.

"Yes," Chris replied. "She has insisted on coming."

Hector appeared to become rather dismal, but he called a cheery "bye" as Chris and Jackie left the tourist park. "See you at six in the morning. It will be a one-day flight, with one fuel stop. He smiled a little as he said; "I did receive a very nice cheque from Rex. The letter attached to it said it was the annual dividend from that share you gave me. I blew it all on another Chinook, it's called Daisy. Daisy is a bit quicker than old Donald."

Strahan and Riley could not believe their own eyes as Chris and Bill walked them through what was Quo-Vadis.

"This is incredible," Strahan had said. "I'm supposed to be a professor of mining, and should know all of this, but you lot are teaching me. I did not teach you all this, Chris; there is much to learn about mining here. This whole escarpment is a geological wonder. It has been thrust up from God only knows where, by forces of such magnitude it belies description. Look at the dimensions you have taken. It is rectangular about twenty kilometres wide. You say it is over four-hundred kilometres long and generally three to five hundred metres high. Is that right? And look at this. You think it may be honeycombed with caverns, with rivers running through it. This is like a giant skyscraper laying on its side. It would take ten lifetimes to learn all its secrets."

"Well, now you can see my problem. How would you set up a mining complex here?" Chris bluntly asked. "You would know of all the newest and best equipment, how I would use it, and how I could best set it up here. I only envisage something relatively small. I have no wish to enter the big league."

"You will not have to set up all that big, Chris," Riley offered. "The richness of your claim only requires smaller but top-quality gear. Ray and I will give you a list of the machines you should look at and suggest how you can best set up. That small flow in the second cavern can be tapped. We believe it comes directly from the river before it enters the lake in the cavern. Chase it up and enlarge it, and endeavour to divert a strong flow—strong enough to drive a number of power generators. I see you propose to have three hydro generators; whatever do you need three for?"

"I thought to use a large generator to power the smelter, a mid-size one to drive the crusher, and a smaller one for general use," Chris answered.

"Extravagant, but I cannot condemn your thinking. It is about what I would expect from you," Riley quipped.

The two learned men stayed for two weeks. They did not mind living rough and contributed their bit to the chores. Evenings were spent around the campfire in rich comradeship. Much conversation was based on mining and engineering.

Jackie quietly whispered to Bill one afternoon as they sat by the river "wetting a line" endeavouring to catch the evening's dinner. "Have you watched Chris as those three, talk, Bill? Chris is in a different world."

Chris was a very happy fellow; things were starting to take shape in his mind. Regrettably there were still many gaps.

"I just cannot put all the engineering complexities together. I will have to go back to university for a while and do a few semesters in the engineering department. My mining degree will enable me to skip a year or so I may be able to go straight into year five. I guess I will have to revise a fair bit of the earlier years."

With their return to the regional city, he quietly set about gaining entry into the University. Professor Strahan was instrumental in using a little of his *"influence"* to ensure Chris achieved the entry he required. He only vaguely mentioned what he was doing to Jackie.

It was only a day before he was to leave for university, that Chris told her the details of what he intended to do.

She did not hesitate. "I will come with you," she said. "Everything here can look after itself for a while."

"No Jackie!" Chris in an endeavour to soften the impact of his decision said. "I will need to be able to apply myself totally to my studies. You would be an undeniable beautiful distraction. You could keep an eye on this office and I am sure Hector will be happy to see more of you at the park. I truly mean this when I say, I will be lonely as a hermit, but if I am to set up Quo-Vadis properly I must do this my way. Please understand?" he pleaded.

Jackie burst into tears and rushed from the office. She sat by the river in their special spot until late that night. Chris had searched the town for her and finally decided to go back to their apartment, hoping she would return. She had returned and sat on the bed waiting for him.

He rushed to her in relief and quietly said, "I am so sorry, I did not think." That was as far as he got.

Jackie gently embraced him and replied, "It is alright, Chris, I have given it much consideration. I know it is important to you, so I will not hinder you. Now would you hold me and make love to me please? It will need to be just so special that I will never forget how it is to be with you."

There were no words to describe the gentleness of their loving that night. Little was said in the morning. Jackie only quietly whispered, "I am going for a walk, please be gone before I get back. I could not bear to say goodbye."

"Jackie," he started to say, "come with me."

She stopped him by placing her fingers on his lips and saying," Shush, not another word, just go." She turned and fled out the door so he did not see the tears that had started to flow.

On his way out, Chris stopped by the tourist park and told Hector of his plans. "Please take care of Jackie while I'm away," he said to Hector.

"I will," Hector answered. That was all that was said, and Chris headed Goliath for the highway and made a quick exit from their lives.

He threw himself into the study, even taking several overseas trips to study at those very good universities that specialised in mining engineering. He visited many manufacturing plants, viewing the latest and most up-to-date machines. For over one year he had no contact with Jackie, nor had she contacted him. He would just not allow her memory to distract him from his studies. The lecturers of all his subjects were most impressed with his devotion to his studies and assisted him wherever and whenever possible. As a result, he graduated from the Schools of Mechanical and Civil Engineering with flying colours.

Today he sat with Professor Raymond Strahan discussing the merits of the diagrams and plans spread out over the professor's normally very tidy desk.

"All this is what I propose to do," Chris was saying.

Strahan was most impressed. "You have progressed far beyond what I can teach you, Chris; when you are set up please allow me to see it. I am very confident there will be nothing to equal it anywhere," the professor sincerely said.

"I am returning to the provincial city tomorrow," Chris said and added, "Our good friend, Ed, has been looking after Goliath while I have been at University. He tells me he has affected some pretty 'fancy' modifications and has added a few new things. I am anxious to see exactly what he has done."

"Have you heard from Jackie?" Strahan asked, rather hesitantly and with a strange note in his voice.

"No!" was all Chris answered.

He was on the road by early morning, and drove all day, arriving at the apartment he and Jackie had shared just before 8 pm. As he opened the door and stepped in, he could feel it was strangely empty. No Jackie. It was obvious the apartment had not been occupied for some time.

"Wonder where she is?" he asked in his mind. "Well, I will just surprise her and walk into the office tomorrow. No, I will go early and just be sitting there." His plan pleased him and he ordered in a burger for his dinner.

He was in the office early. "What's all this? What's that crib and baby stuff doing here?" The unanswered questions ran through his confused mind. He sat at his desk. It was neat, everything exactly in place as if he had never left. He got up and walked to her desk—it too was all in order. He slumped back into his chair his mind rampant in confusion. At exactly 8.30 am he heard a car door slam and a baby wailed.

He heard Jackie say, "Hush Jack, I will feed you in a minute. You are always hungry."

She pushed open the door and stepped backwards in, lugging all sorts of baby paraphernalia. She stopped short as she saw him. The only thing she said was "Chris!" and promptly fainted. Chris rushed to catch her and relieve her of the baby before she hit the floor. As he took the baby in his arms, the child stopped crying and started "gooing" happily.

"Hello, young fellow. Where did you come from?" Chris bemusedly said as he placed the baby in the crib.

Jackie had recovered and sat up. She was still sitting on the floor. "He is mine," she said.

That comment hit Chris as if he'd been hit on the head with a blunt axe. "Yours?!" he stuttered. "When? Who? How come?" the questions just poured from him.

"You should have told me you were coming back," Jackie cried loudly. "I would have met you and warned you. I will leave now if you want me to."

Chris's mind was spinning; he only managed to stutter. "Jackie please do not leave. Give me a moment to get my shattered brain around all this." Then added, "I will make a strong cup of tea and you can tell me all." He paused for a moment then firmly said, "Please do not be concerned. I have to accept this has happened and remember we only had a deal."

Chris had never heard Jackie swear and was further taken back when she blasted out, "That bloody deal! No sane person ever makes a deal like that; I must've been mad." She was back to the efficient Jackie he knew. "Get me that cup of tea while I feed Jack," she said. "What did you do to him? He is laying there watching you,"

"I did nothing," Chris instantly replied. "I grabbed him before you dropped him and put him in the crib."

"He's not hurt, is he?" she asked protectively.

"I don't think so," Chris again replied.

Jackie lifted the baby from the crib and without hesitation let him have her breast. "Lucky little bugger," Chris thought. "I used to be allowed to do that," then stopped himself short. "What the Hell am I thinking," he admonished himself.

Little was said while the child fed. Chris only asked a few general questions, like, "How's the park going? Is Bill about? How's Hector?" These questions were met more or less with a grunt. The child had finished, burped loudly and promptly dropped off to sleep. Jackie lifted him gently and placed him back into the crib, rearranged her clothing then came to sit next to Chris on "that" settee.

"Where is that cup of tea you promised?" she asked. "I hope it is still hot."

"I have not poured it yet. I was waiting for you.

"That makes two of us," Jackie most sarcastically said.

"Ouch!" Chris thought to himself. "I suppose I do deserve that."

He poured the tea and gave her a cup and made one for himself, then resumed his seat next to her.

Jackie appeared to be endeavouring to compose herself. She took a large sip of the tea and started hesitantly. "You must not interrupt me even once," she softly said. "There is much to tell, I have practised many times for hours as to just how and what I would tell you, if and when this time came, but for the life of me I cannot think of one word I was going to say. I think I will answer the easy questions first. The park is going extremely well, Bill is still out at Quo-Vadis, your third question is much more difficult to answer. Hector is dead! He died over two months ago."

Chris could not restrain himself. "How?" he asked quietly.

She ignored his question and continued. "After you left I was devastated and lonely. Hector took me out a few times and we became very close. No! Don't look at me like that Chris. Just let me go on. I found I was pregnant. This is where it gets very complicated. Hector had always wanted a son; he had the two girls; but fate is a strange thing. He was badly wounded when he was serving in the air force in the Middle East—he nearly died. He lost all—everything; all of his wedding gear, you know what I mean. He even lost the urges that go with them. He was discharged on medical grounds and sent home. His wife was unhappy with his loss and found satisfaction elsewhere. She finally left him with two young daughters. They are beautiful girls—they are living with me. When I told Hector I was pregnant, he didn't ask any questions but was extremely happy and asked me to marry him, so it would appear that the child was his. As we had that bloody deal, I was pretty down and desperate and since I had not heard from you, it looked to be a good alternative. So, we got married. Hector was wonderful and when Jack was born he was over the moon. He did not even blink when I told him the baby was yours; all he said was, he could not have wished for a better person to be the father of the child and that a blind man would have even seen you and I were made for each other. I had to explain the deal. He called you all sorts of a blasted fools for that."

"I do agree with that," Chris interrupted, then very quietly said, "Jack, you called him, is my son? WOW!" The word just exploded from him, then remembering he was supposed to be quiet, whispered, "Sorry I am not supposed to interrupt. Please go on."

"It didn't work out as it was supposed to. Like I said, Hector was wonderful, a better father a boy could not have wished for. You have a bit to do to match up my man. Regrettably, Hector's dreadful wound to his genital area flared up. It was found to be malignant. He went quickly and died over two months ago. The girls were hit hard. They are still coming to terms with their father dying. I have told them I will look after them—they have nobody. Their mother has gone, goodness knows where too. I have a home out near the park. I never loved Hector like I loved and still love you. With Hector our marriage was only something of a convenience. You must be warned, that with being an instant father for Jack, and becoming a good dad for the girls; Susie and Annie; you will have your hands full. Oh, I overlooked one other thing, you will have to be a most wonderful, wonderful lover and husband for me."

Chris teasingly delayed any answer, then softly said with deep emotion, "Jackie all this has put my mind in a whirl. This very foolish man has a simple but very important question to ask you. JACQUELINE ELIZABETH CARTER" he shouted, "WILL YOU MARRY ME?"

Jackie sighed deeply and kissed him lightly. "This has been a long time in coming. I never really gave up. My answer is also very simple, Yes! Christopher John Kennedy, I will marry you and you can become Jack's rightful dad."

Jack was fussing.

"Time for your first dad lesson. Come with me into the bathroom and I will teach you how to change a soiled nappy," Jackie laughed.

Chris had found much to do. Within one month he had moved his now "family" into a large house in the best part of town, had cleaned up Hector's estate, which included some outstanding debts. The girls were beneficiaries of Hector's assets. He made very sure the girls were advised by the highly respected legal firm, the upshot being he was able to purchase their interests in the tourist park. He was fortunate enough to find and engage the services of a very experienced senior pilot, with good administrative experience. It took little time, with Jackie's and Vanessa's assistance, for him to set everything right. Chris was anxious to get out to Quo-Vadis and discuss his plans with Bill.

Jackie deeply regretted she was not prepared to subject Jack to the rigours of living rough; however, she did suggest that, as it was holiday time for the girls, he invite them to go with him. The girls were a little hesitant at the suggestion. Jackie told them just how beautiful it was out there, and on her say so, they did agree it sounded a good idea.

Three days later with the two girls comfortably ensconced in the back seat of Goliath they set out for Quo-Vadis. The girls were a little reserved at first, but by the second day of travelling and being totally entranced with what they were seeing and learning about the Golden Outback, and camping out, they were chatting to him like a pair of canaries. They had fallen in love with the Outback.

"Jackie had told us all about this place," Susan, the older girl, said. "I can see why she loved it so much."

They had arrived at the Quo-Vadis campsite. A dust-covered Bill wandered into the camp. "Hi girls," he happily called. "I thought I warned you about bad company."

"Uncle Bill!" both girls screamed and regardless of his dust and grime threw their arms about him.

"Chris tells us you are the boss. We want you to show us everything."

"First things first," Bill laughed. "Chris is the boss, regardless of what he has told you. Next is; Chris here discovered this underground lake, I'm going for a swim to clean up."

The girls were hot and sticky and gleefully chatting incessantly, followed Bill into the now floodlit cave.

"I wonder what he has been up to?" Chris thought.

Bill had been busy: both entrances to the underground caverns were enlarged and clear, lights had been installed in the caverns, and a very strong looking winch frame had been erected over the top of the "dark hole." All it needed now was a winch and cable fitted and they had another way of accessing the sinkhole.

The girls and Bill, all glowing red from the chilly, water, returned to the camp.

The girls were laughing and smiling. "We could not find the hot water tap," Annie, laughed. "The cold water was deliciously refreshing."

.

That night by campfire light, he shared his plans with Bill and the girls. They listened intensely.

Annie interrupted their discussion, and asked, "Where is all this gold you talk about? Jackie had told us you were very clever and had found lots."

"That is something I will show you tomorrow. Now off to bed, you pair. You sleep in the back of Goliath."

"Where do you and Uncle Bill sleep?" Susan asked.

"We just perch in the fork of a gum tree like the possums," Chris very solemnly answered.

"Oh, I do like you," she laughed, and she came around the campfire, hugged him and gave him a light kiss on the cheek, bade him "night" and together with her sister clambered into the back of Goliath. There was a fair bit of giggling, then all went quiet.

Chris heard Susan say, "Jackie was so right—he is something special."

"Looks like you have made a conquest already," Bill laughed.

The next morning, breakfast over, and camp chores done, beds in the back of Goliath made, not without the girls having to be told more than once, "it has to be done."

"Do we have to do this every day, Chris?" Annie complained.

"You most certainly do," Chris growled.

"I now see why you and Uncle Bill sleep in the gum trees," she giggled.

"All done," the girls shouted.

Chris inspected their work. "Huh," he laughed, "my spot up in the gum tree looks more organised than this."

"Do you really sleep up in the gum trees?" Annie innocently asked.

"Shush, you ninny," Susan snapped. "He's joking."

"Come on, ladies," Chris called. "I promised to show you some gold today. You will have to be very brave because we have to have Goliath lower us down the cliff face."

"Oo, that sounds scary," Annie whispered. "You are joking again, aren't you Chris?"

"Nope, no joke," Chris laughed. "You and Susan will ride piggyback with Bill and I."

"I *bags* riding with Chris," Annie quickly said.

"I wanted to do that," Susan cried. "I am the eldest. I should have first pick," and a very noisy squabble ensured.

Chris put an end to it by saying, "Susan can ride with me on the way back."

Argument resolved; they were lowered down the cliff face. Annie darn near choked the life out of him as she clung on so tightly.

Halfway down Chris asked, "Can you see the river pouring from the cliff face, Annie?"

"No," she quietly replied, "I have my eyes closed."

All safe and sound on the sinkhole floor, Chris led them to the river. As they stood on the bank he pointed into the shallows of the river. "There is your gold," he said.

"Where?!" quizzed Susan. "I can't see any gold."

"Look again," Chris laughed.

"You are joking again, aren't you, you rotten thing," Susan laughed.

Bill was near bursting trying to hold in his mirth.

"Here I will show you", Chris said as he reached into the cold water and picked up a thumbnail sized pebble and tossed it to her.

Susie caught it. "It's heavy," she said, and commenced to examine it. "It's gold!" she shouted. "Look Annie, it is real gold. Oh Chris, can we pick some up?"

"Yes, you sure can," Chris replied, "but remember what you pick up you have to carry about for the rest of the day."

"I will pick up a great big pile of them" Annie shouted. "I will be very rich."

"Typical female," Chris sighed to himself.

An hour later, sodden wet and blue with cold, the girls halted their collecting only because every pocket was bulging and threatening to burst.

"Now where are you going to put the rest of the real gold I have yet to show you," Chris wickedly asked.

"Is there more than this?" Susan cried.

"This is nothing compared with what I have to show you next." He took pity on the girls and took them back to camp and provided them each with a wooden box to store their souvenirs in.

"You would have done better to give them tea chests!" Bill laughed.

Earlier, Susie had shrieked with excitement as she clung to Chris's back, as Goliath hauled them back up that cliff face. "I am never going to leave this place," she yelled into Chris's ear," darn near deafening him. "It is so beautiful and look how that water pours from the cliff face. It is marvellous."

"After lunch, I will show you where all that water comes from," Chris told her as they reached the cliff top.

Lunch was a noisy affair; the girls could not talk fast enough relating the marvellous morning adventures.

"Are you up for more?" Chris asked solemnly.

146

"You said you would show us where the river water comes from," Susie reminded him.

"And you said you would show us lots more gold," Annie added.

"I am a man of my word," Chris laughed. "As soon as we clean up here, we will get underway."

"Must we always keep things neat and tidy?" Susan complained. "We only mess them up when we use them later."
"Tidy mind, tidy heart," Chris most philosophically said. "We never leave the camp untidy—it invites all sorts of uninvited visitors, like rats and flies and fleas and snakes."

"OO!" gasped Annie and set to, to assist in the tidying up.

They had been into the cave for a swim when they first arrived, but were enthralled when Chris explained things in detail, including the sight of the water pouring in at the head of the lake and the whirlpool as it found its way out. "It comes out the cliff face we went down this morning. It is out there," he explained to them waving his hand in the general direction.

"You mean this is actually an underground river, Chris?" Susie excitedly said.

"Yes," Chris replied. "Tonight, I will tell you how I believe the sinkhole was formed."

"All this is so interesting," Susan exclaimed.
Chris had carried the lamp that could be refocused. He shone the beam onto the quartz reef. "How beautiful," Susan whispered. "It is the most beautiful white."

"That's not quite so," Chris corrected her. "Look closely."
The beam focused on a thick golden slash.

"Is that gold?" Annie all but choked. "There is tonnes and tonnes of it."

"You are right, Annie. Look at these blocks in the rock fall."
He shone the beam over the huge pile of fallen quartz. The girls

were quiet for a few moments, then burst into unintelligible chatter. "Pick up a small block of quartz and look at it closely, you will see a seam of gold. That seam runs all the way through the reef. How far that reef runs I have yet to find out. I have not had time to establish that." Chris offered.

"I cannot even think of how much this is worth," Susan quietly said.

"Well, I am only guessing, mind you, but I estimate in this pile of fallen quartz there is many hundreds of millions of dollars' worth of gold. I cannot even envisage just how much gold is up there waiting to be mined." Chris attempted to explain. Now you can see why it is called *The Golden Outback,*

"Can I have a small stone for my box?" Annie innocently asked.

"Sure, no worries. I am sure one small stone will not affect my lamb chops buying power," Chris lightly replied.

"What's this about lamb chops?" Bill asked in a bemused voice.

"I'll tell you later," Chris started to say, but was interrupted by Annie getting in before he could answer.

"He is just joking again, Uncle Bill. Isn't he just the rottenest thing? But he is great fun and wonderful to be with.

# Chapter 3

For three weeks, the girls revelled in the enchantment of Quo-Vadis and were most tardy about preparing to leave.

"Can you wait a while, Chris?" Annie pleaded. "I want to go back down and collect a couple more nuggets that I can take back to show the kids at school, just to prove to them that all I say about Quo-Vadis is true." The girls had mastered the art of using the hoist and were now quite confident to travel up and down solo.

"There goes your wish to keep this place secret, Chris, old chap," Bill chuckled.

They eventually got underway, and, after a laughter-filled trip back, they arrived at their new house. To try and describe or recant the scene as both girls at the same time tried to tell Jackie of their holiday at Quo-Vadis was not possible, except to say it was loud and long.

After a delayed dinner as the girls were preparing for bed, Jackie and Chris took a quiet opportunity to sit closely together in the lounge room.

"Well 'Mr Don Juan', you have done it again. Any female that comes within your influence, falls for you. I of all people know the problem."

The girls insisted he came to their bedroom to say good night. Each hugged him tightly. Susan whispered softly, "You love Jackie, don't you Chris? Are you going to marry her?"

"Yes," Chris gently replied. "We will tell you the story of our love one day. We have only delayed getting married since I got back because we wanted to be sure you girls would approve."

"I approve!" Annie piped up from the adjacent bed.

"So, do I," Susan almost reverently added. "It will be wonderful to have you as our daddy. We shall call you Daddy Chris."

"Daddy Chris," smiled Jackie, obviously happy with the development.

"Don't you laugh, Mummy Jackie. That's your name now. How do you like that?" Chris bounced back.

"Very much," Jackie answered. "After all, I am a mummy."

It was a bit strange to crawl into that large bed with Jackie at first, but old memories soon overcame that and their loving was gentle and complete.

"The girls seem very happy," Jackie drowsily commented as she lay satiated in Chris's arms.

"They are wonderful kids," Chris replied. "It is going to take little for me to learn to really love them. They are both a bit like you, you know. They have threatened to do all sorts of nasty things to me if I do not take them back to Quo-Vadis for the Christmas holidays. I did a deal with them," he laughed.

"You and your deals," Jackie growled.

Chris became a little defensive. "All I said to them was if they both got exam results with marks over eighty percent I will let them spend the whole of their Christmas holidays out there. By Christmas we will have a liveable place for you all. Those Italian builders you put me onto are arriving next week, Vanessa has made Donald available, and I am flying them out the day after they arrive. Giuseppe, the boss, had said the thought of working with natural stone sounded interesting. I hope his interest does not wane when I show him exactly what I want."

"Just what are you building?" said Jackie with natural woman's curiosity.

"That's a secret. It is a present for you and Jack," Chris answered. "Be patient. It will take a while, and your patience will be well rewarded."

"You better be ready by Christmas, my man. Jack and I will be coming out then," Jackie very firmly told him.

"You are sounding more and more like a real mum," Chris bravely commented, and received a playful whack on the right ear.

There were many tonnes of shattered rock at the base of that sinkhole cliff—mainly granite and greenstone. He even found a very big pile of quartz blocks not far from the site where he proposed to build the house. After careful examination, he declared "that the quartz contained no worthwhile gold and he would use it to decorate the interior of the house."

"Should put the whole lot through the crusher, boy," Bill complained.

"We do not have a crusher yet," Chris reminded him. "The ship with the crusher on board is scheduled to arrive in a week or two, but the Switz. generators are on the train arriving at the rail depot in the regional city tomorrow. The generators are too much for even the big choppers to carry and I have had to get a trucking contractor to bring them out. I warned the contractor it will not be easy. He was a bit blasé about it. He does have some good trucks and he reckons there is no track that has ever beaten him. Just in case, I have bought a big multi-wheeled Cat. front-end loader and have hired an experienced loader driver to track along with them. I will be taking Goliath to show them the way."

For three long weeks the laden trucks battled along the track. Each day the loader was busy digging or towing bogged trucks free.

"Hells Bells, Kennedy!" the trucking boss wailed, "you were not joking when you said it would not be easy. I should have listened to you. OH HELL," he shouted, "another truck is stuck."

Chris and Bill patiently watched all this. "There is much more gear to come out, Bill," Chris said. "Hopefully Donald and Daisy will be able to handle most of it. I have ordered stainless steel rails and everything that will allow us to install a lift of sorts in the black hole. An installation crew will be coming out with all that stuff. I have told the suppliers their tradesmen should be warned they will be living rough for a while. I hope we can get all the accommodation block ready quickly. It is going to get a bit crowded around here for a while, especially when the boys installing the crusher and the smelter arrive. Engineers from Switzerland are due here shortly too. With a little good management, we can have the lift operating and the generators in position very soon. The crew chasing up that water flow the professors suggested would be adequate to drive the generators has made good progress. In fact, the foreman told me he expects to break through to the river upstream from the lake early next week. The 1.4 metre diameter steel pipes you ordered to bring the diversion to the caverns; are in the railyard at the regional city and the big choppers are going to start delivering them almost straight away."

"You have taken on a big task. Chris," Bill commented, "With all that is going on, there is over one-hundred bodies working out here. I do not know how you are managing to keep it all flowing so neatly. Everybody seems to be fitting in, even the girls, and the cook in the tent city are happy."

"I am not getting much sleep, mate," Chris replied, "but I find all this so exciting I don't think I could sleep all that much; even if I had the opportunity. Thankfully Jackie and Vanessa are organising much at their end. I do not have to worry about scheduling deliveries by the choppers."

Chris had called upon his mining and engineering skills to design and have constructed, a false floor forty metres up, in the space at the top of the small cavern. The floor was adequately supported by precisely-placed concrete steel reinforced pillars. Now a team of carpenters were busy fitting out 170 very comfortable two and three-bedroom, accommodation units. Each unit had its own ensuite and kitchenette . A complete kitchen designed to attend to the needs of the ever-growing workforce; fitted out with the most modern equipment, had been installed and now a substantial portion of the smaller cavern resembled a large community hall that doubled as a mess hall. Several well-appointed offices and store rooms graced almost all of the remaining space.

Bill growled a bit with all this. "Miners and tradies do not expect this type of treatment," he grumbled.

"This miner does," Chris laughed, "so why can't any bloke who works for us expect less."

With the increased use the track out to Quo-Vadis had become compacted and now delivery trucks managed to wend their way to the mine site three of four times a week. These trucks were back loaded with a good quantity of quartz, sealed in solid boxes for delivery to the government crusher and smelter.

Chris spoke by satellite telephone to Jackie at least once a day. Their calls had a regular pattern. After a fond greeting Jackie would give him an "up to date -financial report of the banking activities of Quo-Vadis Holdings and associated accounts. Each day she would report details of what the last load of processed stone earned and what money had been lodged with his bank by the mint. Monday's reports were rather detailed; and often included comments of the like-- You are keeping ahead of your spending," or "Don't forget you have a crusher and 'Whilie' smelter to pay for next month." All this information gave Chris an insight into how they were; *"going"*; and enabled him to make the necessary arrangements and as each account was paid he would tell her the details; and to have little concern about the bigger accounts, explaining; "Rex will attend to those bills. He has negotiated extended terms with the manufacturers; by the time they are due we will be in full operation, often adding; "Jackie, my love, it is just so wonderful that you are there to do all my housekeeping." They would then move on to the important stuff—such as Jacks recent activities, and more personal things. This morning she had been particularly chipper as she told him; "I have to tell you I have hired a housekeeper so I can spend maximum time with my family and you when you get back." Chris would keep her well informed of all that was happening at Quo-Vadis.

"It is like an ant's nest that has been stirred up out here at the moment, Jackie girl; you would not like it. I have programmed most of it to finish by Christmas. I think you will like the house—it is looking good," he proudly said. "Giuseppe has fourteen tradies working on it—plumbers, electricians, painters, the lot. How he organises them is amazing. The crusher and smelter have not arrived yet. It is just as well, as we're not ready to send them down yet."

Sometimes they only talked of their love for each other and the children. They had become a very close complete family; he often included the girls in his phone calls.

Jackie was laughing as she told him, "The two girls adore Jack and all but compete for his attention – they obviously loved their little brother. They are a wonderful help."

They never ran out of "things to talk about??

Jackie and Chris did get married while all this was happening. It was not a lavish affair, only a few very close people attended. Chris asked Rex to let his sisters know of the marriage and asked that they endeavour to keep the news from his mother.

# Chapter 4

Chris's lecturers from University, Professor Strahan, and now Professor Riley—the head lecturers of the mining faculty—approached Chris with a request: "Would it be appropriate to arrange for a number of their current students to spend a whole semester, or at least a good part of the semester, in the Quo-Vadis precinct." It was their considered opinion that the escarpment and the sinkhole, did present a very real opportunity for intense mining studies. They did concede it may take some very questionable arrangements to be made with the University board. They were successful and did obtain the necessary permission to go ahead. The fact that both professors were of very high reputation and were in good favour with the board helped.

Students wishing to attend this unusual activity were advised they had to be prepared to "*live rough*" and would have to meet a fair bit of the additional costs. The few students who declined the invitation to be part of this unique venture were told they would be continuing their studies under the guidance of other tutors.

Chris would receive notification of the numbers of students attending so he could have all the logistics covered. More than once the professors would bring to Chris's attention the matter of a potentially fine young student who could not afford the additional cost of the excursion. Very few knew it was Chris who sponsored that young student.

The professors' enchantment with the area stimulated the students immensely. Often students who had previously shown only a little interest in gaining their degree, suddenly became most enthusiastic with what they were learning. There was very little in the form of complaints from them. One particular activity everyone found very pleasurable was to sit around the crackling campfire in the evenings just talking over the day's activities and asking questions of the professors. From time to time, Bill and Chris would join them at their evening campfire. Chris would relate to the students the story of finding and developing Quo-Vadis and telling them of the difficulties he had encountered; and what measurers he had adopted to overcome them. Often the students would take notes of the types of machines he had used and the plant he had installed. One evening he told of what was presently happening, and some of his future plans. The Professors and students, were totally amazed at all that was happening. Chris did invite the students to make any suggestions with what they could see could improve things in the future. Their young minds had been stimulated and some very good suggestions were forthcoming.

They all listened avidly when Bill related his experiences. Not one of them had been able to master the art of identifying minerals by smell. They would often try and set Bill up just to test him. They ceased doubting Bill's authenticity when, one evening, Bill threw the sample he had been asked to identify at them shouting, "YOU BASTARDS, YOU PISSED ON THAT!"

Riley apologised profusely for that misdemeanour and the culprits were allocated dishwashing duties for the remainder of the campout semester.

Chris was more than once admonished by the professors for not developing the whole escarpment. "You hold leases for over 85% of this monolith," they growled, "and yet you sit here planning to spend millions developing one small section. With what we believe exists within the whole of this escarpment you could be immeasurably wealthy."

Chris had not hesitated and had humbly replied, "Thank you gentlemen; at the moment, BY THE GRACE OF GOD, with what I have planned to do, I have more than enough to do each day. Isn't enough, enough; what would I do with more?"

Nevertheless, Chris did bring his drilling contractor out to Quo-Vadis and sent him out to the surface of the escarpment. He and Bill surveyed and mark out one-hundred proposed drill holes. The majority of the holes were aligned with the known reef. Chris deliberately nominated quite a few holes at random over the length and breadth of the escarpment.

"That will keep Tom busy for six months," Bill laughed, "and maybe keep your learned friends happy. I haven't forgiven them yet for the rotten trick those kids tried on me. I owe them one," Bill snarled.

Chris was weary to the bone. Giuseppe had finished the house in good time and had asked Chris for permission to photograph what he had built. The proud builder took hundreds of photographs and even made a short video. "I can use all this to show people what a little imagination can do. It is a shame this house it is not in the city; I would open it as a show home and sell many from it.

Giuseppe was very proud of what he had constructed. "All you have to do now is hook up water and power." That was not as easy as the builder had made it sound. It required running both water and power feeds about 400 m from the water points and the generators in the large cavern to the house. Chris didn't want to ruin the natural appearance of the sinkhole, and with all his men very gainfully employed in their allocated tasks, he and Bill applied themselves to dig the required two-meter deep trench from the larger cavern to the house.   Those three hydro generators along with the two crushers and the very modern electric smelter had been installed in the large cavern and were fully operational.

After diligently applying themselves for the best part of the first day they had only managed to dig a shallow trench about five meters long. The ground was hard and unyielding. With perspiration running down his face cutting rivers in the dust that had accumulated there; Chris threw down his pick, which was worn almost to nothing and cried, "This is madness! I'm going to buy a great big backhoe to do this. Can you operate a backhoe Bill?"

"Never tried, Chris," Bill replied, as he examined his blistered hands. "If I can avoid all this confounded digging, I will try anything. I am sure the suppliers will send somebody to instruct us when they bring the machine out."

The backhoe was trucked in and arrived one week later. The trucking contractor smiled broadly as he unloaded the backhoe. "It is so much better getting out here now that the track is firm," he commented. "Not one of the ten trucks that bought those bits and pieces of your crushers and smelters out got bogged. It was most generous of you, Chris, to make sure I was not out of pocket over that first attempt to bring the generators out."

The backhoe supplier did send an experienced operator out to teach Chris and Bill the fundamental use of the machine. Not missing an opportunity, Chris coerced the supplier to allow his man to delay his departure from Quo-Vadis until that trench had been dug and all the pipes bringing the water and power to the house had been installed. The two much relieved miners stood back watching the backhoe work. Bill was laughing as he happily said; "my aching back and sore hands all agree that getting this machine out here to dig that blasted trench is one of the smartest things you have done so far Mister. Now we can get back to work to get your Gold mine working."

Bill had questioned the need for two crushers as they were being installed. Chris had bought his engineering knowledge and research to the fore, and told him, "I saw a set up in the States where they used a heavy crusher to reduce the rock to about the size of marbles. They would then run those marbles through a lighter machine bringing it to fines. You know it all from there."

With all the machines now operating, Bill was in his element. They had built a chute from the original cave now aptly named "The Animal Cave," down what space was left available in the black hole after they had installed the elevator. Quartz ore was fed down that chute straight into the first crusher. Those first small particles from the first crusher were sent by a short conveyor belt to the second crusher. The fines from the second crusher were conveyed this time directly to the smelter.

Bill was most happy with the set-up; "Those two crushers were a smart move; he complimented Chris. The wear and tear on the jaws of the machines is definitely reduced, and what was being run into the smelter was *BEEE-UTIFUL*. That smelter, by the way, is far more advanced than my old government smelter. We are pouring ingots that are all 24 carat 0.9999 Gold. Are the fellows from the city mint coming out soon? There are already more than 158 ingots in the strongroom. I do get a little jumpy with all that sort of value hanging about."

"I hope they get here soon," Chris seriously said. "Jackie told me this morning I had better stop spending, and that I am now on the bones of my bum." He had continued the conversation saying "It is just as well I have managed to pay for everything, even the crushers and the smelter. Rex has had to increase the loans to the company. He used most of the money in my private accounts. What the mint are going to pay me for all that Gold will take the pressure off for a while, until they pay up we will all be on dry bread and water."

Chris had arranged with Vanessa, that as soon as the mint officials arrived she was to send them out to Quo-Vadis in Daisy, which was the quicker of the two big helicopters. He was of the mind that if those men from the mint wanted to expedite things; they could load all the gold onto Daisy, give him a receipt and take it back with them.

The officials from the mint were gobsmacked, after having to fly over the Outback for over five hours, to be dumped down on the copter pad in the sinkhole. "We were told there is a mine and a big amount of gold here. Where is everything?" one very perplexed man cried.

"It's about here, somewhere," the helicopter pilot smiled, and took off leaving them standing like the proverbial "*shags on a rock.*" There was little to be seen that declared this was a mine site. All the equipment, crushers, smelters, generators, the lot, were placed inside those huge caverns, and all the tradies were now accommodated in very comfortable suites high up in the smaller cavern. All that the mint officials could see of any habitation was a very large house at some distance, a large backhoe that was filling in a trench containing red and white pipes, and two rather dirty men walking towards them.

"We are looking for a Mr. Christopher Kennedy," one of the mint officials shouted. "Is he about?"

"That's me," Chris answered with a smile, stepping forward with his calloused hand extended. "You would be the chaps from the mint I assume?"

The two men had regained their composure and answered, "Yes, that's correct. We are from The AUSTRALIAN GOVERNMENT mint. We were told to come out and inspect a volume of gold we had been advised was for sale. From what we can perceive, there is nothing here to interest us."

"Don't be too hasty with your thoughts," Chris said, endeavouring not to burst out laughing. "Please come with me. This other chap is Mr Bill Bailey; he used to run your crusher and smelter in town."

"We have heard of Mr Bailey," one mint official replied. "He has a very high reputation."

"Don't give him too much kudos please gents," Chris quickly said. "He is difficult enough to live with, without you blokes swelling his head any further."

With those *"introductions"* over, Chris led them towards the cliff face. Two large disguised doors automatically hissed open and Chris led them on into the Quo-Vadis mine.

The two officials could not believe their eyes and remained speechless for a whole minute. "One would not even guess all this was here," one stuttered. The noise level from the machinery had been controlled by building the generators; crushers and smelter into the large cavern and installing a heavy soundproof door in the access between the two caverns. The only sound in the small cavern was a soft incessant hum from the three shining Swiss. hydro generators.

"I have seen many mines, Mr Kennedy," one said, "but I do have to say, none come close to equalling this. It is quite amazing."

"Thank you for the compliment, sir. Perhaps you would care to follow me into 'Chris's Cave.'"

A large-hand painted sign said: "MAN CAVE! No entry for sheilas unless they bring a coldie and some tucker." The very proper mint officials were overcome with that congenial atmosphere and soon relaxed.

"Come in and take a pew," Chris said, inviting them in to sit down onto two very comfortable chairs. Chris nodded his head to Bill, and without a word Bill opened what looked like cupboard door. On closer inspection, the mint officials could see that the cupboard door was in fact a very substantial strongroom door. That door was electronically opened only after the insertion of a key code. Chris had unbeknown to the mint officials already tapped in the coded PIN, using the handset sitting in the top draw of his desk. Behind the cupboard door was a strongroom set in the confines of the granite of the escarpment rock. Very few knew that the black granite had been carefully mined to form that strongroom. Further entry was prohibited by fifty-millimetre-diameter, high quality steel bars that retracted to disappear into the floor. Solid shelves were set precisely along three walls. A solid looking bullion trolley had its place under a shelf adjacent to the door.

Chris did not hesitate to say, "The gold we have for sale is on the right-hand set of shelves. You are welcome to inspect it. I think you will find it meets all your requirements."
The two bemused mint officials stood hesitantly, then stepped quickly into the strongroom. There was a sudden flash. "Sorry gents," Chris apologised, "there is a camera set to recognise us regulars—it does photograph any new faces."

Both mint officials went a shade or two paler as they saw row on row of gold ingots stacked in precise formation on the shelves. "There are 158 ingots for sale," Chris announced. "They are all 24 carats 0.9999 pure, and better; and guaranteed to be 438.9 ounces each."

"Oh, my goodness. We were told by your accountant to expect a surprise but all this Mr Kennedy far surpasses our expectations," one quietly said.

"Should you be prepared to give me an official receipt," Chris said, "we will load the 158 ingots into the helicopter and you can be back in town shortly after teatime. I will give you the details of the account to credit the net proceeds to. There is a satellite telephone on my desk—you can telephone ahead to your office to make whatever arrangements you may require. The helicopter will have to make one refuelling stop; it can then bypass the regional city and take you straight to the capital city mint. It will be quite late when you get to Perth."

"GOOD GRIEF, KENNEDY! You are asking us to take custody of over twenty-five million in gold bullion and just fly it to the city," one of the men exclaimed almost in horror.

"Why not?" Chris strongly said, "It is only you two, Bill and I, and a couple of trusted workmen who know what will be in those heavy wooden boxes, which will in fact be disguised strong boxes. Should you delay, it will only increase the security risk, which at the moment is absolutely zero."

"If I may, I will use your telephone for a moment, sir?" the apparent senior member of the duo asked. He spent about twenty minutes on the telephone. He returned to Chris saying, "My chief did not believe me at first, but now he has asked can you have the helicopter land in the park at the rear of the Government House Gardens. We are to be met by an armoured car and escort and will be driven straight to the mint. Mr Kennedy, he has asked can you personally call at his office as soon as possible. He wishes to establish a more functional modus operandi, should this again happen in the future."

"It most certainly will," Chris laughed. "Look here." On the shelves on the opposite wall a further twenty ingots were carefully stacked.

The senior man swallowed deeply; he could only whisper, "Mr Kennedy." The senior man finally said, "We will be in touch with you immediately when we get back to our office. It will be early tomorrow; there is much to discuss."

Chris called in two stout men and asked, "Can you kindly stack this lot of junk," indicating the 158 ingots, "into my special boxes and haul it out to the chopper?"

Daisy had been refuelled and was waiting.

"I heard her come back about fifteen minutes ago," Chris said, "she can leave immediately you gentlemen are ready to leave. Be prepared for at least an eight-hour flight with one stop for refuelling. The pilot had anticipated you would be returning today and has already lodged his flight plan." His two men had returned.

"All loaded and ready boys?" Chris asked.

163

"All done, Boss," one replied.

"Good work," Chris complimented them. He turned to the two thoroughly perplexed mint officers, saying, "I will walk out with you, and if you will excuse me, I have to get back to filling that blasted trench. Do you have that receipt ready?"

The senior fellow rifled in his briefcase and came out with a government receipt pad and started to write. "Who do I make the receipt out to Mr Kennedy?" he asked.

"Please make it out to Quo-Vadis Mines," Chris proudly replied.

The senior man wrote for a few minutes then handed the receipt to Chris, and with his colleague climbed aboard Daisy. Minutes later Daisy lifted off and disappeared out into the Outback.

"I hope the security guys got all this on tape," Bill chuckled. I will get a copy run-off immediately. You can take it back with you when you go. Jackie is going to laugh herself silly when she sees it." Unbeknown to the mint officials every minute, every expression on their faces, every word, had been filmed and taped.

The backhoe made filling the last of the trench relatively easy and the water and electricity were all hooked up the next day.

"Thank goodness we had licensed electricians and plumbers on the staff; it made sure it was done correctly and everything is legal," Chris said.

Chris and Bill stood at the house switchboard. Chris was a little apprehensive as he reached for the main switch and flicked it to on. They stood back and watched the whole house light up.

"You are going to cop a fair power bill if you light up this lot often," Bill seriously said.

Chris was laughing as he replied, "Not B likely mate. I own the power station."

They were both laughing heartily as they stepped from their work boots and proceeded to walk through the house. Eight very large bedrooms, each with its own ensuite and generous sitting area. The house had a very modern kitchen, and fine large lounge room. There were also facilities for a library, a game's room large enough for a full-size billiard table with room to spare, and an extremely large family room with a curved window that ran the complete length of a wall and faced out onto the lake and included double very large sliding doors that opened out onto an extensive patio. A very sumptuous sized dining room abutted the kitchen area. There were many other features, it would take pages to record them all here.

"Jackie tells me she has engaged the services of the decorator who did my apartment to help her decorate all this," Chris said. "What's that?" he exclaimed. "Look at that, Bill! That blasted Giuseppe has painted a sign on the door of what was to be my office." The sign read, "*Man Cave*." "I'll kill him when I next see him."

Two weeks before Christmas he received a long letter from his mother. It read: "I hope you are organised, my boy. We have made all our bookings and will arrive in your city on the eighteenth; please be there to meet us. If Rex and the girls can be there I see no reason why you can't be."

Jasmine had apparently accidentally let it slip that Chris and Jackie were married. The letter continued on: "I am very angry that I am the last to know you and Jackie got married and that you kept the news from me. You better have a pretty good excuse or I will box your ears for a week. What clothes should I bring? Rex has told me that we are going straight out to Quo- Vadis for Christmas. Where is it? I have tried to find it on the maps. Is it far? I did read somewhere that distances over there are of little consequence."

The letter did continue on further mainly containing questions and admonishments.

Chris read the letter to Jackie and the girls saying, "Your grandmother will never change; once you get to know her you will love her."

"I do hope she likes us," Annie softly whispered.

Jackie and the girls "chickened out" and pleaded to be left behind when Chris left to keep the appointment to pick up his mum and dad. "I will have Bill take us out to Quo-Vadis and make sure everything is ready for you when you and all the family arrive." Jackie had said as she endeavoured to justify her decision.

"That sounds like a cop out" Chris grumbled. "There is nothing left to do as far as I know," Chris defensively said. "The decorator has finished. I am still amazed at what the pair of you have achieved," he complimented Jackie.

"There is still much to be done, mainly girl type stuff, like check fridges and cool rooms, and ensure all the linen cupboards are well-stocked. I also have to be sure there is plenty of baby food for Jack." Jackie was wanting Chris to not still feel badly toward her for not coming to the airport,

"That kid of ours would eat the leg off the kitchen table if he had the chance. You would think the way he puts away the tucker he would never get hungry," Chris commented.

"He is only a growing boy," Jackie defensively replied. "Babies his age do need good nourishment." Then with a laugh added, "Even a table leg or two for dessert now and then helps. He is growing quickly," she proudly said. "He put on two-and-a-half kilograms last week."

"At that rate, it will soon be time to introduce him to a pick and shovel," Chris lightly said. Then getting serious added, "I am sending four girls out to give you a hand—later this week, before the mob arrives. With you being out there you will be able to organise them and their activities."

"You think of everything, you beautiful man. I am so glad you are mine. How many will actually be coming?"

"I believe about ten and counting: Bill, Strahan, Riley, and their wives. It looks like you may have twenty or more for Christmas dinner. That does not include Jack, the girls, you, and I."

"Where will I put them all," Jackie cried. "That is at least seven couples and kids."

"You have enough rooms; all the kids can doss down over in the men's quarters with Bill. With it being Christmas and all the men going home to their families, the quarters will be empty for about eight weeks. I think I had better get a couple more girls to help you. It is easier to organise opening a new mine rather than setting up all this domestic stuff," he thought to himself.

# Chapter 5

His parents arrived exactly as his mother had advised. Rex and his sisters had declined, with scorn, Chris's advice to be at the airport.

"Mum has never been on time in her life," they had laughed.

"We are sure they will let us know as soon as they arrive," Rex commented. "I gave them my mobile number and explained to them the idiosyncrasies of our transport system."

"Okay," Chris had rather ruefully replied. "I will be going out to the airport to wait for them. You lot can risk Mum's wrath when she sees you are not there to meet them."

It would be impossible to accurately describe what happened when his parents arrived. His mother joyously hugged Chris and exclaimed loudly how well he looked and that married life must be agreeing with him. She was searching over his shoulder and snapped rather aggressively, "Where are the others?"

To say the roof of the arrival's lounge lifted about twenty millimetres with the explosion that ensured when Chris said, "They are not here, Mum," would give the reader an idea of her reaction.

Chris quickly grabbed his phone and called Rex. He tried not to laugh as he said, "No, bro. The 747 has not crashed into the airport building. It is just Mum's reaction to you not being here."

Chris attempted not to be a *"know-it-all,"* as he added, "I did try to tell you. See you at the Majestic in twenty minutes. I have booked the Executives Reception Room for us at the hotel," and had it closed off for our exclusive use."

As soon as they arrived at the hotel, Chris attempted to tell Rex what Mum had said. He didn't have time to complete the discourse before his mother started on his siblings. It was just as well the reception room was well soundproofed. Chris was sure that by the time his mum had finished her tirade, the paint on the walls of that room would be peeling. He had copped a bit after he had tried to answer her question, "And where is your wife, Christopher?" His mother had blasted at him.

"She didn't want to bring the baby to the city." That was as far he got.

"You have a baby!" his mother screamed. "Please, God, forgive me if I kill him here and now. Why was I not told these things?"

"I will tell you everything later, Mum," Chris softly said. "It is a very long story. It will be better if Jackie and I are together when we tell you. She is waiting at Quo Vadis for us."

The tone in Chris's voice warned her to "back off" and she did settle down a bit after that and did even start to enjoy the reunion.

As they separated at the end of the evening his mother loudly announced, "We will meet everybody down stairs at 8 am in the morning."

At 8 am, everybody, kids included, were waiting patiently for "The Oldies". Nobody was prepared to be the brunt of another of their mum's tirade by being late. A small fleet of taxis took them out to the airport. Daisy sat on the tarmac adjacent to the first-class lounge.

"Are we flying in that?!" Chris's mum exclaimed.

"Yes, Mum," Chris firmly said, and introducing the pilot added, "This is Captain Herb. He and his crew will look after you. You will find them equal if not better to the crew on the 747 that you came over in."

His dad placed an arm over Chris's shoulder and conspiratorially said, "This is building up to be the most different Christmas we ever had."

"You do not know half of it," Chris whispered in reply.

First stop was the tourist park. "From here you have a choice of travel," Chris announced to the party. "You can opt for five to six very interesting days living and riding rough, or for another five hours flying in Daisy. Bill, here," he thrust Bill forward, "will look after those who choose the road trip."

Chris's dad and the kids all decided on the road trip, particularly after Bill announced, "they would all be sleeping in the forks of gum trees."

"I think the kids were a bit disappointed," Chris told the kids' parents, "when Bill told them he was just joking.

Chris's mum had enjoyed the flight in Daisy during the first hop. "I will fly, thank you, son," she announced.

After an early lunch, the party separated to go their chosen ways. In short time, all the problems resolved themselves quite beautifully. Mum and Jackie bonded very deeply. Upon her arrival at Quo-Vadis, and after greetings were out of the way; Jackie had made them each a cup of tea and had sat on the patio by the lake edge. She had told Mum the story of how desperately unhappy she was when Chris left her to further his studies and how she had married Hector. She did not mention Jack's parentage. She then took Mum to the nursery to meet Jack. He was sitting by now and smiled as they walked in. Mum looked rather closely at him but said little. She had assumed Jack was Hector's child.

She paused at the edge of the cot and reached in. "May I Jackie?" she politely asked.

Jack was very happy to be nursed by this lady and nestled close to her.

Mum suddenly burst into tears. "He is Chris's child, isn't he Jackie," she stuttered through her tears.

"Yes, Mum, he is truly your grandchild," Jackie replied. "I will tell you the rest of the story now if you want to hear it."

Mum was totally overwhelmed for the moment, and blubbered, "Oh Jackie girl, he is the spitting image of Christopher at that age. He is beautiful! Yes please, finish your story now, but first get me a handful of tissues, I am so happy I cannot stop crying."

The two women sat in the nursery for an hour; they talked about much.

"Where are Hector's two girls you and Christopher adopted?" Mum asked.

"They are waiting in their rooms," Jackie was a little hesitant in answering. "I told them to wait until I called them."

The girls were a little tardy in answering Jackie's call. Jackie had to go and knock gently on their bedroom door to get them to respond. "Chris's mum would like to meet you. Come along now, you will find she is a very special person."

The girls followed Jackie into the nursery and were greeted by the smiling Mrs Kennedy senior.

"Hello girls," she said. "So, this is the rest of my new family. You are lovely looking girls. I do hope we can become close friends."

By teatime, a warm gentle relationship had grown between Mum and the girls, possibly enhanced by Annie saying, "This is wonderful: now I have not only a proper mum and dad, but a grandma and a grandpa too."

That started Mum weeping again.

Chris was unaware of all the "women" in the nursery and innocently barged in. He got such an intense look from them all, he hastily backed out thinking to himself; "I would even defy Daniel to enter that den!

"Go away you wicked boy," his mother cried. "We girls are busy. Fancy hiding all these wonderful people from me all this time. I should box your ears."

"Can we watch?" Annie giggled.

Jackie had often found Chris in the nursery. Without her knowing he would creep into the nursery and would sit on the floor with Jack perched in front of him generally playing "Boos", as Chris called it. Jack was usually bubbling with laughter.

The Christmas weeks went by far too quickly for all. Chris's dad had grabbed for a chair when Chris and Bill took him into the strongroom. They had waited some weeks for the arrival of an armoured car and escort to collect the latest consignment of gold for the mint to purchase. The shelves were heavily laden with gleaming ingots.

"How much is here?" he gasped.

"We are shipping out three-hundred ingots. It is last months' melt. The blokes from the mint are a little hesitant to make the trip with this much gold.

"After making that trip myself," his father had chuckled, "I know their problem. What's all this gold worth, Son?"

"About two-hundred million dollars," Chris nonchalantly replied. That was when his father grabbed for that chair.

"Did I hear right?" he wailed. "I am looking at two-hundred million dollars' worth of gold?"

"That's right," Chris replied.

"You do me proud son," his father respectfully said.

Chris relieved the mood which had become very serious. "All the kids want to take the boat out and do some fishing. Are you blokes coming?"

It was enthusiastically and completely unanimously agreed: all Christmases in future were to be spent at Quo-Vadis. Chris's mum and dad decided to move into the regional city.

His mum justified the move by saying it made sense. "All the children were over here," and quickly added, "What's more important, I must be able to watch that darling Jack grow up. With all the other grandchildren being over here I missed all that with them."

Chris made sure they moved into a very fine, large house in the best district in town.

Before Rex and his family left, Rex cornered Jackie and Chris. "You have a very big problem Chris," he growled. "Your balance sheet has become topsy turvy—you know what I mean? Your cash holding is ridiculous; you had better spend a bit."

"I could go shopping," Jackie mischievously pushed into the discussion.

"And send him bankrupt within a week," Rex smiled, then becoming serious said, "You will have to make some strong capital purchases."

"If I install more mining equipment, with the increased production that would only exacerbate the problem," Chris said. "Any suggestions, Bro?"

"Not really, Chris. A problem of this nature does not come across that often. Most companies I know would kill to be in your position. Because Quo-Vadis Holdings is not listed on the stock exchange very few actually see your accounts in detail, and with you holding all the shares, except for a few non-voting shares, you have no fear of anybody making a takeover bid. As a matter of interest, I had to distribute nearly one-million dollars per share to those few shareholders last month. That distribution hardly made a dent in the cash problem. You could employ a lot more people."

"To do what?" Chris quickly asked. "I have permanent electricians, plumbers, crusher mechanics, miners etc., etc. Because all the machines are the very best, and are all relatively new, all those blokes have an easy life."

Rex was becoming quite frustrated. "You might as well buy a blasted airline. That would cost a mint to run and may soak up some of all this excess cash; some of the smaller shows are lucky to break even at the moment."

"Buy an airline? I do not want an airline." Chris thought for a moment, then with a laugh added; "but a good aeroplane would allow more efficient travel between here and the regional city. Also, it could be used to travel to the major city. That's a good suggestion brother Rex. To build a landing strip will cost a bit. I know there are three of the pilots flying for the tourist park at the moment, who have flown jets. I think Max, the head fellow, has even flown some of the really big commercial jets. This may work out very nicely. Instead of you having to stay in town with the girls each week, while they go to school; Jackie my love; at the weekends or whenever you like, you could all flash out here. It would also allow me to have a little more time with my family."

"I think it would be a great idea. Please put one aeroplane on your shopping list immediately," Jackie happily said.

"One aeroplane coming up," Chris laughed.

"You pair are impossible," Rex sighed, threw his hands into the air and walked out mumbling, "I'm just going to see what the sane people are doing."

As Rex walked out Jackie moved to sit on Chris's lap. "Are you really going to buy an aeroplane for me, Mister," she softly whispered.

"It has extraordinarily good merit," Chris replied as he endeavoured to nibble her ear.

"Stop that you insatiable beast!" Jackie cried, "unless you want to suffer the consequences. I am trying to be serious here and all you are doing is turning me on."

"Okay, you have one and a half minutes, then be prepared to be eaten alive," Chris very forcibly said.

"Yes, please," Jackie giggled.

Later they found time for some serious conversation. "Look at it this way, Jackie," Chris said, "Mum has been hinting that, that big house we bought for them needs children in it. She would like you and the girls to move in with them while the girls

174

are at school. It is a pretty sound argument as she believes she could look after the girls and would see much more of us and Jack and give you a little more freedom. With the availability of a fast aeroplane we could do this. There is also a long-term feature we should consider: Jack's schooling! That is a fair way in the future but it would do well to give it some thought."

He did buy an aircraft, all $28 million worth. When fitted out to Chris's requirements it cost him $34 million.

Rex's comment was, "You have made a good start; how much will the landing strip cost?"

"I will have to tell you that when it is finished," Chris had laughed.

With Christmas behind them and the girls residing with Mum and Dad and being back at school, Chris and Jackie had much more time to themselves. Those two girls Chris had hired at the last minute pleaded to be allowed to "stay on." They had become very good housekeepers indeed and were most happy to be nursemaids to Jack.

"I'm not sure who has the most fun: Jack or the two nursemaids. They spend half the day playing with him," Jackie told Chris.

It was a most beautiful day, conducive to taking a walk. Chris and Jackie had decided to walk over the other side of the sinkhole. The cliff-face over there was astounding, and Chris was in his element. There was little sign of quartz but plenty of Greenstone reef. "This would warrant investigation if ever the reef in the cave petered out, although for the time being that was not worthy of one second of worry."

Tom, the drilling contractor, had conscientiously drilled those areas Chris had marked out on the surface of the escarpment. He had confirmed that the reef in the cave was present a long way along the escarpment.

Tom nonchalantly mentioned, "Several of those randomly selected drill points had struck another quartz reef. It was a little deeper than their known reef. The core samples were a bit of an eye-opener—they all contain gold and Bill had appeared to be quite excited with the ore samples. He has asked me to try and collect enough material so he has something worthwhile crushing. Said something like, 'Looks as if the kid is even more wealthy than he thinks.'"

When he had heard this news Chris, at considerable cost and much blasting, had constructed several access roads up the escarpment face and had sent a small team of miners to sink a shaft to acquire the material Bill needed. That was over two weeks ago and the team was still at work and had not as yet mined down to the reef. Tom had been further engaged to drill more holes to endeavour to plot this new-found reef.

All this was far from Chris and Jackie's mind this day. They were enjoying the peacefulness of this side of the sinkhole. The peacefulness was destroyed by the bellowing of two large scrub bulls. The bemused couple strained to see what was happening high above them atop the cliff. The younger aspirant was trying to take over the herd. Their battle was most violent. Suddenly the clever old bull manoeuvred the younger protagonist to the edge of the sinkhole cliff and forced him over. Bellowing plaintively, the younger bull crashed down onto a pile of loose rock fall about thirty metres from where the hypnotised couple stood.

In fear, Jackie grabbed Chris who enveloped her in his arms. "Is it dead," Jackie whispered.

"I think so" Chris replied. "Sit here for a moment and I will check." The bull was dead. "What a shame," Chris thought, all that prime beef just wasted. "No!" he snapped to himself, "There is no reason why we cannot butcher it here and now, for our own use."

Jackie had overcome her initial fright. "What a good idea," she had responded to his suggestion. "I love fresh beef. How would you get that much meat back to the house? There is too much for the two of us to carry."

"I will get Bill to bring a couple of men over in the work boat. They can help us cut it up, and then take it straight back to the cool room. I believe the butchers usually allow it to 'hang' for a short while before it is used for cooking."

Many of those living at Quo-Vadis enjoyed meals of prime beef for quite a while.

All this remained in the recesses of Chris's mind for many days. "There are many scrub cattle up there in the park," he was thinking. "They have never been rounded up or claimed. The environmental people reckon they are a confounded pest and do destroy much of the bush. I wonder?"

Jackie could almost hear his mind ticking. Finally, three days later, as they sat at the curved window of the breakfast nook, Chris told her what he had been thinking. "Jackie, love, how do you think you and Jack would handle it if we took a six or seven-day trip in Goliath, roughing it?"

Jackie was protectively hesitant for a moment, she did miss those days and freedom of being out in the Outback with Chris, roughing it.

"I would adapt Goliath so you and Jack would suffer only a minimum of discomfort," Chris added.

Temptation got the better of her, and she softly said, "I would love to. I know if Jack got distressed you would turn back, wouldn't you?"

"I would return without a second thought," Chris quickly responded.

"Where are we going?" She asked.

"Remember those bulls we saw fighting," he replied. "Well I have given it much thought and I think we will go looking for some cattle . . . What do you call it?"

"I think you mean, cattle station" Jackie laughed.

"Yes! Cattle station, is the explanation I was searching for. There is a cattle station about 150 kilometres out. I have searched it on the satellite maps. It looks a bit rundown. I would like to have a good look at it from the ground and maybe, just maybe, buy it."

"If you do that, it might get Rex off your back for a while," Jackie excitedly said.

Jack was just turning one. He sat strapped in the specially designed seat, in between his parents, ardently watching the Outback roll slowly past. Jackie had great fun making animal sounds she thought befitted the animals they saw. "How do you make a kangaroo sound?" she asked Chris.

"I don't know. We'll ask the next one we see," he humorously replied.

"Smart arse," she snapped and went back to an easy one, a kookaburra.

It had taken over two days to get there and as they pulled into the area in front of the homestead, an elderly man and woman hobbled out. Introductions over, they were cordially invited to come on in and have a cup of tea.

"We have not seen White Folk for some time, and it will be good to have a yarn," the old man happily said.

The old couple were Graham Simpson and his wife, Jillian. Their families had actually owned over one-hundred-thousand hectares of land, for some time, and had grazing leases for, goodness only knows, how much of the area. They had lived there all their lives. "I think that is getting close to eighty years," old Graham reminisced. His family had lived there for several generations. He was the last of the line. "We have no kids," he sadly added. "Jilly lost three, and we decided to call it quits. We are both a bit crook. Jilly is supposed to go into hospital, but she reckons she will never get out. This joint has gone to rack and ruin. All the men have gone. I have to rely on a small tribe of natives to help out. We would leave in a flash and move to town if ever we got a chance. Can't see that ever happening; we will most probably only ever leave here in a box." Graham's discourse was filled with deep regret.

"What do you believe the whole place is worth?" Chris rudely asked.

"Dunno, son, the old man had replied. "Really it is only worth what somebody would offer."

Equally as rude, Jackie quickly said, "Is the title clear?" She could see where Chris was heading.

"I owe the bank a few bob," Graham was slow to reply. "They have a charge over about half of the title."

"I know I am being very rude," Chris very humbly said, "but would you tell me what you owe?"

Simpson became a little more alert. "You interested in buying it," he slowly asked.

"Depends on a few things," Chris replied, "but, yes, I know it will cost a packet and will be very costly to bring it up to scratch. What's the water situation?"

"Woah! Slow down a bit, lad," Simpson quickly replied trying not to sound over eager. "One question at the time. I am into the bank for about one-hundred-and fifty grand; they are getting a bit stroppy and are threatening to sell me up, miserable bastards. Jillie and I would get nothing. As to your question about the water situation, all I can say is, what water? The cattle find water for themselves. We have not had a dinkum roundup for ten years. The cattle could be here, there and everywhere. The tribe kill one for me now and again; it depends on their needs really. I cannot get a cattle buyer to come out here; the lazy buggers say getting cattle into market from here is too much trouble. Would you and your missus like to look around?"

"May we," Chris replied. "We can take my unit."

Jilly shouted in ecstasy when she saw Jack. Goliath had been parked in the shade of one of the few large gum trees. He had been settled in his crib on the back seat in air-conditioned comfort.

"May I pick him up, Jackie?" she quietly asked.

"Hold a moment," Jackie said. "I will pass him to you. He may not get quite so surprised with a new face if I do it that way."

It was no problem for Jack—he gooed a bit then tugged Jilly's long black hair.

"He is beautiful, Jackie. We could do a clean swap: you can have the station; I will have Jack."

"Dream on, Jilly! Even ten-thousand stations would not buy him," Chris rather passionately said.

Jilly nursed Jack for a while then placed him gently back into his crib. "Thank you, Jackie," she emotionally whispered. "It has been such a long time."

They drove around the station for about two hours. "Haven't been out here for a while myself," old Simpson said. "It is a much bigger mess than I remembered," he honestly conceded.

They drove back to the house. As Goliath rolled to a stop, Chris turned to Simpson and quickly said, "twelve and a half million dollars, cash, lock stock and barrel, vacant possession within six months."

"Far too much!" the old man cried. "I would not like to rob a couple of nice kids like you pair. One-and-a-half million will set Jilly and I in a nice house in town and pay for some decent treatment for her."

"Sorry, Mr Simpson, I do not like to haggle," Chris laughed. "My bottom line is fifteen million. I want no further argument."

"Fifteen million!" the old man exclaimed. "You gotta gold mine or something?"

"You guess right, Mr Simpson; he does have a gold mine," Jackie laughed.

"Must be a *good 'n*," the old man smiled and turning to his wife softly said, "What do you reckon, Jilly girl?"

"Yes, please," she whispered, obviously elated. She took Jackie's hand and said, "Come on in and I'll show you the house. You may want me to leave a few things, although there is little left. We have had to sell all the good stuff just to survive."

"I want you to take everything," Jackie replied. "Knowing this man of mine as I do, he will just bulldoze the house and rebuild it somewhere else."

"Is that an airstrip over there, Graham?" Chris asked.

"It was," the old man replied. "It's a bit overgrown. You got an aeroplane, lad?"

"Yes," was all that Chris replied, then added, "I can have a crew here in three days. They will bring a truck and move you to town. We will put you up in a nice motel until you find a home. The fifteen million dollars will be in any account you wish by tomorrow morning. As soon as you hit town I will have the paperwork for you to sign. Will you need a lift into town?" That was only one of the many questions Chris shot at the old man.

"My old bus is not working at the moment, Chris. I will need a day or two to fix it. We should be okay," Simpson answered hesitantly.

"Just leave it, you can buy yourself a new car when you hit town. I think you should have enough spare cash to do that," Chris said. "We will fly you back to town," then gently putting a hand on Jilly's shoulder said, "This is all a bit sudden, Jilly. Are you alright?"

"Mr Christopher Kennedy, you and Jackie are the answer to my prayers. I could walk out of here right now and not have one moment of regret." Her reply was without a trace of emotion.

Jackie came and sat beside her. "All this will take a bit of getting used to," she said to the old lady. "I would like to introduce you to our parents. They are the type of people who would love to help you."

"Are you kids for real?" Old Simpson cried.

"Very real," Chris laughed. "And just to prove it to you, I'm going to get on that telephone in Goliath and by 6 am tomorrow I will have workmen everywhere, and by 9 am you will be on your way to Quo-Vadis," Chris very positively and forcibly said.

"To where did you say? What's this Quo, or what-ever you called it?" the confused Simpson stuttered.

"It is our home," Jackie softly replied. "If it is okay, Chris, Jack and I will fly back with the Simpsons. For the next week or two this will be no place for a baby and his mum."

Chris excused himself and spent the next hour on the phone to Bill, ten minutes to Rex, and five minutes to his parents. It all happened as Chris had said. No! That's not quite correct, it was not until 8 am when both Donald and Daisy settled down in the station yard.

"Both birds were at Quo-Vadis," Bill told Chris. "It was opportune and I loaded them both with as much gear as they could carry. Workmen, machines, and a multitude of building material were quickly unloaded. The Simpsons, Jackie and Jack were quickly bundled aboard and the choppers rose and roared away.

"Back in four hours," Bill loudly called to Chris. "I told Giuseppe and his mob to get ready and to be waiting to come back with us. He made me laugh when he loudly complained, "That blasted Chris again; never gives a man a moment's peace."

Chris immediately directed the men to repair the airstrip. A small portion had been kept operational for use by the Flying Doctor to answer calls when Jilly required urgent treatment. Repair of the rest of the airstrip was not a major task. It only required removal of weeds and very small trees and the airstrip rolled many times.

Immediately when Bill arrived back, Giuseppe bowled up to Chris and in a very loud voice demanded, "Well, big man, tell me all."

"I am thinking a big six-to-eight-bedroom place with all the extras—you know, ensuites, sitting rooms attached; big kitchen well-fitted out, and a high-pitched roof. A big air-conditioner and a 20-kVA generator should be here early next week. You can use your imagination for the rest," Chris replied. "Oh yes, I would like to see it made mainly with natural stone," he added. Still answering Giuseppe's initial enquiry, Chris continued saying, "Tom, the drilling rig operator, is bringing his new very big rig out in the next couple of days. We have to find water very quickly."

"Find water out here! You joke?" Giuseppe loudly and quite rudely shouted.

"Have faith, my Italian friend. I know there is water somewhere hereabouts," Chris counselled him. "Just let the site foreman know whatever you want and when. The choppers will bring it in as quickly as possible."

A week later the very big drilling rig rolled in. Chris's large Cat. front-end loader trundled along behind.

"Bloody Hell, Kennedy," were the first words Tom's number two shouted. "One day you will find us a job where we do not have to spend days digging out equipment. It is just as well your loader was working on your new track; the gang foreman had laughed his socks off when he saw our rig bogged to the axles. He had started laughing again when I told him where we were headed and that you were out here. He said something like: "That boss of ours is unreal. You do not know what he will be up to next." He asked me to ask you; "do you want them to commence building a decent road to this cattle station?" The number two driller was still complaining as he added; "that blasted road boss was still laughing when he had said to me, 'I reckon I will be 'old bones' before he finishes with me." He did send that loader to dig us out and told the driver to follow along just in case we went down again." Tom's number two had smiled now as he had continued saying loudly; "by the time I got here we had needed that loader at least twice a day to dig the rig out."

Tom stood rather aggressively in front of Chris, and demanded, "Where do you want us to poke down the first hole."

"I am not so confident with locating water as I am to find minerals," Chris humbly replied. "I have marked out ten spots; try them. You will have to go down around eight-hundred meters or more. Maps show the artesian basin is out here so let's hope you find good water."

Tom gave a loud snort, and cynically said, "Knowing you Mister, ten will get you one we strike water in the first hole."

"You are on a five percent bonus and the boys are on a keg if you can do that," Chris laughed.

"I'll dig your bloody hole with my bare hands, for that sort of bonus," Tom laughed and strode to the first marker shouting, "Back him up here boy's, you are on a keg if we find water." His crew responded and with the precision and expertise of long experience, set to, to put that big rig into operation.

Giuseppe, the amusing Italian builder, confronted Chris. "Why did they build the station house here!" he exclaimed. "It is disgusting—you couldn't think of a worse spot."

"I cannot answer that, Giuseppe," Chris quietly replied as he attempted to dampen the builder's, repine. "Probably all the yards were here first and they had thought it best to be close to the action. They didn't have motorbikes or mini choppers in those days; if you had to go anywhere it was 'Shanks's pony' (walk) or on horseback. Give me a day or two and I will have you a new site."

Chris flew back to Quo-Vadis that day. Jackie and Jack met him out at the airstrip. Jack bubbled in delight as he saw Chris and enthusiastically reached for him. The pair laughed gleefully as Chris ruffled his hair and hugged him. After dinner, as they prepared for bed, Chris and Jackie sat on the side of the bed and Chris talked incessantly of what was happening out at the cattle station. Then, when he noticed Jackie had a wide smile on her face, he asked, "Did I say something funny?"

"No, my love, you have not said something funny. It's just that I have some good news for you. I have been trying to tell you, sir," she laughed, "but as usual you always have so much to tell me I am lucky to get a word in edgewise, so just shut up for a minute, give me ten big kisses, and listen."

"Better make it three kisses," Chris very lightly said. "Any more than that and I will not be responsible for my actions. I will probably just whizz you off here and now."

"Four very big kisses coming up," Jackie giggled and flung her arms about him. It was that fourth kiss that did it.

Two hours later as they lay on the bed, Chris softly said, "Now, as you were saying, shut up and listen, I am listening now." As he spoke he was running his hand gently up and down her beautiful naked back.

"Just stop that!" Jackie cried. "At this rate I will never get to tell you about the talk I had with Izzy this morning."

"Izzy! Is that your sister?" Chris innocently asked.

"Yes, I have told you about her and her husband, Peter," Jackie said. "Peter is the fellow the big ranchers in the States often ask to fix up a problem or two on their ranches. My call was most opportune. Peter has finished his present contract and is looking about for a new job. Both Izzy and Peter are fed up with constantly having to move from place to place and now with little Joshua, they would love to settle down. I told them nothing but did tell her to hold on for a while and I would have you call them, and that you may have something that would interest them. So now, my beautiful lover, I may have found you a Station Manager. You can say thank you and start rubbing my back again," she giggled.

"Thank you, Jackie girl; once again you have come up tops," Chris very appreciatively said.

It wasn't until early next morning when the loud demands for attention from the adjacent nursery woke them. Jack was again filled with delight when he saw Chris on the bed. Jackie set the happy child beside Chris and a violent wrestling match ensued.

"I'm getting out of this," Jackie cried as she got dressed. "I'm going downstairs to get you hooligans some breakfast. Be downstairs in ten minutes." She had to shout to make herself heard over the ruckus.

Breakfast over, Chris and Jackie sat very contented at the breakfast table looking out over the lake. "You have spoken of Isabel before, Jackie love," he said," Tell me about her."

"It is a long story, Chris," she very softly said.

"I have nothing too important on at the moment," Chris quickly replied. "I told everybody I was going walkabout for a while, looking for a site to build the new station house, so go ahead—tell me all."

"It is really my story to. I have never told you of my early life," she very emotionally whispered, "and right now is as good a time as any to fill you in."

Jack had been spirited away by the two housekeeping girls for his morning bath, and from the sounds emanating from the bathroom it would appear they were having a great time. Jack did enjoy bath time, so his parents now sat in the quietness of the breakfast nook.

"Like last time I had something serious to tell you, I again ask you just to listen and not interrupt. I will answer any questions later." She took a deep breath and started, speaking hesitantly and softly at first, then as the memories returned, spoke more strongly. "Izzy and I never knew our father, and never knew why he departed. After he left, my mother had many *'gentlemen'* friends, some of rather questionable character. Being so young, we knew nothing of this and only found out some details in later life. For more than five years we existed, God only knows how, we were often dumped here, there, and anywhere. There were no relatives to help. Our mother was finally put into jail for an extended term for being an accomplice on a serious drug charge. Both Izzy and I were placed in an orphanage and, later, with a great variety of foster homes. We became separated. It was only some years later I caught up with Izzy and we have managed to keep in contact since then. The lady of the house in my last foster home did see to my education, and after seeing me through high school she did put me through a basic secretarial course at TAFE. I did well and went on to study bookkeeping at nights. I was lucky, and landed that job with the building developer, where you first saw me.

You know the rest of my story, except I have to tell you, despite any impression you may have had with my brazenness, when I told you that bed badly needed attention, I had never known another man before you. I do thank God that you were my first man, and I know now you will be my last."

"Jackie," Chris softly said, "thank you! I knew you were a virgin the first time we fixed that bed. I felt deeply honoured, and now, for what it's worth, I tell you I have had a few girls in my life, but I have never loved them as I love you."

"Hush! You booby, don't keep on," she whispered. "Just let me finish. Izzy had not done so well. Where I had found a pretty good home with that foster family, Izzy continued to float from family to family, finally getting a job as a domestic with an American family. To cut it a bit short, the family took her back to America with them. She married Peter, the youngest son of her employers. His work did have them travelling all over America, while he worked on contract after contract. He developed a very good reputation and was very highly regarded. He was constantly sought by many cattle breeders."

Chris waited a moment to be sure she had finished, then stood and walked around the breakfast table, took Jackie in his arms, and gently said. "Thank you for telling me all that. If it is possible to love you more and for knowing you even better, I now do." He spoke with deep sincere emotion, then added, "Get your brother-in-law on the phone—I want to talk to him."

Sometime later, after the completion of a long telephone conversation with Peter, they were still sitting at the breakfast table. Chris stood and stretched, picked up Jackie's hand and quietly said, "Thank you, again, my very efficient Personal Assistant," then correcting himself instantly added, "My beautiful wife; your sister her husband and son will arrive in the city in about a week. Peter wants the job, 'Hell or High-Water'. He could not believe he will have to look after tens of thousands of square kilometres of cattle station. We will have to get Rex to organise entry permits et cetera as soon as possible. Our next task will be to quickly find just where to build the new station house, so they will have somewhere to live. It will have to be a little larger than I first thought, as Peter did say to expect a continuous stream of Yankee visitors."

Finding a site was not as easy as it sounded. Jack was left in the care of Chris's mum who had insisted on being nurse maid while they were, as she put it, "out gallivanting around the outback."

This arrangement suited Jack, because "Granma" spoiled him rotten.

Goliath had pushed his way through the scrub of the Outback for three days. They had found a couple of "maybe" sites but Chris wanted better. They came upon a worn cattle track. "I wonder where that goes to," he said to Jackie.

"Not another cave like the one at Quo-Vadis, I hope. I think you have quite enough gold at the moment, sir." That set them both laughing.

Goliath pushed through a particularly thick barrier of scrub. A flock of colourful parrots rose from the scrub with noisy agitation. The cattle track had wound its way through the thick scrub. Chris continued to follow along it. After fifteen minutes of heavy bush bashing, they cleared the thick scrub, and a beautiful scene was revealed to them. A substantial artesian spring had forced its way to the surface and a strong flow of water had formed a sizeable pool. The pool was surrounded by tall white trunked gum trees. Many species of birds fluttered angrily as the peaceful scene was disturbed by the intrusion of that mechanical monster.

Chris exclaimed with delight in a voice that held the small degree of regret. "It would be a shame to disturb the tranquillity of this place, but it is exactly the sort of place we have been searching for; it even has a very substantial flat area over there under the trees where the house could be built. There is even an adjacent flat area, a little further, on where sheds and a workshop could be built. Another thing which makes it so appealing, is it is less than fifty kilometres from Quo-Vadis."

Giuseppe was most enthusiastic about the new site. He carefully listened to Chris's ideas, added a few of his own, searched nearby seeking out suitable natural material, gathered his crew, and commenced building.

Orders and workmen flew in all directions, machines commenced preparing the site. It was not long before the peaceful place was turned into a construction site.

Peter and Izzy arrived. Jackie and Chris had great pleasure in showing them the plans of the proposed station house. They had reviewed the plans, made a few minor alterations and commented, "There will be lots of hard work necessary, and lots of money to be spent. How much are we allowed to spend?" Peter asked.

"Do not be concerned with that. Quo-Vadis Holdings will look after all that," Chris replied. Then, as an afterthought, said, "The one thing I do ask is that you install only the best of the best. Giuseppe your builder is well versed in the standard I insist on. I will take you out to the building site and introduce you to him tomorrow. While your house is under construction, we invite you to stay here with us at Quo-Vadis."

"You seem to have everything well in hand," Peter commented. "I cannot contain my impatience to spend time looking over the ranch."

"You mean, station! Don't you, Peter?" Jackie corrected him.

"All right, Miss politically correct Aussie. As I was saying, I cannot wait to see the station property."

Isabel had burst into tears when, arm in arm, she and Jackie first walked into the proposed house site. "Is this where my home is to be?" she asked in awe.

"Yes, Sis—do you like it?" Jackie asked.

"Like, does not adequately describe my feelings," she exclaimed. "I adore it," and promptly burst into tears as she searched in her pockets for another tissue.

Giuseppe was happy to show them exactly how the house was planned to be laid out and showed them much of the natural material he was going to use, emphasising how much he enjoyed working with the natural stone. "As Mister Slave Driver Chris is not pushing me too heavily this time, I believe this house will equal to anything I have worked on—even Chris's and Jackie's house at Quo- Vadis."

Two days later, Chris bundled Peter into Goliath and drove him around the station. They paused at the first drill site.

"How does it look?" Chris asked Tom, after he had introduced him to Peter.

"Looking good, Mr Miner. I do not know how you do it. You already owe the boys a keg! We are down 1100 meters and have already struck water. We are continuing to push the drill a little further to ensure that it is an extensive strike. The water quality is very good. I think you will find it is more than satisfactory for human consumption. Do you want me to go any deeper?"

"Just go to 1200 meters, put down the pipes, then start on the next hole," Chris quickly answered his question. "Peter here may have a few thoughts later, where he feels he would like to see water points; in the meantime, just go ahead and search where I have indicated.

"You certainly do not muck about, Chris," Peter commented. "I am not used to things being organised for me—I have always had to bear the burden myself."

"I would not let that worry you, Mister. As soon as things are organised, you will be thrown in the deep end and left to run things exactly as you see fit. Do not ever be concerned with any expenditure you may incur. Quo-Vadis Holdings is a very substantial company and can comfortably bear the brunt of anything, and I mean anything, you may wish to spend."

"Izzy did tell me you are most successful. I didn't know until now what to expect. Now can you please show me the rest of the station and show me what stock I have to work with." I have not seen one beast in all the time we have been here. Where are they?" Peter asked.

"We will not have time to do that today, Peter. By the time we finish looking over the place it will be quite late. The home paddocks are over 50,000 square kilometres. The leases extend far beyond that. To tell you the truth, I have yet established exactly the boundaries of those leases. The northern most point is over two-hundred kilometres north. That's all I know."

"Did I hear right?!" Peter cried. "Did you just say two-hundred kilometres?"

"Yes," Chris replied. "It is only an average-sized station."

"If that makes it 'an average-sized station' it would be frightening to hear just how big a big station is," Peter bemusedly commented with a voice loaded with awe.

Chris spent the rest of the day showing Peter only as much of the station as they had time. Peter was trying to make an assessment of exactly what was there and what condition it was in. "Much of this is very new to me," he commented. "The land is totally different from everything I know. It's dry and the scrub is sparse, but in its own way is magnificent. There will be much work to do, and I have to warn you, Chris, it does need to have a lot of time and money spent on it. I will consult with you each time, how and where I will need to spend the money."

"Peter, my erstwhile brother-in-law," Chris very sternly growled, "we did not engage your services for any other reason than knowing you are the best. You are the cattleman and know cattle and their needs; I am only a miner who knows mines. I have already told you to please just spend whatever it takes but do it right."

While the two men spent the day looking over the station, Jackie and Izzy had returned to Quo-Vadis. They had much to catch up on.

"I have much to tell you about that man, Sis," Jackie said with a sigh, as she indicated who she meant with toss of her head in Chris's direction. "By the time I finish talking about him and Jack your house may be finished."

"Well, sister of mine," Izzy pushed in, "I have a few things to tell you too. By the sound of things, our men will be running for cover."

192

The following morning, purely in self-defence, the two men, did find a good reason "To get the hell out of the way," and had laughed as they made a hurried exit out the back door.

"That is no place for any self-respecting man to be; those girls will not even know we have left," Peter laughed.

Chris had driven Goliath slowly around the perimeter of the sinkhole to where he and Jackie had witnessed the fighting bulls. Peter questioned the origin and make of this vehicle they were travelling in. "Am I correct in assuming it has been manufactured to specifically be used in this Outback!" he asked.

"His name is Goliath," Chris chuckled. "Yes, he has been especially built. I will introduce you to his maker at a later date. You may have use for him from time to time; his name is Ed."

As they reached the boundary of the National Park, Peter alighted from Goliath and searched around. "There are many animals around here Chris," he commented. "Do they belong to the station?"

"They belong to nobody," Chris answered. "They are what we call, *Scrub Cattle*. Most of them have never been rounded up, and it is uncommon to find one that is branded. They are more or less free for the taking."

"My mind boggles at that thought," Peter quickly said. "Does the station staff include a few good *'cowboys'* and a herd of good horses?"

"We don't have 'cowboys' Peter; here they are called stockmen."

"You are as paranoid as your wife about being politically correct," Peter cried. "All right! I will ask my question again: does my crew include some good stockmen, and lots of good horses.

Chris could hardly contain his mirth; he was grinning from ear to ear as he said, "I think we had better arrange for you to spend a little time up north on one of the stations up there, to see the Aussie way of cattle *'farming'*. With your experience with cattle for so many years, you may even be able to give them some worthwhile advice. Don't be surprised if they just laugh at you. I don't see either of the girls wanting to accompany you, particularly if they've got a youngster in tow."

Peter was quiet for a short while, then softly said, "What you are saying has great merit, and I can only gain much from such a trip. When I return, I hope you will not object if I introduce a few of my own tricks around here. I can already see a few places that can be improved greatly, if introduce them.

"You can be very confident," Chris replied. "It is like I said, you are the cattleman and I will stick to being a miner."

"All the properties I have heard of have names. What is the name of this property?" Peter enquired.

"It's called Quo-Vadis Station," Chris said.

"That's interesting," Peter said, obviously thinking deeply. "That's old Latin, isn't it Chris? Quo-Vadis. Where are you going? Was that name here when you bought the place or did you give it to it?"

"It's the name I have given everything around here," Chris quietly answered.

Chris and Jackie took Peter and Izzy on a tour of the Quo-Vadis mine. Needless to say, they were struck wordless as Chris showed them firstly the gold reef, and then the gold ingots stacked precisely in the strongroom, adding, "I am about to open another reef up on the escarpment."

Peter did comment, "Now I can see why you were so unconcerned about what I was about to spend."

Izzy made them all laugh when she immediately reacted saying, "What's this about you spending money, Mr Cattleman? Not without me, I hope?"

Peter left for a short sojourn on the cattle stations up north the next morning.

Jackie and Izzy visited the site of the new house regularly on one of their trips out there, and with it being such a short distance they would drive rather than fly. This morning, as they headed to the new house, they spotted Bill out there on the Outback just "*sniffing*" around.

"What's he doing, Jackie?" Izzy enquired.

Jackie had only laughed wickedly. She had no wish to try and explain Bill's gift and simply said, "It looks like he's got a bad cold."

Upon Peter's return he was loaded with many ideas. As they all sat in the family room the next evening he told them, "With what I have learned and what I know and since Chris has told me there is no budget limitation, there is a real opportunity we can make Quo-Vadis Station the epitome of cattle stations."

"All this talk," Chris chided him. "Just get on with it. I cannot wait to see the outcome."

"I will need a string of really good horses, and will have to recruit some stockmen," and, looking questionably at Jackie, said, "Did I get that right?"

That made them all laugh.

"Do you have any ideas where I might find all them, Chris?" Peter added.

"No fixed ideas about the horses," Chris said after thinking awhile. "They are your province, but for stockmen, I would have a look at using the men of the people, they are naturals. They have an inbuilt instinct about the Outback and a special understanding of its animals, even those scrub cattle.

After eight months, things were starting to come together at Quo-Vadis Station. It would be an understatement to say Izzy was pleased with her new home. You could not even say very pleased— her exuberance went far beyond very pleased. Jackie had introduced her to the decorator who did their house, and between the decorator and the pair of girls, they did give Chris's bank account a good hammering.

Peter had often enquired of the progress of the water location. Chris took him to a multitude of drill holes which were spewing water, drawn up from the great depths of the artesian basin, by powerful electric motors which were powered by an array of nearby solar panels. The very thoughtful electricians wiring those pumps had told Chris, "They had included a couple of weather proof power points, in case anybody needed a cup of tea, or in the case of that 'blinking yank', a coffee!"

The two men, Chris and Peter, had developed a strong friendship as each recognised their respective in-laws as the best in their field.

The first muster had been most rewarding. Over ten-thousand beef cattle now grazed contentedly in the home paddocks of the Quo-Vadis station. They had been driven from the National Park and induced to remain there by the lush green fodder growing as a result of Peter's experiment with irrigation and application of trace elements into this small portion of the Outback. Peter had never contemplated an irrigation scheme until Chris had said, "I could put down a pattern of bores for you and you could get all the water you would need for your sprays." Two experts working together. When they had first approached environmental people in town with the idea, and requesting their permission to go into the National Park and rout out some scrub cattle that were in there, the environmental people did not hesitate,

They quietly said, "Go in and drag out as many as you can, unofficially of course. We will not see you. Those confounded cattle are wreaking havoc in the park; there appears more and more of them every year."

The second muster from the park was most rewarding. Nearly thirty-thousand prime beasts were driven from the park.

"There are many more further in," Peter told Chris, "but I must see how this lot go first."

They had often flown over the national park in one of the new small helicopters, one of the fleet of small helicopter '*workhorses*' now attached to the station. This was one of the ideas Peter had brought back from his trip up north. They often used those mini choppers to locate those herds of cattle in the park. The men conscientiously perused the thick scrub that grew down below them.

"What's that?!" Peter cried excitedly. "Run back a bit mate," he called to a pilot. "I saw something." The chopper swung about slowly and retraced the section of the park they had just flown over. "There!" Peter yelled, "There is a herd of horses down there."

Chris was with him on this trip, and quickly said, "Brumbies, they are wild horses, very shy and the lead stallion is usually very aggressive."

"Can you get a little closer, Mike?" Peter called.

"No problem, "Mike the pilot called back, and dropped down to almost tree level. The wild horses scattered in alarm.

"Look at them," Peter shouted. He was still very excited. "They are prime animals. That stallion in the lead looks as if he has some very special blood lines."

"That is possible," Chris replied. "From time to time over the years some of the stations have lost some of their breeding stock. He may have been bred down the line for some time."

"I am not in the least perturbed by all that," Peter growled. "All I can see is a very beautiful animal and a herd of horses completely adapted to the environment. The horses I have bought in, are not doing so well. Do you think we can capture that group?"

"In this land, Peter," Chris very solemnly and softly said, "there are many secrets. They are revealed to us only by God, and if it is his will, you will get your horses."

"That's very deep, mate. You make it sound easy, especially for an unblemished and pure kid like me," Peter rather sarcastically replied. "From what you just said, I'll never get my horses."

"You will never know unless you try," Chris chided him.

"I'm going to get those horses, one way or another. With or without your philosophy." Peter was getting a little hot under the collar.

To get those horses was much easier said than done. The stallion was a canny creature, and after three attempts they were unable to drive the herd from the park by hassling them with the helicopters. As soon as the helicopters appeared the stallion would hide the herd.

"That darn animal is just too smart. This way we are never going to get them out of the park," Peter growled.

They erected a substantial fence to form a trap and attempted to drive the herd into the trap using the station motorbikes. Fifty meters from the jaws of the trap the stallion ploughed to a halt and viewed the fence in alarm, and promptly drew the whole herd in a totally different direction.

"Plurry smart horse," one of the Stockman cursed. "He has more brains than all of us together. He's just too smart to go into that trap."

"What next can we try Mr very clever engineer?" Peter asked Chris.

"I have a bit of an idea. It is different, and it will take untold patience. If we persevere we will win," said Chris, and added, lifting his eyebrows to the sky, "I hope."

The horse hunt was delayed while Chris made a quick trip to the veterinary surgeon in the regional city. Chris explained his need, and for a substantial fee, the vet agreed to help them. Environmental people had followed their activities and when Chris explained to them what he was about to do they quietly smiled and said, "We know *notheeeeeing.*

He had applied for and had been granted permission to acquire a special rifle.

One of the stockman, when he saw the rifle, laughed. "You *gunna* shoot that big bastard, Boss Chris?"

"In a way, Jimmy boy," Chris replied. His plan was to hike quietly into the park, unaccompanied, and attempt to get close to the herd; close enough to put a drug filled dart into that stallion. Peter was most enthusiastic with the plan. He hoped without their leader the herd may become disoriented and be a little easier to get into the trap.

Mr Stallion was skittish and led the herd away from even that one lonely man walking toward them. "It looks like we have to get him used to one man being about," Chris said to Peter. "I do not really have time to hang about in the park for goodness only knows how long. You will have to organise your boys in rosters to sit horse-watching."

Peter did set up a roster. In turn, each member of his crew would spend a few days in the bush camp adjacent to the horses' preferred grazing area. It took over two months before the herd had appeared to accept the presence of one man as the norm. Each time the roster was changed it had to be affected overnight and preferably when the horses had bedded down.

Chris received regular reports of the progress and had now decided at the next change that he would be the replacement "*horse watcher.*" He took his appointed position on a prominent knoll and was pleased to see the herd wander nonchalantly around him. But where was Mr Stallion? A loud indignant snort came from behind a large bush about twenty feet to the right of his camp. It made him jump with fright. The stallion stood there for all intents and purposes viewing him with what appeared to be curiosity.

Chris regained his composure, and softly said, "Hello, Mr Stallion." His voice was greeted with another angry snort. The stallion's ears laid back, and with bared teeth he took a strong step towards Chris, whose only thought was, "I do not think he wants us around here anymore. This could get messy."

Very slowly he reached for his loaded rifle. The angry horse had now assumed a very aggressive pose and reared up. All Chris could see was a mountain of horseflesh and two pounding fore-legs. "I hope this drug works quickly," the thought ran through Chris's mind. "I am in trouble if it doesn't."

He swung the rifle towards the angry horse and fired. The dart lodged deeply in the stallion's neck. It gave an annoyed grunt and dropped back down onto four legs, only to rear up again. It was now almost on top Chris. Halfway through that mountain of horseflesh rearing for the second time, it appeared to dissolve and crashed down almost at Chris's feet.

"That was far too close!" Chris thought. "For a minute there I thought I was a goner." He staggered back to his pack and fumbled for his two-way.

Peter answered. "You okay, mate?" he asked with concern.

"Yes," Chris squeaked.

"What's the matter with your voice, Chris?" Peter quickly asked. "You sound like you've seen a ghost."

"Just come and pick me up. Bring a few boys and plenty of rope to tie this hay burner down. By the way, bring me a couple of extra rolls of toilet paper—he gave me quite a fright. Only joking about the dunny paper, but it was a near thing."

Peter and the crew arrived after thirty minutes. Peter saw Chris sitting on a large rock sipping a hot coffee. "Coffee?!" Peter quizzically asked. Then when he saw the nearby drug-induced form lying so close to the camp he quickly knew why "the coffee."

The stallion was most unhappy some hours later when it awoke and stood on four wobbly legs. All those restraining ropes did not help his disposition. As if for protection the herd had bunched together and when four men dragged the angry stallion from the park the herd reluctantly followed along into the wire closure. The stallion was loaded into an awaiting horse float, not without much cursing and running for cover by the men.

Peter had designed a two-hundred-hectare paddock to be constructed not far from his proposed house, immediately adjacent to a breaking yard. Chris had passed a critical eye over the design, of that breaking yard and although he saw no reason to change the actual design, in his opinion, humble though it may be, the quality of the structure left much to be desired, so it was consequently inevitable that the two men would have a clash of mind. Peter could not concede that the breaking yard as he knew it was; good enough; and was taken back when Chris very forcibly said, "Good enough is not enough—it must be perfect."

They had located a suitable area only 150 metres away from the house site, strategically placed out of sight of the house. Now Quo-Vadis Station boasted the most modern and up-to-date breaking yard, one would be hard placed to find one like it elsewhere. As for the house paddock—the one that adjoined the breaking yard—that was a different matter. For this project the consensus was generally mutual, apart from the fact that Peter could not see that steel rails to a height of seven feet were necessary around the whole perimeter.

Chris had nullified his dissention by saying, "I have seen up close, far too close, just how very large Mr Stallion is, so I am of the firm opinion a fence of this nature will be needed to keep him secure." Chris did concede a little and allowed the installation of fifteen-inch diameter wooden poles as gate posts and at many places in the perimeter. Peter was rather obtuse with his reply to Chris's enquiry "Whatever for?"

"That's for me to know and for you to guess," he had replied and added in a very jocular manner, "Now go and play with your bulldozers and trucks like a good boy. All things will be revealed to you in good time."

These facilities had been installed in the interim period while the men were attempting to capture the horse herd, and one of Tom's drilling rigs had completed its exercise of finding suitable water for the irrigation of the paddock. It had had reasonably good success and for the moment an array of sprinklers poured a volume of life-giving water over the newly-seeded pasture that had been sown in one third of the house paddock. The drilling rig was still operating in the remainder of the house paddock.

One by one, members of the herd were selected by Peter. They were those he considered the best of them. "I would like to keep the lot," Peter told Chris. "It will be a big enough task just to break the ones I have selected." In his travels to the north, Peter had befriended several "horse wranglers,", and when he contacted them, offering them good money to assist him, they all had agreed and had descended on Quo-Vadis and Quo-Vadis Station.

After three months, Peter had a very fine herd of what he called "cow ponies." He got corrected innumerable times. "They are horses, Mister." The herd had been acquired only after much hard work, several broken bones, and sore heads. The wranglers were so impressed with Quo-Vadis Station that most of them wanted to stay on. Peter did ask two of them to stay. The wranglers would not even think of trying to break the stallion. He had his own big compound to himself. Still he never did cease trying to escape. He would rush up to the seven-foot-high steel bar fence when anybody walked near there and did his hardest to get at them through that fence.

Almost daily Peter sat high up on that fence, on one of those fence poles he had especially requested be installed, watching the stallion.

"What's he doing?" Chris asked Izzy. "He is whispering to him; you know, talking to his mind," Izzy nonchalantly replied.

None the wiser, Chris walked away muttering to himself, "When I come out here it is better to attend to whatever business I came out here for. I have a chance I'll understand that. All this horse whispering stuff is beyond me. I'll stick to being a miner!"

Peter's "special pasture" now covered the whole of the house paddock with a verdant green, and the selected herd of horses grazed contentedly in their own section.

It took a little time before the stallion allowed Peter to ride him. It did surprise Chris and Jackie as they drove out to the station one afternoon to see Peter rounding up cattle mounted on the stallion.

"How much did you have to bribe him to do that," Chris had asked.

"Not a cent—he likes me," Peter laughed. The stallion would allow no other to ride him let alone touch. The once wild stallion would tolerate people near him now, but woe-be-tied anybody who touched him. Little Joshua was the exception. One day he had wandered away from the house embarking on a boyish adventure of some description. Izzy found him in the stallion's yard nonchalantly sitting on the ground in front of "that" animal, poking his small fingers into those cavernous nostrils. The stallion snorted with annoyance when she quickly picked the child up and raced from the paddock.

"Shows you that horse is smart. He recognised that Josh was my son," Peter very proudly said.

# Chapter 6

A good road ran from the 110-kilometre peg on the main National Highway to Quo-Vadis mine and the airport which was situated nine kilometres from the mine. An offshoot of this road would take you out to Quo-Vadis Resort and on to Quo-Vadis Station. The road, as a country road, was quite busy at times, with cattle buyers now prepared to make the trip to buy the beef cattle that, after being husbanded in those lush paddocks of Quo-Vadis Station, had become prime quality beef. Their visits were soon followed up by monster six-trailer trucks sent out there to pick up the buyers' purchases and get them to market in the city. One thing Chris did insist on was no mining trucks used the road—those massive multi-tonne many-wheeled monsters would have destroyed the surface in very little time. Many tourists did choose to drive to the resort. It was a long two-day drive; they were rewarded with their choice with magnificent vistas of the untouched Outback.

We must step back a little to tell the story of Quo-Vadis Resort.

Some three or four years previous, about the time Chris had pulled Jackie from the then "black hole" and had taken the time to trace the route taken by the ancient river, he had diverted a relatively strong stream from the underground river in the cave to flow down the ancient river bed and onto what he had deducted to be a fairly substantial lake basin. Chris and Bill had believed that a good amount of gold had been washed down the ancient river bed to the lake, so before the lake started to refill they had scraped the old basin clean and ran the scrapings through their gold processing procedure. Their belief was well-founded and they were well rewarded for their effort.

"That old riverbed will have a lot of gold sitting in it," Bill commented. "We should scrape that too."

"That's nearly ten miles of very difficult work. I think we will put that on the back burner, just for a rainy day," was all Chris said.

The stream flowed strongly from Chris's diversion and the lake filled quickly becoming a haven for much wildlife. Over time, the area adjacent to the lake and the river became a verdant green delight. Many picnicked in this special place. It was one of Bill's and the Kennedys' favourite spots.

One lazy afternoon, as Chris lay *"cloud watching"* he told his friends, which included Jackie by the way, of Hector's plans for this place. He thought to couple it with the tourist park and be able to offer resort accommodation.

Jackie had listened intently and added her experience to the conversation. "When I was working in the tourist park we did have many enquiries about the availability of some form of longer-term accommodation. These tourists were looking for an opportunity to experience the Never-Never but were severely limited because of how far they would have to travel each day to even reach that which they sought. The idea of a resort, smack in the middle of a patch of the Outback, is a very good idea. I can see what Hector was aiming at. It does have another side to it; my dearest *friend,* Chris (*being female, she had not missed Chris's FRIEND quip.*) brother Rex will be happy to see you spending up big on a new project."

Needless to say, the development went ahead, and now a luxury resort overlooked the lake. Vanessa had been rather sceptical at first but after one year of operation, the resort became so popular, reservations were having to be deferred for over twelve months.

Jack put on a major "wet" when he was told his mother and father were going away for a while on an extensive prolonged research program without him. They just *had* to visit many highly rated resorts throughout the world. The only problem they struck was that there were so many king-size beds that needed attention.

Rex had viewed the accounts and sarcastically commented, "Now this is what I call a tax dodge." They had listed their accounts as research. Despite Rex's sarcasm, the upshot of all this was the designer of that very beautiful South Pacific resort who had shown great initiatives in his design had been voted by; The Kennedys; to be without peer and he was invited to apply his skills to the design and development of the Resort at Quo-Vadis. Giuseppe, who was contracted to build the resort according to the designer's plan, had threatened to resign three times, after altercations with the designer. Surprisingly enough the designer had capitulated under certain conditions; namely, Giuseppe had to agree to "look at" building all of the future developments the designer was involved with.

In all due time sixty-four luxury class lodges were built on the shore of the lake. Chris and Jackie were very pleased with the completed resort and agreed it was up to the standard of the best they had visited.

Although a little rough in places, the road into Quo-Vadis complex was quite a pleasant drive. As Vanessa would explain to intending travellers, the distance was formidable, and for a small additional cost, travel to the resort by flying in one of the Tour Park's luxury jets could be arranged. The Quo-Vadis tour group now had three small private jets amongst their fleet. The airstrip at Quo-Vadis had been developed considerably and was now equipped with men and equipment which enabled even some of the interstate air traffic to land there.

Many of travellers opted to drive.

Vanessa quickly recognized a business opportunity existed and ran her idea past Chris. She had recognised that it is a full day's drive to even get halfway to Quo-Vadis from the regional city, and by the time they had stopped at least four or five times to take in some of the spectacular views of the Outback Chris had surveyed for the road to pass through, they were looking for a break.

"We need a stopover point somewhere about halfway," she argued, "and perhaps even have some motel type units available. We should include a basic but good restaurant where they could get a meal. Not everybody would want a meal, so we should consider several types of fast food outlets. Some will be pulling caravans. I am sure they would appreciate some decent toilets and shower suites."

Chris agreed; he could see the wisdom of the idea and did have Giuseppe build the stopover in the traditional natural stone style which had become synonymous with Quo-Vadis. The stopover became known as the Quo-Vadis Stopover, and had become fully functional in just over one year.

Chris had chosen the site where the road passed within half a kilometre of the escarpment, and where he had found another of those holes where the river in days past, had flowed. It was only a much smaller aperture which could only be accessed by one man crawling. Still it was enough to enable the installation of an eight-inch pipe to tap the underground river to service the needs of the Stopover.

The venture and provision of staff came under the jurisdiction of the tourist park. Vanessa now happily ruled over a multi-story office with twenty-five or more staff. With the advent of the resort and it is stopover, she had "demanded" and obtained a substantial increase in her staff levels. She had embarked on an advertising program endeavouring to bring the virtues of the Outback to a much larger audience. Her advertising program was most successful.

One of the very popular activities amongst the younger folk, who were visiting the resort with their parents; was gold fossicking. Children under the age of ten years were allowed to search that small creek bed looking for Gold. A limit of five nuggets per child per visit was strictly enforced. Bill and, at times, Chris; did enjoy watching these children as they fossicked. It gladdened the miners' hearts as they saw the rapture in the face of a young child as he or she found a stone.

Sometimes, Chris, after watching one of the younger children search over a picked dry section of the creek, would quietly slip ahead of the child and drop a good-sized nugget on the creek bed for that child to find. Bill was more surreptitious, albeit generous. When he became aware that the resort at that particular time held a large number of children, early each morning, around about dawn, he would wander nonchalantly along the creek with a pocket or two full of pea-sized grains of gold and "*salt*" the creek (*an old- miners' term meaning to place gold to make the claim more valuable than it really was*). Very few children left the resort without having at least one piece of gold as a memento.

Vanessa, one to not ever miss an opportunity, had done a deal with a local jeweller to manufacture accessories from gold supplied by Quo-Vadis mines, so that the adults; not just the children, could take home a memento to remind them of the wonderful times they had at Quo-Vadis Resort. The accessories bar did quite a brisk business which proved to be a nice little sideline for both the jeweller and the Tourist Park.

Rex's only complaint was that the blasted Resort and Tourist Park and now The Stopover were making far too much money.

# Chapter 7

Chris had left Goliath with Ed—he was due for a full service and check over. He had travelled to town by private jet and had intended to drive the big SUV back to Quo-Vadis. As was normal with Ed, Goliath was handed over in perfect condition, fully fuelled, a few new up-to-date pieces of equipment installed and tuned to perfection.

In a spate of nostalgia, Chris decided to try and follow his original track back to Quo-Vadis. Jackie made her repine very obvious when he announced his intention to her during the telephone call which had to be made if they were not together overnight.

After calling him "mean," "miserable" and many other things, she softly said, "That first trip we ever made was the best; it sits high in my favourite memories. I do not blame you for wanting to make it, only envy you that you will do it. Please take extreme care. I have never seen weather like it is here at the moment. It is absolutely rotten, cold and raining. It's been like this for the last twenty-four hours. The rain is so heavy you are limited to being only able to see twenty to thirty metres away. I have never in my life seen rain like this. They have even stopped flying. Jack is happy—he was here when it started and cannot get back to school."

"Are there any problems?" Chris enquired, full of concern. "There is little I can do to assist you from here. I left the regional city this morning and will continue to try to push my way through the storm. I am about eighty kilometres out from the main road at present. It is not raining here yet."

Chris had shopped quickly the previous day and stocked up all the chests in Goliath with *"lazy man tucker"* predominantly tins of nutritious vegetables, meat stews, and packets of dried food that only needed to have water added and heated. He did acquire a good amount of variety of tinned fruits, for dessert should he feel like it. Several loaves of bread, eggs, bacon and tubs of margarine and many packets of the ever-important tea leaves were all there.

As he stowed all this on- board Goliath, he admonished himself, "Good Grief, I have certainly gone overboard with my purchases. After all, I only expect to be out there for one week. There's enough here to feed a man for a month."

He had travelled about two thirds of the old track. Now he was much more experienced with driving in the Outback and instances of getting bogged were the exception. He had entered the rain-sodden area early the previous morning. "Jackie was not joking when she described the weather as absolutely rotten," Chris thought to himself. "It does not look like it's going to ease up."

It was getting close to midday when Goliath lost traction and slid sideways and lodged his front wheels over a large rock. Chris tried valiantly all the tricks he had learned, but he could not get Goliath free. "There is no alternative: I am going to have to do get out and fit the caterpillar tracks. This was another of Ed's devices. The tracks fitted around the dual drive wheels on either side of Goliath, converting him into a mini caterpillar tractor. Unfortunately, the tracks could only be fitted when the wheels were off the ground. Goliath was fitted with hydraulic jacks designed specifically for use in situations such as Chris now found himself. He reluctantly dragged himself from the warm interior of is SUV, into driving, freezing, pelting rain, and by the time he had completed the task he was soaking wet and freezing. "I had better get myself dry and changed fairly quickly. Getting pneumonia out here would not be good. This spot is too exposed. I will go on a little bit further. I do remember there is a good stand of trees not all that much further up the track. I will stop there, get a warm fire going, get myself warm and dry out."

Now he was fitted with the tracks, Goliath made child's play of extracting himself from his predicament. "This darn rain appears to be getting worse," Chris mused, and despite his discomfort he lightly thought, "I can just see Peter's face as he envisages all that beautiful green fodder that will appear after the rain ceases. The way it is coming down looks like it could last for a hundred years."

His mind was spinning about and he quickly followed up that thought with, "Perhaps this is one of those one in one-hundred-year deluges some of the old-timers talk about."

His musings were interrupted as the stand of trees where he intended to set up camp came into view. "I will set up camp here," he thought. "I don't like the idea of driving on in this rain; even with those tracks on Goliath may get into trouble again." His practical mind refocused and he drove Goliath into the shelter of the trees. "I am already wet so I will set up the annex quickly then get that fire going," he said to himself, and so saying clambered once again out into the downpour from the warm cabin of Goliath.

He was already wet and the cold biting wind exacerbated his discomfort. He felt the coldness right through to his very bones. "One could hardly believe this place could be so hot one day and then within a day or two one could quite easily believe they were in Antarctica. BRR!" he muttered.

As quickly as he could he dragged the annex from its container on the roof of the SUV out its full distance. He did not bother to set out the steel poles that normally supported the annex, but for expediency he simply attached the tie ropes to some conveniently placed trees. He spread a thick waterproof groundsheet, attached and anchored the side panels, and using the skills the people had taught him he managed to get a strong fire going in the open front of the annex. He hovered over the fire for a few moments, all but devouring the heat. "This fire will not last long. I must collect much more wood now while I am wet so that hopefully I will not have to venture out again later."

He walked briskly out of his camp onto the track. He had traversed about thirty meters when something odd caught his eye. "What's that?" he exclaimed almost out aloud. It had all the appearances of a bundle of rags somebody had dropped in the middle of the track. "If I'd kept going I would have ran over that," he angrily thought, and went to drag it aside. As he lifted the bundle he realised it was more than a bundle of rags, but a girl coiled in a foetal position. "Good grief!" he cried, "She looks like she is dead."

Hesitating no further, he picked up the sodden pile of rags and its contents and rushed back to the camp. He set her down on the dry groundsheet, adjacent to the fire, and gently uncovered her face. In unconsciousness the face was relaxed; even so, he could see she was very beautiful. He very carefully moved her a little closer to the fire and managed to remove her wringing wet outer garment. "It used to be a fine quality overcoat," he remorselessly thought. He replaced the coat with a dry blanket. Her clothes underneath were only light cotton, they too were soaking wet. "They will dry much more quickly if I leave them on her," he thought. "I won't take them off."

He pushed her even a little closer to the fire and stoked it up. "At this rate I am soon going to need more wood," he urgently thought. "I'll have to leave her for a minute or two while I grab some." He snatched up an axe and once again ventured forth into the pouring rain. Within ten minutes he had accumulated and stacked a fine pile of wood under the cover of the annex, including some good-sized logs. "That will keep us going for a while," he thought. "Now, what to do I do with her?"

She had regained consciousness and now sat almost devouring the warmth of the fire. "That's good," Chris thought to himself, "at least she is not dead," and rather stupidly asked, "How do you feel?"

"Cold," was a very quiet reply.

"Get yourself warm," he said, and passed her another blanket, which she promptly wrapped around her legs. "I am Chris Kennedy, I found you in the middle of the track. You are lucky I didn't run over you." She did not respond, only sat blankly staring into the fire.

"I will make you some hot soup; do you think you could eat it?" he asked.

She just bobbed her head as if agreeing. Chris emptied two cans of instant soup into a large saucepan and caught a measure of rainwater as it ran off the annex roof and set the saucepan on a bed of red coals he had raked slightly away from the main fire. He cut two large slices from his last bread loaf. They were a bit stale, so he set to toast them. She had watched his every move and when he poured the soup into a large mug and handed it to her with a well-buttered slice of toasted bread, she quickly slid a hand from the blankets and grabbed them. They were devoured in very short time. The warm food look to be reviving her a little.

"More?" he offered, as she drained the first mug.

"Yes, please," she answered this time and held out the mug. He added the second slice of toast to the offering. The second serving she ate more slowly, still looking to relish every morsel.

"Feel up to talking?" Chris quietly asked.

She replied rather hesitantly and rather softly, "I will try," then added, "Thank you for the soup. I have never tasted anything so good. It is the first food I have had in a week."

"Good grief, girl! What the Hell are you doing out here? Are you by yourself? This is no place for a girl by herself," he scolded.

She tearfully responded, "I was painting."

"I think you better get some sleep, young lady," Chris very firmly said. "Perhaps after you've had a good rest you may feel more like talking. Are you warm enough?"

"I don't think I will ever again be warm enough," she quietly replied. "I am a bit warmer, but I am still very cold."

"You are still wearing wet clothes," Chris said quite sharply, then added a little more softly, "I will get you a dry T-shirt, and some thick socks. Crawl into the back of the wagon—there are some towels in the cupboards on the right-hand side, grab one and get yourself dry, then slip into these dry clothes. Chuck your wet things out. I will place them about the fire and try and dry them. You will find more dry blankets in the chest on the other side. That chest will contain a thick under blanket and a pillow. Make yourself a bed on the floor. It is lined with a special surface so you should be quite comfortable. Before you get settled I want to get into the front seat to get my phone. I want to let my wife know what has happened. The track ahead is probably impassable and I know of several places that will be next to impossible to get through, so it looks like we may be stuck here for a bit, and I do not want her to worry."

He retrieved his phone and as he crawled out, he chuckled, "I bet she makes a comment like, 'just like you Christopher Kennedy I would not be surprised if somebody told me you had arranged for all this rain so you could get stuck with a young pretty girl.'"

Jackie answered the telephone, obviously relieved to hear from him. She was dismayed to hear of the girl's predicament.

She naturally asked, "Is she, all right? Is she hurt? Do you need any help?" and quickly added, "I wish I could get out to the airstrip. If necessary, I would fly a helicopter myself and come and pick you up. Captain Henry, our chief officer, did tell me earlier, he will definitely not let any sort of aircraft out until this weather clears. Please be careful Christopher J. I will die if anything happens to you."

The girl had set herself up as Chris had ordered; a pile of wet clothes sat on the open tailgate. She had heard the whole telephone conversation, and very cheekily said, "You lose your bet, Mister. She did not mention you setting all this up."

"You are obviously feeling better," Chris laughed. "Another comment like that and you will sleep out in the rain." She appeared to chuckle as she snuggled into the pillow and looked to fall instantly asleep. He followed suit shortly after. He made himself some soup, changed from his wet clothes, stoked up the fire by adding a couple of large logs, thinking to himself that it should keep it burning all night, rolled out a sleeping bag and crawled into it. He also dropped off to sleep quickly.

He awoke at dawn. The first thing he noticed was the heavy rain persisted , black heavily laden clouds still hung low. "Could be a bit more wet stuff still about," he thought to himself. Despite being carefully arrayed around the fire; her clothes were still very damp. He glanced into the rear of Goliath, through the open tailgate, and saw she was still asleep. "She must have been totally exhausted," he thought. "I reckon if I had been wandering around the Outback in that freezing rain, I would have been a bit weary too."

As quietly as possible, he gathered pans and plates and utensils along with a container that contained eggs and bacon and salvaged enough bread to cut two good slices. The fire had died to red ash. "Ideal for some quick breakfast cooking," he thought. It did not take him long to have eggs and bacon sizzling in the pan and the bread toasting. He could have used the cooker in Goliath, but he wanted to avoid disturbing her.

Breakfast was nearly ready when he heard her disturb and say, "That smells good. Can I have some?"

"Most definitely," Chris answered. "By the time you get yourself decent, breakfast will be ready."

"Where are my clothes?" she asked. "I gave them to you last night."

"They are not dry yet," Chris replied.

"Then you will have to put up with me in your T-shirt. It is very big so do not worry. I am quite respectable and decent."

As she clambered out of the tail great gate, Chris wickedly thought, "Not quite that respectable and decent—that T-shirt leaves very little to the imagination."

She obviously enjoyed her share of the breakfast and even asked for a second cup of the tea brewed in the traditional style in a tea bucket.

"That is good tea!" she exclaimed, as she downed the second cup with gusto. "Did I tell you my name last night? I cannot remember very much of the last five or six days. What I do remember vividly is being so freezing cold. I am Penelope Carstairs. I think you did tell me your name last night, I have forgotten that also." She hesitated as if awaiting his response.

"I am Christopher Kennedy—Chris to my friends," he responded. "I am a gold miner. I have a mine about two-hundred kilometres further north. I was on my way home when I found you. I have a wife, Jackie, Jacqueline to be correct, who I love very deeply, so be assured, that despite what I can see, which is plenty, and regardless of the fact that you are a very attractive girl, you are perfectly safe with me. I have a son, Jack, and many friends at the mine. You told me last night you're out there painting—it was all a bit garbled. Is that right?"

"Yes," she replied. "I am a painter and an artist and enjoy painting scenes of the Outback. They sell very well. When the rain started, my car got bogged. I could not get it out. It ran out of fuel with all my attempts. I had no idea where I was—I just locked up the car and started walking. The rain was so heavy, it had washed out my tracks, so I got hopelessly lost. I found this track two, no, it may have been three days ago and was following it hoping it would take me to civilisation."

"That's quite a story," Chris quietly said. "Now I have to tell you, you were going the wrong way. You were heading away from civilisation toward my mine. You were in such a bad way when I found you I can tell you here and now, you would never have made it. You would have perished on the way. By the look of you when I found you that was as far as you were going. As soon as we can clean up here, I want to call Jackie, and tell her I am going to attempt to get through. I should make it by late afternoon."

"He is used to organising things," Penny thought, then quietly said, "Please make your phone call. I will start cleaning up."

"I think your clothes are dry now, Penelope. Sorry, you'll have to put them on without them being ironed," he laughed.

"I can do that later," she replied. "Please call me Penny. I like this T-shirt—it is very comfortable. Do you mind?"

"I do not mind one little bit," Chris quickly replied, "so long as you don't mind me spending half my time perving at you."

"So, I am not quite as safe as you said, Mr Kennedy," she laughed. "I will have to make sure that I keep my distance," she giggled, and started to pack up the camp.

Chris spoke to Jackie for a while assuring her all was well and the girl was up and about. "She is putting on a good front, but I can see she is still very weak and should get some treatment very quickly. The rain is not easing here so I am going to strike out for the new road. That way, I am expecting to get home sometime this arvo. If you do not hear from me by sundown, better get Bill and the boys to come and look for me."

Jackie's response to this was a little hesitant as she said, "If you think that is the best thing to do, do it—I have learned to trust your judgement."

Chris helped Penny with the last of the packing up and within the hour they set off.

"You are not following the track," Penny cried in alarm, won't you get lost?"

"I will not get lost," Chris replied. "I have surveyed this area and have a fair idea where I am. We are heading for a new road I have had constructed; had we kept to the track we would have been required to battle through several difficult and dangerous stretches. This way, although fairly rough, will work out much better. Goliath here was designed and specifically built for this type of terrain, so sit back, buckle up, and enjoy the ride."

His voice was strong and confident and gave Penny the assurance she sought. After about an hour the rain ceased and the clouds lifted; enabling them to look out at the magnificent vista of the rain washed Outback. From time to time she gasped with apparent delight. "Look at those hills, Chris. They are an artist's dream. I must come back here and put onto canvas what I am seeing. The colours in those cliffs will challenge the most talented of artists."

They cut the new road just before noon.

"You really do know your way in the wilderness," she commented, and added, "Could we stop for a moment? Nature calls," she whispered as if divulging a great secret. She disappeared into a low scrub.

"Don't go too far," Chris called as she disappeared. "I do not want to have come and search for you."

She had taken her now dry clothes and returned respectfully clad. "I guessed on this better road you may be travelling a little faster, and I thought it wise to remove the distractions you have obviously been enjoying," she giggled.

"Killjoy," Chris growled, and packed her back into Goliath with a cup of hot tea in her hand, swung Goliath onto the new road, and continued their trek to the mine.

Penny was not strong and on the second day at Quo-Vadis, after running herself ragged trying to see everything, she collapsed. The weather had cleared and Jackie did not hesitate to immediately call in the Flying Doctor.

He examined Penny and told Chris and Jackie, "Penny is totally exhausted and needed much rest and intensive care."

Penny was most upset with this advice and in confidence told Jackie, she had nowhere to go back to.

Once again, Jackie did not hesitate. She and Penny had formed a deep friendship and had spent many hours talking over a multitude of subjects. "You must stay with us Penny, at least until you are well," Jackie insisted. "You are most welcome."

As Penny recuperated she started sketching again. Jack would hurry home from his play group and sit with Penny and discuss her sketches, pointing out little deficiencies as he sees them; things like: "Kangaroos do not have tails that long, or fluffy ears."

That had caused the pair of them to laugh heartily when Penny had replied, "My kangaroos are special: they do have long tails and fluffy ears."

Jack, not to be outdone, simply said, "Then I will have to catch one of your kangaroos, just to prove you are not a fibber."

Her recuperation continued, and she began to fill her sketches with colours she produced from various pigments, obtained from the sap of a variety of trees and various finely crushed ores. Bill often contributed some very fine dust collected from his crushers. Penny would make these crushing's into a fine smooth paste for her use. Her equipment was supplemented when Jackie had reason to travel to the regional city. She made it a priority to purchase a full set of brushes and "artist's gear" and the most complete case of coloured pigments that was available. Penny's paintings began to take form. To give her space to work, Chris did convert a vacant workman's shed into a makeshift studio for her and overcame Penny's shortage of material to paint on by cutting up an old tent into appropriate sized squares.

Penny was a great favourite with the native women, who would sit for hours watching, OOHING and AHHHING as she constructed a painting and did often gift to her some of the pigments they used as they painted stories on the walls of caves. She became most adept at using natural pigments . Now days rarely used the tubes of colour Jackie had bought for her.

The lifestyle at Quo-Vadis obviously suited her, and she, obvious to all, was enjoying good health. She usually dined with Chris and Jackie, and, of course, Jack, and one evening she humbly asked them, "Could I stay a little longer?" following the request by saying, "I will travel to the city and sell some of these paintings I have done while I have been here. I will then be able to pay my keep." She was totally bemused when the pair of them burst into peals of laughter.

"Penny, dear girl," Chris managed to stutter, "I think we can manage to accommodate and feed you."

Giuseppe was fully occupied building numerous comfortable cottages for the permanent staff employed at the mine. The staff did bring their families to live in those colleges; regrettably the lack of educational facilities did make things most difficult. Once a child's needs went beyond kindergarten, to further their education they had to be billeted in the regional city.

Chris and Jackie from time to time would wander through the newly-erected cottages. "The way things are progressing, Jackie girl," Chris said during one of their walks, "a small community is growing here, and I can see a need for some community facilities."

"I have been thinking along those lines for some time," Jackie replied. "With so many families here with small children we do have a need for a school, and while we are on this line of thinking we should be looking to provide many other things, like a post office, a nursing post and things like that."

"There is probably a mountain of paperwork to go through. I will see if Rex can get things underway for us."

"I think is most important to get the school here first," Jackie quickly said.

"You always were a conniving female, Jacqueline Kennedy. You are setting it up so Jack can come home each day and share his day with you."

"Can't get away with a darned thing, can I, Mister? I have to admit that did come to my mind when we were talking about a school here. As it is on those days he is with the play group, I hang out in near the lift in the cavern, waiting for him to come home.

Rex had taken the task to have community facilities approved. "It is well our office has staff with the knowledge of what is required; he told Chris, "They are pressing ahead, but are delayed by those Government instrumentalities, whose hands are tied by regulations, consequently approvals are painfully slow.

Although Chris was the registered proprietor of all the mining leases, he was extremely limited with what buildings he could build on those leases; consequently, he and Rex decided it would be a better move to try and obtain freehold title to the block of land where Chris envisaged the village could be built. The Crown Lands Department procrastinated for some time to even agree to look at the proposal, but when they were notified by the State Treasury, and The Government Mint via Her Majesty's mint, of the importance to the state of the Quo-Vadis venture, approval was forthcoming.

Nevertheless, Chris was required to submit a comprehensive survey covering the land he required. "I am not going to go through this again," he told Rex. "The survey will embrace thirty-thousand hectares and covered all of the ancient riverbed, the resort and lake. With all the protocol satisfactorily behind them, and payment to The Crown Lands Department of an amount of $165,000, Quo-Vadis Properties Proprietary Limited became the freehold owner of thirty-thousand hectares adjacent to Quo-Vadis mines. Quo-Vadis airport was included in the title. Chris also had his interest recorded for the whole of the area of Quo-Vadis Station. He was told that it was highly unusual; however, for an annual fee of $2000 a note would be attached to the file, and no guarantees were given that he would have any other rights than those covered by grazing leases, and where applicable mining leases.

# Chapter 8

Bill and Chris had watched Giuseppe as he built the homes and town facilities, and it was decided; as it was time for Bill to move from the tradesmen's suites into a home, and with Giuseppe being preoccupied with the urgent need for the homes and facilities in the township, the intrepid pair, decided building a house did not look too difficult and they would build Bill's house themselves. They decided on a site, about two-hundred metres further along the lakefront from Chris and Jackie's home. It was in a delightful little sheltered cove, and in the old measurements about two acres in area.

Bill approved of the site with great enthusiasm, after he had run his fingers through the black earth. "Look at this, Chris," he cried. "There is nothing I cannot grow in this. Now I will have the garden I have long dreamt of."

The miner in Chris instantly calculated the rich deposit of black earth was placed there about the time the sinkhole was formed and was a by-product of water swirling around and around in the cove dropping topsoil washed down by the river. Much debris had been in that swelling melee, and when the river had found an escape hole, the built-up retarded water receded, and the debris was dropped in the cove. Over many years, the debris had been reduced to black humus. Chris look closely at a handful of the dirt and reeled off a list of elements it was lacking.

Bill took a long sniff at the handful and immediately agreed. "I am sure we can find many of those elements about here," Bill said, and smiled as he added, "With your brains and my nose we will be able to create a magnificent garden."

With great enthusiasm, the amateur builders commenced the project. After two months of blood, sweat, and curses they stood back and took a long analytical look at their progress.

"I have to tell you, mate," Chris chuckled, "it looks nothing like a house; I think we need Giuseppe."

Giuseppe could not stop laughing as he viewed their effort. Bill and Chris were most offended when Giuseppe nonchalantly said, "I'll get a bulldozer in here tomorrow and clear this away, and start to build a proper house," and had the temerity to burst into another long bout of laughing. "Best laugh I've had in years," he stuttered as he gasped for breath.

Jackie had watched, encouraged, and supported the boys in their endeavours. In a way she was happy to see Giuseppe take over. "Now that Giuseppe is on the job," she thought, "it was an appropriate time to suggest they should have, a proper studio and maybe even a house built for her friend Penny."

Penny had been going up to the children's group at least twice a week, and was teaching them how to use colours, and how to paint. It was less than a week later that Jackie very proudly showed Chris Jack's painting of "My Dad".

That did it! The harassed Giuseppe was immediately commissioned, as a matter of priority, to build a house for Penny. As usual Chris did not stint, and the house did have a very substantial and functional studio attached. The fact that it was built with the major portion of the windows looking out over the river as it most spectacularly poured from the cliff face, was *"purely incidental"*

The sinkhole at Quo-Vadis had begun to take on the appearance of a small community. Bill's garden enhanced the scene. He had planted every conceivable vegetable, most of which was growing quite successfully in the enriched soil and the protected cove. He had even cultivated about half an acre of spuds. Closer to his house it was a blaze of colour. Flowers of many, many species grew in profusion. Chris and Jackie's home were rarely without beautiful vases of flowers. To walk in Bill's garden was not unlike walking into a perfume shop where half the bottles of perfume had been spilt.

Penny was ecstatic with her new home and studio. Chris had Ed build her a mini Goliath. When Chris presented the mini to her, she flung her arms around him, kissed him very soundly, and turning to Jackie shouted, "When you have finished with him can I have him."

Jackie had laughed and quickly said, "You are down the line a bit. Susie, Annie, and Steph have already put in bids. I do suggest you do not hold your breath while you wait your turn—it will be a long day before I am finished with him. He has much bed fixing yet to do. In fact, there is a large bed upstairs that needs attention immediately." Without hesitation she took Chris's hand and drew him towards the staircase.

All this went over Penny's head. In her contentment, Penny produced some very fine paintings. Her efforts reached the pinnacle with one particular piece. Chris had been doing his miner's thing and was poking around a small watercourse out near Quo-Vadis Station not so far from the people's village. The watercourse ran on a short distance to form a swamp. A stand of old paperbark trees had grown up in the swamp. Chris watched with interest as several native women were stripping one of the larger trees to acquire a slab of bark to perhaps make a dish or something similar. The slab of bark came off in one large piece about four-feet square.

He instantly recognised a potential use for that slab of bark, and politely asked the women, "May I have that?" Chris was a great favourite with the people. They knew Boss Chris was responsible for many of their young men being gainfully employed and being introduced in the ways of working cattle. The young men had become very competent stockman. The women were happy to give Chris the slab of bark, and very proudly showed him how he could "*shave*" and flatten it.

In early course, Chris presented Penny with the flat four-foot square of paperbark. The surface still contained some colour and texture.

Penny had viewed the gift rather sceptically at first, and then after thinking for a few moments longer, shouted, "How marvellous! Thank you. Chris. I know just what I can do with this," then rather seductively whispered, "Has Jackie finished with you yet?"

Chris simply answered "No", and as quickly as he could, "Got the Hell;" out of her studio.

Penny took the slab of paperbark, and all her painting paraphernalia to the people's village. She sat quietly with one of the stockmen and his family and carefully asked of them, "May I capture your spirit on the paperbark slab?" and added with genuine meaning and sincerity, "I believe when I have completed my work your spirit will live forever."

The painting was nothing short of amazing. She used only pigments from ore gathered from creek beds and cliff faces. She prepared them all with great care, some were as smooth as silk, others rich and grainy. The family had been good models, the stockman, his woman, and two children—a boy about ten years old and a girl about five. They were clad in their traditional cover. A mongrel dog had joined the party and sat at their feet. They were all very proud to be chosen by Missy Penny and it showed.

Chris and Jackie were spellbound when Penny set the final product on an easel in the bright light of the curved windows of the lounge room in their home. The backdrop of the lake enhanced the scene. Penny had captured it all. If one looked closely you could see the pain and suffering of the years of persecution of the people; and looking deeper you could see a proud and generous people still existed. The eyes of the children looked toward the skies and glistened with hope for the generations to come. To all who looked at the deepness and the way she had used those pigments and colours, they could all but feel the emotion captured in that painting.

"Holy cow, Penny," Chris enthused, "I knew you were good, but not this good. Where are you going to hang it?"

"I was going to give it to you and Jackie," Penny whispered. "I owe you both so much."

"NO!" Chris all but shouted, "This is far too fine to be left hidden from the world in the confines of a mining camp. You must have a *"full on"* exhibition and display much of your work. Sell some if you want to, but never, I mean never, sell that one."

Jackie did not dally, and immediately set out to ensure the exhibition would be done properly. "It must be in the 'big *smoke'*—your work demands maximum exposure," she told Penny.

Setting up the exhibition did take a little time. Rex assisted immensely by making available the whole of the ground floor of the accountancy firm. The location was perfect. Annie enthusiastically joined in; she had left school and had joined Penny in her painting pursuits. In her own right she had become quite a talented artist. Penny insisted Annie showed some of her work too.

Was the exhibition a success? The first day it was a little quiet. On the second day, many of those first-day visitors returned bringing their friends with them, who in turn returned with their friends. Word reached the curator of the City Art Gallery. He stood silently before the paperbark painting; it was his third visit.

One of his colleagues stood beside him open-mouthed. "This is a National Treasure!" the curator exclaimed, "We must advise the National Gallery what we have found."

It was the last day of the exhibition. All but one of the paintings, including all of Annie's, had "Sold" signs attached, not so the paperbark. A large sign had been placed below it: "Not for Sale."

Four suits from the National Art Gallery stood before it. These four men were recognised, and very highly respected critics. Many budding artists had had his or her dreams smashed by this lot. Penny's paperbark painting left them speechless.

"What's it called?" one whispered to Penny, almost reverently.

"I have called it 'WE ARE AUSTRALIA.'" Penny shouted.

At that, two of the men simply slumped down on a nearby padded bench seat.

"Miss Penny," the head curator whispered, he still had not regained his voice to any degree, "we cannot buy your work—we do not have and will never have enough money. We would like to take it with us as we return and hang it in pride of place in the National Museum. We would ask you would you kindly attend an official opening of a display of your paintings. Our colleague here has told us he has purchased a number of them and will lend them to us for the purpose of the opening." He had regained his voice, and very loudly said, "You are a marvellous, talented young woman; where have you been hiding all these years?"

"Out in the Outback," Penny replied. "Nobody disturbs me out there and I can indulge my passion uninterrupted."

She and Annie were invited to exhibit in many overseas venues. Annie in her own right had achieved a very good level of success. When she exhibited, in conjunction with Penny, her recognition was exacerbated, and even when she exhibited independently she was most successful. By now Annie had grown to a very attractive young lady. She was highly sought after as a guest speaker at many art displays. To maintain a level of sanity, and to escape from the conglomeration of functions they had been pursued to attend, both girls would return to the studio at Quo-Vadis for at least six months every year, only returning to the hectic round of appearances when insistence, their attendance became so intense they had no alternative.

As they left, they always carried with them a carefully packed crate of their latest creations. It was never long before that crate was returned empty.

There was one matter that did occur during one of the times the artists had returned to their studio. Penny had recalled she had left a good number of paintings in her bogged SUV and asked Chris could he help her retrieve them. She had little idea where the SUV had been abandoned, so Chris had enlisted the aid of one of the natives who was reported to be a very talented tracker. He took the tracker to the place where he had originally found her. Penny worked with the tracker for over three weeks. She was totally amazed how he worked and eventually returned to Quo-Vadis rather disappointed. The tracker had led her to the edge of the sand plane, a vast inhospitable barren wasteland.

He had told her, "Missy Penny, your car is out there."

Upon her return to Quo-Vadis; Penny had told Chris and Jackie; the Tracker would not enter onto the sand plain under any circumstances; and had said, "It is the land of many evil spirits."

"I could not make out exactly what he was trying to say except to understand he would go no further. I deduced; he believed it was the land from which the people were forbidden," she whispered in a very frightened voice, "After my previous experience, I tend to agree with him. He did say, "Only Abdiel Boss Chris, would be safe out there. Is that you Chris?" Penny softly asked; Jackie answered for him. "It is Penny, the people of the land have a special regard for Chris."

The thought of the paintings "out there," weighed heavily on Penny's mind and she eventually asked Jackie; "Do you think Chris would help her find those paintings?" When Jackie told Chris of the request, Chris had emphatically answered; "No way,"

Regardless of her fears, Penny persisted, and after Jackie had sarcastically chided Chris saying, "If you won't do it for Penny, do it for me; after all she is my very best friend," Chris reluctantly agreed to help.

They had set off from Quo-Vadis in a very well stocked Goliath. Penny took him to the point where the tracker had said the SUV entered the sand plane. They did not travel far onto the sand plain before Chris was forced to stop and fit the tracks which converted Goliath into the mini caterpillar tractor.

Chris was no native tracker, and they meandered far out onto the sand plane, hoping to find her SUV. Time just slipped away, and regrettably the satellite connection failed to work. Something in the sand of the sand plain interfered with the reception.

"That's the evil spirits at work," Penny whispered.

For two long weeks they searched and could not find the vehicle. It was purely by chance that one evening at sunset a flash of light reflecting a partially-covered rear-vision mirror caught Chris's attention. The SUV was all but covered by windblown sand—only a few small sections remained visible. Fortunately, that partially covered rear vision mirror was one.

"It is fortunate we have found it," Chris told her. "I am down to the last few drums of fuel and I was getting a little worried about getting back. I do not have enough fuel to be sure I can tow your vehicle out. Goliath would use a lot of fuel to do that. We'll only salvage what we can and head back in the morning. We are a long way out and it will take a bit of time anyway."

The interior of the SUV was relatively clear of sand. "The manufacturers must have fitted good seals on those doors and windows," he commented as he loaded over thirty very good paintings into Goliath and set off on the return trip.

It was as if the "evil spirits" were yet to have their way, as overnight it started to rain heavily.

"This is completely unseasonal," Chris grumbled. "It should not be raining at this time of year."

"This is what happened last time," Penny cried. "We will be alright, won't we, Chris?" she near hysterically cried.

"I hope so," Chris replied but to himself thought, "This rain will make it heavy going, and fuel consumption is going to dictate whether we make it or not."

He drove most carefully on. Fitted with those tracks, Goliath slugged his way through the wet clinging surface and on the second day spluttered to a stop. The rain had persisted and now it was accompanied by a freezing cold wind.

"That's it," Chris softly said to her, "We walk from here."

"Chris! Chris!" Penny cried, "I cannot go through that time again. At least before I die make love to me so I may die happy. I have wanted you so badly for such a long time, but my respect for you and my love for Jackie would not allow me to offer myself to you. If I am to die I want to go knowing your love."

Chris was a bit taken back by this outburst. "Penny," he softly said, "You offer me the greatest honour a girl can offer a man. You are a beautiful and most desirable woman, but I cannot take you. My love for Jackie took many years to manifest and grow; now it is so strong it gives me strength to live each day. Without that strength, yes, we will surely perish; if I do perish I will know I die having honoured Jackie and my love for her."

Penny sat dry-eyed through his discourse. "Oh, Chris," she cried. "I am truly sorry to have burdened you so. Yes, I can feel that strength you say, and are now confident we will see this to the end and survive."

And survive they did. After seven days and nights of rain and freezing wind, laden with sand blasting them most of the time, they staggered into one of Peter's far out stockman's camps. Two stockmen on routine maintenance inspection had got bailed up there by the inclement weather. They were still in radio contact with Quo-Vadis Station. Their supplies were limited, still they managed to rustle up a warm meal of sorts.

Chris laughed and said, "It is like you said, Penny, when I fed you that soup and toast so long ago—that was the best meal you have ever eaten."

Peter arrived at the hut five hours later driving a huge multi-wheeled earthmoving machine. "It is not a Rolls-Royce," he laughed. "It was the only machine I had that I was sure I would get through this weather with. If you are up to a long rough ride through the night, we can leave straight away. You may not be very comfortable but at least you will be warm and dry. This monster has a coffee machine built in. Pretty neat, eh!"

A long rough ride through the night not exposed to the rain and freezing, howling wind after what they had survived did not cause Chris and Penny one little bit of distress and when, after about three hours, the wind and rain stopped and much to Peter's surprise, Chris hugged Penny and shouted, "THE EVIL SPIRITS HAVE GIVEN UP! WE ARE FREE."

Peter tried not to be distracted from his driving and cried over the roar of that monster machine's motor, "What's this Evil Spirits business?"

"Tell you some other time, Peter," Chris was laughing as he replied. "Believe me, we are two very happy and grateful people to be here."

Jackie had braved the ruminants of the storm and had driven hell for leather out to Quo-Vadis Station and was impatiently waiting for them. After darn near strangling him with hugs and kisses, she cried softly into his shoulder, "Do not ever, ever go out there without me again. If it wasn't for Annie locking me in our bedroom, regardless of the storm, I was preparing to come out to look for you. Please tell me you both are all right."

It only took a short time before things were back to normal; that is, as normal as life at Quo-Vadis could be.

Chris did tell Jackie of Penny's outburst. "I would not have really minded Chris if you had been with her," she whispered. "I have known for a long time she wanted you. I love her so much as a sister and friend. I nearly suggested to you it was all right by me if you had some time with her. You are such an honourable man, I see now  that will never happen. Is there any way I can love you more?"

"There is a way," Chris lightly said. "You can start learning this very minute," and gently took her in his arms and kissed her deeply.

Early next morning a very happy Jackie loudly cried, "If that was lesson one last night, I cannot wait for lesson two."

"Wanton woman," Chris laughed and reached for her.

# Chapter 9

Bill had been marooned in the regional city by the unseasonable weather. He was booked into an extremely nice hotel; nice as it was it did not have an extensive amount of facilities for guests. Bill could not tolerate the forced inactivity. He wandered through the streets more or less window shopping. He visited all the machinery distributors to see if there was any type of new machine to have recently hit the market that perhaps they could use at Quo-Vadis. He even gave his bank people much anguish as he rearranged his accounts. He did visit his old mates out at the Government crusher and smelter, scoffing at the antiquity of the machinery compared with the up-to-date modern machines he had at Quo-Vadis. He also shared a few coldies at the Royal with a few of his old friends. No matter what he did he could not alleviate his restlessness.

He had been sitting in the reception area of the hotel reading, for want of something better to do. "I feel like a good cup of tea and a cake. The hotel can provide one," he thought. "I think I prefer the tea and cake they serve at that great little tearoom down the street. Some of their cakes are really mouth-watering," he mused.

The hotel provided large umbrellas for the guests. He grabbed one and walked out into the rain. He didn't envisage a long absence from the hotel and called to the concierge, "back in one hour."

The concierge acknowledged his call with a nonchalant wave. Bill was taking little notice of what was ahead in his path, concentrating more on avoiding any deep puddles, and was forced to pause mid step, not to avoid a puddle, but the bedraggled form that lay across the footpath. "What the hell!" he gasped to himself. "Looks like somebody has slipped on the wet surface and come a cropper."

True to his gentle instincts he reached down saying, "Here, mate, let me help you up."

A distorted, agony-filled glazed-eyed countenance look back at him.

"Good grief, it's a woman!" he exclaimed. "Are you hurt, madam?" Bill quickly enquired.

The reply surprised him completely; it was garbled and he had no hope of understanding what was being said. The last bit hit him hard: "Please help me." He understood it clearly. He stood for a long moment looking at it; that pile of sodden cloth and flesh that was all that was left of a human being.

"Blazes, she is off her face." The thought almost threw him into a panic. Old memories erupted through his very being. The blurred images of awakening, lying in a filthy gutter, looking up at a sodden sky that poured rain down on him, hungry and cold and that insatiable demand by his mind and body for more and more of that stuff.

"Please help me." The message filled his mind.

"Come on 'mam'", he whispered, "I will help you."

He removed his expensive waterproof jacket and wrapped it around her. Several couples passing nearby stared briefly at him, then turned away in disgust, some saying: "Blasted filthy junkies."

Totally unperturbed by any of this, Bill gently lifted the form and walked as quickly as he could back to the hotel. She was not heavy—she was little more than skin and bones. He paused as the automatic doors of the foyer swung open. A receptionist, standing behind her highly-polished counter, saw him enter with his burden and immediately summoned the concierge.

"Mr Bailey has returned, he is carrying an injured person," she called.

The concierge dropped the sheet of notes he had been studying and rushed up to Bill.

Before he could say one word. Bill loudly said, "She needs immediate medical attention—get an ambulance."

The concierge hesitated, "I know her, Mr Bailey. She is the town slut. You should not worry about her."

Without putting the woman down, Bill looked hard at the man and shouted, "I don't give a rat's arse who or what she is. Just do as I say and get that bloody ambulance here now. You and I will sort this out later." Bill's features, his stance and voice emanated an aura of intense anger and a very frightened concierge rushed to his desk, quickly searched a list of emergency numbers and dialled the ambulance depot. He had to make eight attempts to get it right he was shaking so badly.

Bill laid the rain-sodden figure gently onto a very expensive lounge suite. That did stimulate the concierge and he burst into action. Within a minute he stood beside Bill bearing a large blanket.

"Here, sir," he quickly and somewhat humbly said, "perhaps you could wrap her in this." Of course, he was only endeavouring to minimise the damage to his precious settee.

"Thanks," Bill snapped and did wrap her securely in the blanket. She was still out of it, out somewhere, to where even her befuddled mind did not know. The pity that welled up in Bill's mind almost made him weep. She looks so bad he thought she will be lucky to survive this one.

Two paramedics rushed in. Bill had not heard the ambulance arrive.

One pushed Bill aside, "Is she dead? What happened?" Then in a moment of recognition exclaimed, "Oh hell! It's that mad junkie bitch. This is the fourth time this month," and turning to Bill demanded, "Who are you?"

Bill had taken a step back to give them room, now with the aggressive behaviour of the ambulance man he stepped forward and stood eye to eye with him, and very sharply replied, "It doesn't matter who I am, just get her to hospital, now."

The "now" was said with such force that the paramedic raised both hands in surrender, and quickly said, "Take it easy mate; we will get her to the hospital as quickly as possible."

"I will come with you and fill in all the paper work at the hospital." Bill was still very agitated, and shouted, "Move, man. She needs help urgently."

The medic hesitated for a moment then thought better not to say anything and did spring into action. As they loaded the patient into the ambulance he called over his shoulder, "You cannot ride with us, Mister; you will have to follow in your own transport."

Bill had watched them slide that bundle of humanity into the ambulance, which paused for a moment, then disappeared into the street with sirens wailing. He didn't have a car and looked around. A taxi stood at an adjacent rank. Bill quickly commandeered its services and sat in the front seat alongside the driver. "To the hospital please," he ordered. "There is an extra ten bucks' tip in it for you if you can be there before they enter her into the wards."

The taxi and the ambulance arrived almost simultaneously. "Well done, mate," Bill told the driver as he handed him a fifty dollar note. "Just keep any change."

"Thank you," the driver politely and gratefully said.

Bill walked in beside the trolley on which the woman lay. The receptionist saw them coming in and quickly came out from the receptionist's cubicle. "What have we here?" she professionally demanded, "Accident?"

"No," Bill interjected before the paramedics could answer. "Severe OD. Please place her in a single room, in the private wing. I will give you as much detail as I know, which isn't much. I picked her up out in the street."

The receptionist very quickly returned to her cubicle picked up her telephone and urgently punched some numbers, spoke briefly for a moment, then turned back to Bill saying, "The orderlies will be here in a moment. Is she violent?"

"No! She is not violent; she is totally non-compos," one of the paramedics interjected. "It is Elasia. She was in here about four weeks ago."

"What surname?" The receptionist demanded.

The paramedic just shrugged his shoulders. "I haven't got a clue," he replied.

The receptionist rolled her eyes and typed something into the computer. After a moment, she loudly said, "Here we are, ELASILA SKLOSKI, female, age thirty-eight, no fixed address. She will have to go into the public ward. I will let them know she's on the way up."

Bill had heard all this, and in a very angry voice said loudly, "That is not what I want. I want her in a private wing with your best specialist to take charge. I will meet any costs."

"And just who are you?" the receptionist growled equally as loudly. "Are you a relative or somebody of authority?"

"My name is Bill Bailey; my address is care of Quo-Vadis Mines. I am not a relative. When I see another human in need, as I see this lady is, I must help. The hotel will confirm for you that I am more than able to meet any costs. If you need any further information you can get it later; for now, stop this mucking about and get this woman to where she can be treated. All the stuffing about is not helping her one bit." Bill presented a very firm forceful demur.

The receptionist hesitated for a moment then quickly said to the orderly, "Private wing, now. I will ring ahead. They will be waiting for you. The resident doctor is up there at the moment. He will assess her and get a specialist in straight away. I think I saw Doctor Mayo go up about twenty minutes ago," and turning to Bill quickly explained, "Dr Mayo, is the senior consultant for the drug and alcohol wing. His rehabilitation record is extremely good."

"Thank you, miss," Bill quietly said. "May I go up with her?"

It was the receptionist's turn to be very firm, and she left no room for argument when she very quickly said, "No, if you wish you may wait down here. Firstly, come over to my desk—I require some details from you."

After ten minutes of a virtual inquisition, Bill signed a document that confirmed he would be responsible for all costs. Having done all this, he sat in a hard, impersonal chair in the waiting area. He watched intently as the receptionist made numerous telephone calls. A tea lady wheeled her trolley in and the receptionist pointed to Bill. The trolley was quickly wheeled to where Bill sat.

"Tea or coffee, luv?" the tea lady very respectfully asked.

"A strong tea with milk would be good, and can I have one of those sandwiches, please? I missed lunch with all this action." Bill gratefully replied.

Bill endured the discomfort of the waiting room for a further forty-five minutes before impatience got the better of him and he stood and walked to the receptionist's cubicle. "Any news, miss?" he asked through the glass panel.

The receptionist responded quickly: "Dr Mayo has only just called to confirm if you were still here. He would like to talk to you. He is waiting in his room, suite 1A on the third floor."

Bill caught the lift to the third floor, found suite 1A, and did not hesitate to walk in.

A young nurse arose from her desk. "Mr Bailey?" she asked, and not waiting for an answer said, "Dr Mayo will see you straightaway. Please follow me."

She led him to an adjacent door, knocked and walked in. Bill had obediently followed her. Mayo stood pouring over an x-ray screen. An MRI image of the head was displayed; he then briefly referred to a pile of pages, then turned to Bill with a pink hand extended. "I am Jason Mayo. Bill Bailey, isn't it?" he enquired. "May I call you Bill?"

Before Bill could reply, Mayo had continued, "You have taken on the task of assisting Skolski I see. Do you know her?"

Bill could only laugh and quickly replied, "Give me a break doc, I haven't answered the first question yet."

The specialist paused midst his discourse. "Sorry, Bill, I do tend to get a bit abrupt and carried away at times."

"That's okay doc," Bill now warmly replied. "Most busy men are like that. The answer to your first question is yes, please call me Bill—everybody else does. Now the answer to your second question, "do I know her?" The answer is yes and no."

"Yes and no? That's a strange answer, Bill," the bemused specialist said.

"Not so strange if you know the whole story," Bill softly said.

"This sounds most interesting," Mayo said. "Would you tell me of it?" He was now totally intrigued.

"It's a long sad story," Bill answered. "It is my story, and, in a way, it is reflected in what we see in that girl you are treating."

"This sounds well worth the while to listen to, sir," the specialist whispered. "I have finished for the day. Please sit and I will have my nurse find us a cup of tea."

Bill was quiet for a minute, then softly said, "Firstly tell me, how is she?"

"You are not a relative; but I see you care, so why not. She appears not to have any known relatives. The woman is a mess. Physically she has been extensively abused. There is evidence of much abuse—some old, some recent. She has extensive bruising, some quite deep to at least fifty percent of her body; from the positioning of those injuries it would suggest she has been kicked many times as she lay in a prone position. Her skull is intact, the brain scans show considerable trauma, the most recent would have been the cause for her collapse. In addition to all this there are many quite severe abrasions and burns. Those burns appear to have been inflicted by a glowing cigarette tip. Despite all this, there is no reason why her body would not heal. She is not that old and the body does have wonderful regenerative power. I cannot at this stage ascertain her emotional and mental state. With all her physical trauma I expect that damage would be considerable. Any recovery will require extensive nursing. I am not confident she will ever recover from her addiction without removing part of her brain; that would leave her to be little short of the zombie."

"Thank you, Jason, we must avoid any further talk of that operation." Bill very quietly but firmly said. "Now I will tell you why I am here."

Bill took a large drink of tea from the cup the nurse had placed beside him, then continued speaking softly. "There but for the grace of God go I. I well know the pain of being drug dependent.

I have to go back some twenty-five years, about the time I left High School and was introduced to marijuana. You have most probably heard all this before—how a young life is destroyed by unscrupulous dealers. Once they get you started there is no turning back. Much to my parents' dismay, I quit school and headed out on my own. As you well know, the craving multiplied and soon I turned to all manner of criminal pursuits, just to get money to buy drugs and feed the habit. I think my parents died of shame and I was left alone in the world to slip further and further down into the world of the hell of a drug addict. It ended up I was incarcerated for armed robbery in which a policeman was severely wounded. Prison was a living hell; drugs were sometimes available but never enough. I received many beatings for not paying up. I was shot trying to escape prison. While I was in hospital, a kindly lady came to visit me. She never knew why she had been sent. She did tell me in later years, she had no option, she just had to do this. When I was discharged from hospital, of course I was sent back to jail. That kindly lady continued to visit me, even in jail. I was twenty-six years old when I was released from prison. The parole conditions were very hard. To this day I believe it was only because that lady told the parole board she would take me into her home and look after me, that I was given parole. She was an elderly widow and had very little. With her help, I managed to stay clean for twelve months and got a job at the Government crusher. It was dangerous hard work in those days. Still, I survived. The crusher boss recognised that I had a unique gift and was able to identify types of ore by smell, and he often used me to assist him in the daily running of the crusher. I stayed on that job for fifteen years, and when my old boss retired he recommended to the higher-ups that the job be given to me. His recommendation must have carried good weight, and I got the job. I had been clean all the time. The kindly lady had died in that period and had willed her home to me. I now had a good job and a home; but I was restless— I could not settle. I knew I was good for nothing but running a crusher and set to learn the intricacies of smelting. The upshot of this was I was asked to take the position of crusher and smelter boss, from which I resigned just recently to take a job with a young prospector at his goldmine—the Quo-Vadis goldmine. It is a long way out in the Outback, and a combination of peace and the comradeship of the owners having taken me in to be part of their very beautiful family, has filled the void of my restlessness. This is the part you may take or leave—it matters little to me—but I will tell you anyway. Very often in my journey I would suffer the strong power of drug addiction calling me. You may ask me how I overcame this. I cannot answer that for you—I do not have a real answer, except to say by God's grace I was given the power to fight it. By that grace I have survived and the need for drugs has left me completely. I am a very happy man. When I looked at that lady earlier today, I saw myself twenty years ago and I knew I had to help her. That's about it, doc."

The specialist stood and took Bill's hand saying, "Bill your story inspires me to try even harder to help these poor souls buried very deeply in their dependence on drugs; how I can do that I do not know. I have much knowledge of their problem. You, sir, have even greater knowledge than I, having been there and done that. I would ask you to work with me; however, I see before me a very contented man and I think an offer to work with drug addicts would not be what you would want, as you have found that which you need."

"Thanks for that, doc," Bill humbly replied. "You are right: I do not see myself as a man who could do that which you are doing. I do have a need. I wish to take that very sick lady with me back to Quo-Vadis. I sincerely believe out there, with the help of my now family, we can lead her to find a good life free of that insidious disease she has suffered with for so long."

Jason Mayo, the drug and alcohol specialist, thought deeply for a minute. He stepped up to the window of his room and looked down on the courtyard, deep in thought, then turned to Bill and said, "Bill, I cannot make her go with you to your Quo-Vadis. I can only tell her of your offer."

"That will not work, sir," Bill quickly said. "It would be better, before you discharge her, I tell her of what I am offering. Can you keep her here for about five days while I go back to Quo-Vadis and talk this over with my family? I am very sure they will not hesitate to agree to her coming out there."

"You expect to travel over one-thousand km, and travel back those one-thousand kilometres in five days? How will you do that?" the perplexed specialist asked. "Do you have a fast aeroplane?"

"Yes sir," Bill replied. "Three or four at the last count. The kids use one to get to and from high school; Jackie, that's the boss's wife, uses one to go shopping. I have free use of another. Chris, that's the boss, just has to get in line, and to wait his turn."

"I think I would like to meet this family of yours, Bill. I will have to program regular visits to my patient," Mayo said with a laugh and added, "You are a fine man, Bill Bailey," and once again shook his hand.

"Thanks for that, doc," Bill whispered, "but I know what I have become is purely a gift of God's Grace. I believe the weather will clear tomorrow so if you will excuse me I will leave you and prepare to make all the arrangements for her and try to be back on Friday morning. Can you keep her here that long?"

"She will be sedated for a couple of days and provided she does not get violent I will keep her here for her own good." Then, with a suppressed smile, he very lightly asked, "I assume you have the wherewithal to pay for this long consultation."

"I reckon you are covered, doc," Bill replied with a laugh. "My last dividend that the mine paid was just on four million dollars. Most of that is still sitting in the bank."

"Four-million-dollar dividend. Good grief, man. It is obvious I'm in the wrong business. I was just joking, Bill—there will be no account."

"That's good," Bill laughed. "I would have sent it back with an attachment—my bill—for twice your account for specialised storytelling."

On that note Bill took his leave of the specialist, and next morning returned to Quo-Vadis. Upon his arrival he sat quietly with Chris and Jackie and told them comprehensively all that had happened, and what he wanted to do. He explained, "As she rehabilitates there will be some special moments. I would like to keep the kids and you two from seeing them, so I will have her move into my house. It will all be kept aboveboard I promise you. I only want to see her well."

Chris and Jackie did not hesitate. "You do whatever you think is best, Bill. Do you have any experience with addicts?"

Bill simply replied, "Lots. I will tell you a story one day that I think will surprise you," then to lighten the moment, cried, "Hey, where is my grandson, Jack? I have missed him. You will have to run the joint for a while Chris. Do you think you can do that without leaving me a mess to clean up?"

Chris contemplated just how to reply to that remark; he hesitated, for a moment then snarled, "Just for that you grumpy old bugger, I'm going to leave you such a mess it will take you all next year to sort it out."

Bill returned to the provincial city next day. He nonchalantly strolled into the hotel, booked into his preferred suite, and asked for an additional suite. The receptionist was most gracious and without hesitation replied, "Certainly, Mr Bailey. Will you be staying long this time?"

"No," he replied, "I do not expect to be here very long. Maybe only a few days. I do expect myself and my guest will leave on Monday morning." Immediately after he walked into his suite he telephoned the hospital and asked to speak to Dr Mayo, in the drug and alcohol wing. There were a few clicks and Mayo's girl answered.

"It's Bill Bailey, miss," he quietly said, then asked, "Is the man in?"

"He is in, Mr Bailey," the girl said. "He is in a consultation with a patient at the moment. Can I have him call you back? I know he is expecting your call, so I do envisage he will not be long."

Bill lay back on the bed trying to compose what he would say to "What's her name? ELASIA—that's right. I wonder how you pronounce that correctly, I think I will call her Ellie."

His musings were interrupted by the impatient buzzing of the telephone. "Jason Mayo here, Bill," came the voice through the receiver. "Good to see you back. You really covered a lot of distance very quickly, just as you said you would."

"How is she? Can I move her today, or even tomorrow?" Bill impatiently asked.

"First things first," Mayo answered his questions. "It would be best if you came and saw her, Bill, and offer her your proposal. If she is okay with it I will discharge her into your care. What time could you be in here tomorrow?" the specialist asked him. "I do want to be with you when you talk to her. She is still a bit irrational at times."

"8–8.30 too early?" Bill quickly replied, to which Mayo answered, "Those times are good with me Bill, I have no appointments until 10.30."

Bill arrived at the hospital at 7.55, caught the lift to the third floor, walked straight into the medical suite and bowled in without knocking.

Mayo's receptionist/nurse had obviously just arrived, as evidenced by a make-up kit being hastily stowed into a drawer. She was obviously a little hassled and said with a laugh, "You do not even give a girl a chance to repair last night's damage, Mr Bailey. You are early. I don't think Dr Mayo has arrived yet. He usually does not get in until 9.30. He did call me last night and told me you would be in between 8 and 8.30. Knowing most of his clients I did not expect you before 8.30. I am making tea. Would you like a cup while you wait? I hope Dr Mayo hasn't forgotten your appointment."

"No! I have not forgotten his appointment," a voice blasted from the open door of Mayo's room. I have been here since before 7.30 and am a little concerned that my visitor gets a cup of tea and I am overlooked. Come in and sit-down Bill."

In a flustered panic the receptionist/nurse prepared and presented them with cups of tea in record time. Bill and Mayo sat sipping the tea, while Mayo related all that had developed with their mutual patient. "I am sharing all this in confidence with you, Bill. By rights, I should have a written authority from the patient, but she is in no condition to consider that. I am trusting you will treat our discussions confidentially."

"Jason!" Bill answered quickly and speaking very sincerely said, "You had no need to even think of asking that of me. Be very well assured our discussions will be kept between you and me. I appreciate it that you are prepared to trust me."

"It is as I said," the highly respected drug and alcohol specialist, Mayo said softly, "She will require extensive care, not so much for her physical healing, all her bruises and lesions are responding very well to treatment; your big challenge will be treating her mind, and somehow taking from her that horrible demand her body literally screams out for. I have seen and treated many addicts over the years; her condition is equal to the worst of them. Yesterday she went into an almighty spasm, demanding drugs and thrashing violently about, Do you think you can handle that?"

Bill was not affected one little bit with what he was hearing, and did not hesitate to reply saying, "What I hear you saying, Jason, does not deter me one iota from my decision to help her."

Bill had a tone of finality in his voice. "Whether or not I win or lose it will not be from want of trying. So, to what you ask, can I handle her irrationality, I can only reply, regardless of what I have to face I will continue to try."

"I hear you Bill," Mayo said. "I believe you of all people are the only one who will succeed. Have you finished your cup of tea? Finish it up and come with me and we will say hello to your challenge."

Elisia lay on an impersonal hospital bed. Her hands and legs were restrained by thick straps. Mayo walked to the head of the bed and smiled benevolently down at her and said, "Hello Elisia. You have a visitor. His name is Bill. He would like to talk with you. Are you up to it?"

She looked questionably at Bill for a moment then whispered, "Yes."

Bill stepped forward and took one restrained hand in his and held it gently. "Hello Elisia," Bill softly said, "I am happy to finally meet you."

"Who are you?" the prone figure demanded, then hesitated. "That face! That face! I keep seeing it. Have you come to haunt me?" she screamed.

Bill placed a hand gently on her shoulder and spoke to her with great sincerity. "No, not to haunt you. You recently asked me to help you, and I promise you I will do my very best to do just that."

As she listened she appeared to settle a bit and then asked in a rather plaintive voice, "You will not hurt me like the others did, will you?"

"Again, no, Elisia! I also promise I will never hurt you," Bill assured her, and then turning to Mr Mayo firmly said, "would you kindly have your nurses remove those straps."

The nurse interrupted him abruptly saying most firmly, "I don't think that is a wise thing to do, sir. She does have moments of great violence and may hurt herself."

"I don't think that will happen nurse," Bill quickly said. "I am sure Elisia will be much more comfortable without them, and I have much to say to her."

A look of gratitude flashed across Elisia's face. "Thank you, Mister. I am all right now and those straps were hurting." She continued speaking in a quiet, wistful voice. "Your face has been all that has kept me sane. Have I met you? Did you know me? You know what I mean? When? Where? How? My mind or all that's left of it cannot recall you."

The straps were off by now and she wriggled herself into a more comfortable position. Mayo signalled silently to the nurse, who raised her eyebrows a little, but followed the specialist out of the room.

"Good," Bill laughed, "now we can talk without those nosy parkers interrupting. The first thing I want to ask you is, may I call you Ellie, I am not too sure I can pronounce your name correctly. Polish, isn't it?" She only bobbed her head by way of answer. "Well Ellie, I want you to believe me when I say, if you're willing to try, I reckon between the both of us, we can beat this crap-filled world you find yourself in. I will ask much of you: the first thing is, you will have to give me your absolute trust. It will not be easy at first, but I know that we two together will win. I tell you this with all sincerity, I know where you are at the moment, and well know your pain."

Bill's voice was so deep and sincere, Ellie lay as if hypnotised. Then after a moment of hesitation, whispered, "Bill, that's what Dr Mayo called you. Do you really believe there is hope for me?"

"Not only do I believe, I know that if we work together we will heal you. Do not think for one minute it will be easy," Bill cried. "There must be not one moment of one day when we take our eyes from the goal we pursue. It will not be easy at first. Yet, I know. Don't ask me how I know. I just know one day you will awaken, and you will smile again.

Ellie reached to him and took his hand and squeezed it. She said nothing.

"The second thing I have to ask of you, I need for you to agree to allow me to take you to a place, far, far from the clutches of those drug-dealing bastards. This place I talk of is truly wonderful, and you will be amongst some of the most beautiful people to ever walk this earth. I will tell them of your sickness and they too will help us. When you find I speak the truth you may start to give me all your trust. Between you and I, we must have that absolute trust, regardless of what happens."

Ellie started to cry and through her tears she blubbered, "Look at me, I have not cried like this in….., I do not know how long. The only time I ever cried was when I was in pain. Please take me to this place and those people Bill. My heart tells me there is hope."

Bill squeezed her hand lightly saying, "Thank you, Ellie. Let's make that first step right now."

He called loudly, "Dr Mayo. Ellie and I are leaving now. Would you be so good as to sign her discharge papers quickly? Every moment she spends here is a moment lost in Ellie's way to happiness."

The nurse started to object.

Mayo silenced her as he snapped, "You heard Mr Bailey, have those discharge papers on my desk in less than an hour, and get Miss Elisia dressed immediately. And you, Bill, wait for Elisia and both of you come straight to my office before you leave the hospital."

Three people were patiently waiting in Mayo's reception room for the specialist. Regardless of this, Mayo's receptionist walked them straight into his consulting room. Mayo sat behind his desk and motioned them to chairs. He paused for a moment, as if he was trying to put together some special advice, then having come to some satisfactory resolution he addressed them. "Please listen very carefully to what I am about to say. You pair of idiots are about to commence a journey to God only knows where; you both are fully aware this journey will not be easy and will be filled with pain and anguish. You, Bill, will have to be strong, stronger than you have ever been in your life; and you, Elisia, always have to hold hard to that face that has ridden with you in these last terrible days. I cannot give you any special advice other than, trust God and trust each other. Now go. I am not going to prescribe you any medicine, young lady. This is one journey you have to make by yourself without being propped up with medicines. And you, Mr Bill Bailey, in six months from today would you kindly arrange for me to visit you at your fabled Quo-Vadis so that I may monitor Elisia's progress and check on how you are faring?"

"Quo-Vadis? What's that?" Ellie asked.

"Didn't he tell you? That's his goldmine," Mayo laughed.

"Not mine," Bill quickly interrupted. "I am only part of it. Do you have a family, Jason? Why don't you make a holiday of your visit and bring your family? This is something I can guarantee: you will find any time you spend there will be most agreeable."

Bill stood quickly and took Ellie's hand and growled, "Come on, Ellie. This bloke will go on and on if we do not get out of here."

Mayo stood, shook Bill's hand, hugged Ellie and said, "Go with God, you pair," and shooed them out the door.

As they walked through the hospital foyer, Bill told her, "I will have to go back to my hotel and collect my gear. It will only take a moment, as I had not expected to be stuck in town for long and had packed very little."

Twenty minutes later they were in a Quo Vadis resort jet on their way to the mine. They were in the air for only a short while before Ellie hesitantly said, "All this is too much for me to take." She gasped, "Do you have a little something I could take, just a little bit to see me through?"

"No way!" Bill all but shouted. "Scream and shout and kick and bite all you like. From now on there is nothing like that for you, Ellie girl."

She started to become rather agitated with this, and started shouting, "I cannot survive without something. My whole body is screaming for it."

By the time they reached Quo Vadis she was a writhing screaming bundle. Bill gently lifted her from the jet and carried her to where Chris and Jackie sat in Goliath waiting. They both looked with concern at the gibbering female Bill carried.

"You did warn us," Chris said softly, "but I didn't expect this."

Bill sighed deeply, and softly said, "There is a long story to be told—my story. In the meantime, you'll have to trust me or send me away."

Chris took Ellie from Bill's arms saying very forcibly, "I didn't hear that, you silly bugger," then very forcibly added, "You are family, Bill, no matter what, never, never ever forget that. Grab your bags and we will take you home. The kids are all at school so don't worry about them. They will be told all they need to know in due course. Are you going to stay with us?"

"Thanks for that, mate. I think it will be best if Ellie lives at my house for a while."

There were times in the next months that did tax Bill's resolve to a maximum. Despite that, not once did he falter. Ellie did not meet any of Bill's "family." In that time, she was often seen walking through his garden and lately working alongside him. A large package was delivered to Quo Vadis Airport. It was labelled "Handle with Care, PLANTS" and addressed to Mr Bill Bailey c/o Quo-Vadis Mines via Quo-Vadis Tourist Park. The sender was a well-known rose farm in the eastern states.

"Rose Plants?" The postal bloke quizzically asked Bill when he had called to pick up that special parcel. The postal bloke was an inquisitive type and asked, "Do you reckon you can grow roses out here, Bill?" then thinking twice, added "If anybody can, you will."

The bare root rose cuttings did receive a level of pampering that would befit a level of protection a mother would nurture her favourite child with.

Ellie had nonchalantly mentioned to Bill that she remembered her dad had grown roses, and that she loved roses. It had been many years since she had seen a rose. Bill had spent hours researching the intricacies of rose growing and had had several prolonged telephone conversations with the owner of the rose farm. The roses, to Bill's great satisfaction, thrived.

Chris did regularly visit Bill to keep him in touch with the activities of the Quo-Vadis group, and to always enquire, whether he needed anything. Ellie made a point of keeping herself elsewhere when he did visit. Bill did make an opportunity to share a very deep and meaningful time with Chris and Jackie as he told them of his early days.

"That's quite a story, mate," Chris said. "We can now really understand your need to help this girl."

Jackie did not say one word. She held Bill close and gave him a light kiss on the cheek, then said, "I will say it again; you are a good man, Bill Bailey."

Susie and Annie would often walk along the lake edge, chatting on girly things. Today they had decided to alter the direction of their walk to pass by Bill's garden.

"What's that beautiful perfume?!" Annie exclaimed. "Bill's flower garden must be in full bloom."

There was no fence around that garden so the girls meandered through the flower beds trying to locate the blooms that were responsible for the beautiful perfume. As they got closer to the rose beds, the perfume became more intense and they paused to admire the beautiful flowers.

"I think they are roses," Susie cried.

"They are," came a girl's voice from underneath the nearby large shrub. Both girls stepped back in alarm.

"Who?" Was all Susie got out?

"I am Ellie. Bill's friend. You must be Susie and Annie. Bill has often spoken of you. He refers to you as being his adopted nieces. I have had enough of weeding today and was looking for an excuse to call it quits and make myself a cup of tea. Would you care to join me? I do have some of Bill's fresh lemon drink if you would prefer that."

The two girls were totally perplexed. Curiosity got the better of them, and after a moment's hesitation answered, "A glass of that special lemon drink Uncle Bill makes would be nice."

"Good," Ellie responded. "Come on in. I have not had a chance to talk to anyone for quite some time."

True to form it was not long before the three of them were chatting amiably. Ellie explained her presence by simply saying she had been very sick when Bill bought her to Quo-Vadis. "It is such a beautiful place. And Bill is so kind—I am well on the way to full recovery."

Unannounced, Bill strolled in and stopped short when he saw the two girls. "What's going on?" He demanded.

"It is alright Bill," Ellie replied. "The girls were admiring your roses and I invited them in. They are even more special than you said they were."

"I hope what he told you was nice, Ellie," Susie laughed. "Uncle Bill does tell a lot of tales. You are very naughty Uncle Bill. You could have told us Ellie was here. She is going to come walking with us sometimes. We want to show her all the things you and Daddy have done."

That night as Bill and Ellie sat quietly reading, Ellie put her book aside and quietly said, "I think I am about ready to meet people again, Bill. Can I meet the rest of your family? Their adopted mother Jackie and her husband Chris sounded so special, and the way the girls talk about their little brother Jack you would think the sun, moon and stars all shine from him."

"I like the sound of that," Bill replied. "Tomorrow when I take the fresh flowers to Jackie, I will make it a big bunch of 'Ellie's roses', and you can give them to her yourself."

"Oh, you beautiful man, Bill Bailey," she exclaimed and threw her arms about him and kissed him very soundly. Bill was quite shocked for an instant then responded with equal enthusiasm. "Bill, Bill, Bill," she cried, "Take me to bed right now please, so I can show you just how much you have come to mean to me, and how much I love you."

Bill drew back a little and whispered. "No, Ellie, not yet. I do share your feelings, but I do not believe you are healed well enough just yet. We must, and I say must, give it a little more time. It would be a shame and an absolute disaster for us to do anything that would set you back. Dr Mayo is coming out early next week. I would like to hear what he has to say about your progress. Please understand, and do not get upset if I do not take you to bed this very minute. Believe you me I am sorely tempted. It is a beautiful evening; let's just go for a walk down by the lake, come back and make a strong cup of tea and sit and enjoy each other's company."

"I hate you, Bill Bailey," she whispered. "Why do you have to be so wise, and so good," then very seductively whispered, "Please don't make me wait too long. You have aroused a demand in me which is far stronger than any demand I ever had. It is a wonderful feeling, and it grows greater every moment I am with you."

Jackie was absolutely delighted when both Ellie and Bill wandered into the kitchen the next morning bearing the beautiful roses. She gave Ellie a warm hug of greeting, called loudly, "Chris, Bill and Ellie are here; come and join us."

Chris came immediately and commented, "This is a pleasant surprise. Welcome, Ellie. Those roses are beautiful. It is obvious they have been grown with a woman's touch."

"Oh, no," Ellie quickly responded, "nobody but Bill could ever grow something as beautiful as these flowers. He did grow them for me."

The four of them sat in the kitchen chatting over many things. Ellie did ask Jackie, "would you mind showing me your house?" adding, she had admired it from a distance for all that time she had been living at Bill's. She had met Susie and Annie. "They are beautiful girls. They had told me that Chris and Bill, had done many wonderful things here. I can barely wait to see all that."

Jackie had only laughed at that saying, "Believe me, Ellie, even though I have been here all the time, there is much I have yet to see."

The drug and alcohol specialist Dr Mayo was nothing short of amazed at what he saw of Quo-Vadis. "What a wonderful rehabilitation clinic this is," he laughed. "It is little wonder Elisia has progressed so far." He spent many hours every day for a week with her. His examination was complete and comprehensive. He had bought his wife and two sons with him; they were billeted at Quo-Vadis Resort. His wife was delighted with the Resort and Quo-Vadis in general, telling the doctor, in no uncertain terms, "Jason, this is where I want to spend every one of your holidays in future. Chris is taking the boys out to Quo-Vadis Station tomorrow to show them a real cattle station. He said something about that they are branding at the moment, and the boys will be put on a horse and have to help the stockmen bring the cattle into the yard. They are very excited. I hope you have your cheque-book with you; the genuine twenty-four-carat gold accessories that are being sold in the gift shop are really beautiful. I may want to spend a dollar or two or three in there."

Mayo laughed, "What with the boys wanting me to buy them a pony each when we get back, and you taking a bucket full of gold home, this could become a very expensive consultation for me."

"You don't know half of it yet," my very clever doctor husband. "Did you know that that very celebrated artist, Penelope Carter, has her studio here? She has invited you and I to call in tomorrow and have a browse through some of her latest creations. I can see the looks of pure envy when my girlfriends come to visit our home next and they see the collection of her paintings you are going to buy me."

"Isn't she the artist the national television featured in the series of up and coming young Aussies."

"Yes," his wife had replied. "Her paintings are given accolades all over the world."

"I do not think I can afford to come out here too often," the doctor sighed.

Mayo called Bill aside. "Bill," he said, "you have worked wonders with Ellie. I believe she will now be able to deny the addictive urges, and within the year she will be completely free of that compulsion and be more or less completely healed. She had told me, very confidentially of course; that she wants to marry you and remain at Quo-Vadis for ever with you. She cried when she told me that. She has integrated into the Kennedy family rather comprehensively. Little Jack had made her cry, she said, when she told me he called her Auntie Ellie."

"Marry her?!" Bill exclaimed. "First I'd heard of that. Come to think of it, that would be a great idea; do you think next week would be too early, doc?"

"Keep me out of it," Mayo laughed heartily. "That's a decision you and Ellie have to make on your own."

Bill and Ellie did get married the following week. Chris made a healthy donation to the building fund of a church in the regional city to induce a pastor to fly out to Quo-Vadis to perform the ceremony. In its simplicity it was a wonderful ceremony, attended by all Ellie's new family. Dr Mayo and his wife delayed their departure so they could attend.

Bill did not change that much, but all could see the happiness that exuded from him and Ellie. Ellie did tell Jackie her story. Jackie had wept with her joyously when Ellie confessed she had found love, not just from Bill but from her whole new family at Quo-Vadis.

# Chapter 10

Things got back to normal at Quo-Vadis, whatever that is at Quo-Vadis, until Chris received a call from Rex. "You had better expect a call from two Middle Eastern suits. They called in here demanding to see the owner of Quo-Vadis mines. They had a writ issued by some local court. By the look of it, the document had been prepared in a Chinese laundry but it did bear official stamping and recording numbers. I have my office checking them out. They do appear to be authentic. Chris, my erstwhile brother, they are suing you for trespass and illegally mining of their lease. The writ claims the land was granted to their family by some Spanish King way back in the sixteenth century. They claim their ancestors explored much of the Outback and the Spanish King granted them the land in gratitude. Their story also says that the same King granted their ancestors much land in South America and they are preparing to sue, in their words, many Spanish and Frenchmen. Despite that document having an official look about it, the whole thing has a pretty rotten odour to it. They have charted a private jet and are on their way out to Quo-Vadis to serve the writ."

"Oh, struth!" Chris exclaimed in horror. "I'd better hotfoot it to the big smoke and organise a legal team. Those jokers will just have to turn around and chase me."

Jackie was more worried than he was. "You won't have to go to jail, will you?" she cried, then growled, "This is not fair. Why now, when everything is so right."

Chris had always worked with one of the best (and most expensive) law firms in the whole state. They were most conversant with mining and all the legalities and acts associated with it. It had been they who had been instrumental in preparing all his lease purchases from Morris, and the recording of the leases over the sinkhole and the escarpment. The senior partner of the law firm made himself available immediately when Chris contacted him. He assured Chris that he personally would attend to the brief, and as soon as those people, he nearly said boogies, serve you we will have an injunction lodged. "That will give us plenty of time to investigate their claim," then scoffed, "Land Grants by a Spanish King, in the sixteenth century; now I've heard everything. It is important and we must get the matter heard in our courts here. Where the hell is that local court that issued the writ in the first place?"

Chris spoke with Jackie that night, assuring her the matter was well in hand and he would keep her informed. Now all he had to do was wait for those suits to show. He had lunch with Rex the next day and told him "If those people show up again, send them to the law firm. I have given instructions for them to accept the writ on my behalf." This apparently did not suit the protagonists, for he heard later on that day they had sought him in many places.

The following morning as he sat at breakfast in the hotel cafe, the maître d' walked quickly to his table. "Reception have directed this call here Mr Kennedy. Do you wish to take it?"

Chris took the call—it was the lawyer, Norton Bellamy. "Sorry to disturb your breakfast Chris," Norton said. I have two very obnoxious agitated fellows sitting in my office. They refuse to hand over the documents to us and are demanding to see you personally. I have a strong feeling they are aware we will examine those documents minutely, which of course we will. For some reason or another, that we should do that does disturb them."

"Can you put them on, please, Norton? Use your speakerphone so you can hear all that is said," Chris instructed him.

"Okay," Norton replied. "Here is the senior man. I cannot pronounce his name."

Before Chris could say a word, a voice blasted from the phone. "Where are you hiding? We want to see you."

"I am not hiding," Chris very firmly said. "Listen to me, and listen very carefully, you are a very rude person. I see little point in disturbing my breakfast to meet you. Hand those papers to Mr Bellamy NOW!" Chris shouted. "He is fully authorised to accept them on my behalf. Give him the details of your law firm and the lawyers can sort this out. Now get the hell out of my hair."

He disconnected the call and handed the phone back to the smiling Maître D'.

An hour later Chris's mobile buzzed. "Norton Bellamy here, Chris. What a confounded mess. I finally got the details of their law firm from them. They are domiciled in a Middle Eastern city. They sure do things differently over there. I finally got to a fellow who claimed he was the lawyer for the plaintiffs. He rattled off a great list of numbers, saying they were rulings of matters of this nature, handed down by the court in that city. Apparently, if you ever travel there, you'll be locked up—no hearing no nothing. You will be grabbed and locked away and all your assets will be seized. How they think they can do this I do not know. Chris, you must be very careful. I got the distinct impression these two want to grab you and drag you back to their country. They claim they are police officers and have been authorised by our immigration department to do just that. We are checking this out even as we speak. May I suggest you return to Quo-Vadis as soon as possible and closely monitor all incoming flights, especially any unauthorised flights. By the way, the Spanish King's grant is a load of codswallop; the ink is hardly dry and the paper it is written on was only manufactured a year ago. All your lease documents are beyond dispute. I'm off to the High Court now to lodge a denial of claim on the primary basis of fraud. The villains are supposed to come back here tomorrow. I'm going to try and have them detained and charged with misrepresentation and attempted intimidation." Bellamy then added with a gleeful chuckle, "You can expect a hefty bill for all this, and you owe me lunch."

Chris laughed, "Norton you amaze me. Do you know you said all that without taking one breath? Be here at the hotel dining room at 12.30 tomorrow. I will get my brother Rex to come also. I think you know him—he is a senior partner of Kennedy and Dixon, the accountants."

Lunch was a very interesting affair. Norton had hardly sat at the table when he said, "Chris, those fellows are part of a group who have tried this all before. Had you agreed to meet those 'gentlemen'—I use that term most liberally—they would have tried to intimidate you and would have offered to have the action withdrawn for the payment of one-million Australian dollars. Had you resisted their intimidation they would have possibly become physical, even resulting in your murder. There is some record of this happening before."

"Wow!" Chris loudly whispered, if there is such a thing as a loud whisper. "How did you find all this out?"

"When I called at the judge's chambers," Norton replied, "I'm well known there, I got to talking with a couple of the judges. They had agreed, without pre-empting the case, that the bona fides of the writ and the grant were dubious and they did initiate several proceedings. The first was to disallow the lodgement of the writ on the grounds of denial of the authenticity of the grant. The next thing they did was to issue an order to the telecommunications people to trace the address of the lawyer. They then required the immigration department to check on the entry permits of our friends. It appears they are here illegally. The authorities did contact their counterparts in that country who were shocked to be informed what was happening, and most emphatically confirmed that no such procedure exists or has ever existed in their country to incarcerate an individual without trial. There is much more, Chris. Do you want to hear it? It does involve you."

"Since I am involved, yes, what is it?" Chris asked.

"It's like this," Norton replied, "the presiding judge would like to set down a date for the hearing of the claim. Do not worry—lodgement of the writ has already been denied. Despite that, their lawyers have lodged an appeal. I do not understand their thinking; they have no hope of success. The authorities are hoping, this is where you come in, you will agree to continuation of your defence. Their idea is to see if they can drag our gentleman and all their friends, and hopefully the cohorts in this scheme into one place, preferably into court. They are hoping to nip this thing in the bud, as they can see that, should these nefarious activities be allowed to continue, many small companies and people with less intestinal fortitude than you may get hurt. They do recommend, and I endorse that recommendation, that you avoid any contact whatsoever with those two fellows."

Chris laughed rather sarcastically and said, "Norton you expect me to sit here and now calmly eat lunch with you. I am not so tough and do have a wife and family to worry about, yet when I think about it I have to agree with the authority's thoughts. This sort of thing will not go away by hitting it with a powder puff. We must use a sledgehammer. Yes! I will go along with what is planned. What date has been set?"

"Three days from today. That makes it Thursday at 11 am, at the High Court."

"I'll be there, Norton; and thank you," Chris very sincerely said.

"I should thank you," Norton said with a laugh. "All this has brightened up what was shaping up to be a rather dull month. You can thank me after you get my account. QCs don't come cheap you know."

The whole matter turned into an almost humorous charade. Three high court judges sat and listened patiently to a very sleazy lawyer and twenty witnesses, drawn from sources unknown. Their evidence was a parody of lies and contradictions. Chris noticed that ten, or was it twelve, uniformed police officers quietly stationed themselves about the court room, and placed themselves discreetly behind the lawyer, those witnesses, and the two fellows who had pursued Chris.

It was all over by 11:57 am when the presiding judge addressed the court. "We have heard more than enough, and are astounded," he spoke very loudly to ensure everybody heard clearly, and, directing his address at the lawyer, said; "that you and all your witnesses have the temerity to come into this court room with what is obviously a bundle of incomprehensible untruths. We find that Mr Kennedy has no case to answer to, and secondly, we find that the contempt you bring into this court is intolerable, and sentence each and every one of you to six months incarceration. It would appear most appropriate for the authorities to confirm the bona fides of your immigration papers. There is another matter which we have allowed to be bought into this court. You two fellows should be arrested before you leave these rooms and charged with attempted major extortion. Your lawyer may remain in this country, and retain his license to practice here, only for the time it takes for your trial to be heard. Unfortunately, that trial would be in another court. Should it have come before this bench, and you were found to be guilty, I personally would see to it that you got the maximum term of *'free board and lodging'* regulations allow."

With very quiet efficiency, the policemen moved up to all the accused and handcuffed them. As they were led away, the senior of the two men who had pursued Chris so relentlessly, turned and shouted at Chris, "This is not the end of it Kennedy. I will come for you and kill you."

The judge hesitated in his leaving. "What's this!" he exclaimed, "Add a violent threat to kill to the list of charges."

Chris quietly sat down beside Norton. "Is it over," he softly asked. "When I went to Uni. to study mining, this was not part of the course. They only taught us about digging into good clean healthy dirt—not into stuff like this filth."

"All over," Norton answered, "and by the sound of it I do not think something like this will ever recur in this state again, thanks to you. That bloke who made that threat will go away for I believe about twenty years and will be deported the moment he steps from jail." Norton placed an arm across Chris's shoulder, he was smiling broadly. "How do I get to your fabulous Quo-Vadis? Since hearing all about it, I do want to see it."

"Nothing could be easier," Chris quickly replied. "Let me know when you want to come and I will have a private jet waiting for you and your family, if they want to come. I will book you into the Quo-Vadis Resort, and expect you to stay for an extended time. Not like a certain QC I know, there will be no charge."

Chris had kept Jackie well informed of all this, and she was waiting at Quo-Vadis Airport when his jet touched down. She could not contain her tears of happiness as she scolded him softly when she held him. "Please do not do that ever again," she whispered. "Yesterday I found two grey hairs."

# Chapter 11

It was that time of the year between the incessant cold sand-blown winds and the unmerciful heat of the Outback. Peter and Izzy had been visiting Chris and Jackie and after dinner they had sat discussing the progress of the station.

"We are shipping out another five-thousand prime steers next week," Peter had very proudly told Chris, and added "I have never seen cattle trucks, the likes of what are used here." He spoke with a touch of awe in his voice. "Those fellows who drive those monster six-trailer rigs amaze me. They roar into the cattle yard, unhooked their trailers, then one at a time back those trailers into position at the loading ramps, load up, and within three hours re-hook their six trailers, waved goodbye, then thunder off. Those water feeders you had built into the trailers enable them to make the two-day trip without stopping. They carry sufficient fuel, and drive day and night. Did you know they have three drivers in the prime mover so they can drive in four-hour shifts? Those prime movers are amazing. Your friend Ed sure can build a good unit. Fully air-conditioned, cookers, fridges, coffee machines—they are almost like a kitchen on wheels. It even has a sleeping compartment at the back of the cabin. I must do a trip with them one day. The stock is very well cared for. Ed has fitted cameras in each and every trailer, and the drivers can see if there is any animal in trouble. I was told if an animal is distressed or falls down it is the only time they stop and unload it, leave it a bail of fodder and a drum of water, and look for it on their return trip."

"You appear mighty happy with your lot, Peter," Chris commented.

"Happy?" Peter quickly replied. "Never been more content in my life. Those native stockmen are real winners. They are a pleasure to work with. They are a happy lot. Even Izzy is all but bursting with happiness. Hey! that was a funny thing to say in the circumstances. Did you know she is pregnant again; and could not be more content? What about you Chris? You have the whole of this huge Quo-Vadis complex so well set up, everything seems to run itself. It must be time for you to sit back and start enjoying the fruits of your labours."

"I'm glad you bought that up, Peter," Chris quietly responded. "There is much I wish to do yet. There is just so much out there," he waved his arm to encompass the Outback. When I first left Uni. I started out to see it all. Quo-Vadis interrupted that. Jackie and I have talked about that only just recently, and she is adamant that I should continue with my exploration. She did put a proviso on that, only if she was with me. She did question why I had to do this, saying I already had much more than many other men, and was very understanding when I did explain to her that I believed everybody has an addiction of some sort. Fortunately, it is not the dreadful addiction that Bill and Ellie talk about—it is more meaningful than that. Grab your drink and we will go and sit in the lounge room and I will tell you of my thinking. Jackie was quite surprised when I spoke to her of my thoughts. Mark you, they are my thoughts only, of people and their addictions. I had never been able to come to a satisfactory conclusion about addictions. How does one explain an addiction? Can they explain why that very rich man grasps every cent that comes his way? It is more than greed; it is built into his very being. And why does Penny paint? Why does Bill love his garden? Or an author writes? Why does a teacher teach, or a doctor strive to heal? Closer to home, why do cattlemen live to spend their lives herding cattle? It is easy to answer all this by simply saying it is their calling; their profession. In my own twisted way, I believe that is neither right nor wrong, and that their need goes deeper; so deep my limited mind cannot grasp the answer, and I will lie in my grave not knowing."

Jackie and Izzy had crept silently into the lounge room and sat quietly behind Chris and Peter. Unbeknown to Chris, they had heard all he had said. "He told me all of this just recently," Jackie whispered. "All I could answer him was that I admired his wisdom so very much and that there are things about him that I did not even know. You can perhaps see why I love him."

Chris had heard her whispering and quickly asked, "How long have you pair been there?" He appeared a little embarrassed that they had heard his discourse.

"Oh, quite a while, Mister Philosopher. Only long enough to hear all you have said," Jackie very proudly answered him.

"You have given me much to think about," Izzy softly said. I have to agree with you—there are many, many things that remain unanswered. Just to lighten up the conversation, has Peter told you I'm going to have another baby? You had better get to work Christopher Kennedy. I will be one ahead of my sister."

"Give me a break, Izzy," Chris laughed. "I do my best."

Chris renewed their drinks and they sat quietly just sipping and chatting. "I do need something from you Peter old chap," Chris seriously asked, "I require two or three of your best horses for riding and four sturdy pack horses. Don't include Mr Stallion— he hates me. Jackie and I have decided to look over the northern grazing lease; you know, that very big one that everybody says is worthless, and would not fatten a flea."

"Why horses?" Peter exclaimed. "Wouldn't you be better to take Goliath?"

"No," Chris exclaimed, "Not this time. I want to be able to feel the land. You cannot achieve that from the cabin of Goliath. Old Mallee, the native elder, has told me that until I have felt the land I will never know its secrets. We are only waiting to hear from my mother to see if she can come out to Quo-Vadis for a week or two or maybe more to look after Jack."

Izzy had not hesitated: "If your mother is not available I will have Jack with us; he and Josh are great mates."

"You are very game to take on two five-year-old boys at once. They will wreak havoc in your home," Jackie lightly said.

Izzy only laughed at that and replied, "Not if Peter puts Jack on a pony. Josh has his own pony you know. If they are true to form they would just disappear each morning and come home when they are hungry."

"Just like their fathers," Jackie giggled.

The weeks had flown past. Chris and Jackie had never enjoyed such a level of peace and harmony. Their relationship had always been the source of envy of many of those who knew them; now something new had entered their closeness. Together they had developed a great love for this harsh land—The Outback. Each day was now filled with exciting new discoveries, some as small as a coloured beetle, or as huge and spectacular as those magnificent Outback sunsets. The enjoyment they were finding in the sharing of their bodies had reached a proportion that belies description.

"You know Christopher John Kennedy," Jackie had whispered after a particularly fulfilling interlude, "I will most probably be well and truly pregnant by the time we get return to Quo-Vadis."

"Nothing would please me more," Chris had softly replied and added, "Regrettably, it is near time to head back."

Next morning, as they broke camp and were reloading the horses, a bright flash of the first rays of sunlight was reflected from the hillside about one-hundred meters ahead of them. That flash rested in his brain for a minute, only to be discarded with a rather angry retort, "It's probably only a reflection from a discarded can some uncaring bloke had nonchalantly tossed there. I'll pick it up as we go past and take it back with our rubbish."

As they rode toward the "discarded can," the morning sun was just rising.

Jackie cried loudly, "Look, Chris. The whole hillside is sparkling. Isn't it beautiful?"

"It's more than beautiful, Jackie girl," Chris nearly shouted, as he jumped from his horse and miners pick in hand and raced excitedly toward that glittering hillside. In a matter of a moment, he was hammering away at a rocky outcrop. He stood up and shouted triumphantly. He held a fist sized piece of grey rock he had dislodged for her to see. It sparkled in the sunlight. "This is a pegmatites reef Jackie girl. It will probably contain many beautiful gemstones. When I look at it more closely I believe it is heavily laden with spodumene crystals."

Jackie was caught up in his excitement. "That's all above me. Chris. You are so excited—I know it is important."

"Important!" Chris cried. "That's only half of it. Spodumene is a known source of lithium—you know, the mineral they use in the manufacture of those rechargeable power storage units, batteries and the like. It can be worth a fortune. This looks like a substantial deposit. We must get back as quickly as possible and try and find out if this area has ever been pegged. I know we hold the grazing lease, but that does not give us the right to mine."

"Do you really need more money, Chris?" Jackie asked with a concerned voice. "Your Empire is huge as it is."

"I take your point, Jackie my love," Chris quickly replied. "You remember I was talking about addiction the other night. This is exactly what I meant. I am a miner, and if there is something to mine, I must do it. Please understand."

"I will, my very clever mining man. I can see where you are coming from. Would you please help me down on this horse, and make sure our baby number two is on the way? You have got me so excited with your exuberance and enthusiasm, I must have you here and now, this very minute."

Without a moment of hesitation, and with a monstrous grin on his face, Chris complied with her request, and baby number two was definitely "on the way."

"You have your new mine, and after that, I am pretty sure I will have my new baby," Jackie sighed with contentment. They did not dally or let themselves get side-tracked further; consequently, it was only six days later they rode sedately into Quo-Vadis Station. With greetings and salutations out of the way, Chris waylaid Peter, and quietly asked, "How's your Internet connection? I need to look at some satellite pictures of a certain section of our grazing lease, and hopefully be able to identify something we have found."

"The Internet connection is fine," Peter replied quickly, and asked, "Anything interesting?"

"Yes, definitely, Peter," Chris replied, almost bursting with the need to share his discovery. "I think we have found a pretty good deposit of pegmatites—that's the ore that can generally contain spodumene, from which they extract lithium."

"Holy cow! Peter exclaimed. "That stuff is worth a fortune. Is it a mineable deposit?"

"I would have to prove it up, to be able to answer that. First thing I have to do is check out if it has been pegged—you know, if it is already held by somebody under a mining lease. I know it is covered by our grazing lease, but I do not think that authorises me to mine. Our grazing lease does prevent anybody from mining on it unless they have our permission; anybody wanting to mine there must first of all approach us, so I will be forewarned."

For the next two hours, much to the annoyance of the girls, Chris and Peter poured over satellite maps, and having been able to establish the exact location of the deposit, had set about searching mining leases that had been granted over it.

271

"This lease is one of the biggest of our grazing leases," Chris told Peter. "Sorting it all out is going to be a bit tricky. See these numbers here," he said, "they represent three separate mining leases that have been granted. I am going to have to negotiate with all three of them, and endeavour to purchase them from them. One of those people I have to negotiate with is a registered company in Singapore. To make things a little more complicated, the whole of the northern grazing lease is covered by native title. This is going to be fun," he rather sarcastically said to Peter, who had been watching him as he worked.

"It's like you said, my super-smart brother-in-law, I see now what you meant: you are the miner, and I am just a cattleman, who would not have a clue as to how to go about all that you are talking about."

"The first thing I have to do is to see which group of the people were granted the title."

That was as far as he got that day, as Jackie and Izzy pushed their way into Peter's office.

"It's time you pair stopped playing games on the computer, and spend a little time with us," Jackie said, but her curiosity got the better of her, as she then enquired, "How did it go, my man? Is it a goer?"

"It is going to take a lot of work before I can answer that, Jackie girl. You may have to put up with me being a little distracted for a few days."

"Your plane is here," Peter's number two called. "Hop on the wagon and I'll run you out to the airstrip.

"Keep in touch," Peter said as Jackie and Chris strolled arm in arm out to the SUV.

"Jackie is looking so very well," Izzy softly said to Peter. "Perhaps we should do exactly what they have been doing and spend a couple weeks doing nothing but wander through the

Outback. Jackie said a strange thing; she said she has come to love this wonderful land."

On the short flight back to Quo-Vadis, Chris explained all he had found out about the pegmatites deposit. "First thing tomorrow, I will go out to the native camp and find out from the elder, Marlee, who are those native people who hold the native title. I have found a name of a tribe. I have written it down, as I have no hope of pronouncing it."

Once again providence smiled upon him. After several attempts at pronouncing the name of the tribe to a very amused elder, once he had got over a laughing session, old Marlee, simply said, "I think you are trying to say," and rattled off a comprehensive native title. "That's us. There are not many of us left. There is another camp out there; they and us are all that's left."

Chris did not hesitate, and told the elder what he had found, and his wishes and plans to investigate the possibility of a mine on their land. To do this he would need their permission.

"Have you found gold, Mr Boss Chris?" Marlee asked.

"No, not gold this time," Chris answered. "I do not know yet if what I have found is even worthwhile exploring. I do need that permission to even start exploring and conduct a survey."

The old native elder thought for a while, then softly said, "I will talk to our people, and go and talk to the other mob, and let them all know what it is you request. I will let you know later what they all think."

"Later!" Chris sadly thought. "That could be a few days or a few months. I will have to be patient. One good thing about having to slow down for a while it will give me a chance to talk it over with Bill."

When Chris mentioned pegmatites and spodumene to Bill, all Bill answered was, "Getting a bit fancy now, mate. I never heard of any deposits of that stuff in this area. There are a couple of big mines operating down south. Before we get into it too deep, it will possibly pay for us to duck down there and have a *bo-peep* at their set up."

Several days later and after many hours of research, and a handful of telephone calls, Chris, Bill, and now Jack, who was home on school holidays, and grasped every minute he could to be with his dad and uncle Bill, especially if they were doing something special, were heading down south to one of the mines.

As they approached the mine site, Chris growled to Bill, "Look at all that processing plant and machinery. It will not be a cheap exercise to set up and get underway," and called to the pilot, "Would you be able to do a circuit or two over the mine site, Bruce? Have that nose camera I had fitted running as we make the circuit. It will help us to look at things later."

A mine boss, whose name he said was, "Geoffrey, Geoffrey, Jeffries" was a little nonchalant and offhanded at first. Then, after establishing these blokes were not on a tourist jaunt, he proudly took them on a comprehensive tour of the whole set up. He liked the look of these fellows, especially since the questions they asked were intelligent and seeking.

After the tour, and back in his office, over a cup of tea he confidentially told them, "I am not sure how much longer the mine in its present form would continue to operate. The production level is above expectations, but interest on the borrowings to fund the cost of the initial setting up and associated expenses, are bleeding the company's cash reserves dry," and added almost philosophically, "I may be looking for a job myself before too long."

Bill only winked at Chris, with what was a knowing look on his ugly countenance.

The flight back to Quo-Vadis was filled with much discussion. "Can you fund a set up like that, Chris?" Bill asked.

"If I find the deposit is sustainable, I will not hesitate," Chris replied. "You will only have to push the boys in the 'animal mine' to lift production, and if it becomes necessary, we can always lift the mine on the escarpment into full production. The people from the mint are always asking whether we can supply more. It appears those ingots you produce are so perfect they can virtually on-sell them without having to process them in any way."

"Later" turned out to be two weeks, before Marlee hesitantly knocked on the door of Chris's office and said. "I am very uncomfortable here, Boss Chris. I do not like it. It is the land of The Eulooway. I do have a reply to your request."

Chris did not hesitate and quickly said, "Go back to your camp my friend. I will come to you as the sun rises in the morning. I will have a helicopter take you home straight away.

The sun was just rising as one of the swift helicopters from the Quo-Vadis Station fleet settled down about one-hundred metres from the native camp. A handful of children rushed up to see what it was doing here. Chris jumped out and grabbed one boy and shouted, "I have come to catch you all and EAT YOU," as he placed the laughing boy inside the helicopter, and laughed as he shouted, "WHO ELSE WANTS TO BE EATEN UP."

"Me! Me! Me!" He was assailed by a multitude of young voices. The children all knew, Boss Chris loved to joke. He grabbed two of the jumping kids and poked them into the open door of the chopper, then reached for the other exuberant kids who had at great game just keeping out of his reach. Eventually he shouted, "All right you mob, into the chopper," and leaning over the front seat quickly and quietly said to the pilot, "Take them for a quick spin Bruce. See if you can scare the devil out of them. Come back for me in about twenty minutes."

Old Marlee had stood watching all this, and quietly said, "You are a good man, Boss Chris. The children think you are *plurry beaut.* Come to the camp and we'll talk. Two elders from the other mob are here and wish to listen to what you have to say."

The native elders all knew of Boss Chris and listened intensely to all he said.

"It is good you are honest with us Boss Chris," one elder very firmly said. "You do not hide anything and you say you have not taken the liberty of exploring without our permission, and do not know if the mine is even worthwhile but are prepared to spend time and money to see if there is anything there. You have said if it is a 'good thing' you would like to start mining, and that it will cost much money. Our people have to do very little, only to give you our permission. That land you speak of we know well. It is forbidden to us. It is a place of evil spirits. You are a man of great courage, Boss Chris, we can only believe you are ABDIEL, in our language that means, BEING A FAITHFUL SERVANT OF GOD. That is good. Marlee speaks to us of all you have done and we can clearly see, and believe your spirit is very powerful. You have also told us that if the mine does make any money you will give the people ten percent of that, and after building costs are repaid you will increase that amount to fifteen percent. Will that be much money?"

"I can only hope so," Chris earnestly replied, and added, "I would be most happy if you would talk with the White Folk lawmakers and have them read the agreement I will have prepared for you to mark and seal all this we have spoken of."

The chopper had returned, and the group of laughing children poured into the meeting. Each one was devouring a chocolate covered ice cream cone. "I see you found my stock in the chopper fridge," Chris laughed. He had stocked that fridge, simply because he knew the kids loved chocolate-coated ice-cream, and it was a certainty he would run into a few of them.

"You are a great favourite with our people, Abdiel Boss Chris," one of the elders said with a laugh. "We will help you all we can."

Jackie only smiled as he related to her the outcome of his visit to the native camp, and softly said, "I know someone else you are a great favourite with, Mister," and kissed him deeply.

The very expensive firm of lawyers had prepared a comprehensive document. It was 168 pages of legalese and complexity.

"Hells Bells!" Chris cried. "The native people will not understand this. I hope they get some good advice from somewhere."

He handed the document to Marlee with a sincere apology saying, "Please take this to your lawman and have him speak to you of what all these words say."

Marlee had only replaced the documents into the large envelope and said, "It will be done as you say, Abdiel Boss Chris."

Ten days later, Chris received a satellite phone call from Vanessa at the tourist park. "Chris," she said, "there is a fine specimen of the native people here asking to be taken out to Abdiel Boss Chris at Quo-Vadis. He says he is a lawyer for the people."

"Thanks Vanessa. I have been waiting for him. Please make sure he is very well looked after and send him out in my own personal jet as quickly as possible. A native you say?"

"Yes Chris," Vanessa replied. "He's a very fine, up-right looking fellow; speaks very well indeed."

An hour-and-a-half later, Chris and Jackie drove Goliath out to the airstrip. His jet was just arriving. The only passenger stepped briskly out.

"Vanessa was not kidding when she said he is a fine-looking fellow," Chris softly said to Jackie.

The man walking towards them was well over six-feet tall, slim and loose limbed, immaculately clad, and moved with an easy grace. Chris did not hesitate and stepped forward, hand extended and shook the man's hand that had been extended in return.

"Welcome to Quo-Vadis, sir. I am Chris Kennedy. I understand you wish to see me?"

"Thank you for your welcome, Mr Kennedy," the man replied. "Yes, I am here to discuss with you the matter of your need to explore and possibly mine on the people's land. I am Matari, or if you prefer Mathew, Matthew Blackstone. I have been engaged by the people to advise them in this matter. May I say, I have done much research about you and Quo-Vadis Holdings. I find now that the information available does not do justice to what I am seeing."

"Thank you, Matthew. May I introduce my wife, Jackie; she shares my great interest in your people and was with me when we found the pegmatites reef. That's the reef I am hopeful we will find worthwhile developing."

Matthew offered Jackie his hand, saying, "Ah, yes, Abdiel Boss Chris's woman. The people talk much about you. I have to say, you have made this part of our land into a beautiful place. It is forbidden to us. That is why it was excluded from the initial native title claim. The forbidden lands encompass the whole of the escarpment to a fifty-two-kilometre perimeter boundary. Stories from the Dreamtime tell of a tribe of the people who ignored the warnings and had climbed down the face of the cliff and set up a camp down there. The stories tell that only one man came back. He told of the dreadful things which had happened to the people. So, for an unknown number of years, not one of our people had dared to enter the sinkhole. The elders now speak confidently that they enter the forbidden lands without fear, understanding they are protected by the spirit of Abdiel Boss Chris. That makes you a very powerful man in their eyes Mr Kennedy."

"Please call me Chris, Matthew," Chris quietly said. "I am really a pretty ordinary bloke, who is blessed enough to be in the right place at the right time."

"Don't believe a word of that," Jackie lightly interrupted. "He really is something special." Matthew only laughed at that and said, "Your love for him shines from you Jackie."

"Enough of all this," Chris snapped. "Let's go to the house, have a cup of tea, and talk about what Matthew is here for. I am expecting it to take at least two days to cover everything, and perhaps later we can make a little time so I can show Matthew over Quo-Vadis."

The two men did spend the next two days discussing the application to mine and its conditions and implications. The outcome was all but a foregone conclusion from the outset, save for one or two sticking points. The elders of both groups had vehemently insisted that nothing was to be paid to them until and if and when the mine went into actual production. Chris held to the thought that he was morally obliged to compensate the people right from the start. He argued that once he had been granted the right to mine on their land, there was nothing to prevent him from selling that right to another miner without having done one thing further with what the people had granted him.

Matthew put an end to the conflicting point by simply adding a clause which precluded any other party from developing the deposit. Chris had suggested that while Matthew was making that amendment to the document he add a further clause that said that all monies held on behalf of the community by Quo-Vadis Holdings was to earn four-percent per annum interest, payable monthly on the first of the following month on the maximum balance held during the previous month. The elders also demanded that none of that money held could be used for any other purpose, other than payment for the cost of education of any of the known and recorded children of the people, or for meeting the costs of any special medical needs of the people.

"I will leave all this accounting to my brother, Rex," Chris said. "I think we should make a note that his company, Kennedy and Dixon, be appointed accountants for the people. They have a department that solely handles the affairs of the Quo-Vadis group."

"This is all very satisfactory," Matthew said, addressing Chris. "I know the elders have already discussed Abdiel Boss Chris's request with the people and two days from today they are all to meet and sign or put their mark on the agreement. You will be required to be the first signature on the documents. I should warn you Chris," he said with a sparkle in his eyes, "you should be prepared, a gathering like this does always require to be part of one huge corroboree that will last all day."

By sundown the next day, the agreement had been danced to, and signed and sealed by every member of both groups. Their signatures had been duly witnessed by one of the High Court judges, Chris had previously met, and had flown in especially for the purpose. The High Court judge had, upon Chris's invitation, bought his wife and four children with him. They stayed at the resort for over two weeks.

"It has been amazing how Matthew had organised all this," Chris told Jackie with a note of admiration in his voice. "He is one smart lad, that Matthew. The judge tells me, Matthew is highly respected and is very experienced, having won many cases in his court relating to the Native's Titles Act."

With the Judge and his family and Matthew having departed, and as they lay contentedly in their bed, Jackie whispered softly, as she snuggled a little closer, "There is another matter you must be told of my man. The daughter of Abdiel Boss

Chris has made her presence known. She will be with us in about eight months."

"You mean we did it?! You are definitely pregnant?" Chris cried.

"Yes, I am very sure. I think it happened at the time when we discovered the pegmatites reef. Do you remember?" Jackie happily asked him.

"I remember the occasion very clearly," Chris answered, and then rather enthusiastically whispered, "Is it too late to do it again right now?"

"If you think for one minute I am going to forego my greatest pleasure, just because I am pregnant," Jackie giggled, "think again, Mister, and come here right now."

Chris was a very happy man, things were working out extremely well. "Now the thing I have to do next," he thought, "is to contact those three existing mining lease holders and try and buy them out. That company in Singapore may hold things up a bit."

The office of the Department of Mining in the regional city were able to provide him with some details of the leaseholders, including a contact number for the Singaporean holder. It listed a number in the big smoke. "I will pursue acquisition of that lease first," he thought. It was not all that easy as he had to make several telephone calls before he received an answer. The telephone was eventually answered by a heavily Asian-accented fellow who was unable to assist Chris with his enquiry. He did inform Chris, "That Mr Tay-Chan was a property developer and to his knowledge his employer had no interest in mining"; however, he did give Chris a further telephone number in Jargon in Singapore, the head office of the company. Chris immediately followed up that information, and after fifteen minutes of being transferred from one department to another he was finally transferred to a European voice.

"Mr Kennedy, is it? I am James Henderson. I am the head of Tay-Chan Australia. I am told you wish to discuss a mining lease registered to Tay-Chan Australia."

"That's correct," Chris replied.

"I do regret to have to advise you, Mr Kennedy, I have no knowledge of any such mining lease," Jamerson said. "Mr Tay-Chan is busy at the moment; when he is free I will enquire of him for you and call you back with his reply."

"Thank you, Mr Henderson," Chris quietly said, and before he could say any more the line went dead. "Looks like I will have to practice being patient once again," Chris thought to himself. Still deep in thought he decided while he was waiting he would pursue the other two lease holders. He had little difficulty in arranging the purchase of those two leases.

They were held by an old prospector and his son-in-law, who fortunately lived in the Regional City. Chris visited the old prospector who enquired, "Why are you interested in this flea-bitten bit of dirt, Mr Kennedy? We have checked it over. There is no gold on it."

"Your mining leases form a section of our grazing lease," Chris quite correctly said. "I want to try and remove any possibility of the area being mined at a later date."

"They are useless to us," the old prospector said. "With them being covered by a native title, it is impossible to do anything much with them. What are you offering?"

"They constitute a very large area of almost known useless land. Would $10,000 each sound okay to you?" Chris said with his tongue in his cheek, and thought to himself, "After all, I am not even sure they are worth anything myself."

"That's twenty-grand better off in my pocket than a couple of pieces of worthless paper. I will agree to that," the old fellow said, and shook Chris's hand.

"Thank you, for that, sir. I will have some documents prepared and have them ready for your signature in a day or two," Chris quietly said.

"Two down; only the messy one left to sort out," Chris thought.

Bill had spent a lot of time studying the processing of pegmatites to extract the spodumene crystals.

"Good grief, Chris!" he complained. "It is nothing like processing ore for gold. Setting up the processing plant will cost a small fortune. I envisage the plant alone will cost about two-hundred million dollars, may be even as much as two-twenty. That's using the best equipment available. Top engineers to install it, and maintenance workshops, and mining machinery will set you back a few shillings more, if you get out of it for under three-hundred million I will be surprised."

"That cost will be spread over the next twelve months, I reckon," Chris said, and thought deeply for a moment. "Okay," he said as if resolving a major problem, "It is time to increase our gold output; we will start to mine that section of the reef Tom found on the escarpment and put it into full production. In addition, we will strip the overburden off that other section of the reef that Tom had found was only twenty metres down. I will have Ed build eight or more thirty-cubic-metre trolleys, and prime movers to haul the ore to an enlarged chute running from the surface of the escarpment down to the crushers. That's a bit more expense; fortunately, we have enough machinery about here for us to accomplish that. Will your crushers and smelters be able to handle this increase in ore we will be feeding them?"

Bill did not hesitate for one moment, and quickly said, "When you bought all those crushers and smelters, I did wonder if we would ever use them to capacity. I am very confident they will handle whatever you load onto them. You had better warn the people at the mint of your intentions."

"I will ask Rex to prepare a forward projection of our costs and seek his advice," Chris very seriously said. "I am quite sure with careful planning I can handle all this, although it is a little bit scary. If we proceed with this spodumene venture and it turns out to be a bummer I will be hurt badly, but I don't think it will actually kill me."

"Have you got all the lease bit cleaned up with that bloke from Singapore, Mister Miner?" Bill asked and thinking further added. "All this research and calculating will have been a waste of time if that bloke does not come to the party."

"I believe I'll have an answer to that question sometime tomorrow," Chris replied. "I am expecting a call from his Australian manager then. It does appear that that bloke, Tay-Chan, is the only one who has any idea that his company actually holds that lease."

He did receive a call from Singapore later that day, and a soft female Chinese voice softly asked, "Is Mr Christopher Kennedy available?"

"Christopher Kennedy speaking, miss," Chris swiftly replied.

"Thank you, Mr Kennedy. Would you kindly hold for Mr Tay-Chan," the caller purred.

There were a few clicks, a slight delay, then a deep voice spoke, "Lee Tay-Chan speaking, Mr Kennedy. I am told you are inquiring about a lease I hold over some nebulous piece land in Central Australia. I have never seen that land. I had forgotten about it. What is your interest in it?"

"I have the grazing rights for a good portion of that lease, sir," Chris respectfully said, "and I wish to run a herd of cattle there. I am a little concerned that should you wish to start mining there I will have to move those cattle. You know of course you cannot start mining without my permission or the permission of the natives who were granted rights to it under the Native Title Act."

There was a slight pause—Chris thought the line had been disconnected—then Tay-Chan came back on. "James Henderson, my Australian manager, is here with me, Mr Kennedy. He tells me what you say is absolutely correct. I came by that lease seven or eight years ago, a client of mine had defaulted on payment for a small block of apartments we had built for him. That lease came to us as part of the settlement when I wound him up. Like I said, I have forgotten all about it. Do you propose to start mining it? Have you found it contains gold?" Tay-Chan abruptly enquired.

"That is to be seen," Chris replied equally abruptly. "Like I said, I do wish to ensure undisturbed grazing rights. The cost to set up a mining venture out there would be a major risk. It is an unproven area and any expenditure would require much consideration. I have searched and have found no exploration reports. It would be foolish to even commence thinking of mining the area without a comprehensive study. Do you have any reports?"

"No, not at all. I have not given the area a second thought since it came into my possession," Tay-Chan answered. Then, without hesitation, asked, "How much are you offering?"

"How much would you consider to be a fair price, sir?" Chris nonchalantly asked.

"It is a very big area, and there is still a debt sitting on those apartments. I would consider selling it to you for five-million Australian dollars."

"That is ridiculous," Chris snapped. "It is useless to you or anybody else while I have the grazing rights. Your mining lease does not affect those grazing rights. I can continue to graze there. Fifty-thousand dollars is all I am offering."

"That is a long way from my price, Mr Kennedy. I believe we have no chance of a deal," Tay-Chan rather softly said.

"That's fine by me," Chris sharply replied. "I only pursued the possibility, thinking to round off the leases I hold for the area and to ensure any attempt by a mining company to even investigate the area could be deferred without any further dispute. I will never, and I repeat, never diminish my grazing rights."

"You are a very forceful and positive man, Mr Kennedy," Tay-Chan said, again using that very soft deep persuasive voice. "I can see something is better than the nothing I already have. Would one-hundred thousand keep your interest?"

"Still too much to pay for a whim, sir. Try seventy-five-thousand. Take it or leave it," Chris very strongly answered.

"It is very clear to me, Mr Kennedy, that you have spent a deal of time in our markets," Tay Chan laughed. "You have acquired a high level of bargaining skill. Seventy-five-thousand Australian dollars it is. You carry all the costs for document preparation and statutory registration. You appreciate that with the whole area being subject to a Native Title it will always be impossible to do anything but graze that land." Then almost gloating, added, "you have made a bad bargain Mr Kennedy."

"That is to be seen Sir," Chris replied without hesitation. "My solicitors will provide you with a copy of the proposed agreement at a very early date," and was about to discontinue the call, when Tay-Chan interrupted saying, "You sound to be a very interesting person, Mr Kennedy. I would like to meet you. Would you personally deliver the documents and we can sign them together?"

"Like you said, sir," Chris replied, "although I am a very busy man, I would like to meet you, and will deliver the documents myself. Would you object should my lawyer accompany me?"

"You are a very wise young man," Tay Chan said. "I have no objections to your lawyer being present. I am assuming we will have the opportunity to peruse a copy of the agreement before we actually finalise the deal."

"Yes, that is to be expected and will present no problem. Goodbye for now," Chris sharply said and disconnected the call. Chris had placed the call on the speakerphone, and Bill had sat listening to all this.

"Bargaining in a Chinese market. That would be right. You sure have plenty of guts young fellow. You are looking at spending around $300 million and you nonchalantly argue over $25,000," Bill chuckled.

Chris laughed with him, and said, "More like bull-dusting in the main bar at the pub. First things first," Chris quietly said to Bill, "I will have to get Tom and a drilling rig out to the reef. The mining leases I bought from the old prospector cover a good patch. We will have to work within that until we stitch up that Tay-Chan bloke. It will take a few days to get the rig out there. There are no roads, and with a bit of luck we will be able to avoid any soft spots. I will lead the way in Goliath. Would you be okay to follow along behind the rig in a big loader, just in case we do strike any trouble? Tom tells me his big rig is out at the station, drilling for water.

"That's helpful; that's part of the way out to the reef."

After eight long, hard days, the rig was finally in position over the reef and had drawn up the first core samples from twenty metres. Chris had been able to leave the drilling to Tom and Bill. Bill had studied the sample intently, and after sniffing it for a minute, said, "It's good. Would you now get me a core from one-hundred metres?"

"No worries, old fruit," Tom cheekily said.

"I'll old fruit you, you bent banana," Bill chuckled in response. "Just get me my samples."

He used the satellite telephone to let Chris know of their progress.

"I'll grab a chopper and be out there first thing tomorrow morning. Jackie will let me know if Tay-Chan calls," Chris replied.

Upon his arrival at the rig the next morning, Chris could not sit around doing nothing while he waited for the rig to draw up the hundred-metre-deep sample. He commandeered the loader which had not been committed to any particular task, and commenced to strip the overburden from the reef, starting from that exposed outcrop Jackie had discovered, and he nostalgically thought, "It was there her baby had been conceived." He studiously worked to push that overburden from the reef.

He had worked for about two hours and had uncovered about thirty square metres when Bill jumped up on the running board of the loader shouting, "You have done it again! Good Grief man! You have found something that belies explanation. Tom is still pulling up good samples from over four-hundred metres. The reef is not showing any signs of bottoming."

"Take him down to five-hundred; then, if there is no bottom, pull him out and set him up again over here." Chris had shouted over the roar of that big Cat motor.

"Will do!" Bill excitedly exclaimed. "Will you be here?"

"No. Would you please take over here and cut a trench about ten metres wide to a depth of say five meters. Stockpile what you dig out. We will take it back and run it through your crushers. I will be in Goliath. I am going to park on top of that bit of a hill, away from all this racket and ring the professors and try and get them out here. I think we need better brains than ours to look at this. I would like to be able to establish a rough measurement of what sort of a yield we can expect. It looks all too good to be true at the moment. I do want to contact Rex to see if he has heard from Tay-Chan. I believe the documents may be ready by now, and I do want to see them signed and registered before we do too much more out here."

Chris and Bill loaded Goliath from that stockpile of pegmatites ore, gave Tom instructions of where and how deep he should drill, and headed back to Quo-Vadis. The trip back took four days. Jackie, naturally enough, was very pleased to see him and asked a never-ending stream of questions, which he tried to answer between kisses of welcome.

He was able to ask a question of his own. "Have you heard from our Singaporean friend?"

To which Jackie answered, "No, I was talking to Rex last night and he has suggested we ring him. He has had plenty of time to go through the copies Rex sent him."

Chris did immediately call Rex; who laughed as he said; "Chris! Your timing is spot on; I have only just a minute ago received a call from Tay- Chan's office and an appointment has been made for two days hence. "It's like I said to Jackie, he has had plenty of time, and has either been making a parcel of alterations, or just playing you like a fish, waiting to see how important you considered the matter and how long you would wait before your patience gave out, and you would call him. I see him to be a very slippery character, and I think we should take our friend from the law firm with us."

"Thank you, brother," Chris said. "I agree with you and will go along with everything you say."

When the trio—Chris, Rex, and Norton; that very senior lawyer—arrived at the offices of Tay-Chan Developments two days later they were immediately shown straight into Tay-Chan. The offices of the development company were not large, but very functional.

"Not bad for a building developer," Rex whispered to Chris. "There are a lot of staff; they all appear busy."

Tay-Chan sat at a large well-ordered desk. Two suits sat on one side.

"You are very punctual, Mr Kennedy," he complimented Chris.

After quickly completing all the introductions to his suits, Tay-Chan sat back in his chair with a self-satisfied smirk on his face and loudly said, "Mr Kennedy, I have read through the copies of your document. They have been prepared in a most professional manner. I will be happy to sign my side of the agreement only if you agree to one small alteration."

"Here it comes," Rex very quietly whispered to Chris, whose anger level had apparently started to rise.

Tay-Chan was continuing. "I have increased the sale price to AU$250,000."

The amount did not worry Chris, but the flagrant breach of principle irked him. To Chris, a deal was a deal—not something to be altered without mutual agreement. Chris controlled his anger, stood and turned to Rex saying, "We are out of here brother, and Mr Tay-Chan, you can stick the whole deal up your arse."

"What are you saying, Mr Kennedy? Are you saying you will not agree?" Tay-Chan quizzically asked.

"I am," Chris very softly said, his voice was loaded with venom. "I am accustomed to dealing with honourable men—not men who wallow in skulduggery and cheating. You have had over one week to advise us of your proposed alteration, but, NO!" Chris shouted, "you wait until the last moment when in your contorted way of thinking, by having me here and to quickly finalise the deal, I would just accept the alteration without question. NO SIR, I WILL NOT!" Chris had continued to shout, "Now my brother and I and my solicitor will leave you, and you will be stuck with a block of land I will control for now and ever. You will never be able to dispose of it for any gain whatsoever, without my permission. To get that permission will cost you much more than the AU$75,000 we had agreed upon. Please do not try and contact us, we will not accept your calls."

The two suits quickly stepped up and stood before Tay-Chan and started prattling in some Asian language. After several minutes one of those suits looked hard at Chris and threw his hands in the air in apparent surrender, and said, "Mr Kennedy please be seated; we understand your anger. Mr Tay-Chan does wish to address you further—may he?"

"He has one minute," Chris, not sitting, very fiercely said.

Tay-Chan rose and stepped before Chris. He had an enormous genuine smile on his face. "Mr Christopher Kennedy," he said quite formally. "In my many years of business I have never met a man so resolute and strong and may I add, as honest. You have very firmly said, "Take this deal as we discussed, or I will take it with me to my grave." If you will be good enough to allow, I will sign that lease over to you now."

"Thank you, sir," Chris said. "It does please me to find that my time has not been wasted. We have our own copies of the document; it is those we will ask you to sign. They are precisely the same as the documents that were sent to you. My people tell me these documents have been drafted most comprehensively and have no loopholes for either of us."

"You are an extremely careful man, Mr Kennedy; that is good," Tay-Chan said as he signed the documents Rex had presented to him, and handed them to Chris saying, "How do you Aussies say it? I do not ever want to hear of a 'bloody' mining lease ever again."

"That is totally up to you. I am sure you can advise your own people of this," Chris snarled. "I had arranged to take you to lunch. In my present frame of mind, I would not be good company, so if you will excuse us, we will leave now."

"What time is your flight?" Tay-Chan asked. "Perhaps we may take a minute and share a cup of coffee?"

"My flight leaves immediately I arrive at the airport," Chris replied.

"Do you have your own aircraft?" Tay-Chan gasped.

"Yes," Chris said by way of reply. "I have four or five at the last count."

Tay-Chan laughed a genuine laugh, and promptly said, "It looks like I should have hung out for much more."

"It is well you didn't," Chris chuckled. "Had I been put in a position to have to reconsider the deal, my next offer would have been considerably less."

The three men sat in the taxi on the way back to the airport. Rex laughed loudly, and said, "I have never seen you angry before, brother; you are quite frightening."

Chris only gave a deep chuckle to that comment, and said, "I was not angry, Rex; it was all an act on my part. I have forgotten how to get really angry. If we get back in time, do you think you can get those documents registered today? I do not trust Tay-Chan. The sooner we can get all this well and truly tied down the happier I will be. Where are those documents by the way?" Chris asked.

"Haven't you got them?" Rex quickly asked. "Don't tell me you left them with Tay-Chan?"

"Oh! stuff it," Chris cried, and yelled to the taxi driver, "Take us back to Tay-Chan's as quickly as you can, please."

Rex burst into a spasm of laughing and only managed to splutter, "Keep your shirt on mate; they are all here, safe and sound in my briefcase."

"If I didn't know better, I would call you, a rotten bastard Rex; you darn near gave me a heart attack," Chris laughed.

Fifteen minutes before closing time, Rex's legal team registered the lease in the name of Quo-Vadis Holdings.

"I will change that to Quo-Vadis Lithium as soon as you can get that name registered. I want to keep all the accounts separate if possible," he told Rex, then added lightly, "Have I got five-hundred-million dollars lying about? I am going to need it."

"That's a big bite, Chris. Our forward projection does show you will accumulate around that much in fourteen to fifteen months; in the meantime, your cash flow, on your present production will give you about thirty-five million a month."

"Bill and I have discussed doubling our output," Chris slowly said. "So, on those figures, we will be able to fund the development of the mine. I will have to stop buying aeroplanes."

"The mining lecturers from the University, Professors Strahan and Riley, who were now good friends of Chris and Jackie did not hesitate to grab Chris's invite to Quo-Vadis, especially when the invite was flavoured by Chris's statement that he had something special and rather interesting he would like them to look at. They had found their visits to Quo-Vadis stimulating, and always, even those very learned men, returned edified in some way.

The spodumene project was nonetheless exciting for them. They spent several days either walking back and forth over the area from which Chris had had the overburden removed, examining the drill cores Tom bought to them under a very high-powered microscope or wandering at large over the surrounding Outback. Chris had already installed a hard-packed earth airstrip, and despite his comment to stop buying aeroplanes, had purchased another aircraft that was more suited to this type of work rather than use the private CL300 jets of his passenger fleet.

The professors had been at the new mine site for a week. On the evening, of their return, as the meal was finished, and the two ever-helpful girls had cleared away, the professors, Chris, Jackie, Peter and Bill sat dallying over a coffee.

Strahan started the conversation without hesitation saying, "Your deposit is most interesting. It is extremely rich in crystals—predominantly spodumene. Our sampling, if we bring it down to layman's language, is generally around 7.3% spodumene per tonne of pegmatites. By industry standards, that's a very rich load." Strahan paused for a moment to take a sip of his QSV brandy one of the girls had placed beside him. "Thank you, I needed that," he chuckled. "This next bit is most interesting," he continued. "We have been able to ascertain the crystals contain Lithium at an average of 9. Should this be so, I have to tell you, there is no other deposit in the world that has figures as high as that. We will take a sample back to the University with us and conduct further tests under laboratory conditions to confirm these figures," then looking at Chris asked, "Have you proven up the extent of the deposit yet, Chris?"

"No, sir," Chris replied. "All we have found so far is that the pegmatites sheet is an average thickness of, would you believe, five hundred and forty meters. To date we have only established, by diamond drilling, it is at least twelve kilometres wide. Lord only knows how long. The drill is twenty-eight kilometres from the first hole in one direction and continuing on, we have gone two kilometres in the opposite direction. The thickness has remained about the five-hundred meters. Some holes are a little thinner; others a bit thicker. Tom our driller wants to go deeper; he reckons since this is known to be part of the artesian basin, there may be water down there. I hope so. From what I have learned this evening I know I have a decision to make," and looking softly at Jackie said, "What do you think my love? Do I go ahead and mine this deposit?"

"What else are you going to do Christopher Kennedy? I suppose you could stay home and make babies," Jackie chuckled.

"Oh, hell and damnation," Bill cried as he jumped up in alarm, "There is no decision to be made. You have been told this is a full on economic proposition; all we need is a few expensive machines, some smart fellows to put them together, and a bloody big stepladder so Chris can reach the top of the pile of dollars he will make. I checked the price of spodumene concentrate this morning; it is worth around seven-hundred dollars a tonne. At the professors' figures, 100,000 tonnes of pegmatites with the yield of 7% spodumene gives us 7000 tonnes of concentrate, or, if my maths is correct, that's over half one-million bucks. With the machinery we have talked about buying we can easily process 2 to 250,000 tonnes of pegmatites a week." Bill took a large gulp of his drink mumbling something to Jackie who sat next to him, which sounded like, "The only problem I see is how the hell you pair are going to spend it."

"That's easy," Jackie whispered back, "I do need a new dress or two."

Chris pushed back his chair and, addressing the professors, said, "Thank you, gentlemen," then rather resolutely added, "There will be much to do before we are up and running with this. Bill, I do not want to use you too much more; you have enough to do looking after Quo-Vadis gold. Peter is fully occupied with the station; Jackie and I, I am told, have a heavy schedule ahead, with Jack now ensconced in that live-in college in the big smoke and with our new edition not due for six months, this woman," he growled pointing an accusing finger at Jackie, "has booked us onto a world cruise. I had to agree to it or have my love life modified."

"Ouch," Riley laughed.

Bill leaned forward a little, resting his elbows on the table. He plainly had something he wanted to say. "Chris, what do you think of the idea, of contacting that bloke on the spodumene mine we visited down south?" he asked. "You know the bloke with a funny name. He struck me as a 'good-un', who knew his job. Perhaps we can get him interested in joining us."

"That's a very good thought, Bill," Chris replied. "Tomorrow you and I will duck down there and have a yarn to him; perhaps he will know some good engineers who can help us set up the plant. They would know if there is any better equipment than what we are looking at, and where to get it from. If that manager will 'come on' board it will be a good start."

The trip down south the next morning proved most fruitful for Bill and Chris. After quickly perusing the professors' figures, all Geoffrey exclaimed was, "My Goodness Gracious, Chris, these figures are remarkable! You say they were prepared by two senior University mining lecturers; on the strength of these figures, I can see a wonderful project ahead. I would love to be part of it. You can definitely count me in. Did I hear it correctly when you said you have no need to embark on raising the capital, and that you were going to fund it, in its entirety, yourself. That almost belies belief and does avoid the major problem that this project has always had. When do you want me to start? I have been told to finish up here; would next week be too early?" he asked.

Chris had only smiled at the exuberance of his discourse, and replied, "If you can start next week that would be okay, unless of course, you could make it earlier. Let me know exactly when you are ready and I will send an aircraft to pick you up."

"He does not muck about does he, Bill?" Geoffrey chuckled.

Chris and Bill returned to Quo-Vadis that afternoon. On the flight back, they examined many of the specifications of the array of machines available for what they were planning to do. They had pondered over a comprehensive diagram the professors had prepared. The diagram and notes appended set out the processes involved. Rather nonchalantly, Chris said, almost as if he was speaking his mind out loud, whispered, "We're going to need a whole lot of water to be able to operate effectively. Tom had better get that new big rig of his out to the site straightaway. I will go out to the site first thing in the morning and select exactly where I want him to drill. Jackie will want to come with me; she says she has many fond memories of our time out there and would like to see what is happening."

Bill had been taking notes as they looked over the diagrams and softly said, "I think I can see a couple of places where we can add some different things to improve even this."

"Go for it, Bill," Chris had replied. "I know whatever you suggest will be for the best."

Two days had passed before the two friends met again in Chris's office. "I have been trying to establish exactly where we are at," Chris told Bill. "The way I see it we, have moved forward very well and have overcome most of the earlier matters that were presenting problems. This is what I have ascertained we have accomplished. Firstly, we had to confirm that the pegmatites deposit was viable. We have done that. That deposit is definitely viable. Secondly, we have found somebody with experience to help us set up and run the operation. Geoffrey has filled that space very well indeed. Thirdly, with Geoffrey Geoffrey's and the professor's advice, we have ordered a comprehensive list of plant and machinery which I believe will be what we will need to get this operation underway. When you get a moment, Bill, please run your eye over the list just in case I have missed something. The fourth and final thing, is a big one. We have yet to resolve how we are going to get all this processing plant and auxiliary gear to the mine, and later getting the concentrate from the plant to market. Trucks would need to make the nine-hundred-plus kilometre trip from the railhead in the provincial city to Quo-Vadis, then crawl their way a further 350 kilometres through the Outback from Quo-Vadis to the mine; that's a twelve-hundred-plus kilometre trip each way. The costs of getting the plant on site blows my mind; fortunately, those costs are non-reoccurring; it's the costs of transporting the concentrate we produce that is the concern. It would be a major expense and if we don't resolve it, it would be on-going. Do you have any suggestions, mate?"

"None I can think of at the moment," Bill replied. "How do the big boys, you know the iron ore miners, handle this problem?"
"

They usually transport it by rail," Chris replied slowly as if he was thinking of something. He sat quietly for a while, then as if he had been jabbed with a pin, he quickly spun his chair around and switched on the very up-to-date PC that had sat on the shelf behind him. In short time, a satellite image of the  Outback appeared on the screen. It was focused on the pegmatites deposit. Chris slowly scrolled the cursor northward. After a few minutes, Chris excitedly exclaimed, "You are brilliant Bill—look at this."

Bill rolled his chair a little closer so he could get a better view  of the screen. "What am I looking at Chris?" he asked. "It looks like an iron ore open cut mine to me."

"It is," Chris quickly answered, and scrolled a little to one side of the mine site. "See here," Chris whispered as he pointed with a pencil, "that is a railway line. I saw it there some time back. That open cut mine is about 380-400 kilometres north of our site. If I were to build a spur line from that iron ore mine to our mine site, and hook the line up with theirs, our problem would be overcome. Tomorrow you and I are going to pay that iron ore mine a visit."

The Operations Manager, that's what he called himself, was a little hesitant with giving Chris a reply to his request. All he would commit to was to put it to the Mine Board at next week's meeting, adding the comment, "Don't hold your breath, Mr Kennedy, the members of the board are okay, but I have found most of them are very closed in their thinking." He did suggest, "Perhaps it will be good for you to present your proposal to them personally—it may help; I can arrange for your attendance if you so wish."

"I would appreciate it if you would do that," Chris said.

The board of the iron ore company listened intently to Chris and asked many questions about the spodumene deposit. One asked point blankly, "You are an experienced mining engineer, Mr Kennedy; do you think there could be a deposit of pegmatites on our lease?"

"I cannot answer that," Chris answered him. "There is a fairly substantial ridge between our mines; one never knows what's next door." Chris could see the board member was already planning to send his geologists out to have a look.

The chairman wound up the meeting by saying, "We will consider your request, Mr Kennedy and let you know our answer next week."

"A further lesson in patience once again," Chris resolutely thought.

Rex was very positive about the whole project. He travelled out to Quo-Vadis for the sole purpose of learning all the details. "All this expenditure you intend to proceed with will alleviate much of the holding company's tax burden for the next financial year, and even if the mine runs at a loss for a while it will not hurt. We can raise the five-hundred million and a bit more for the construction works, overnight. The increased production from Quo-Vadis gold can be used to top up any losses incurred by the venture, however once the production of spodumene gets fully underway I cannot envisage the project ever incurring any loss."

"I am so very glad that you are there to attend to all this economic hoo-ha, Rex," Chris meaningfully said, adding, "I only want to be involved with mining, not sitting in some corner trying to do all those sums. I prefer the numbers associated with surveys and exploration results."

Chris had often noticed three or four, sometimes more, natives standing silently on the hillside watching all that was happening all over the mine site. He had made a habit to wander up to them and explain bits and pieces of those things they were seeing.

"It is well you are protected by KORORA (the GOD of Creation)" the witch doctor whispered, at one of those times, and had softly said, "the land does not like holes being drilled into it or all these great machines destroying its peace."

"I hear you, wise-one" Chris had replied, "I hurt the land as little as possible. I am grateful it gives up its secrets to me."

That appeared to please the witch doctor, who had replied, "I fear your power Abdiel Boss Chris, it is good you are our friend, and understand our ways."

Chris had walked humbly back to the turmoil of the mine site thinking, "Some people say I am lucky. I do not call it luck; to me it is a blessing."

# Chapter 12

Chris and Jackie did take that six months' cruise. He had laughed quite happily as Jackie warned him, "One word about mining in the next six months and you will swim home!"

They returned to Quo-Vadis, feeling as good as new. Chris was bursting with energy; Jackie was very large, she was near bursting also, but for another very obvious reason.

Bill met them at the airport of the provincial city, and on the flight from there to Quo-Vadis told them of the progress out at the pegmatites mine and a multitude of other things which had occurred in their absence. He told them with a note of regret in his voice that none of the larger machinery had arrived. The manufacturers had all advised the machines, "Had had to be made to Chris's specifications and were on the way."

Bill said, "I have organised the trucking contractor—the same bloke we used to bring the machinery for Quo-Vadis Gold out. He said he will keep a watchful eye out for its arrival at the railhead and bring it out immediately. He was extremely pleased to hear we have a half decent road now days." Bill was so full of information he wanted to pass on to Chris, he had started on one subject, and halfway through would get way-laid by something else he wanted to say.

Chris had laughed at all this and held up his hands in surrender. "Slow up a bit, Bill," Chris cried, "It will take a little adjustment for me to get back into the swing of things."

"Okay, mate," Bill chuckled, took a deep breath, saying, "There is much more to tell you."

"I do want to hear it all," Chris replied, "Just slow down a bit and breathe now and again."

"Sure thing, Chris boy," Bill started again. "Now, where was I? Oh yes, that's right, the mine. Geoffrey is really earning his keep. He has bought three of the mechanical engineers who

301

installed the plant at that mine down south with him. Those engineers have gone through the diagrams of the proposed set up of our machines, made a few suggestions, and commented, that the machines we have ordered are far superior in quality and capacity than the machines they did install for Geoffx2, they called him, down south. Oh Hell!" Bill cried in alarm, "I nearly forgot. The directors from that iron ore mine next door, have been calling at least twice a week, every time asking when you will be back. There is one other thing," Bill could not keep the smile from his face, "Jack has wagged school and is waiting at home for you."

Jack was not waiting at home; immediately he had learned his parents were on the way back he rushed out to wait for them at the Quo-Vadis airstrip. Jack's exuberance was unbounded as he welcomed them. He cried as he hugged Chris, and took little regard of Jackie's condition, and all but pounced on her, and through his tears of sheer happiness wailed, "I have missed you both so much; please do not go away without me ever again."

A couple of days later, after having taken time to look over the gold mines, the resort and the station, he flew out to the newly-registered pegmatites mine, now called Quo-Vadis Lithium. He did not recognise the place at first. Some ten-square kilometres had been stripped of overburden. That overburden had been crushed and mixed with crushed quartz tailings from the gold mines and crushed dolomite ore from a deposit Chris had located in the cliff face off the escarpment before he had left on the cruise. Load after load of this mixture had been utilised to fill in trouble patches in the road. Now a rough road, ran all the way between Quo-Vadis Lithium and his home at Quo-Vadis.

The native elder, Marlee was particularly overjoyed with Chris's return. His first comment was simply, "All will be well now, Abdiel Boss Chris has returned."

Despite the absence of the processing plant, it was obvious that a big amount of mining had been affected. Orderly lines of pegmatites ore marched up to what was obviously the site where the processing plant was going to be. Buildings, sheds and workshops had been erected in a specific pattern.

Geoffx2 bounded up to him, darn near shook his hand from his arm and cried, "It is so good to see you, Mr Chris. There are several major decisions to be made." He looked hard at Bill, his whole face was a mask of humour, "Mr Coward Bailey would only say, 'better wait for Chris.'" Geoffx2 continued without taking an apparent breath. "We have had six visits by people from the iron ore mine, a couple of geologists and engineers. They said their visits were only social, I think they only wanted to have a sticky beak. They could not believe what was happening here. The geologists near blew their minds when I showed them some of the core samples. They are very keen to see you push a rail line through to link with theirs. They did ask whether you surveyed the route and how you will do it. They seemed a little sceptical—said something about there being some pretty wild country between us and them."

"I have done a survey, Geoff," Chris replied. "It's all on file in my office. I will run through it with you when you are next at Quo-Vadis. There are some bits you may be able to help me with."

"When are you meeting their directors?" Geoff asked.

"They have made me wait for over six months without giving me a decision; they can wait for a couple of weeks now—it will not hurt them. What's more important to me is the water situation."

"Oh, yeah," Geoff somewhat humbly answered. "I forgot to mention, seventy percent of those sites you chose for Tom hit the artesian basin; the water is plentiful and beautiful. We can use it to wash the crushing's without having to treat it to remove any impurities. I am using both of Tom's rigs to try and establish the extent of the pegmatites sheet. It is a monster. From what we have found so far, it will take over one-hundred years to even make a dent in it."

"Slow down a bit mate," Chris interrupted him. "Everybody seems to have one-hundred-and-one things to tell me, all at the one-time. My mind is still half on that cruise ship. All I can say is the pair of you have definitely earned your keep."

"And loved every minute of it," Geoff laughed, adding, "All the people here are an absolute pleasure to work with."

Chris had intended to fly back to Quo-Vadis in one of the delivery aircraft.

As he climbed aboard, the pilot said, "Sorry, Mr Chris, it is getting a bit messy out there. It looks like the daddy of one of those dry thunderstorms is about to hit. They are very bad this year. One last month hung around for over three days. Nothing could fly during that time. It should clear overnight."

Jackie was most uncomfortable; several spasms of pain racked her body. "These are not like the pre-delivery spasms I had when Jack was born," she thought. "Anyway, I am not due for two weeks." Those pains increased throughout the day and culminated when she collapsed onto the kitchen floor. Ellie was nearby arranging a vase of flowers and saw her fall. She rushed to the writhing form and assisted her to her feet, announcing very strongly, "It's off to bed for you young lady," and called for the other girls to help her get Jackie upstairs to her bed.

"Is her baby coming?" one of the young lasses asked.

"I cannot tell," Ellie softly answered. "I better tell Mr Chris what has happened."

Chris did receive a storm-distorted message. He had tried to tell Ellie, "Get the doctor quickly!"

That didn't work. The thunderstorm and lightning had intensified to such an extent it precluded any further contact. "There is no point in even contacting the doctor; he will not fly in this storm," Chris thought and in panic-stricken haste decided to grab an SUV and try and drive through the storm and get home that way. He consoled himself by thinking, "Ellie has a good head on her shoulders these days; she will see to it Jackie is okay."

The mine site had closed down and all the vehicles had been stored away from the lightning that conducted a near continuous dance across the exposed pegmatites. He paused for a moment, totally in awe as a brilliant fork of lightning blasted into a majestic gum tree, one of the very few, that grew on the nearby hillside. The blast displayed the awesome power of the lightning bolt and left the tree a blazing sentinel. "A man could get fried by being out in this," he thought almost in panic and he hesitated for a moment, then contained his fear, his strong desire to be with Jackie prevailed.

The workshop foreman, where most of the SUVs had been stored away from the harm of the storm, protested vehemently when Chris demanded a vehicle. "You must be insane to drive out in this."

Still, ten minutes later Chris, roared off into the storm.

"Bloody fool," the workshop foreman said to himself as he watched the SUV disappear. "I hope he will be alright."

It was no Sunday drive. Chris was forced to use all his driving skills to keep the SUV on the road, battling the lightning storm and sand-laden wind blasting at the SUV from seemingly every direction. Still he drove on. Nothing, but nothing, was going to keep him away from Jackie when she needed him.

Jackie lay on the bed bathe in sweat. The girls sponged her continuously with cool wet cloths. At times, Jackie nearly twisted herself off the bed as another spasm of pain rose within her to near intolerable heights.

"We need help," Ellie cried. "I do not know what to do to help her. I feel absolutely helpless."

It was as if they had heard her. Four native women adorned in the traditional way walked quietly in and stationed themselves one at each corner of the bed. They stood quietly with their heads bowed, as if they were preparing to guard the bedraggled form that lay before them. Without a word being said, they rose their hands and in unison started to chant. The chant was very soft and rather beautiful.

"What are they doing?" one of the girls cried in alarm.

Old Marlee had, unobserved, quietly followed the women into the room. Normally men were forbidden to be present at a birthing. As Jackie was not a native woman, he believed in this instance he was not contravening tradition. Even so; he too was painted with the many intricate designs of the native people.

He softly replied; "the women are taking Missy Jackie far, far away from the EULOOWAY, the evil ones of the night. They are who she battles. They wish to take and eat the soul of the child of Abdiel Boss Chris. those evil ones think, if they can do this they will take away the power of Abdiel Boss Chris."

Jackie had appeared to be resting a little more comfortably, although from time to time she would scream and reach out her arms as if she was trying to push something way.

Old Marlee sat at the bottom of the bed apparently in a trance. "She is a brave woman, is Missy Jackie; see how she fights the Eulooway."

All through the night, the four native women and Marlee kept vigil over Jackie, at times revolving, each to take a new position, or to step back and join hands to dance, never once ceasing that haunting chant. Ellie and the girls had stood the whole night through, totally hypnotised by what was happening.

It was nearing sunrise as Chris in the storm-battered SUV roared into Quo-Vadis. He did not stop for one instant but drove the SUV straight onto the elevator that dropped him to the house level in the sinkhole. He clawed urgently out of the vehicle and even before the elevator stopped he had jumped from it, and rushed to the house, as if he was being pursued by the devil himself.

"Where is she?" he shouted at the girl who had come down to the kitchen to make a cup of tea.

"Mistress Jackie is upstairs, sir," she stuttered as she managed to recognise the madman standing before her. Chris took the stairs three at a time and pushed into the bedroom just as the sun rose.

There is no explanation for what happened next. At the moment he crashed into the room the native women ceased their chant and commenced a rhythmic clapping. From high up on the window, through a small chink where the curtains had not been fully drawn, a ray of bright sunlight poured into the room. That ray of sunlight appeared to dance about the room for a moment then flooded over the still form of Jackie as she lay on the bed. As that bright ray of sunlight appeared to caress that dishevelled body; the child entered the world.

In unison the women whispered, "Yindi has come."

One woman lifted the child and presented her to Chris, saying, "Her name is Yindi."

Chris took the child gently in his arms and held her as if she was a piece of fine precious porcelain. "She is so beautiful," he whispered to the native woman and stepped up to where Jackie lay.

She was now completely relaxed, all pain had left her, although she did look like the outcome of a train wreck.

"Yindi; that is a beautiful name. Yindi, I wonder what that means?" he whispered softly to himself.

"She is the blessed child of the sunbeam; it is she who has given her the name," Marlee had heard his whisper.

Chris laid the babe beside Jackie's cheek and softly said, "This is Yindi. She is as beautiful as you."

Jackie held the baby close and smiled at Chris. "Now I have a complete family," she cried a little as she whispered, "I have a wonderful man, a very special son, and now a beautiful daughter. I can ask for nothing more than to be allowed to love them as I love each and every one of them at this minute."

Chris reached over and gently kissed Jackie's forehead. "I too have a complete family," he said. "At last I can be a contented man."

Ellie gently took the baby from the reluctant grasp of Jackie saying, "Let me clean her up and wrap her, Jackie. I'll bring her back shortly; in the meantime, the girls will help you into the bathroom so you can get cleaned up too; you Mr Dad can make yourself useful and find this beautiful child a crib."

Marlee, the wise old native elder, stepped forward to confront Chris. "I will tell you, Abdiel Boss Chris of the child's name. The name of Yindi is, as I have said, means, Child of the sun or a Sunbeam," and continued, "I have to tell you, what has happened here this day will be told and retold many times around the campfires at night. It will be the story of how Missy Jackie fought the whole night through to keep her child from the Eulooway, the evil spirits of the night, and how the evil ones fled as Abdiel, the faithful servant of his God, Boss Chris, appeared and how at that moment NGANAGK YIRA, the rising sun sent one of the sunbeam children to show the child the way into the world. The story will also tell how the thunderstorm MINALKA had taken fright and had drifted far away."

With the storm gone Chris called in the Flying Doctor to check Jackie over. "After a session like you have just been through a thorough check out is warranted," he told her.

The doctor completed his examination and called Chris aside and said, "I have found that Jackie herself is physically okay and will recover quickly. Regrettably I have to tell you that birthing of the child has done severe damage and Jackie will be unable to live through another pregnancy. When she is well enough I want you to bring her to the city where she will be able to have several small operations to correct what damage we can. I do most strongly repeat: no more children."

Jackie was quiet for a short while after Chris told her what the doctor had said. "I am okay with that," she said. "I never want to go through that again; the things and images I experienced when I was in labour were bad. They were so bad, so very bad, I was terrified; then you were there and I felt safe. It will take me some time to push those horrific images aside. Your love will help me," she quietly said.

Yindi Katrina Kennedy grew into a particularly beautiful woman. She was loved and admired by everyone. Big brother Jack practically worshipped the very ground she walked on. As she grew, she did spend countless hours with the native peoples from near and far. At seventeen years of age, contrary to all tradition and at the invitation of a very powerful witch doctor she walked in the Dreamtime with him. Her books of the people were acclaimed as bestsellers.

One thing worthy of report is the story of the Yindi Stone. Those groups of native men continued to stand stoically on an adjacent hillside watching the huge machines as they worked. One morning one of the men idly commented as a huge front-end loader lifted a bucket full of ore into a truck, that the machine has the strength of fifty horses. Chris who was passing nearby had heard the comment, quietly said, "That is not so, it has the power of six-hundred horses."

That impressed the group and they watched more intently. The loader had dug its bucket deep into the pegmatites and as it raised it to dump the ore in the waiting truck, a crystal of spodumene about one-metre long and half a metre in diameter fell from the bucket. Call it what you like, but by providence as that crystal fell it caught the sun and a flash of sunlight flowed over the hillside almost blinding the native men standing there.

Open mouthed, one exclaimed! "Yindi (the sun) has sent us a gift; we must take it back to the camp for all to see."

Chris recognised their need and had that loader carry the crystal to the camp. The camp elders were unanimous and the crystal was placed where the very first rays of the morning sun hit it, sending a blaze of sunlight throughout the camp. The crystal was immediately named, Yindi's Stone.

# Chapter 13

Chris had been ensconced in his office in the big cave. He had heard a vehicle pull up and the elevator being used. "I am not expecting anybody. Who can this be? Whoever it is I hope he is a bearer of good tidings," Chris had thought.

There was a soft knock at the door and Chris called in response, "Come in, if you are bringing a couple of coldies and good news," to which his visitor responded, "Sorry, Mr Kennedy, no coldies but maybe some news of interest."

The visitor stepped into the office and stood before Chris's desk. "I am Michael Tomlinson, the Operations Manager of the iron ore mine. You may recall we have met some time ago when you first called on me to discuss the possibility of using our rail network," he quickly said.

"Yes, I remember you, Michael," Chris replied. "I have not given up hope of constructing a railway line between our two mines. It may sound a weak excuse, but every intention I have had to pursue that request and follow up my visit with your management, is either interrupted or waylaid by the needs of something or another developing out at the mine site."

"That's why I'm here, Mr Kennedy," Tomlinson quickly said.

"Please call me Chris," Chris interrupted him.

"Thank you, Chris. As I was saying, I am here because the board has become more than a little impatient—in fact I think are quite frustrated—with not hearing from you, and in an endeavour to expedite your thinking, they will visit you."

The full board of the iron ore mine descended on the pegmatites mine site a week later. As they attempted to enter the works area they were accosted by a very belligerent Safety Officer who told them, "he did not give a stuff who they were, or why they were here," and almost shouting; told them in no uncertain terms,

"You wear full safety gear, or you can get back into that helicopter and *kiss off,*" then compromising a little added, "Wait here, and I'll get you all a full kit, and tell the boss you are here."

The managing director was most amused with all this, and laughingly said to the board members, "I can see that this is in no nonsense site; we will have to be on our best behaviour.

An unshaven, dust-covered man walked quickly up. "YOU WANT TO SEE ME," he shouted over the roar of a passing loader. Then in a moment of recognition cried, "Holy Moses! What are you mob doing here," then quickly apologised saying, "Sorry, gents, you caught me off guard."

The Chairman laughed heartily, and said, "Since Chris Kennedy would not come to the mountain, the mountain has come to him. Is there somewhere we can talk without having to compete with all these machines, and afterwards, would you mind showing us what all this construction is about."

"My office is soundproofed; follow me, and we will all move into there and be able to talk without shouting," Chris answered. "It will be a little crowded, and I will have to raid the mess hall for a few extra chairs. Anybody for a cup of tea or coffee?"

After a few more preliminaries and introductions all around were completed, the unscheduled conference got underway. Chris had organised Bill and Geoff to join them.

The Chairman opened the discussion and started to waffle on about the iron ore mine. "Sir," Chris interrupted him, "Let's get to the guts of your visit; have you made a decision as to whether or not Quo-Vadis Lithium could ship concentrate using your facilities," Chris snapped.

"You are right, Mr Kennedy; that is all I want to talk about. You are most direct, sir. I see you are a man not to be trifled with—a bit like your Safety Officer. Do you think he would mind if I remove my helmet while we are in here?"

Chris had regained his good humour, and with a smile said, "We have a one-hundred percent safety record, which the men protect with great zeal. I have offered a good bonus to all if we can maintain it until the plant is operational."

"Most meritorious," the Chairman commented, and continued, "To get to, what did you call it? Oh yes, the guts of our visit, we would like you to consider this. You build and pay for the rail link including all the rolling stock and pay us, one-hundred dollars per ton of material you ship."

Chris heard Bill take a very deep breath and almost choke as he loudly said, "That's nothing but a load of bull shit, Chris."

The Chairman looked very sternly at Bill, and said, equally as loudly, "If you would kindly let me finish, sir, there is a little more. We will issue you 400,000 primary class shares in Iron Ore Mines Limited——that's the company that runs the iron ore mine; in return you will issue our company one million shares in Quo-Vadis Holdings Proprietary Limited."

"Have you finished, sir?" Chris quietly asked.

"Yes, son," the Chairman answered. "You do not have to give an answer today; also, at a later date, we would like to discuss pegmatites mining and processing with you."

"Thank you, sir," Chris respectfully said, then raising his voice so all could hear clearly, very forcibly said, "I cannot understand how you have the temerity to make such an offer. That is the biggest insult to my intelligence I have ever received. Now I must ask for you and your board TO GET THE HELL OUT OF MY FACE! He shouted; I have more important things to attend to, like cleaning a toilet."

"There is no need to be so rude, Kennedy," one of the board members cried. "We have given you an answer to your request."

"YOUR ANSWER IS A LOAD OF CRAP," Chris shouted again. "Your deal requires you mob to do nothing. You have offered

400,000 near worthless shares. Your shares as at yesterday's price were priced at 8.31 cents per share, down from the issued price of one dollar per share. Your production is at a barely sustainable level and the company is in debt to 72% of any equity. There is a strong risk that you will go down the tubes within twelve months. Perhaps if I am a little patient I will be able to pick up what remains of your company for almost nothing and get that blasted rail network for free. Quo-Vadis Holdings is worth many, many, times your company. We carry absolutely no debt and enjoy a very comfortable cash flow. I must suggest you go away and do your homework. Just to show you I am not completely unreasonable, I will offer you an alternative. Your geologists have located four good pegmatites loads. I am not aware if you have confirmed their potential yield. You are most hesitant to commit to developing those loads, as you fully know: firstly because of the cost of mining the ore; and secondly, because of the costs to install machinery and the processing plant is well beyond your present resources. Should you be prepared to execute a comprehensive and binding document that you agree to Quo-Vadis Lithium, mind you, only the Lithium arm of Quo-Vadis Holdings constructing the spur line with costs equally shared, we would immediately commence to build the line. We have the men and machines that will build the 340-kilometre spur line within twelve months. By that time our processing plant will be operational. We would send our highly experienced team of analysts to your pegmatites deposits to assess their viability. This will be done free of charge. All their findings will be made available to you. Should you decide the sites are worthwhile and proceed to mining those sites, at your cost, with the interconnecting rail line being complete, the ore mined could be shipped to our processing plant for reduction to spodumene concentrate in your own rail wagons. We would charge your company a premium for processing your ore. That premium would be calculated on 32% of the value of the concentrate we extract from your ore. You may have as many inspectors where ever you wish to ensure your interests are protected, providing those inspectors do not detract from the efficiency of our operation. Those inspectors will be at your cost. Once the link construction is complete, Quo-Vadis Spodumene concentrate will be transported via that link to your mine, then on to the coast, using your existing railway network. Adjacent to the loading dock, we propose to set up our own storage facilities to store the ore awaiting shipment to the purchases. Their ships will be loaded by our own loading plant. Our own locomotives will haul our own specially-designed concentrate wagons. Those trains will be much faster than your ore trains and will be given right of way, both coming and going. Should you wish, you may attach your concentrate laden wagons to our trains. We would not charge you for this service. We are aware at the present you do not have the available cash to pay for your share of the railway line construction. As a temporary measure, the Iron Ore Company are to issue one million fully paid shares to Quo-Vadis Lithium. Those shares will have full voting rights, and may be redeemed by your company on payment, in full, of your share of the costs of the railway line plus interest on the debt at 8% per annum. We will also require to have two seats on your board."

One director, thinking he was being so very smart, spoke out loudly, "I am surprised you overlooked demanding our jocks and socks, Kennedy," he snapped.

"Another smart-arse comment like that and I will not only take your jocks and socks, I will include your balls too," Chris growled sarcastically in retort.

The Chairman stood, took a deep breath, and very angrily said, "That's quite enough," then in a not unfriendly tone said, "Christopher you have given us much to think on, and to debate. Some of your demands will require shareholder approval; fortunately, we have the full annual general meeting next month and do have time to include all this in a letter of advice we will have sent to them. I believe all this, including the meeting, will not be concluded within three months. I will undertake to give you our answer to all your requests then."

"Understood," Chris replied, adding, "Now if you'll excuse me I have a new bore-head that is spewing a big volume of water that urgently must be attended to."

As the board members filed out, the Chairman made sure he was the last to leave. He paused in front of Chris and said, "Chris, I for one, would welcome you as a member of the board."

They shook hands and proceeded on their separate ways.

Chris called Rex that evening. "Thanks for all the information on the iron ore mob, bro," Chris very sincerely said. "I think they were a bit surprised I knew so much about them, and their company's very weak position."

"Do you think they will accept your terms, Mister Miner?" Rex asked.

"It doesn't really matter at present," Chris replied. "When we are ready to move the concentrate, if they do not want to be part of it, too bad, we will have to go back to our original plan and have to truck it through Quo-Vadis."

"That is going to be darn expensive; it is going to be a bit of a wait and see game, eh bro!" Rex exclaimed. "Let me know if you need any more help."

Regardless of the fact he had not had a reply from the iron ore people, Chris had Strahan and Riley quietly do a study on the pegmatites deposits of their company. The learned men had reported to Chris, that their analysis was quite encouraging. Of the five deposits they had examined, they had unearthed a further unknown deposit; four, were good, the fifth deposit, the one they had found, although a little smaller, was extremely rich in spodumene crystals. In all, their deposits are commercially viable.

"Are they going to develop them?" Riley asked. "With their shares being around eight cents a share at present, it would be a good time to grab a few."

Chris had pondered that comment for a couple of days, then spoke with Rex about it and together they agreed, the idea to buy into the iron ore company had good merit. Rex surreptitiously mentioned to a financial journalist he knew that the iron ore company had unearthed viable pegmatites deposits adjacent to their mine. The two-inch column in the next edition of that journalist's magazine caused little excitement in financial circles.

Chris set to, to pick up whatever shares in the iron ore company came on the market. Even before the board came back to him with their answer to his proposal, he held nearly twenty-two million of their shares, all purchased at eight cents or less per share. Dividends by the iron ore company for the last three years had been non-existent, and investors were happy to grab whatever they could. Should the board come up with the one million shares he had asked for, he would hold nearly 32% of the iron ore company. Chris and Rex did attend the annual shareholders meeting and sat quietly in the midst of the remaining shareholders listening to the board waffle around the true position of the company.

Two things did engage Chris's attention. The first was a question raised by an elderly gentleman sitting in the front row, who rather forcibly stood and asked, "You have retired two board members; who will replace them?"

The Chairman rather confidently replied, "We are awaiting the outcome of an offer we are about to make to a very experienced mining man. The Chairman had not observed Chris and Rex sitting well back in the hall.

The second matter that had caught Chris's attention, did engender some heated exchange between the board and the shareholders after one shareholder had loudly, more or less demanded, "What are you doing about the pegmatites deposits reported in the financial journal last week?"

"We have undertaken and are awaiting assessment reports," was all the Chairman said.

"Confounded waste of time and money to even have them investigated," the shareholder very crossly said. "Everybody knows there is no worthwhile pegmatites in the area.

Shares in the iron ore company dropped to an all-time low of four cents per share after that meeting. Chris continued to have his brokers buy whatever shares came on the market and had those brokers advise the stock exchange for the moment he was not intending to take over the iron ore company.

Construction works at Quo-Vadis Lithium had proceeded very well under the guidance of the engineers of Geoff x2 and the two university professors who from time to time would suggest alterations to the original design. As to be expected, every alteration did improve the function of the plant.

# Chapter 14

The Kennedy family—Chris, Jackie and Jack, Baby Yindi was not with them she had been left in the care of the two-house girls, who loved playing-nurse maid— Bill and Ellie made up the party; they had decided to spend an afternoon fishing.

"I would like to try our luck over in the lake outlet," Chris had nominated.

"I have not wet a line over there," Bill had said. "There may be some good-sized trout swimming around in there just waiting to be hooked."

It was a very pleasant afternoon, and the men, that included Jack, had had moderate success, and eight good-sized fish, had been hooked. Those fish included a fine five-kilogram trout, Jack, after much excitement, had landed.

Chris had been dreamingly watching the river as it flowed majestically on its way." What a magnificent sight all this is," he thought; but he was a little perplexed. "Bill," Chris, quizzically asked, "is it my imagination or is the outflow of the river past here considerably greater than the volume of water which is flowing into the lake from the river that comes from the face of the escarpment?"

"Never gave it a thought, mate," Bill replied. "Give me five and I will have a look." He was quiet for a while—he too was watching the river flow past. After about ten minutes he said, "You know, I think you are right, Chris: this outflow is many, many times greater than the inflow. How can that be?"

"All I can think of," Chris replied, "is that an underground river does enter into the lake somewhere."

"Here we go again," Bill laughed. "Mr Smarty mining engineer on the job again. All right Mr Smarty, tell me what you are thinking."

"Very well, Mr Grumpy, you remember that small stream of water we found when we walked into the secondary cave—you remember the cave that opened up in the wall of the sinkhole. Think on it mate, that entrance would have been large enough to contain an enormous flow of water. I am guessing a little here and thinking, mind you, when the escarpment was pushed up, that would have been a sight to see, I would have liked to have been here to see that happen, I can see that that big river was cut off and forced to find another outlet. That outlet was probably somewhere further down the sinkhole, and the lake has formed over it. Now, I am still guessing, that outlet is in the lake bed somewhere. It is a huge volume of water, hence all this increased flow down here."

"If I didn't know you better, Mr Miner," Bill sighed, "I would say you are dreaming. Now knowing you like I do, I can believe what you are saying is possible. There is little point in wasting time and money to satisfy our curiosity. All we can be sure of is a river flows from the escarpment into the lake, and a river of a much, much greater volume, flows out."

"Let's walk down stream for a while, from what I can see here, the river flows straight into the cliff face," Chris suggested.

The women and Jack were happy to accompany them as they explored. The prospect of sharing one of Chris's new discoveries caused some excitement. The party walked along the riverbank for about three kilometres, just admiring the scenery.

Chris, who was in the lead, stopped abruptly. "Look at this Bill," he cried. "The river does not go all the way to the cliff face— it disappears down a great big hole here, it is about one-hundred metres short of the cliff face. I would not like to get caught in the current here and washed into that hole; you would be a goner for sure. Better warn everybody never to swim in the lake outlet, even if it is a couple of kilometres upstream from here."

Chris had gone very quiet. "Uh Oh, what are you thinking now, boy?" Bill asked with a touch of resoluteness in his voice.

"I suddenly have something important to think on," Chris softly replied. "What is the one big question we have never really answered?"

"There are several questions in that category," Bill quickly replied.

"I was thinking of the question of supplying adequate power to Quo-Vadis Lithium. The several acres of solar panels were the only solution we had come up with. Here we have an unlimited source of power. All we have to do is harness it. A couple of big Hydro generators will give us more than enough power for our needs out there. I will bring Tom and his rig down here and have him poke a big hole down about fifty metres parallel to that big drain-hole and go down, say two/three-hundred metres and see if it is feasible to build a generating station down there."

Chris was off with the fairies, his mind racing in 1001 directions at once, totally absorbed in the possibilities of such a project, and how he could utilise all the benefits that such a power source would bring to the whole of Quo Vadis.

Bill brought him back to earth, with a jolt, when he demanded, "And how the hell, supposing you do build your generators? are you going to get the power from here to the mine?"

"That will be the easy bit," Chris replied. "I will build a transmission line."

"Oh yeah!" Bill exclaimed, "and bugger-up the scenery for miles around."

"To keep you happy, Mr Grumpy, I will run a cable underground," Chris replied. "I will make sure that cable has at least five times the capacity of our immediate needs. I do envisage the possibility of requiring that extra capacity at a later date. It will cost quite a bit more to transmit the power this way; however, there are some attendant advantages. With the cable being buried it will be protected from the weather, especially those thunderstorms and sand-driven winds, and grumpy old men."

"Don't mind me, Chris," Bill grunted. "I actually see your idea is great, and only stir you to make sure you use that can of worms you call a brain to consider everything, and every possibility. It's a bit late to do any more exploring today; let's call it quits and come back in the morning."

Everybody, the women and Jack, had listened intently to that man they knew as either their husband, their father, or their friend. Jackie whispered softly to Ellie, "It is small wonder that his brain does not explode with all this; I got lost about the time he said we will have to warn everybody not to swim in the lake outlet. Everything after that just went completely over my head, but those two are very excited so it must be something special."

"I understood it all, Mummy," Jack piped up. "They are going to make 'lectricity here for the mine."

"You are getting more like your father every day, young man," Jackie rather proudly said, then added, "I think it is time we women took our men home; I cannot see them doing any more fishing today."

Like a runaway horse with the bit in his mouth, there was no stopping Chris now. Early next morning he and Bill stood on the riverbank overlooking that swirling nightmare where the river disappeared down the hole. "There is far too much water flowing past here for our needs," Chris said softly. "We will have to build a diversion of some description to capture only the amount of water we require to drive our generators. Hopefully we'll find a way to be able to run that outflow from the generators back into the river."

The episode of bringing that very big drilling rig down the escarpment cliff face was a parody of fear and humour. There had been much debate as to whether it was better to dismantle the rig and lower it piece by piece or leave the machine intact and lower it without dismantling it in any way.

Tom would not hear of anybody pulling his machine to bits, he finally conceded that to lower the rig intact was the best idea. Tom was beside himself with concern for his baby, as that huge gleaming twenty-four-wheeled monster, that he would spend hours polishing, was lowered down. He had hung desperately to the long guide ropes, only to get entangled in a stray rope and ending up suspended, swaying upside down some hundred feet in the air. He was eventually brought down to earth and the rig was finally successfully lowered to the floor of the sinkhole. Tom immediately set to, to inspect his precious machine, and after an hour of crawling all over it, loudly announced, "all was well and he had found there was no damage, not even so much as a scratch on its precious paintwork.

Four hours later, the huge drilling rig was in place. Chris had selected a position about fifty metres back from the river and adjacent to that ugly whirlpool. The diamond tipped drill bit into the granite surface and the project commenced.

"It's black granite," Tom shouted above the roar of the diesel motor of the drill. "It's gunna take a bit of time to get down three-hundred meters, Chris. You say you need to have a hole twenty metres in diameter. All I can do is to cut a pattern of holes over that area; you will have to take over from there and excavate. I will drill your blasted holes—after all, I am a driller; you are the bloody miner—digging holes is your lot."

"I am out of here," Chris laughed, "Just call me when the first hole hits three-hundred meters." He turned and hotfooted it back to the house for a quiet cuppa with Jackie. "She, at least, doesn't yell at me."

It was 4 am, three mornings later when the bedside telephone demanded attention. "It's Tom, Mr Miner."

The near-hysterical voice cried, "You better get down here quick; we've got an almighty big problem."

"What sort of problem?" Chris drowsily asked.

"I've run out of rock. I'm drilling in mid-air at the moment, we have struck a bloody big hole."

Chris was instantly fully awake. "How deep?" he almost screamed the question at Tom.

"210 meters with an 80-mm bit," Tom answered with a plaintive voice.

"Hold as you are," Chris ordered. "I'll get Bill and be there in twenty minutes."

Bill was extremely reluctant to get out of bed at that "Godforsaken" hour. However, he and Chris did arrive at the drill site in less than twenty minutes. That's not exactly correct, Chris did arrive in less, having run all the way. A very red-faced, gasping-for-breath Bill arrived ten minutes later.

"Look at this! I am much more in control now," Tom, said. "I have pulled the drill and have poked a camera down the hole. There is limited light. If you watch the computer screen, it has a cable attached to the camera, you will see we are in a very big cavern. The drill broke through the middle of the roof. Don't tell me you knew there was something like this down there."

"I'm not that good, mate," Chris replied. Then asked; "how far had you lowered the camera into the cavern before we got here?" About fifty-eight meters, Tom replied, "Please take the camera lower, say about twenty metres." Chris ordered. The camera cable reeled off another ten meters. "Hold," Chris sharply said. "Look at this Bill, even in this limited light, the computer screen is showing something that looks like water. Very slowly now Tom, take the camera down a further ten meters," Chris ordered. At eight metres, the camera became submerged in flowing water. "That's it," Chris whispered.

"Tom, that cavern is around 230 feet deep before we hit that water. How solid is the roof Tom? And is there any sort of a floor or even a substantial ledge" he asked the driller.

"The roof is solid granite," Tom answered. "We were in hard solid granite all the way down until we hit this. As for a floor of any description, at the moment; I cannot answer that until I get a bit more light down there."

"It's wonderful," Chris laughed. "You know what this means, Bill? By the Grace of God, I have been given a two-hundred-foot-plus cavity, a bit over two-hundred-meters down, in which I can build our power station. A ten-meter diameter pipe carrying a two-hundred meter head of water, will be more than enough to drive even the biggest turbines. We do not have to do worry about a tail race for the outflow; we can run it straight into that stream."

"You can sure pick them," Bill laughed. "Did you know this was here, or is there something about this Abdiel business the natives talk about?"

"I had no idea. I only selected the drill site at random. I did not even hope for something like this," Chris humbly replied, then turning to Tom quietly said, "To maximise the full benefit of this wonderful discovery, I will need that pattern of holes over an area of; say a diameter of twenty to twenty-five metres. If you use the eighty mm bit, how close together can you get those holes?"

"No closer than seventy or eighty millimetres," Tom replied. "It will be a pick and shovel job after that."

"More blisters," Bill growled lightly.

For the next six months, the peace of the sinkhole was shattered by a continuous racket of compressors, jackhammers and heavy machinery. From time to time, Chris found it necessary to blast away some particularly hard stubborn sections of the granite. Scoops attached to long cables drew the broken rock to the surface where it was promptly hauled to crushers to be returned as gravel and used to create a firm thin road to the excavated hole. Bill was amazed how Chris compiled logistics of the whole project, even the installation of that ten-meter diameter steel penstock (the pipe bringing the water to the generator under great pressure), the large capacity lift and the four generators. The generators, by necessity, had to be lowered by huge cranes even before the pipes and the lift were installed. Chris had prepared for the future by having foundations for a further two 150-Megawatt generators surveyed and poured. It had taken over eighteen months-- from the time he and Bill had sat by the river fishing, --- for the first drops of water, instantly followed by that huge volume of diverted water poured its kinetic energy down that shaft and those beautiful 150-Megawatt generators started to spin with a hypnotic hum. During the hiatus of the discovery of that wonderful cavern and the completion of the power station project, Chris had surveyed the route, and had several crews digging and installing the very expensive high-voltage underground cable, including an appropriately located voltage regulation plant, and branch lines to supply power to the resort and the cattle station. The power station and the installation of the cable was completed only two weeks before the final nut and bolt was tightened to complete the installation of the spodumene processing plant.

Chris had derived much malicious pleasure from juggling the very spirited negotiations for the purchase of the spodumene concentrate by the many foreign lithium producing countries, all of whom had been given samples of the concentrate Quo-Vadis Lithium would produce. He finally reduced the contenders to a British firm and a Japanese Conglomerate, agreeing to supply each of those two proposed purchasers 250,000 tonnes per annum to each of them. He could see to have two reputable purchases did ensure a continuation of the sale of spodumene in the highly unlikely event one of those companies struck difficulties.

"That's another $350 million per annum I have to find a home for," Rex had lamented.

Chris had only laughed as he replied to Rex, "Don't worry, old chap." Although Rex was only twelve years his senior, Chris did love taking the "Mickey" out of Rex by referring to his brother as "The Old Chap." "I have a thing or two in mind to spend a bit on."

"Will you ever stop, you madman?" Rex complained to him. "Over the last thirty months, what with the spodumene set up out at Quo-Vadis Lithium, the power station and transmission cable, purchase of aeroplanes, and the Iron Ore company shares, just to nominate a few you have spent darn near two-billion dollars. Not a bad effort for a kid! It was a good thing that all your other operations, referring of course, to Quo-Vadis gold, the cattle station, the resort and the tourist park all kicked in while you have been playing miner."

"Only two billion? That was cheap even at twice that price," Chris chuckled. "I thought I had done better than that. It is a shame that the iron ore mob haven't come to the party with their share of the rail line. Do I have about four-hundred million lying about brother? I feel a take-over coming on."

"Give me a break, you maniac. I have only this week moved into our new building. If I have to include all the accounting procedure of an iron ore mine in your portfolio, I will need at least two more floors." Rex had hesitated for a moment, then lightly said, "It may be quite fun and rather edifying to manage a take-over. Do you really want to make a complete buy-back? You already hold thirty-two percent of the stock."

"All the way, please, Rex," Chris replied, "I do not want some old codger putting his oar in and interrupting our operation."

A week later there was a long editorial by the finance editor of the daily newspaper announcing: "Quo-Vadis Holdings Proprietary Limited have announced they are to make a take-over bid for Iron Ore Limited. The firm of accountants controlling the bid have advised the offer to shareholders registered at today's date will be 6.3 cents per share. With the current listed price of Iron Ore Limited at 4.8 cents per share, the offer is most generous. Quo Vadis Holdings Proprietary Limited is wholly owned by one Mr Christopher John Kennedy. We have been unsuccessful in our attempts to contact him for comment. We were advised he is presently on an exploration expedition, and his date of return is unknown. Company Office searches revealed very little, and we do confirm that all statutory requirements are complete. A senior man from the company's office, did say in confidence, 'Quo-Vadis Holdings Proprietary Limited is very strong, with substantial unencumbered assets.'"

Chris and Bill uninvited bowled into the hastily convened directors meeting of Iron Ore Limited and positioned themselves at the head of the conference table. Chris did not hesitate, and in a voice that allowed no room for dispute, spoke very loudly. He started by extending his arm and pointing: "You, You, You, You and You; all five of you, are no longer required by this company. Make immediate arrangements to vacate your offices."

"You cannot do this!" one very angry ex-director snapped.

"I can, and I have," Chris very forcibly said. "I presently hold over eighty-percent shareholding in this company and am enforcing a takeover. All of you who I nominated leave this room now. I do invite all others to remain, and suggest you hold onto your hats—it is going to be a very exciting future. Mr Simpson, sir, may I ask you to remain as Chairman and Managing Director, and place these remaining gentlemen, who will remain as board members, into positions you consider much more appropriate to their talent. Quo Vadis Holdings will not interfere with the running of the company unless we see room for improvement. Frankly speaking, we have identified areas where there is need for much to be done."

There were a few minor hiccups before the takeover was complete. Several stalwarts were slow in parting with their stock. They had bought their shares some years before and had paid over the issued price for them. They were, understandably, without enthusiasm to sell their shares at the offered price and lose a lot of money. Rex advised them of their statutory rights, gave them the prescribed fourteen days to accept the offer, then acquired their shareholding by simply paying them out..

The last stand-out did reply to Rex's advice and had written saying, "With the involvement of the Quo-Vadis group, I could see a better future for the Iron Ore Company and wish to be part of it." He did institute legal proceedings to prevent the forced sale of his shares.

Chris had admired this old codger's tenacity and invited him to visit Quo-Vadis.

"Where the hell is that?" the old gentleman exclaimed.

"Its way out in the Outback," Chris explained, then added, "Have little concern, I will get you there and back with absolutely no discomfort."

After one week of staying at the resort, and bludging on Chris's generosity, the old fellow emphatically announced, "After seeing all this, there is no way you are getting my shares Mister. With what you have done here, and the brilliance of your management, I can only see a bright future for the iron ore company."

"I was expecting that," Chris had replied to him. "I do have a proposition that may interest you. You hold 50,000 shares in Iron Ore Limited. For many years you have watched their value decrease and have not received any dividends. You did pay a premium for those shares—they owe you $65,000."

"You know it all," the old fellow interrupted.

"Let me finish, you cranky old bugger," Chris laughed and continued. "I will issue you with 0.25% of a B class non-voting share in Quo-Vadis Holdings in return for your shares. We could go ahead with the court action. I have no doubt in the final analysis, you will be forced to sell me your holding at 6.4 cents per share, and possibly be landed with court costs. I would prefer not to do this; it is not my nature. To let you know a little of the value of what I am offering, be advised, Quo-Vadis Holdings is worth several billion dollars, and last year the dividend on one B class share was $1 million. You cannot sell those shares I offer you to any person other than me."

The old gentleman stood quietly for a minute, then softly said, "Can I sit down for a minute young fellow," he stuttered. "You are telling me your B class shares pay $1 million dividend a year, and that my 0.25% will return me about, $250,000 a year?"

"That's correct," Chris laughed. "I am willing to do that just to get a cranky old bugger off my back. As a matter of interest, I am anticipating the dividend may be a little higher this year."

The old gentleman stood quickly and offered Chris his hand saying, rather enthusiastically, "Done deal, lad," then with a smile on his face added, "Cut out the old bit, you have made me feel twenty years younger."

One month later, after the takeover being officially complete, Chris and Rex again sat at the head of the conference table.

Simpson, the Chairman, sat next to Chris. He was a different man to that oppressed individual who had sat there one month previous. He stood tall and straight and announced. "Gentlemen of the board, Mr Christopher Kennedy will now address this meeting. He and I have discussed in depth what he has to say to you. All I can add at this point is—and using his words—is 'hang onto your hats', there are exciting times ahead. I do welcome Mr Ambrose to the board, as an alternative board member in the absence of Mr Kennedy. Mr Ambrose was the last shareholder to relinquish his holding, and Mr Kennedy believes his maturity and wisdom will ensure we keep the ship steady." Simpson turned slowly to Chris, saying with a chuckle, "Okay Chris, your turn. Hit them right between the eyes."

"Thank you, Mr Simpson. I promise you I will only brighten up their day," Chris said. "Gentlemen! You will have to be a little tolerant at my lack of expertise in delivering a long discourse. Protocol is not my forte—I prefer action. There are a number of matters I have to inform you of. Matter number one. As from yesterday, all debts of Quo-Vadis Iron—that by the way is the unlisted company for whom you are invited to join—have been absorbed and cleared by the parent company, Quo-Vadis Holdings. You will not have access to the accounts of Quo-Vadis Holdings. Be well advised; here and now; I am going to require a greater input from each of you; consequently, your fees will be increased by five-hundred percent. You may draw all or any of those fees at any time in each financial year. The financial year for our purposes commences on the first of September each year. The Chairman's secretary, the very delightful and efficient Ms O'Connell will hand each of you a contract drawn up by our solicitors. The contract will require you to commit to the company for ten years, and in special circumstances is open for negotiation should the need arise. It will also be renewable after ten years. Read these documents very carefully, and if you find them acceptable return them to Ms O'Connell by Friday next week. We are open to negotiate any point you may wish to discuss. I am very confident you will find the terms of the contracts are most agreeable; consequently, I am going to pre-empt your signing, and talk of matter number two. For your information, these are the things we have put into action. Construction of the railway link proposed by Quo Vadis Lithium has commenced; on present progress it is anticipated to be fully functional in ten more months. The pegmatites deposits of Quo-Vadis Iron have been explored and have found to be considered most economical. The mining of Iron Ore has been changed from the old traditional ways to more modern ways, suggested by two very learned university mining professors, who by the way have been engaged as permanent consultants. Rail wagons and locomotives have all been updated. We have completed comprehensive negotiations with an overseas group, who will purchase under contract all the ore we can produce. We are investigating replacing the very old crusher at the mine with a newer, more up-to-date efficient machine. This will reduce crushing costs considerably and produce far better ore fines. The ore buyers have advised us they will be prepared to increase the contracted price, should that occur as the better product would decrease their smelting costs by an estimated fifty percent. As a matter of interest, we are looking at the prospect and economics of doing our own smelting."

Chris took a long drink of water, and, with a touch of humour in his voice, said, "Goodness Gracious, I have not had to talk for this long for some time; usually my wife never lets me get a word in edgewise. Rex will take over now and give your ears a rest from my monotone."

He promptly sat down, and Rex stood and took over. "You have all possibly guessed by now, Chris and I are on this board only in the interests of Quo-Vadis Holdings Proprietary Limited. It may be of interest and to your benefit for you, before signing those contracts , to be aware of just what a monster you are *getting into bed with*. The conglomerate is wholly owned by Chris. There are a few B class non-voting shares on issue; by the way if you are interested, each of you will be able to purchase 0.25% of 1 of those B class shares. Ms O'Connell can give you all the details later. The holding company is the sole owner and operator of Quo-Vadis Gold, Quo-Vadis Resorts, Quo-Vadis Tourist Park, Quo-Vadis Station, Quo-Vadis Power, Quo-Vadis Properties, Quo-Vadis Lithium, and now Quo-Vadis Iron."

One of the more senior board members, Johnathan Perry, the finance director, stood and all but stuttered, "You are saying one man, Chris Kennedy, owns the lot?"

"Yep!" Rex exclaimed. "Not bad for a twenty-nine-year-old miner; he is a bit of a smart arse if you ask me. I can get away with comments like that because I'm his big brother. I had best stop mucking about; if we are going to get home tonight, there is much to discuss. Firstly, I wish to hear from each of you how you see your area is going. Should you have any thoughts of any changes that could be instituted, do not hesitate to suggest them. Secondly, I wish to see any conflict between departments resolved to everybody's complete satisfaction and resolved quickly."

One particular subject was a matter of spirited discussion. Every board member had his own idea as to what the allocation of staff should be.

Rex didn't hesitate to intervene. "This matter will not be resolved here in the boardroom; each of you will submit to me a comprehensive schedule of what staff you want and what will be their duties. You may object to some of the changes I will suggest," emphasising the word *suggest*. "What I suggest will be instituted immediately," then with a smile on his face added, "Tom, I do not want to see your schedule contain a postscript, *all girls to be pretty*. As each of you consider your needs, focus on what you know of the individual. Consider each staff member carefully, their strengths and weaknesses and in particular their attitude. I expect you all to follow the guidelines of advice Ms O'Connor will hand out to you. Within the next month I expect each of you will call a general meeting of all your departmental staff, where you may advise them of the new structure. Their individual reaction will be a guideline to your assessment of their suitability of remaining with the company. It may sound harsh, but you should divest yourself of anyone you see as a problem or even a potential problem. A happy co-operating office is an efficient office. You will always have problems—have them dealt with quickly; and Jeff, your number two is unsuited for that position. He is a likely type—obviously a talented man; it would be a shame to lose him; see if he would like to join the exploration team of Quo-Vadis Lithium. Transfers between the companies of the group are not out of the question. Chris could tell you he worked as a non-entity for many of his early years and moved on mainly at his own initiative; what I am referring to here is initiative, so encourage suggestions of improvement to anything within your department. Keep a watchful eye on attitude. Anybody within the department with a bad attitude is like a cancer and can corrupt the whole department. Don't hesitate to get rid of any semblance of a bad attitude. If in this washout you end up short staffed, we will attend to that quickly by conducting an extensive recruitment program and engaging only what we see as top-quality people. Each of you will be involved in that recruitment program; so, you can see for the next few months you will be really earning your keep. When it all boils down, the efficiency of your department is your responsibility, and in the big picture does have repercussions on the whole company. Emphasise to the staff that they are contributing to a highly prestigious and successful group with their efforts each day. That will not be overlooked. It has been a long day, and there is only one matter left for attention. Chris will cover that now, and Chris, please don't chuck in any curly bits—I want to go home in one piece."

"My brother is the ultimate comedian," Chris laughed as he stood. All I wish to advise you is that I have made arrangements for each and every one of you to bring your families out to Quo-Vadis. You will be staying at Quo-Vadis Resorts for a minimum of two weeks, starting from the first of next month. That's the school holidays. The invite is not mandatory—you may already have other plans; it is only there for the taking, and for you to perhaps gain a better insight into the extent of the Quo-Vadis group. You may stay longer if you wish. All expenses, including accommodation are covered for you, you and your families will travel there by aircraft from our Quo-Vadis air fleet. Bring your fishing rods, swimming togs—they are not mandatory," he added with a big grin, and then continued, "and plenty of sunscreen."

In the following months, the company went ahead with leaps and bounds. Mining, transport, finance, administration, right down to the cleaning staff, all worked hand in glove, and what was a company on the verge of collapse now became an efficient, very profitable enterprise.

Eleven months later, pegmatites ore from the deposits on the iron ore mining lease was being railed to Quo-Vadis Lithium for processing and the spodumene concentrate added to the concentrate from the deposit at Quo Vadis Lithium for shipment to the various buyers. Construction of the railway had not been without a problem or two. The biggest problem was that ridge of very rocky mountainous country between the two company's operations. That had been overcome by building a nineteen-kilometre tunnel through those mountains. An extension of that very expensive high tension electrical cable had been made in conjunction with the railway construction and now the very-expensive-to-operate diesel powered generators had been replaced with a most modern electrical switchyard, drawing power from those beautiful generators at the Quo-Vadis sinkhole. With the advent of this new power source, operating costs of all the plant at the iron ore mine had been reduced to almost zero. Although those, now, four massive one hundred and fifty-megawatt generators had more than enough surplus output, Chris did go ahead and, piece by piece, install two more generators. He now had nine-hundred Megawatts of power at his disposal, and laughed as he told Bill, "You can have as many crushers, smelters and processing equipment, you could ever envisage the group needing."

# Chapter 15

These days Bill was a very busy man, now having to maintain constant surveillance over all the plant at their many and various mines. From time to time, the professors would bring to his notice an up-to-date version of a new machine or procedure, which Bill invariably installed or instigated quickly. One of his greatest pleasures was to walk through the spodumene plant with the mine manager, Geoff, and watch that, *you beaut crusher* at work.

He often shared breakfast with Chris and Jackie; they would discuss many of the large and small things that were happening. "What's that bit about a smelter out of the iron ore mine you were talking about at that board meeting, about a month back?" he tossed the question at Chris.

"It's just something I had been thinking of to keep you from getting bored, mate," Chris replied.

"That," Bill exclaimed, "would be a great challenge. It would be something I would really enjoy. The machines in all the mines are nearly all new, and they very rarely need any repairs of any description. I am sure the mine managers could look after them without me constantly bugging them like I do now, so I could devote all my time to that project. Have you talked it over with the professors?"

"I have had a few short discussions with them about this. They were very enthusiastic, saying a smelter out there would open up many possibilities," Chris replied, then very meaningfully, said, "Okay Mister Smelter Master, let's get to it. We'll get Rex and the professors out here as early as possible. In the meantime, you and I will do some research of our own and look at what's involved. I do not wish to spend much time away from home for a while; I am going to spend some time with Jackie and Yindi—I have missed them. A lot of our research can be done on the net."

"You drive, I'll be the passenger," Bill happily laughed. "Those darn computers hate me. They deliberately messed themselves up every time I even touch them. I am amazed with what the uni. boys can make them do."

Chris was quiet for a couple of moments; it was obvious he had something on his mind. He looked directly at Bill and softly said; "as we are looking at something further for you to look after, it is opportune to discuss this before we start.

I have become increasingly concerned with your workload. Bill! You have been involved with everything that has happened at Quo-Vadis; right from the very start. In all the time you have been here; to my knowledge you have never taken a decent break. There is no way I can measure the value of your contribution. You are now pushing 60; you should be thinking of slowing down a bit. Don't give me any codswallop by saying *I'm alright;* we both know at times you are pushing yourself. There is no way I want you to stop working; without you about, the place would fall to pieces.

Do you recall the Mine Manager who works for that gold big mine in town? His name is Jacques Piermont. I had a call from him last week, he had heard much about Quo-Vadis and in particular Quo-Vadis goldmines and he was wondering; *did we have a need for a very experienced mine manager.*

I knew you are under the pump a bit (under pressure) and thought it would not hurt to listen to what he was offering. Jacques came out yesterday and explained; that although the lease they had purchased from us had been most profitable several of the board members had taken exception to his demanding that with the increased profits they could well afford some more modern equipment. Much to his distress the board had appointed another engineer to lead the mining operation on that new lease. He feels he may be getting pushed aside and would like to make a move before that happens. He is going to come back next week.

All our other operations are run by top managers. You have always run the gold mining operation; even the crushers and smelters. Perhaps you would take a little time and think on this. If we appoint Jacques to take over managing the goldmines it would leave you free to continue overseeing all the operations of the group; and devote some time to new projects. You have always been at my right hand and know just about as much of the Quo-Vadis group as I do. You could continue in that role. I would expect without the pressure of the day-to-day dramas of running the goldmines you and Ellie could take a few well-earned holidays. You might even get a chance to spend a little more time in your garden; and even wetting a line more often.

The decision is yours for the making; my friend; but I can see with a pair of us driving this Quo-Vadis monster; the sky is the limit, and new projects of the like of the new smelter out at the iron ore mine could receive your full attention. I have to warn you; I do have several other things in my mind; with which I will need your assistance. So, I can assure you; you're not going to get bored."

"You make it sound good Chris. Yes, I am tired;" Bill rather wistfully said, then rather forcefully added, "there is one thing I want understood here and now! Although I would be 'your partner in crime'; I never; and I say again; never; want you to give me any shares in the holding Company. That company belongs to the Kennedy's for now and all future Kennedy generations. I perceive that young Jack is tarred with the same brush as his old man, so I can clearly see for at least control of the company for the next generation is in good hands.

Okay let's have a talk with Jacques Piermont and see if he is as good as he says he is." Jacques lived up to his word. He was a very experienced and competent gold mine manager and was totally elated with what he was seeing and enthusiastically commented "all this beautiful modern machinery is a mine-managers dream, and all that I will have available at my fingertips will allow me to run your mines precisely as I know mines should be run."

Now Chris and Bill could get back to the thing they loved, exploring and starting new projects.

# Chapter 16

The next morning Chris was working in his office in the house, when Bill walked in saying; did you know you have a visitor waiting downstairs?"

"No," Chris replied, "Anybody I know?"

"It's Susie. By the look of her she has a big problem." Bill replied.

"I wonder what's up," Chris said to nobody in particular, as he quickly left his office and raced downstairs. Bill was right there almost on his heels; Jackie was just coming in from being out in the garden and together the three of them strode into the family room where Chris and Jackie's adopted daughter; Susan awaited.

Susan was far from the beautiful gentle girl they had known. She had lost so much weight, and exaggerating a little, --if she stood side on, you could easily miss seeing her and her countenance was one of total despair.

The first thing Chris thought was, "Good grief, she looks bloody awful."

"Susie! Susie!" Jackie cried. "What's wrong? Are you sick?"

Susie all but collapsed into Jackie's arms, crying, "Mummy, oh Mummy," she cried, as her tears soaked them both. "I need you so badly. Alan is dead and I am all alone, and these dreadful men keep coming and making such dreadful threats and doing such terrible things to me. I am so frightened." She wept copiously as she tried to speak.

"Let's go into the lounge room," Chris softly said. "It is always nice and sunny in there and we will sit and listen while you tell us everything that's causing you so much distress. I am sure whatever it is we can fix much of it."

"Oh Daddy," Susie whispered, "I knew you would know what to do," as she flung her arms about his neck and snuggled into his shoulder, absorbing the sense of security.

"I'll make us a good cup of tea," Bill volunteered.

"I have done that," came the soft voice of Ellie. "A tray of tea and home baked biscuits for five is here and ready."

Bill took the laden tray from her saying, "Thank you, Ellie dear. I think we all could do with it."

Chris, Jackie, Bill and Ellie sat quietly and listened to Susie as she tearfully rambled through what had been happening.

As far as Chris could understand, the problems had all started last year, when four Middle Eastern types had uninvited come to the mine and started calling Alan all sorts of filthy things, claiming he was trespassing and stealing their gold. "They had demanded all their money— everything—and further demanded if Susie and Allan would not sign the mine over to them and give them the money they would come back and kill both of them. Alan had told them to go to hell and the four of them really beat him. They had asked the police in town to help them. The police were very sympathetic but said "They did not have the men who could be spared to sit way out in the Outback waiting for a few baddies who may, hopefully never come back; the best thing the Police could do was to keep an eye out for those fellows and drag them in and question them, and unless Alan and Susie were there to identify them; they could not charge them. Alan and Susie did stay in town for a while but Alan had said he wanted to go back to the mine. The men had been there in their absence and had trashed the place; the house; the mine; everything. Apparently, Alan had wanted to stay and try to clean things up, but those men came back the very next day, then day after day always beating him; it got so bad towards the end she and Alan would run into the bush and hide and wait until they left. Apparently, those terrible men did eventually catch them and beat both she and Alan.

342

"How dreadful!" Ellie exclaimed.

Susie had tried to continue talking. Jackie hushed her; however, Chris very quietly but firmly said, "Let her talk Jackie, love, it will do her good to get it out, and I do want to hear it all."

Susie took a deep breath and continued to tell what had happened next. "I pleaded with Alan to give them what they wanted. He was very brave and said he would never give in. The next time they came and caught us they beat him so badly he could hardly walk." She collapsed onto Jackie almost screaming, "Then they raped me—all four of them. I cannot get the pain of it from my mind and I feel so dirty. Alan was so badly beaten he could not protect me and they made him watch those men as they took turns to rape me. He was in such a mess in mind and body after that, he hung himself. Not a word of goodbye—not a thing; he only went into the bush and hung himself. I found him hanging there two days ago. Please help me!" she wailed.

"The filthy bastards!" Bill shouted. "I'm going to get a few boys and go and pick them up and teach them what pain really is."

"No, Bill," Chris very firmly ordered, "You will do nothing, and you Susie girl, are going to stay here with us. Jackie will get the Flying Doctor in for you; he will give you a thorough check over and give you something to help you sleep. You will never see or hear of those animals ever again."

Jackie poured Susie another cup of tea and they sat together softly talking. At times, Susie would burst into tears and once again collapsed onto Jackie's shoulder.

Jackie sat Susie by the warm sunny window and walked back to Chris. "What are you going to do, Chris?" she asked. "You were so cold when you more or less told Bill to butt out, I am sure half Hell froze over."

"Please do not worry, my wonderful wife. All you have to do is look after Susie—that is enough, I will take care of the rest. This is not the homecoming I expected. I will be away a couple of days; you must not worry—it will be alright," then without another word commandeered one of the fast helicopters and flew out to the station. He explained to Peter what had happened to Susie and told him he needed a good horse and half a dozen of his best stockmen for a few days.

"What are you going to do? Whatever it is, I am coming," Peter offered.

"Come if you must," Chris replied. "You must understand that you cannot interfere or be surprised with what happens."

The group rode for two days and nights to arrive at Susie's deserted home in the early hours of the morning. They did find Alans body and immediately buried him. It was only then Chris explained to the stockmen what had happened and why he needed their help. The stockmen were outraged and shared Chris's anger. They did not hesitate to dig the temporary grave, however they steadfastly refused to touch the body. "I will have to come back later and arrange for him to be buried properly;" Chris sadly thought. The group did not go to the house only lay in wait about a kilometre down the track. They drew a large log across the track to stop any vehicle that would approach. Around about 11.30 am a battered old Land Rover raced rather quickly down the track, so quickly in fact the driver did not have time to stop or avoid the log and ploughed into it, demolishing the whole of the vehicle's front end. Four men extracted themselves from the damaged vehicle, cursing vehemently at the driver in some foreign language. One had a large cut on his forehead—it looked like he had bashed his head on the dashboard as the vehicle hit the log. They walked constantly around the wrecked vehicle, jabbering in a language Chris did not understand, not that he knew any other language than English.
Their main concern seemed to be centred on how they were going to get back.

They jumped in surprise when Chris appeared from the bush. "Got a problem I see, fellas," Chris rather innocently asked.

One of the hostile, very angry men, who appeared to be the leader, blazed with a voice full venom at Chris. "Did you put the log across the track? Are you one of those bushrangers we have read about?"

"Right with both questions," Chris coldly replied. "Now I will ask you a question, what are you doing here? Be careful with your answer—I know what it should be. For your information the girl is not here, and we have buried her husband. I would like to invite you to a little party to show you what happens to nasty people like you."

One of the fellows hastily produced a large revolver and shouted, "I'll show you what happens to people who cross us."

He got no further before the stinging lash of a stock whip tore the gun from his hand and a second lash tore out his right eye. "Sorry boss," a very Aussie voice chuckled. "I missed—I was shooting for both eyes, hang on a minute, I'll get you the other one."

"He's lost interest, Jimmy. Leave him be," Chris said softly.

The man was down on his knees screaming in pain, holding his face in both hands as he tried to contain the pain and to reduce the blood pouring down his cheeks.

"Anybody else like to lose and eye or two?" Chris growled. Ignoring the plight of his colleague one of the other fellows did drag out a large revolver and started blazing indiscriminately into the bush at the side of the track. In seconds there was a whistling of stock whips being plied by experts and that foolish man was divested of ninety-percent of his clothes. "Oops," a voice chuckled, "I seem to have taken his nuts too."

"Anybody else inclined to lose his eyes or his balls?" Chris had sarcastically laughed. There was a slight pause as the two undamaged fellows looked with horror at their screaming compatriots.

"No takers—that's a good move," Chris called. "Just toss out all your weapons and stand back to back, your hands on your heads. A little closer please," Chris said as he stepped out from the protection of a large gum tree and signalled nonchalantly and more whips wrapped tightly about the men binding them securely. "You can put your hands down now," Chris ordered. "You'll need them to help your mates. We are going for a walk, so be good—I do dislike getting angry."

Eight days later the party of stockmen on horseback and four very frightened fellows flung over the backs of pack horses, with Chris trailing along in Goliath, paused at the edge of what appeared to be a desolate, godforsaken land. Chris had declined Peter's offer to accompany him on this section of the journey, telling him, he had contributed more than enough already.

"We are about to enter the land of KINIE GER (the evillest spirits of the land)" Chris announced to the stockmen. "I will understand if you do not wish to come with me." The stockmen milled about, as if in indecision.

One finally asked rather tentatively, "How many days are we to remain there, Boss Chris?"

"Many," Chris replied. "I wish to introduce these men to the KINIE GER. Those two," he indicated the blind man and the now genital-less man, "will return with me and will spend many years in a white man's jail. These other two will give their spirits to the land to be tormented for ever."

One stock man stepped up to Chris and said with a very concerned voice, "Abdiel Boss Chris, we have heard of your powers. What you are thinking of doing is very dangerous. The Kinie Ger are very powerful and may capture your spirit also."

"Thank you, my friend," Chris replied. "I will trust Maarman Yira (God) to protect me. What I wish to do, I must do." With that he dragged the four captive men from the pack horses and securely bound their hands, arms and legs and bundled them into the back of Goliath. Without another word to the stockmen he headed Goliath out into that desolate land.

Goliath had full tanks of fuel so Chris drove on over that unforgiving seemingly endless desert, sand for two-and-a-half days, finally stopping adjacent to a substantial outcrop of formidable looking rock. "This looks like a likely place," Chris thought, "Now I will put the fear of 'old nick' (the devil) into these blokes."

He dragged them from the back of Goliath, and sat them in the blazing, unrelenting Outback sun. Next, he poured the blood of a large pig, the native stockmen had caught and butchered for him; over the two undamaged men. They had watched the stockmen as they carved up the pig with obvious revulsion and now realised why that blood had been saved.

They cried piteously, "You have made us unclean. Should we die we will not be able to enter that place we have had promised to us."

Chris had coldly ignored their cries and almost reverently said, "The natives believe these rocks are the very home of the Kinie Ger, the evillest of the spirits. It is said that they feast very slowly on the flesh of man and prevents his soul from entering the Dreamtime. I do not know what you believe, but it is here I will leave you, staked out naked for the feast." The two fellows wailed in fear, "you cannot do this it is inhumane, they wailed with panic-stricken cries"

"I can and I will," Chris venomously answered. "As your hands and toes are eaten, think about what you had done to that young man and his wife. This punishment is just."

Without a further thought, Chris left those two fellows just as he had said, staked out naked, totally exposed in the intense burning Outback sun. Once again, he bundled those two injured men into the back of Goliath and drove slowly away. He had gone about two kilometres when a large black shadow drifted across his path. Chris looked up into the sky to see what had caused the shadow. Mullian (the wedge-tailed Eagle) circled overhead. The shadow he cast appeared to say, "No further Chris."

Chris looked up into the sky to the eagle and quietly said, "So you do not wish for me to leave them here. Whatever punishment they receive they deserve it, and even worse," he endeavoured to explain his actions. A feeling of intense compassion hit him; the thought pounded in his brain, "They are humans of a sort, so I guess I had best return and collect them and take them back. Maybe they will get their 'just desserts' in prison."

By the time he had returned to that rocky outcrop, a flock of black crows had gathered around those screaming men. The crows scattered as Goliath roared up. Chris stepped out to a pitiful sight. In the short time he had left them there, one man had an eye picked out by those razor-sharp beaks and blood poured profusely from numerous other places. The other fellow had blood pouring from his nether region and numerous other wounds about his body. About fifty metres away, several crows squabbled over the something that had been removed causing all the bleeding. Chris quickly cut the ropes that held the two fellows to the stakes and sat them up. Both cried piteously and writhed in pain.

"Not feeling quite so tough now I bet" Chris snapped. "Wrap these rags around yourselves. I don't want your blood all over my nice clean vehicle and get into the back with the others. Behave yourself or I will find something else for you to enjoy," Chris very forcefully ordered.

As he drove away from the rocks, that majestic bird floated down and drifted alongside for several hundred meters, then with a flap of those mighty wings it disappeared into the blue sky.

After two days of hard driving back along his tracks he reached the edge of the forbidden land. His stockmen had patiently awaited his return.

When they viewed the damaged cargo Chris carried, they cried out loud with fear-filled voices, "You have stolen the meal from the Kinie Ger; they will be angry," they wailed.

"I do not fear the anger of the Kinie Ger," Chris very firmly replied. "I believe the spirit which protects me is much, much stronger than them. My spirit sent Mullian to tell me to turn back and bring them out. I will give what is left of these fellows back to their brothers so all their brothers will see what the Outback will do to them should any of them ever attempt enter this land again, and will think twice before trying to do anything of the nature these fellows had done"

The stockmen all agreed with what he had done, one saying, "You are most wise to listen to what your spirit tells you, Abdiel Boss Chris."

He firmly shook the hand of each one of those stockmen, thanked them sincerely, and instructed them to return to the station, telling them, the less said about your adventure, the better. That last bit was really wasted. Another tale was told over and over around the many native camp fires.

Chris had driven to the big smoke and was now parked in the driveway just outside the gates of the embassy of that mob. It was well past midnight and rather than disturb the Embassy, he unceremoniously dumped those four fellows in an untidy heap outside the gates, blocking the driveway.

Nothing further was ever heard of those four men: no news reports, not one thing.

Chris returned to Quo-Vadis. His return was greeted with mixed response. Bill's response was predictable: he raged about the room shouting, "You blasted idiot, you might have got yourself killed. You could have at least told us what you're about to do."

Jackie's response was the total opposite. She held him with loving arms for a few minutes before whispering, "Is it over?"

Next afternoon he quietly sat by the lake with Susie, not telling her what had happened, only assuring her she would never have to go through that again, and that she would never again have to look upon those men.

Susie cried in apparent relief, then softly said, "Daddy, I never want to go back to that mine ever again. I want you to take it all and do whatever you want with it."

Chris had answered her quietly saying, "We'll talk about that much later. I will keep an eye on the place for you. In the meantime, you are to stay here amongst the people who love you and will help you get well again."

Jackie agreed that was all for the best and added, "You are a wonderful soft and sensitive man my Christopher Kennedy."

"Not so soft," Chris thought to himself. "Those four blokes will be nothing but vegetables for what is left godforsaken live.

# Chapter17

Brother Rex had asked him to come to town for a day or two. There were a few decisions which needed to be bought to his attention and resolved. Leaving Yindi in the care of his mother, Chris and Jackie did accede to Rex's request. Jackie had gone off to get her hair done, and with it being such a beautiful day, and having some time on his hands, Chris decided to walk the couple of kilometres from his apartment to Rex's office. He strolled nonchalantly along the street, musing on one or two things that he should do when he got back to Quo-Vadis. For once, he was finding this short stay in the big smoke rather pleasant.

The traffic light was against him and he paused to wait for them to change. A non-aggressive tug on his right arm brought him back to reality from his musing. "Chris! Christopher Kennedy," the voice excitedly said.

He turned to the voice. "Who?" he asked. He did not recognise the face.

"It's Jamie, Jamie Hill. You must remember me—your old CEO from the Investment Company."

"Mr Hill. I recognise you now. What have you done to yourself? You look far from the man I knew. Have you been ill?" Chris exclaimed!

"Yes! In a way I have been ill, more or less," Hill replied. "But look at you, you look a million dollars."

"Thank you, sir," Chris humbly answered.

"No more sirs or beg your pardons, please, Chris. Things have changed a bit," Hill quietly said, and, as if he was divulging a great secret, whispered, "I am no longer with the Investment Company; a few things got to me and I had to give it away. Did you ever go on with that mining venture? Helen had told me you were studying mining."

351

"Yes, Mr Hill," Chris started to reply, only to be interrupted.

"No Mr Hill anymore please, Chris," Hill quite abruptly said. "Please call me Jamie."

"Okay Mr Jamie," Chris chuckled.

"Full of humour aren't you, lad," Jamie responded.

"If you're not with the Investment Company," Chris enquired, "are you with another investment company? You would have had to pick and choose from all the offers that must have had come your way."

"It didn't happen like that, Chris," Jamie ruefully said. "That rotten little turd—you remember him, Graystone, your old supervisor—created a rumour and made it known all over town I had been sacked for unsavoury conduct. He never specified what I had done that was unsavoury. I eventually learned from another source, he had never quite got over the dressing down I gave him about stealing your kudos and trying to wangle the footy invite given to you by your client. I have managed to get a job as a stock clerk with a motor firm; in my present frame of mind that's about all I can handle anyway."

"Jamie," Chris very sympathetically and quietly said, "there is something wrong in all this. Do you have time to grab a coffee with me? Somewhere quiet. I would like to hear it all if you do not mind telling me. I only have to make a couple of phone calls, then I will be free for the day. I think you and I have much to talk about. If you think I am getting too nosy, please tell me. There used to be a good coffee shop just around the corner—that would be ideal. First a phone call to my brother to let him know he will have to do without me this morning and next to my very special wife Jackie to let her know what I am doing."

Chris and Jamie Hill sat at a window table in the coffee shop. For a while Jamie said nothing. Chris could see he was trying to bring himself together, trying to remember the sequence of things as they happened.

"It must be a very emotional thing he has to talk about," Chris thought, "so I'll let him begin in his own time and his own way."

Chris ordered a second cup of coffee. It was about to be delivered to the table when Jamie started to talk. "Chris," he very hesitantly said, "this is very hard for me. I have never before had to put what happened into coherent words, so bear with me a little if I wander a bit, and at times I may even start to blubber."

"Only tell me what you want to Jamie. Do not think you have to tell me everything," Chris softly said.

"Thank you for that Chris," Jamie whispered. "I think it will help me if I can tell somebody I trust everything that is on my mind." He took a large gulp of his coffee, looked straight at Chris's face and said, "You remember your old supervisor Graystone, he turned out to be a bigger bastard than you thought. In fact, to my mind, there is no bigger bastard on this earth. Did you know his wife was the daughter of the managing director? She is a bigger bitch than even Graystone; she was 'on' with half that motorcycle gang from the north side. How she and Graystone ever got together one would never know. I guess they were made for each other.

Not long after you left, and to everybody's surprise, especially mine, Graystone was appointed onto the board. That meant he now had authority over me, and he progressively went about making my life hell. He was a very poor administrator and the company lost account after account because of him. He blamed me for the loss of those accounts, no matter how hard I tried to save them. The harder I tried, the more he would stuff up my efforts. In the end, I couldn't take any more and physically broke down. I had a small stroke, and Graystone saw to it I was unsuited to continue working for the company, and I lost my job.

To say it was not a good time for me would be an understatement. With all the pressures of my work and my stroke, my marriage suffered and my wife left me. I thank goodness there were no children to suffer with our breakup. She didn't leave me much, and has since remarried, and moved interstate."

Jamie had become a little overcome. He took another large gulp of his coffee and appeared to pull himself together and softly continued. "All this happened a couple of years back. I've been alone since, surviving from day to day as best I can. Thankfully there has been no repeat of the stroke; in fact, I am now more physically fit than I ever was, really, I am quite well apart from being stuffed up in my mind. By the way, the Investment Company no longer exists. I do not know what happened or what happened to Graystone. I hope he got what he deserved and ended up in hell. You may remember Helen, my PA. I met her about nine months ago. She is married now and has a daughter. She was quite a mess for a while after you left. I didn't know you pair were a unit. She told me she eventually got over it all and is now a very happy. That's about it, Chris. There may be other bits and pieces but nothing important."

He sat back in his chair and sighed, "I feel better for getting that off my chest. Thank you for listening, Chris. Please tell me how you are, and why you do look so disgustingly well. You must be in a good paddock. Helen did tell me you were studying mining; did you finish your studies?"

Chris slowly stirred his second cup of coffee and quietly replied, "Yes, I did finish the course. I am now a graduate mining engineer. Quite contrary to your lot, I have been very successful."

It was all very quiet for about thirty seconds, then Jamie blurted out, "Well! Don't leave it at that! Make my day—tell me all."

"Okay, I will tell you some of it. It would be difficult to tell you everything without appearing to boast a bit. I will start at the very beginning. I too had a rough start; I even spent six months living with the native people, they had saved my life. Upon my return to civilization I had been most fortunate to win a few dollars. With those funds I designed and had a very special vehicle made that enabled me to follow a dream and go prospecting. It all turned out very well, but only with the help of some very special people. I am married now to the most beautiful person God created. We have a son and a daughter. There are many others along the way who all contributed to allow me to become what I am today."

"And what is that?" Jamie interrupted.

"That's rather easy to answer," Chris laughed. "I am a very happy man, who by the way is very rich. While we have been talking I have been giving much consideration to something. Would you like to join me and my company? This meeting is most opportune and with what I know of your talent and capabilities, you are the answer to a problem that has been bothering us for some time."

Jamie's coffee was totally ignored now and he was giving his full attention to what Chris was saying. "What's this problem you talk about, Chris?" he quickly said. "If you think I can help, I surely will."

Chris hesitated for a moment then asked, "Are you free for lunch? I would like you to meet my brother, Rex. He is the senior partner of Kennedy and Dixon—they are my accountants. He will give you the details much more comprehensively than I can. Jackie my wife will want to meet you too."

"If you are buying, lunch is fine by me," Jamie enthusiastically answered.

"I like to eat at Stefanoso's," Chris quickly said, "The food is good. Make it twelve o'clock. If I'm not there, ask the maître d' for my table; I will let him know to expect us."

"Stefanoso's, is bit more upmarket to where I normally eat, Chris. I will be there." Jamie laughed

The operation of the conglomeration known as the Quo-Vadis Tourist Park which operated in conjunction with the Quo-Vadis Resort had been an on-going subject and a point of much discussion by Chris and Rex. It was not so much because of the lack of good administration by Vanessa, the Jackie-trained young lady—she managed the two businesses very well indeed and was operating most successfully, without causing them any worries; they were concerned that with all the expansion that had been instigated, that her workload was definitely excessive. They had been told by Vanessa quite bluntly, "Butt out—I have it under control." Because of its growth, the tourist park had been forced to move further "out of town" to that five-hundred hectares of wasteland. The tourist park now consisted of an airfield, which was quite capable of being an alternative landing site for even domestic aircraft. That airfield had been designed to operate the movement of the eighty-plus helicopters of various sizes, in conjunction with aircraft movements, Tour buses all operated out of the extensive bus depot. Workshops, all overseen by highly trained managers. a fully staffed and equipped fire station, a very nice cafe, and several small retail outlets had grown with the airport. Air traffic control officers operated from a most modern control tower. Vanessa had most efficiently overseen the conversion of that wasteland not being used for any particular purpose into attractive parks and gardens. She now operated from a ten-storied administration block, comprehensively staffed by a well-informed and efficient people. Both Chris and Rex had long recognised Vanessa's workload was unreasonable and they must find her a very good assistant, regardless of her objections.

Lunch at Stefanoso's had been most congenial. Before lunch, Chris had bought the credentials and availability of Jamie to

Rex and Jackie's notice. Rex had agreed the idea had good merit, but, typical of Rex, he did suggest only as a precautionary measure, why not give him a twelve-month contract to see how he goes. Chris had agreed that sounded good, and over lunch they offered the position to Jamie who was to say the least, most enthusiastic with the proposition.

"You say the companies involved are the Quo-Vadis Tourist Park, and the Quo-Vadis Resort?" Jamie asked, and waited patiently while the brothers and Jackie pondered the best answer.

After a few moments of a rather embarrassing silence, Chris answered him and spoke for all three. "Jamie, I think it is best we give you the full details of just who you will be working for, and in that way, you may be more aware of what a monster you will be involved with. Your twelve-month contract will be with Quo-Vadis Holdings Proprietary Limited. I am the sole owner of that holding company. The holding company owns the total shareholding of all the other companies in the Quo-Vadis group. I'm not going to go through a list of them at the moment."

"WHOA!" Jamie interrupted. "Did you say Quo-Vadis Holdings; before I unceremoniously left the Investment Company they had been asked to buy into that company by many clients; one enquiry even came from one of an Institutional Investment people. With so many people enquiring I had to find out a bit about it. There is little known other than it is very successful with assets worth many billions of dollars. Is that you, Chris?" Jamie very humbly whispered.

"It is," Chris laughed. "Do not let that influence your decision."

"You do not have to say another word, Mr Kennedy, Sir," Jamie laughed. "I think I had better call you Sir from now on after learning exactly who you now are. Who would have thought that that non-descript investment clerk ever had the potential to become so successful? I need to hear nothing further. When and where do I start?"

"Jackie and I are leaving at 6 am tomorrow. We will meet you at the Tourist Park and we will fly direct to Quo-Vadis."

Jamie had left them shortly after; his head was in the clouds, yet he was still conscientious enough to want to go and advise his current employer he was leaving. Chris and Jackie, along with Rex, dallied a little longer, talking over what had been discussed with Jamie over lunch.

"Where did you find him Bro? He fits our needs perfectly."

"Quite accidentally," Chris answered. "In fact, he found me."

"I do agree entirely with what you are proposing," Jackie said. "I see he fits our needs perfectly. I wonder how Vanessa is going to feel about sharing her "children." She is very possessive about them. Did you know she even told me to bug out when I tried to suggest a couple of changes?"

It was less than one month later before Vanessa called Chris. "Got a couple of minutes, Mister?" she asked. "I have a problem I would like to talk over with you—it's about this new guy. I will fly out to your office first thing tomorrow morning." Vanessa was never one to hold anything back. At twenty-seven years of age, the very attractive administrator, ruled her little empire with the proverbial rod of iron.

"This does not sound good; our little plan might have gone awry," Chris thought as he hung up.

He shared his worry with Jackie that evening. Jackie only smiled and said, "You worry needlessly, my Christopher. I know Vanessa and, although she puts on a tough front, underneath, she is very soft and very feminine. I think you will find she only requires a little reassurance."

"I sure hope you are right, my wise wonderful wife. When it comes to you women, I am well and truly out of my depth," the rather chastened Chris said.

Chris and Jackie met Vanessa at the airstrip the next morning. Almost before she had clambered into Goliath she started blasting into Chris's ears. "This guy Jamie Hill is impossible Chris," she yelled. "He wants to change everything; he even wants me to move my office to the top floor, from my perfectly satisfactory first floor. He reckons it is not necessary for me to see every person who walks into the building and thinks that there are many more important things for me to be doing, and the reception department has very good supervisors and girls and between them they are more than capable of registering each and every person. What's worse," her voice had almost reached fever pitch, "Do you know what that cheeky beggar said to me?"

"No, do tell," Chris managed to squeeze in.

"He said, he said," in her confusion she repeated herself, "he said, I suppose an old spinster like you does want to check out every bloke to see if he is potential husband material. It is just as well the bloody coward struck my rubbish bin over his head for protection and dived out on my office like a cut cat, before I clobbered him. He did make me laugh though, and later offered to take me to dinner so he could apologise."

With all of that off her chest Vanessa appeared to settle down a bit.

"And have you been out to dinner yet?" Jackie innocently asked.

"That's tonight," Vanessa quickly replied. "I came out here today because I wanted you to know I am very unhappy with him."

"Very well," Chris said. "I think it would be good to clear the air of everything that is annoying you. A new coffee house has opened in town. I have not tried it yet. We will drop in there and have a real wongi (group talk)."

Over fresh coffee and freshly baked scones, slathered liberally with raspberry jam and cream, Vanessa really struggled to explain to Chris and Jackie what her problem was. Finally, she sat quietly and almost whispered, "What Jamie . . ."

"Jamie now," Chris mused to himself, "not that guy anymore."

She was continuing ". . . has instituted is really very good. He ran a big office in the city did you know?"

"Yes," Chris replied, "I used to work for him."

"Oh," was all Vanessa replied, then without giving much thought to what she was saying said quite softly, "He must've been quite young when you knew him. He is only thirty-five now you know. He only looks older because of the things that had happened. He was married but is divorced now."

Chris stood as if to conclude the morning coffee break. He winked to Jackie and very firmly said, "I see my little experiment to find somebody to take some pressure from you Vanessa girl, has not succeeded so I will send him packing tomorrow."

Vanessa responded very quickly to that and almost shouted in alarm, "No, Chris, there is no need to do that. I would like to give him a real chance." Then as if realising how that could be interpreted quickly added, "Just to see if his ideas work and when it all boils down the view from the top floor is very good. I can still watch a lot of comings and goings. His office is next door to the one he wants me to use. OH HELL! What's wrong with me? I am saying all the wrong things—you'll get the idea I like him."

"Do you?" Jackie very softly asked.

"Since it is you who asks, Jackie," Vanessa replied, "between only we three, I do," she softly confessed.

"Then I want a full report about your dinner date," Jackie very sternly told her, "and I mean a full report."

Chris was not privy to that report. All Jackie said was, "I do not think we will have any more problems with those two—they look to have sorted out much at dinner and afterwards."

"You don't mean?" Chris started to say, only to be cut off by Jackie smiling and saying, "Just mind your own business Mr Sticky nose—the report is strictly girlie business only."

Three months had passed, and Vanessa and Jamie had asked Chris for an opportunity to meet and discuss many things that had come into their consideration over that time. It was a beautiful morning. Chris had hoped it would be an informal meeting, so he had asked Jackie to join them, The four of them, Chris, Jackie, Vanessa and Jamie, strolled along the lake front. The conversation, although still quite informal, was deep and meaningful.

Conversation had been initiated by Jamie, who had said, "There is much to discuss, Chris. I hope you have plenty of time."

He was a different man to the half human who had accosted him in that street in the big smoke. He had put on flesh and muscle, stood straight and tall, clear-eyed and obviously happy. He held Vanessa's hand as they walked. "Vanessa and I have spent much time talking over what is exactly needed at the resort."

"By the look of this pair, any spare time they had appears to have been utilised in improving senior office members' interrelationships. I do not know where they found the time to talk business," Chris chuckled to himself.

After taking several deep breaths Jamie rather confidently started. "Our resort is very popular, but it caters only for basic holidays. The Tour Park is at capacity with the daily tours, and we only allow the big group tours to be booked four months in advance. We really do need another three or four Chinooks to maximise taking advantage of the amount of business available. We have asked to talk to you not because of what is happening, but what we see would really improve and change the resort from being only an accommodation venue to a full-on holiday resort. We took advantage of our position and stayed at the resort for a week."

"That would have been fun. Doing what? Need I ask?" Chris chuckled with a mighty smile on his face.

"Be serious, you drip. This is important. Just put your grubby little mind back in its box and listen," Jackie admonished him.

"Sorry, Jamie. I could not resist that. Please continue," Chris apologetically said.

"Thanks, Jackie. I'll put that one on my list of 'things to get even with Chris for.' As I was saying, after staying at the resort we had asked ourselves: what does it need? I found all those reports you and Jackie had written about all the resorts you had visited when you were first considering setting up the resort. You never did complete it or do all those things in a way you had envisaged."

Chris was serious now and answered him. "I do appreciate what you are saying, Jamie. Both Jackie and I were unable to come to terms with what was entailed in operating a full-on holiday resort. Please run your ideas past us."

They had walked as far as Bill's garden. The perfume from that garden assailed their senses. "Let's sit here and enjoy this, and I will tell you all we have discussed."

They found seats on nearby rocks. Jamie waited until all were settled then commenced. "Firstly, we must have a comprehensive on-site management staff, overseen by an on-site management. I could look after that, but I recommend we have a live-in manager. Next, we need to provide all those things people like to do when they are on holiday. Fish—they can do that now; swim—no problem; read and sleep—yes. But eat? Eat where? As it is, they almost have to cater for themselves. We would like to set up two very upmarket restaurants with very professional staff, and perhaps a couple of regular eating houses, somewhat along the line of the fast food restaurants. We can see with the intensity of the reservations, there will be more than enough patronage to make all those eating houses rather profitable. Even if they only break even, they will fill what we see as an undesirable deficiency in the present setup. You have a readily available water supply, so we could have a top class eighteen-hole golf course and prepare a few easily-negotiated walking tracks. The Outback here is something that would appeal to the less energetic. A walk up and along the escarpment is really something special. I know that the climb up the face is daunting. You have made roads for trucks further down so a simple pathway should be a little trouble to you. Peter can set up pony rides overseen by the native stockmen, perhaps even with campouts for the more adventurous. We think they will go down very well with resort guests, both young and old. We have talked with the native elders who were very happy to allow the guests to visit their camp and view a genuine corroboree, conducted around the campfire. They would do this once or twice a week—nothing ceremonial, mind you. They believe it would give us White Folk a better insight into native culture. The native women were all most enthusiastic with the idea of giving demonstrations of bush craft and hand painting. We are even thinking to set up a shop at the resort where they could sell their stuff and would like to move the accessories shop out to the resort. Those accessories never really get the exposure they merit at the Tourist Park. The shop would still only stock gold accessories made from gold from your mines. We would like to include pieces that have chips of selected beautiful coloured spodumene crystals in them. The owners of that big diamond mine way up in the north-west have said they would be happy to provide some small stones—at a price, of course—for our use.

Our mate from the jewellery shop in town, can see the potential of this venture would like to provide permanent professional staff to run the shop. Wants half the margin, greedy blighter; however, he would cover all costs except rent. This idea may need a little bit more thought and tuning up. From time to time, other things may come to mind, so please be prepared if we come wanting to do more. We are very confident that with the advent of all this; we will have to be prepared for a substantial increase in demand for accommodation, and envisage—this is the big one," Jamie laughed, "we will need many more bigger and better lodges."

"Poor Giuseppe," Chris thought, then asked, "Have you run this past Rex?"

"That's the good part, Chris," Jamie replied; "With the increase in demand for accommodation Rex is quite enthusiastic with the whole idea. His only comment was, even in the worst event the place would break even. He did say to tell you to call him after you have heard about all these ideas. There is one other small thing: we do believe an early morning flight from town to Quo-Vadis and a late evening return flight, should be added to the park's schedule, to cater for a few possible day trippers."

Chris delayed any answer for a moment, then replied with a big smile on his face, "I do not think you are telling me the main reason you think that flight is necessary. I think I do know what ulterior motives you pair have."

In due course all the conspirators had suggested were instigated, and it became common knowledge throughout the travel industry that holiday packages offered by the Quo-Vadis Resort were undoubtable without peer. At Bill's insistence, they did include a once weekly visit to a working goldmine in some of the packages.

It was found that with the greatly increased patronage many new staff were required. Vanessa and Jamie interviewed each and every one of those applicants who responded to the advertisement in the local and national newspapers. The response to those advertisements was far beyond what had been at anticipated. This enabled careful selection and the new staff were the best of the best. Their selection did prove so very good that, in the ensuring months, not one complaint of any nature was recorded; conversely accolades were numerous.

# Chapter 18

Ed had been commissioned by the mint—in the words of the higher echelon of the mint—to build an armoured car that was totally impervious. What they wanted was a vehicle that could withstand anything but a full on military assault. They were most concerned that the spasmodic delivery of gold from the various small mines out in the Outback were rather vulnerable. Many of those miners had collected their bars of gold, be they small or large, from the various smelters and held them until being collected by the mint-appointed contractor in standard type armoured cars. Now with the contribution to the collection by Quo-Vadis gold, those armoured cars would, at times, carry gold in excess of several hundred million dollars, and every effort had to be made to ensure the gold had to be better protected.

When Ed was told to spare no expense with the construction of the proposed vehicle, his mind went into overdrive. He had spent many hours with Chris, picking his brains, trying to establish if there were any improvements to that initial design of Goliath that could be instituted. The final product that rolled from Ed's workshop was ugly beyond belief.

Bill in, typical fashion, had laughed when he first saw that vehicle, and commented, "You would need one hell of a can opener to get into that can."

Chris had volunteered to run with the first delivery in that ugly new vehicle to ensure the crew were fully conversant with much of the very complex equipment Ed had installed. "What are they picking up from our mines this trip?" he had asked Bill.

"There is seven hundred million dollars' worth of gold to go; it has built up a bit while we were waiting for this van. You will have to do be particularly watchful—there is a whisper about that there could be, somebody who is planning to hit this delivery."

Chris took that news rather flippantly, saying, "Oh well, if that happens it will be a test of how good he is. What did the boys call him, Ed?"

It had become more or less a tradition with Ed's mechanics to give each significant vehicle they built a name. "He is called Dracula," Ed laughed.

Despite his flippancy, Chris did have a high level of concern, and did make the people at the mint aware of the rumour. They took Chris's concern seriously and were most emphatic when they said, "We cannot delay having this delivery completed; our vaults are almost empty. The darn government is spending money right, left, and centre. Did you hear they had actually reduced the national debt by about half by repaying a lot of loans the other mob left them with when they took over after the last election; so now the national gold reserve is needing a good top up. Treasury is relying on the delivery of this gold, so it must proceed with all haste. As a precaution, we will warn the military people they may be called upon to provide an escort. Hopefully it will not be required. Fortuitously the air force has a number of those much-celebrated jet fighters on display at the airport. We will immediately obtain authority to call them in at short notice should the need arise. Thank you for the warning Chris—let's hope it is no more than a rumour."

Dracula rumbled away from Quo-Vadis three weeks later. Behind those quarter-inch steel doors that lined both sides of the cabin were shelves, carefully loaded with seven hundred million dollars' worth of gold ingots.

"This is the biggest movement of bullion we have ever seen from out here; it makes one very apprehensive with the magnitude of the responsibility to deliver it," the senior mint official said as he handed Chris the official receipt. "Funds to be credited to the usual account, Mr Kennedy?" he asked and added,

"The fact that you trust the mint so completely, makes our work so much easier."

"Yes, sir, that account would be good," Chris replied. "I am going to ride along with you and be available should there be something about this monster you missed when Ed explained all his workings. Did Ed run through what of these blue buttons were about? There are ten of them: four within easy reach of the driver, and six placed in strategic spots around the rear cabin. Should you activate any one of them, the air throughout the van will be pumped out and replaced with fresh air from his own tanks in less than five seconds. This feature was fitted just in case you are subject to a gas attack. In those cupboards under your seats, those seats, you may have noticed, are fitted with quick release doors; there are six high-powered, automatic, fully loaded rifles, and six handguns. There is a substantial amount of additional ammo, some already in cartridges. There are also several packs of stun grenades. Let's hope you never have to use any of this. Coffee is brewing, so while we have a few minutes I would like to review the track with you."

He drew out a folder that contained several enlarged satellite maps and selected a specific map. "The obvious place for a hit is here, in this canyon," he indicated with a long finger. "The canyon is about ten kilometres long and has very steep sides. When we built this road, we had no alternative other than to come through here. The canyon has many interesting features. Tourists who have chosen to drive to Quo-Vadis, often stop along its length to admire the many colours in the rocks. Like I say, we had to come through here! The sheer walls of the escarpment were on one side and an area of unstable almost swamp-like ground extended over a considerable area, on the other. We did attempt to put a stabilised track through it; unfortunately, after having lost more than one of the excavation machines, we gave up, and came through here. You can see from the map; to go around that swamp would have added several hundred kilometres to the length of the road. The choice of putting the road through the canyon did in itself present a few problems, and to get a suitable surface we had to do a large amount of excavation. We did find some unusual features as we excavated."

The crew of Dracula studied the map for quite a while, then, after having their coffee, commence their journey. The early part of the trip was rather uneventful.

As they were about to enter that canyon, the driver called, "Heads up fellas—we are about to enter that canyon." In an instant the men in the rear cabin, who were travelling with the gold as escorts, became alert. Chris had taken the seat next to the driver, and before Dracula had even covered half a kilometre, he shouted, "Bogies ahead; they have blocked the road with rocks. Okay driver, engage all the wheels and drive straight into those rocks; the front crash bar is made of the strongest of steel and covers everything that is at all vulnerable."

Dracula hit those rocks, shuddered a little, and then proceeded to either push the rocks side or just climb over them. "He is a mighty machine, sir," the driver shouted. "He is not even getting warmed up."

A rattle, not unlike a hailstorm hitting a tin roof, commenced.

"That's small arms fire," one of the support crew yelled, followed quickly by, "Activating window screens now." All the windows of Dracula were made from armoured glass. As an extra precaution, Ed had added retractable bullet proof screens. The combination of those screens and the armoured windows prevented projectiles from even the highest-powered rifle from penetrating the van.

"How many do you see?" Chris called to another of the support crew who had been searching the canyon top with binoculars.

"At least one-hundred, maybe more of the bastards. They look like those Middle Eastern types you see on the newsreels. It doesn't matter where they come from—they are all ugly looking pricks," then suddenly cried, "HOLD HARD INCOMING!"

A blinding explosion enveloped the van. "Handheld rocket," another of the crew grunted. "It didn't do a darn thing to him—not even a dent. That's bloody good steel you had him made from, sir."

"Damage report, sir," another of the crew laughed, "That rocket scorched a bit of his beautiful paintwork."

"Let's hope that is the worst thing that happens," Chris cheerfully replied, then ordered, "Open up all rifle slots, please, Mister Driver; now you blokes in the back can start to earn your keep. Give those nasty bastards a taste of our medicine. Pick your targets carefully men—individual kills are more effective than random blasting away. I will appreciate it if you would please remember I have to pay for all those explosive headed bullets."

For the next fifteen minutes, Dracula chugged majestically along that canyon floor riding unimpeded over rocks and logs and bodies that had plummeted down from the top the canyon walls.

"You are doing well," Chris, complimented the crew. "I have counted fifteen kills already. We are approaching that very narrow section of the canyon. How does it look, Mr Driver? If we can get through here the rest of the trip should be a piece of cake and we will not need any help."

"Not so good, sir," the driver shouted, "they have a loader or something like it up there and have two bloody big boulders, poised into position to drop down on us; there is one on each side."

"They are starting to play rough. We had better contact HQ and advise them of the position and let them know we will appreciate some help. Hold him here," Chris cried, "do not enter that narrow bit of the canyon. Back him back about ten metres.

Do you see that pile of rock up against the escarpment? Park Dracula so that the front crash bar is leaning against that pile of rocks, rev the motor up to the redline and have him slowly push that stack."

The big V12 diesel motor roared to a scream; after thirty seconds, the driver urgently cried, "He is holding the redline, Mr Kennedy—we cannot keep him there too long for fear of damaging the motor."

Chris appeared not to be concerned with his fear, and over the roar of the motor shouted, "Keep him there, and have him push with all his power against those rocks. Be prepared to wind him down quickly, should he push those rocks out of the way."

Dracula sat there for a full five minutes, motor screaming and all twelve drive wheels digging into the hard canyon floor. Clouds of blue smoke erupted from those spinning wheels and almost hid the monster armoured car. Without warning that pile of rocks suddenly collapsed and Dracula literally bounded into the black void beyond.

"All forward lights now please, Mr Driver," Chris called, and that black void was illuminated, by eight powerful beams. "Take him about fifty metres in and hold him there. On second thoughts, make it a bit further," Chris said, "just in case those bogies try to follow us. Three of you blokes in the back take positions at those rear slots and if any appear give them a hefty blast and dampen their enthusiasm."

Nothing untoward happened, and after ten minutes a much-relieved Chris, softly said, "I think we are clear now, the bogies appear to be reluctant to follow us. Who's for a cup of tea? I think we have all earned it."

"What next, Mr Kennedy?" the driver asked.

Chris was a little hesitant to answer, and replied, "I am not really sure what is the better thing to do. We can sit here and wait to be rescued or we can move on. When we were building the road through the canyon we found this cave. I did walk along it for about half a kilometre; unfortunately, I did not have a very good light and was afraid of falling into a hole. What I know about this escarpment is that it contains things that belie explanation. I am guessing—mind you, just guessing—that this is a very old river bed, and when the escarpment was pushed up, a very big underground river had been cut off. We found evidence of the same thing occurring further down. Our guess was that the river built up huge pressures and eventually forced its way out of the escarpment through a number of caves, creating a number of rivers that flowed out into the Outback. Should that in fact have happened, the Outback as we now know it would have been a far different place. We have established that the huge river did find a substantial outlet in the bed of the lake in the sinkhole. Several of those smaller rivers did continue to flow. The river flowing from the escarpment from that waterfall into the sinkhole is an example of that. With more or less ninety percent of that big river once again flowing unimpeded, a lot of those rivers created by the built-up pressure ceased flowing from their outlets in the sides of the escarpment and dried up leaving the escarpment honeycombed with these caves. I am going to explore all this one day. If we keep going I think we will find this cave does lead to that big river. It may present a barrier which prevents us proceeding much further."

"That is all most interesting, sir," the driver commented. "It is fortunate we have somebody here with us who knows a lot about mines and mining."

"I do wish I knew a lot more," Chris humbly replied.

"What next, sir?" The driver asked with a degree of respect.

"It's up to you blokes what we do," Chris said. "The choice as I see it is, do we go on not knowing what we will find, or do we sit here for a couple of days waiting to be rescued. Unfortunately, the radio does not work in here; there must be some sort of mineral shielding any transmission."

It was unanimous and all the crew agreed with the driver when he said, "I for one think it is best to go on; if those rotten buggars cover the entrance to the cave the rescue crew will never find us."

"That's good thinking. I had not thought about them doing that. I was hoping you would all agree to go on. I think we should fit the tracks; they may slow us down a little but will be handy if we hit some soft stuff, or if it gets rough."

"This has turned out to be quite an adventure; not at all like the average pickup and deliver run," one of the crew excitedly exclaimed as they all clambered out.

Within fifteen minutes tracks had been fitted and secured, turning Dracula into a mini caterpillar tractor.

"We are now as ready as we can be," Chris told them, and turning to the driver said, "If you don't mind I think it would be best if I did the driving for a while. It can be a little bit tricky driving this type of unit with the tracks fitted. I have done it quite often and am quite used to it."

Dracula now crawled slowly along that dark cave. The surface was very rough, and those powerful headlights did a merry dance as Dracula pushed along his unimpeded way. The crew had positioned themselves at the now-open windows, excitedly exclaiming as the powerful spotlights that were shining in every direction revealed the beauty of the multi-coloured minerals that made up the escarpment.

Suddenly, Chris most excitedly cried, "Holy Cow! Look at that!" He had hauled Dracula to a halt, and loudly ordered, "Shine that spotlight back a bit; focus about ten metres up the side of the cave. Do you see that? That is a quartz reef. Climb out and have a close look. You will find there is a seam of gold running through it.

It is the same reef we are mining at Quo-Vadis where all this gold we are carrying came from."

"That quartz reef is on the other side too," another of the crew called. "You sure are right Mr Kennedy; I can see that vein of gold even from here."

"Grab an axe and hop out," Chris suggested. "Chip off a few blocks—you can keep them as a memento of all that has happened today."

"Won't we get into strife for mining without a permit?" one of the younger crew conscientiously asked.

"You do not have to worry one iota about that," Chris said with a laugh. "I hold mining leases for the whole of this monster we call the escarpment."

"Are you saying, Mr Kennedy, that all this is yours?" one of the other crew questioned him with a voice filled with dismay. "You must be worth a dollar or two."

The whole crew were in buoyant spirits and laughed excitedly at that comment. They would have loaded the whole of the rear cabin of Dracula with "mementos" had common sense not prevailed, and each crew member only stowed his memento in his lunch box.

With a crew now filled with excited apprehension about what new discoveries lay ahead, Dracula continued on his way.

They had travelled for a further hour when Chris announced, "Although we have travelled a good distance along the escarpment, by my reckoning we are nearing the centre. Keep your eyes open and those spotlights going; if you see anything that looks like a dark hole or a sunken section, let me know quickly. Those dark holes or sunken bits could be just the surface of a sinkhole. If we go down one of them we will never get out. Because I think we are near the river, there may be washouts that cause those sinkholes."

"Our Mr Miner on the job; thank goodness," the driver who had taken the co-driver's seat, commented. "I am glad you took over driving, Mr Kennedy. I would never have known what to watch for."

As they rolled around a sharp, bend and without warning, those powerful headlights revealed an amazing scene. They had reached a very big river. What had totally hypnotised them was that mighty river flowing out over an eight-foot drop. The crystal-clear water exploded into a shower of fine spray which when illuminated by those powerful headlights created an array of rainbows.

"I told you this escarpment had some wonderful secrets. Take a long, long look at what you are seeing fellas, you may never see something as amazing as this ever again in your life," Chris reverently whispered.

"I have a camera fitted with a good flash," one of the crew cried. "I am going to take a dozen photos of this. Nobody would ever believe me unless I had some proof."

"I would like to have some copies of those photos, please," Chris quickly said. "If they are any good you will be able to sell them to the National Geographic."

He had crawled out of Dracula and was surveying what was ahead. He turned and ruefully said to the crew, "This looks to be about as far as we can go. I can't see any way we can get any further. There is an eight-foot-high little cliff blocking any further progress. We will have to retrace our tracks and see if there is any other way."

"Mr Kennedy, sir," one of the crew interrupted, "I think I can see a wide shelf up there. It looks wide enough for Dracula. If we can get him up there, maybe we can continue on."

"Well spotted, young man," Chris said enthusiastically. Let's go over and have a good look and see if maybe we can find a way."

To even climb up that eight-foot barrier was a problem. The face was smooth, totally devoid of any hand or foot holds.

"Granite," Chris growled to himself. "Worn smooth by tens of millions of years of running water," then loudly said to a couple of the crew, "Bunk me up boys, I want to get up there and have a good look. There is no point in getting Dracula up there if the shelf is only short and does not lead us to safety."

With a bit of effort Chris now stood up on that shelf. His powerful handheld torch revealed the shelf at this point was about five-meters wide and was generally one or two feet above that fast-flowing river.

"I have said it before and I'll say it again," Chris thought to himself, as he carefully walked along that shelf, "this escarpment is truly amazing. I think my earlier theory, that somewhere down stream that river had got blocked and built up even above this shelf, is correct. When the river finally broke free it left this shelf high and dry. We cannot retrace our steps, as I'm sure the bogies will be waiting for us. The immediate problem is to get an eighteen-tonne armoured car loaded with gold from down there to up here. There is no other alternative than to build a ramp of some description and try and drive Dracula up it."

He had to call upon many of his fundamental mining skills to construct the ramp. After three hours of chipping away with the meagre tools at their disposal, they had constructed only the outline a very basic ramp. In desperation; Chris even had the crew, very carefully draw high-powered explosive from some of the rifle shells; he packed that explosive into a couple of cracks in that granite barrier; then precariously detonated the charge by hooking a short electrical cable up to Dracula's electrical system. The explosion was deafening but the result was effective. The crew actually sheltered inside Dracula; it is just as well he was so robustly constructed as projectiles caused by that explosion would have killed them. It still took a further ten hours, in the words of one of the crew, of darn hard work, to construct the ramp and laughed as he said, "I don't think this was on my list of duties."

"Neither is being murdered by bogies," one of the other men cynically reminded him.

Finally, with that powerful winch with cable affixed to the steel pins driven into that hard granite forty meters along the shelf, and with motor roaring in protest, Dracula dragged himself up the ramp. The crew had stood and watched Dracula and shouted joyously when he finally came to a halt upon the shelf.

"There will be no turning back now, fellas," Chris warned them. "I think we all deserve a cup of tea after which we will press on and see what other surprises this escarpment has for us." Nothing of any consequence restricted their progress from then on, although at one section the shelf was about four inches underwater for about one-hundred metres. One of the crewmen was required to walk ahead of Dracula to ensure no nasty surprises lay hidden underneath that water. So that he would have dry footwear, later he had removed his boots and was wading barefooted about thirty metres ahead of the slow-moving Dracula. He suddenly let forth a loud scream and withdrew his right foot from the water with a large crab attached to his big toe. That toe must have appeared to be an inviting snack to that crab. With the crab still attached, he hastily raced back to Dracula. The crab's lunch was terminated abruptly with a forceful blow with the back of an axe.

Not taking any further risks, the crewman donned his boots and after being the subject of several ribald jokes he resumed his duty to wade ahead of Dracula. After that Dracula just ploughed slowly along the shelf. The men watched in apprehension as at times that shelf was so narrow that Dracula appeared almost suspended above that fast-flowing river.

"By my calculations," Chris announced to the crew, "we are at least forty kilometres from where we entered the cave. He had no sooner said this, when he shouted, "Get a couple of spotlights up here; I think I can see what I have been looking for."

Almost immediately, two spotlights focused on another dark hole in the side of the cave. "I was hoping we would find something like this. The river broke out here too, to wash out another cave; let's hope it's accessible all the way."

The washout had formed a cave that was larger than the one they had originally entered.

"The river that flowed down here through it must have been rather substantial," Chris's miner's mind thought. "I wonder if that quartz reef has been exposed in here somewhere. This journey we have been forced to make so far has proven to be not only exciting, but also quite valuable as it has shown me even more of the escarpments secrets .

The floor of this cave had been washed almost clear of obstacles and Dracula was able to progress, although still cautiously, at a much greater speed. Chris suddenly shouted joyously, "I knew and hoped it would be here."

"What? What have you found now Mr Kennedy?" the driver now acting as co-driver, questioned.

"My quartz reef is up there; it looks to be even more substantial here," Chris replied.
"Hell man! That's over forty kilometres of gold-bearing reef we have proven exists. You are not going to tell us you own all of this."

"Yep," Chris replied, his eyes dancing with excitement. "This and much more."

"There should be a law against blokes like you being allowed to be so filthy rich," the co-driver laughed, then with rather intense sincerity, said, "You can keep all your gold, Mister, we owe you much more than that: we owe you our very lives. It was you who got us out of this predicament alive."

"Don't forget I got myself out too," Chris laughed.

For another half-hour, Dracula pushed on. Finally, Chris cried, "Look up ahead, fellas—that's sunlight. We have made it." That two-foot-high bank of soft dirt across the mouth of the cave proved no problem for Dracula, and with many cries of relief the crew crawled from the vehicle.

"Where are we?" one of the crew asked. All they could see was the endless arid Outback.

"I believe we have about four hours to travel, in that direction," Chris indicated with a wave of his arm after having spent a few minutes reading the compass on Dracula's console. "We should be able to strike the main road there," he explained. "After leaving the canyon, the road does veer away from the escarpment quite a bit. I don't know about you blokes but I am hungry—we have not eaten a decent meal for nearly ten days. You tend to lose all track of time in that darkness of those caves."

"Ten days!" the young nineteen-year-old crewmember exclaimed. "Now you have come to mention it, I realise I am starving. Would somebody rustle me up a cow—don't bother skinning it, just cook it skin and all, I will eat the lot."

The whole crew laughed at that, not so much from the humour of his comment, but from the relief they now felt now they were finally safe. That relief was written all over their faces. They dallied there for a while, then, well fed, washed from the freshwater tanks on Dracula, and with a change of clothing, it was a contented group that continued on their adventurous way.

Although a little rough in places, the Outback did not inhibit their progress to any degree. Dracula made short work of any obstacle; it was no problem whatsoever for him to climb that low hill, from the summit of which the primitive panorama of the Outback was breath-taking. The thing that caused most delight was the sight of a small army convoy as it made its way along the main road. The convoy came to a dusty halt, as it found Dracula nonchalantly parked across the road blocking their progress.

The Lieutenant in charge questioned them relentlessly; he found it difficult to believe that these people, which all the search parties had given up all hope of ever finding, just turned up, and were sitting here as if nothing had ever happened. "You say you came through that mountain. That belies belief; however, it must be true for here you are. All the searches covered every inch of the land between that cave and miles around. We should have believed your wife, Jacqueline, sir. She said we are wasting our time and should not worry; you were in your element and would surely be okay. What a report all this is going to make."

"Did you catch those bogies?" Chris asked.

"No, sir," the Lieutenant promptly answered. "The air force was called in and two Hornets, caught most of them camped in the canyon outside the entrance to the cave, apparently waiting for you to come out. I hear the pilots had orders to totally destroy those people who had attacked you. The Hornets had blasted them mercilessly. We found eighty-four dead ones. Two had survived and had told us you had disappeared into that cave, and that some of them had tried to follow you. They had given up rather quickly when they became lost, and two of them perished by falling down black holes. Ten escaped the Hornets. They had not been in the canyon. All sorts of crap is flying about. Questions are being asked of the government as to how such a large group of heavily-armed terrorists get in the country. It turns out they have been here a long time. We call them sleepers. They are the sons of refugees who had gained citizenship and were waiting to be called upon when needed. I have been instructed to escort you to the city. The Treasury people were most happy when we advised HQ, that you had been found and the precious gold is safe."

Curiosity must've got the better of the Lieutenant and he quietly said, "It must be a large amount because the effort to find you has involved a very large number of personnel."

"Yes, it is," Chris replied with a broad grin across his face. "Better tell Treasury we have spent the last ten days down the pub and have blown a fair bit of it on having a good time."

"HA, HA, HAR," the Lieutenant sarcastically laughed. "I have to give it to you, Kennedy, you must be some sort of bloke to have gone through what you have told us and can still make a joke about it."

Jackie had flown to the city and was waiting for Chris at the mint when Dracula rumbled up. She didn't say a word; she only threw her arms around him and burst into tears, eventually stammering, "I did tell them it was a waste of time worrying about you, Christopher Kennedy. I knew our love would keep you safe and well."

"I never doubted for one minute that I would not survive, my beautiful Guardian Angel. I have far too much to live for; after dinner I have quite a story for you and Bill. Is he in town, or is he out at Quo Vadis?" Chris asked.

"He and Ellie are at the hotel; we are to meet them there for dinner," Jackie replied. "They are awaiting any news from the mint people. They were supposed to let them know immediately if anything developed. You caught everyone by surprise with your sudden appearance out of nowhere."

"I would have thought the Army boffins would have let you know we had turned up. How come you knew we had been found, Jackie love?" Chris asked.

"I accidentally—mind you, it was purely accidental— heard the Lieutenant talking to his headquarters" Jackie giggled. "Never mind; you are here now, fit and well and none the worse for wear. I can hardly wait to hear the tale you have to tell."

They had delayed leaving the dinner table that evening while Chris told them of his adventure. They sat entranced as they listened to Chris's story. Jackie and Bill interrupted many times when they demanded more and more details, consequently it was late before they left the restaurant. It was not before Bill said in a rather disbelieving voice, "you have seen that the quartz reef does definitely run at least 240 or 250 kilometres from the Animal Cave, where we are presently mining, and are trying to tell me that the reef definitely runs the full 400 kilometres of the escarpment?"

"I now have absolutely no reason not to believe that," Chris very firmly replied.

"With what I am hearing," Bill ever so softly whispered as if endeavouring not to divulge some special secret, "that it is an extraordinary gold-bearing reef. You say in many places we have ready access to the reef in those caves. I think we will have to at least commence some small mining operations in as many places as possible, just to keep out those greedy buggers; who they are we can only guess. If we are not careful they will be trying to grab a slice of your reef, by demanding that, in the interests of all, the whole escarpment must be fully developed. Just who those fellows are , we will never know, but greed has some strange bedfellows. Our small mines will show that we are doing something. The mines within the caves would alleviate the necessity to sink shafts to the reef as we are presently doing." Bill took a large swig of his beer, and as if he suddenly thought of something more to say, quickly added, "Have you any idea what this discovery makes you worth, son?"

"I haven't a clue, mate," Chris replied, and laughing loudly added, "and what is more to the point I really do not have the time or the patience to try and work it out. Rex can worry about all that. I only wish to be able to spend time with this beautiful creature and her kids."

Jackie quickly corrected him by saying very firmly, "They are your kids too, Mister."

Nevertheless, despite his nonchalance at that time, over the ensuing years, Chris and Bill, did prove up the full extent of that reef. Their exploration discovered a very interesting network of caves that had been created by the river over an innumerable number of years.

The ten bogies who had escaped the onslaught of those air force Hornets; because they were not in the canyon when the Hornets hit—they were stationed on the canyon top acting as lookouts. They had watched in horror at the carnage those jets caused, and when they saw a squad of paratroopers floating down from those high-flying troop- carrying aircraft, they panicked and rushed without knowing to where— into the Outback. They were relentlessly pursued, by highly-trained army troops. Two of the boogies died from snakebites, one broke a leg and had been abandoned. He had been abandoned and had died at the place where the mishap occurred. The remaining seven had survived for six more days. By good fortune; they had come across a remote waterhole that provided them with some respite. Finally, they conceded their flight was hopeless but before they would surrender to the pursuing troops, they vindictively thought, to extract some vengeance and create a diversion by setting fire to the dry scrub of the Outback. With a strong wind behind it, the fire spread quickly. The bogies had not taken into account the peculiarities of this land, and when the wind suddenly changed suddenly they were trapped and died painfully in the circumstances caused by their own folly. The people at Quo-Vadis had experienced scrub fires in the past and were well equipped to handle any threat the fire created. Huge earthmoving tractors quickly cleared a wide firebreak between the fire and anything considered vulnerable. Once all the stock and buildings were safe, the fires were generally left to burn, kept under fairly constant surveillance.

On the first instance Chris experienced one of these Outback scrub fires he was most concerned. His concern was completely alleviated when the old native elder, Marlee, had laughed and said to him, "Do not worry, Boss Chris. It is our way to set a fire when we leave the area to move to a new camp. The fires clear away the old scrub and allow the new grass and the new shrubs to grow better. That brings the animals we hunt back to feed on the new growth, so that when we return to the area, there are many animals."

The fires burned harmlessly for about three weeks and were totally extinguished by one of those solid rain showers that would suddenly appear and disappear almost as quickly as they came. Peter, the ex-American, now Station Manager at Quo-Vadis Station, had never before experienced this. He was most impressed at just how rapidly the new growth reappeared.

# Chapter 19

The village at Quo-Vadis had grown into a small township, caused by the influx of all those people required to provide labour for all the mines and the infrastructure necessary to keep them operating. Chris and Jackie did enjoy strolling through all that was happening within the precinct of the new township. Today they were strolling by the three new homes Giuseppe was building for families who had recently arrived. Four tradesmen working on those houses were sitting out the front of the partially built houses, on improvised seats enjoying their lunch and a cuppa. Boss Chris and his doll of a wife were very popular with all the people engaged in the various activities associated with the construction of many buildings.

The plumber did not hesitate and called, "Wanna cuppa, folks?"

"That's billy tea, isn't it?" Chris asked. "There is nothing like billy tea. Yes, please. I think Jackie would enjoy a cup also."

"I would love one," Jackie quickly replied, "since it is being made by experts."

Seats were quickly found for them, 'Seats' of randomly selected blocks of wood, although perhaps a little rustic, were placed strategically so Chris and Jackie could join the circle. The conversation drifted around the growing town and how the tradies were hard pushed to keep up.

"It is growing quickly," the landscape installer thrust his opinion in. "We could do with a few more shops and things like that. My missus loves the place but typically of a woman, she misses her shops."

The tin of worms Chris called a brain, started to churn.

"Uh oh," Jackie thought to herself, "What's he thinking of now?"

Chris was a little quiet when they continued their walk, and that night as they lay comfortably in each other's arms Jackie very sternly demanded, "Okay Mister, out with it. What's going on in that head of yours? You have been thinking of something ever since we left the tradies this afternoon."

"Cannot get away with a darned thing when you are about can I, you beautiful mind reader. Yes, I have been thinking about what those blokes said."

"You mean about a few more shops," Jackie exclaimed. "I for one would think that would be great. I am sick and tired of going without or having to make a four-hour trip there and back to town, just for a box of cereal or something as non-consequential."

"That is not the major thing that is in my mind; there is much more," Chris quickly whispered in reply. "You have heard Bill and I talking about a smelter out at the iron ore mine, duplicating the plant at the spodumene deposit, opening up Susie's mine and at least one or two more gold mines in those caves in the escarpment." Chris's thoughts had wandered a little, as he tried to bring to mind all that he had been thinking about. "You know Jamie and Vanessa had talked about how the extraordinary demand for accommodation at the resort has necessitated us building eighty additional lodges. You know that pair are unit now?"

"Yes!" Jackie abruptly exclaimed in reply. "Vanessa told me weeks ago, he was the best lay she had ever had, and she was going to keep him about for a while, she did say; the fact she had fallen for him big-time helped her decision. Now Mr Kennedy, keep your mind on what you are telling me. No more of this going off on a tangent," Jackie's good-humoured tolerance had become frustration. Picking this man's mind was like sticking one's head into a box of bees, his thoughts were everywhere.

"Sorry, sweetie," Chris apologised, "my mind is a little rampant at the moment. Now as I was saying, before I was rudely interrupted," that comment earned him a cuff on the right ear, "we are going to need many more people. We can fly them in and out. The logistics of doing that are immense, and with careful planning we can avoid a lot of that by creating a very viable community. That thought does appeal to me. I do like the feel of community. I guess I am still a country lad at heart. I would want you to be part of that planning—a big part in fact. I am very excited with the whole idea. Are you tired? Let's go downstairs and make a cup of tea, grab a couple of pencils and some paper, sit at the dining table, and I can start putting my thoughts onto paper. Hopefully you will be able see a little more clearly what I am thinking, and you will be able to add your thoughts."

And they sat up the whole night scribbling, arguing, and laughing and by dawn a vision had been converted into a comprehensive plan.

"It is all very well to put our plans onto paper," Chris said, "but I think that a plan such as this involves everybody, and before we start anything I feel we should first seek a general consensus from all in the existing village."

As was typical of the man, procrastination was unknown. He immediately had a printer from the regional city run up 250 pamphlets advising everyone; a community meeting would be held at the schoolhouse on the weekend and invited all interested in the future of the town to attend. To ensure people did not get the idea attendance was mandatory, he simply signed the advice, Mr Christopher Kennedy, and for ten cents per pamphlet he recruited several of the local children to deliver one to every household. Rumour was rampant. What the meeting was all about ranged from closing of all the mines, to a possible government takeover. Or had the Kennedys gone broke? The fact that Chris had closed the office in the regional city did not allay a lot of conjecture.

Bill barged into Chris's office waving a copy of the pamphlet. "What's this about?" he demanded.

"It is nothing to get hot under the collar about, mate," Chris softly replied. "Jackie and I only want to talk to everybody about our town; you and I know all too well with all our plans, it is going to grow substantially in the near future. We actually only have a vague idea how many people live here at the moment. The workforce is so transient—it is almost impossible to keep track of numbers. Have you any idea how many men working in all the mines, fly in and out each week? Many of those men are living in camps and are patiently awaiting housing being available so they can bring their families out here. Then there is the Resort to consider. Jamie and Vanessa have told me that with the level of enquiry for accommodation by an increasing number of tourists, the present staffing situation will never cope. I really do consider, if we do not plan now, it could all end up in one hell of a mess."

Bill had stood listening intently to what Chris had said, then plonked down into one of the visitor's chairs saying, "Good thinking, Mister. I had been wondering just how you are going to staff all those plans of yours. What do you hope to achieve by involving the whole of the community?"

"That is to be seen," Chris replied. "I am hoping for some good suggestions to come forward. There is a sort of plan I am going to put up at the meeting; it will be interesting to see the reaction."

On the evening of the meeting Chris and Jackie arrived early at the schoolhouse and mingled with the people. Chris noticed the chap that had been elected at the recent State Government election to represent this vast Outback electorate, accompanied by three other obviously government types, had arrived and commandeered seats in the front row. Chris had purposely kept his nose out of politics. "Not my cup of tea," he had told Jackie. "I have more important things to do other than sitting around all day listening to old farts beating their gums trying to be important."

Chris had met that politician once or twice before. The man had never impressed Chris as a capable person—he was too much of a party man. Chris only paused as he casually walked by him, and politely said, "Hello Ken. I did not expect to see you here."

"Anything that affects my electorate, is my business," the politician abruptly replied, expecting Chris to respond. Chris didn't even slow his casual stroll—he just walked on.

Jackie was already sitting at the teacher's desk, so Chris brought a chair up and sat beside her.

"More here than I expected," Chris laughed. "Word must have got around a bit."

As he sat, the packed room went quiet, so without further ado he addressed the crowd: "I know many of you," Chris firmly said, hoping everybody could hear him, "There are quite a few I have not met; I do hope we can soon change that. I am Chris Kennedy, commonly known as the Miner, and this delightful creature sitting here beside me is my wife, Jacqueline, Jackie to all and sundry. I do bid you welcome and thank you for coming. Despite all the crap flying about, there is nothing for you to worry about. I only wish to discuss our little village. As you all know it is growing like topsy. We have estimated with all the permanent residents, the fly in fly out workers, a variable number of tourists, there are at present upward of 5000 persons, more or less. There may be many more—the nature of the population and with it growing so quickly make it difficult to keep tabs on exact numbers. I do know there are many of you that are awaiting houses, so that your families can join you and live here. I don't blame you—it is a beaut spot. I have called this meeting because I need your help.

Quo-Vadis Holdings is a private company; we have been happy to endeavour to provide homes for you and realise our very strict policy of building only quality homes does slow things down a bit. Take heart; I have spoken with our builder and he assured me he is going to bring his total building company—staff, tradies, the lot—to assist him in the next weeks, and endeavour to overtake the backlog."

Giuseppe was sitting near the front and called loudly. "Yeah, yeah, I will catch up if only you will bloody well slow down a bit." That caused a ripple of good-humoured laughter.

The politician stood and attempted to speak. Chris abruptly cut him off. "Ken, this is not a political event; you are only here as an observer. Please sit down!" That caused a strong burst of laughter and comments of the like, "Skitch him, Chris."

"Now we have finished with the interruptions, I will continue," Chris loudly said as he attempted to regain control of the meeting. "As I was saying, I need your help. Amongst you there are many talented people, and I'm asking you to choose from them those you think have the capacity to bring forth all those things which would create a very special town. My wicked wife has put her oar in already and has very strongly said we need every sort of retail outlet to supply the needs of a vibrant community. To put it in simple words, she has said you women folk like to shop. You all can help by nominating those shops you would like to see."

"Even Uncle Charlie's fish and chip shop? I love his chips," a voice from somewhere in the back of the hall called. That caused another burst of laughter, followed by a flood of suggestions being shouted.

Chris raised his hands, as if requesting quiet. "What we need are people of vision—people who are planners, not just thinkers, but men of action. Not just say, a plumber, but a man of experience who can see the needs of the whole community, now and in the future. The same applies to all; the list is endless. We must decide where the town centre should be situated. It is like I said, we need planners who have a vision, a magnificent viable vision which this community deserves. Quo-Vadis Holdings will fund in total all this—the houses, the shops, any workshops or factories, community buildings, and the like. Should any of you at any stage wishes to own their own house, or whatever, they will be welcome to put their desires forward. I personally will approach the Premier to seek his thoughts of his government providing official people, police, doctors and nurses, teachers, the sort of qualified men and women we will need. I see little problem there as he will be advised, again, Quo-Vadis will carry any costs. There is one thing each and every one must take on board: Quo-Vadis Holdings will not compromise on quality; if it is not the best of the best, it is not good enough. We will set up an office, somewhere about here, and provide staff who will be available and open to discussion. I feel you can ably be represented by, say, twenty of the best qualified and experienced people from amongst you. This is in no way an election; these people are possibly already known to you. The whole project requires deep and meaningful thinking by you all. To ensure and expedite progress, I would like to have those people who you have chosen to put together their plans and let me have them by July first. The plumber should stick to the plumbing plan, the electrician to electrical matters, each of those twenty specialists, to each his own. I know everything I have said this evening is a bit airy fairy; however, I know with diligence and hard work we can make this venture successful for all of us. Let's hope and pray we achieve something very special, not for just now, but for all those who will follow along behind us. No questions tonight; just discuss everything amongst yourselves. Jackie and I are going to be cowards now and duck out the back door. Go girl! I'm right behind you."

They left a stunned crowd, that for a moment were absolutely quiet, then all hell broke loose. Chris and Jackie actually sprinted towards their sinkhole refuge. After about one-hundred metres they paused and looked back. The noise emanating from the schoolhouse was tremendous.

The topic of the new town was on everybody's mind; even the children at school were encouraged by their teachers to paint pictures of their dream town. The twenty-man "committee" came to the sinkhole three days before the first of July. They had to request permission to enter the sinkhole as entry past those diligent guards was by permit only. After the two attempts by bogies to disrupt the Quo-Vadis operation, and the subsequent attempts on Chris's life, security had been moved from lax to tight. Chris had questioned the need of it; however. Bill was adamant that with all the gold, at times stored in the vault in Chris's cave office, the additional security was necessary.

The twenty-man committee were allowed entry without hesitation. Three persons—that darn politician and his two hangers on—were turned aside. After much shouting and waving of arms and making many threats, the three-angry men stormed away.

Chris had arranged for the meeting to take place in the small cavern. Tables and comfortable chairs were set up and Ellie had bought a number of girls from the catering staff who ensured tea and coffee cups were kept topped up. Ellie had even baked especially for the occasion.

"What have you got, fellas?" Chris asked and added, "I did expect to see at least one or two women amongst you."

"Nar," one replied, "we had a few girls to help us; in the end, they were so bloody argumentative we left them behind."

"That was very brave of you," Chris chuckled. "Jackie will join us shortly; she has managed the enquiry office and will present a resume' of the many enquiries we have received. I am confident the interests of the women folk will be well covered. Be warned, she can be most argumentative at times. Each of you committee men have been chosen by the community and your peers for your known expertise in your particular field. For now, I will ask you to present a brief breakdown of that which you feel appropriate to suggest. We will only run through each man's presentation quickly, so please limit your presentation to the particular features. After this meeting I will ask you to leave the documents with me and I will go over them with a fine-tooth comb, not to usurp your plan, only to endeavour to ascertain how your plan fits in with all the others."

To "quickly" run through all those plans was a joke. After six hours, and Ellie having to whip up a quick snack for them, the meeting concluded with Chris rising and saying, "All these plans are very good; they are precisely what I envisaged. Has anybody given any thought to where the town could be sited?"

The landscape designer quickly stood and said, "I was thinking to have the river that runs to the Resort pass through the town. The whole place could be made most attractive with parks and gardens running from the town centre along the river."

Chris thought on that for a moment, then said, "I may have an alternative for you to consider. Give me fourteen days to go through all your plans and see how they fit in with what I am thinking." The whole six-hour meeting had been conducted in a most cordial atmosphere and all left excited and well pleased with the outcome.

Chris, Bill, and Jackie had gone through every individual plan at least five times. "The major flaw remains," a very tired Chris resolutely commented, "how does each and every facet of all these very good suggestions come together? They have all overlooked a plan for the actual town. We need a very good experienced town planner. I am not qualified, and do not want that responsibility. The site for the town is another thing. Consider this! Riley and Strahan, the university professors, in their exploration of the caves in the escarpment have found yet another entrance to the underground river, just here."

His finger poised on the map of the escarpment about ten kilometres from the first cave Chris had found. That cave had since been named The Animal Cave, as it was the animal tracks that had led Chris to it.

"I have named this new cave, The Professors Cave. I have had a lot of aerial photos taken of the area and if you look closely at those photos you can identify an ancient riverbed that after wandering about for about thirty kilometres the riverbed runs from The Professors Cave to the Resort lake. Mr Bailey, old buddy, you and I will have to investigate the possibility to try and divert some of the underground river, like we did before, into this second ancient riverbed. You can see from those aerial maps there are numerous places we could site the new town. I like the look of this place here," Chris pointed to a place on one of the photographs. "You can see it is not so very far away from a lot of the houses we have already built."

Chris stood and stretched. "This is all well and good but useless without an overall plan," adding as an afterthought, "Madam Administrator, I never did get around to hearing your report of all those inquiries that have come into your office."

"I'll Madam Administrator you later, you clown," Jackie laughed as she picked up several sheets of paper and started to read. "Many of the inquiries are rubbish—they want to open shops selling what I consider is nothing but junk. I think we should turn them aside. There were inquiries from three of the major grocery chains. One of those chains in fact did send a deputation to gather as much information as possible. The leader of that deputation did tell me his bosses had expressed a great deal of interest in what was happening out here. It appears that many of the women have been using their stores for online shopping and they wish to protect that business. They did ask for me to send them more up to date information when things are a bit more set-in- concrete. We have had firm commitments from various government departments to provide the personnel we did request. I think they like the idea it will not cost them a bean for buildings or salaries, and that housing would be available at a very moderate rental apparently influenced their decision. I have been thinking over the problem of a town planner, Chris! You crazy man, cast your wicked mind back to the first time we met. You'll recall Jacobson had said he had a meeting down south to go to. That meeting was with the town planner; his name was Henry Grimes. He was young for a town planner; for what I saw later, he was very good, and I mean very, very good. Perhaps we could follow him up."

"That is some of the best news I have heard so far, Jackie girl. Tomorrow you and I are off down to that major country town."

The CEO of that now regional city, did remember young Henry. "He had been poached by the government and has moved east; we were very sorry to see him go. I do have a contact number for him should you wish to speak with him."

They thanked the CEO for his help and as they walked out the door, Chris whispered to Jackie, "We're off east for a day or two, my love; before we do that, I want you to use that contact number and call him. I am willing to wager a shilling or two he has not forgotten that 'honey' who worked in the apartment developer's office."

Henry Grimes had definitely not forgotten her when Jackie told him she would like to call on him. In Chris's words, "The rotten little beggar almost crawled down the telephone line in his urgency to ask 'When? Where?'"

"I usually stay at the Grand when I'm over there," Jackie had purred. "Perhaps lunch, day after tomorrow at that very nice top floor restaurant, at say twelve o'clock?"

"I'll be there," Henry enthusiastically replied.

And he was, bunch of flowers and a box of chocolates included. Disappointment registered clearly on his face when Jackie walked in hand and hand with Chris. Jackie promptly introduced him.

"You never met my husband did you, Henry? This is Chris, Christopher Kennedy, the Miner." Chris shook Henry's offered hand, saying, "I do regret the subterfuge we used to get you here, Henry. I have to tell you we're anxious to talk with you."

"You have progressed from being the planner in the country Shire; what are you doing now?" Jackie asked.

"Not that much really, Miss Jackie."

"Mrs Jackie," she lightly corrected him.

"Oh yes, sorry I forgot. You are a lucky guy, Kennedy," he laughed. "To answer your question, I am one of the assistants to the State Planner; it is a government position."

"Please forgive me for saying, this Henry," Jackie interrupted, "that did not sound like a man who is happy with what he is doing."

"It's okay," Henry rather reservedly replied. "Things in the job do lack any excitement; it is mainly checking over plans that have already been checked over by at least two others, then having to put up with whingeing developers when we insist on alterations. I do not get much of a chance to use my own initiative."

"I'm sorry to hear that," Jackie softly said. "It is a shame that has happened. You struck me as a planner with some brains and the initiative to make things happen. Let's have lunch and we can talk about all the things that have happened over all these years. Nice things like family, children, hobbies, things like that.

Chris and I have two wonderful children; he is a very successful mining engineer; we are living way out back in the Outback in a most beautiful place. I am very content. Now tell us all about you."

Henry was quiet for a moment, and quickly said, "I do not have a great deal to tell you. Being an assistant to the state planner does lack excitement in one's life. The woman I married moved on. No kids to hold her—we could never really afford them."

"Perhaps we can brighten up your day," Chris interrupted Henry's melancholy mood. "Let's enjoy a top meal, knock the top off a couple of very good wines and after lunch we will tell you of why we wanted to see you. We have a proposition for you to consider."

"So, this is not really a social visit," Henry was smiling a little now.

"No, it is not; not another word until after I have eaten," Jackie very firmly said.

After the fine meal and the good red wines, they sat enjoying an after-dinner port. During dinner Chris had perceived as Jackie had said, that here was a real talent. It was being wasted, so he had no hesitation in directing the conversation to that purpose of the meeting by quietly saying, "Henry I have an exciting proposition for you to consider: how would you like to draw together a multitude of ideas, and starting from scratch, plan and direct the building of a complete country town to accommodate say twenty to twenty-five-thousand people. Not just a few roads and buildings; every facet you could envisage to make it the best of the best places to live and bring up families in. You will be inhibited only by your own imagination."

"That is a planner's dream," Henry softly answered. "Who is funding all this? Have you government approval?"

"It is not a government project, Henry," Jackie answered. "We keep as much of our activities as possible out of their grubby little hands. Chris has managed to have them provide some services—as for funding, that's Chris's problem. No, that's wrong—it is not and never will be a problem; you will have an open cheque."

Henry was now obviously interested, and enthusiastically asked, "Where is this dream town?"

"This is about 1000 kilometres north-east of the regional city," Chris replied.

"That's way out in the Outback. Is that where you live? From all reports that is a godforsaken land and you expect me to build a viable township there." Henry growled.

It is," Jackie instantly replied. We will be relying on you to change much of that."

"And when can I see all this?" Henry asked, and added, "I am a conservative type of bloke and do not like to rush headlong into things without giving them proper consideration."

"I like the sound of that," Chris replied. "As soon as you are ready, let me know. I suggest you arrange for at least two weeks' leave. Immediately I hear from you I will send a plane for you."

"You have your own plane?" Henry stammered; he was getting thoroughly bemused with all this.

"Yes, Henry," Jackie quietly replied, "six or seven, at last count."

"All this is getting completely out of shape," Henry cried. "I will call you in two days' time. I have to arrange to take those holidays, and to clean up a couple of outstanding things that are sitting on my desk."

Chris passed him a business card. "Use the mobile number. Only I will answer. Call anytime. I will await your call with much anticipation."

As they all stood, preparing to depart, Henry hesitated for a moment, and said most sincerely, "I see before me two very much in love, happy and very honest people, and believe it will be an honour and pleasure to work with you. This has been a very pleasant and rewarding afternoon, I am pleased you thought of me."

Henry did ring Chris mid-morning the next day. "I commence holidays next Monday," he blurted out without even saying hello.

"That's very good," Chris answered. "You did not waste any time. Give me an address and I will have a car pick you up. Pack only summer weight gear. You will be taken directly to the airport, then flown straight to Quo-Vadis. We will be there to meet you."

From there it all happened very smoothly. Henry spent the first ten days of his holidays going over and talking with those committee men about all those plans they had submitted. Susie acted as an intermediary, introducing the men to Henry and explaining their particular interest in the project. She and Henry worked very well together, and for a girl who had all but given up, she suddenly became that wonderful vibrant person they all used to know.

After much, sometimes heated discussion, Chris and Bill did manage to divert a substantial flow from the underground river to that newly discovered ancient riverbed. The main point of contention had been that Bill had advocated that this time they did scrape that riverbed to harvest what he saw was much alluvial gold therein.

Chris would not agree; the upshot of their argument was that Chris, as usual, did have his own way. "I do derive much pleasure from allowing all those children to find those nuggets."

After Bill and Chris had walked the thirty kilometres of that ancient river bed, from where it left the entrance of the Professors Cave to where it entered the Resort and lake, Bill conceded he could not argue with Chris's generosity. They were absolutely delighted to find two good waterfalls and many large pools would be formed along the way.

"These will be good fishing spots," Bill had chuckled. "We must quickly stock this river with an abundance of good fish." Then because he was still smarting a little about the gold cynically asked, "Okay, Mister Smart Guy, with all this extra water flowing into the lake, when it is full, where will all the extra water go?"

"I wondered that too," Chris answered, "so I got one of the choppers and followed it. We hadn't noticed it before, but there was an exit point in that ancient lake bed. The run-off ran towards the west for about forty kilometres, then the river appeared to disburse over a flood plain. I think that in time it will become a very verdant area. As a matter of interest, I did notice a good number of potential fishing holes along the way. I have spoken with old Marlee the native elder, who was particularly happy with this development. He spoke of tales from the Dreamtime of a green land, abounding with native animals and believed, 'this may have been part of that tale.'"

Henry had requested they all meet the next morning.

Chris told Jackie of the requested meeting, to which she replied, "I think he wants to tell you he wants the job. Susie has told me he is very, very enthusiastic about all he has seen."

To say Henry did want a job would be an understatement; he told Chris, Jackie, Bill and all the committee members, "I can see a wonderful future for the town." In a roundabout fashion, he did offer some apologies to one or two of the committee who had been a little slow in agreeing to his suggested changes to their plans. "I am pleased to see you are all now very happy to have those changes incorporated, particularly when I show you where I propose the town centre could be and how each and every one of the committee's plans would be integrated. That rugged bit of land along your new river can be made into it a very attractive showpiece. It is about five kilometres from the sinkhole and about eight kilometres from the airport. The Resort and cattle station are a bit further away. The earthmoving people are confident they can construct winding roads in and out of all those huge boulders in the area; they say it will be quite a challenge. They can see, with the construction of beautiful homes and their gardens, it will make the whole area most spectacular. Giuseppe had grumbled a bit about having to build his beautiful creations in and around bloody big rocks. The truth, in fact, was he was most excited, knowing full well that the natural environment complimented those houses made predominantly from stone. As for the reaction of the landscape consultant, I think I had best keep his comments to myself, except to say, he did question my sanity."

Henry's enthusiasm was contagious, and without hesitation Chris very forcibly said, "It is your baby now, Henry. Do all or anything you consider to be worth the while. Not forgetting for one moment you are not inhibited by any restrictions whatsoever. Any problems you encounter can and will be overcome. I speak for all here—Jackie, Bill and every member of the 20-man committee will be here to help you. I personally will not interfere, but you will have to be aware I am always available should you ever need anything."

On that note, the meeting concluded. Henry paused at the doorway and quietly said; "you know that girl Susie, you sent to help me Chris, she is just great; nothing is too much trouble for her. Is she really your daughter?"

"She is," Chris replied. "Jackie and I adopted her when her real dad died. In recent years she has had a rough time; you and your vision for this project has drawn her out of her melancholia."

"I have something for you to worry about now," Henry very sternly said. "I need an answer within the next thirty seconds. Should you be agreeable, I would like very much to formalize all this and accept your offer of a job. I have a letter here, for your records to confirm this. I am not going back to my old job and would like to start here tomorrow morning. I have long service leave banked up and they can use part of it as termination notice. What's my salary?"

"First things first," Chris laughed. "Welcome aboard, Henry. I am very sure you will not regret your decision. Now the second bit, your salary; how does a $250,000 contract for one year, to be reviewed and extended by mutual agreement, sound to you?"

"That's a very attractive offer, Chris," Henry replied. "It is at least double my existing salary."

"I can always reduce it should it embarrass you, Mister Town Planner," Chris quickly said with a broad grin on his face.

As Henry walked away, Chris softly said to Jackie, "That's one hell of a fine young man; he will take a big load from our minds."

# Chapter 20

Planning of that township, particularly the shopping precinct, was not without a degree of conflict. At the third meeting, the twenty advisers and counsellors and Henry, accompanied by Susan, had sat in earnest conference for several hours. The counsellors all had a vision for a tree-lined street extending along the riverbank.

Very early in the meeting, Henry had rather forcibly stood and said, "I have reviewed all those ideas you have previously submitted. I have something in my mind that will require you to completely revise your thoughts. The whole area was until recently a very dry intimidating piece of land; with proper planning, we could make it into a most attractive green shady park which would bring people here to shop. The river Chris has rejuvenated, brings a constant good volume of water through here. You have all seen what Bill Bailey has done by bringing in loads of enriched soil, and, now, with all that water and a little expertise we could grow almost anything. Of course, there are many types of plants that will not tolerate the harsh Outback climate; nevertheless, I am sure we can find many that will completely satisfy our needs. It is amazing what a little water can do. Have you looked at the gums along the new watercourse? They are all showing signs of increased growth. Look at the bush and trees growing along the sheltered edge of the escarpment— they are verdant and healthy. Chris tells me they receive a good supply of water seeping from the escarpment. As a matter of interest and as it is not so far from the town site, I propose we preserve much of that area as possible and in time create a very large area of parks and gardens, even a botanical garden containing every type and species of plant from our beautiful Outback."

"It's got to you too, Mr Town Planner; don't let that worry you—it happens to all of us," the transport committeeman rather solemnly said.

There were nods of agreement all around the table. "You have our full attention, Henry," the landscape fellow said. "Fill us in with all the details, especially with what you are planning to do with the shops."

"I was about to come to that," Henry answered, as he undid the large folder Susan passed him. "Here is a comprehensive plan of a mall—a very upmarket mall, with accommodation for all the shops, be they large or small. The design does provide for the expansion, if the need arises. I propose to site it not on; but a little back from the riverbank but within a beautiful parkland setting with lawns and gardens that run down to the riverbank. Most people will choose to drive here to shop, so you will see I have incorporated extensive undercover parking on the reverse side of the mall to the river, making that shopping area traffic free, and consequently very family friendly. There will be several pedestrian entries from the undercover car park to the mall."

The counsellors all gathered around the plan absorbing the details. After about fifteen minutes, Duncan, who had been nominated for his plumbing expertise, simply said, "This plan will mean I have to revise my whole plan for the shopping precinct. I can see where you are coming from Henry and I do agree with your ideas."

One by one all the committee counsellors had a say. There was much forthright discussion back and forth—one or two were rather direct in the criticism.

"Before we do anything," one snapped. "We need to get some feedback from the women folk."

"I do not need a decision today," Henry interrupted. "Why not seek your wife's opinion? Ask her to talk about it with the girls as they meet for their morning chinwags. We meet again next

Friday; perhaps you will have some feedback to report on then. You other fellows could request your women folk in a like manner. From my experience, an attractive, clean mall with retail outlets presenting and pricing their product in a competitive manner are much more popular than a long line of shops. To make things a little bit more attractive, you will see there is provision for a few coffee shops. They are usually very well patronised in the malls where people can take a break while they shop or even to grab a quick snack. The girls often make their favourite coffee shop the venue for their weekly chinwag. I am hoping to receive applications for every conceivable type of shop, apart from the regular grocery shops. Things like butchers, greengrocers, hairdressers, newsagents, bookshops, with a wing of the mall providing specialised personal services, like, a beauty parlour, masseur, counselling services, things of this nature. We are not limited by space so we could give some thought of including a lending library with internet connection. The Television reception, at times out here, is not so good, so as an alternative to TV, we could have a movie theatre showing the latest released movies. Further on with the entertainment facilities, people may welcome a live show now and again, and I am confident that the schools will be pleased to have a venue where they can conduct their presentation evenings and the kids could put on play. This very well positioned large space is designed to accommodate a fully functional restaurant that has an external entry allowing it to operate after hours. In the same vein we could look at another restaurant out in the park and or perhaps several small places where people enjoying the park could get a drink or a nibble. Exactly what; in the way of shops, to come here, is dependent entirely on the level of interest shown? I am confident we will receive many applications, and the biggest problem will be sorting out the best."

At the next council meeting, Henry's plans were approved in total. The road building contractor had made the meeting laugh, when he related his wife's comment. "She had told me in no uncertain terms, this plan is really marvellous; if you blokes do not go ahead with every bit of it, she would organise the girls and give us all the sack."

"My wife said something similar," the electrician said. "She was a bit stronger with her threat, and if I didn't vote for it, I would be sleeping in the spare room for a month."

Jackie added to the humour of the moment by saying, "With or without dinner?"

"I have spoken with Mr Kennedy, Chris," Henry said endeavouring to regain the direction of the meeting. "His only comment was, immediately we agree, we should proceed with the total plans, of both the shopping/town centre and the township without delay. He did enquire of our plans, for a community centre, sporting facilities, and the like—all those things a healthy community enjoy. He doesn't muck about, as you all know; he told me he has chosen the site for a complete hospital with fully equipped treatment facilities for all but those illnesses which require highly specialised treatment and suggested we make provision for an emergency ward. He is even talking about inviting specialists to set up consulting rooms in the hospital where they could provide a regular service. He shook me a bit when he suggested Bill, Mr Bailey, join us. Bill and I had met on the proposed town site. Bill shared many of Chris's plans with me. He started by quoting some statistics which many of you may be aware of, such as: we presently have a population that numbers around 5000 people, varying from 3500 to 6000. He was laughing when he said, 'The mad miner, Chris Kennedy, has plans to expand his mining activities and we can expect the people living here will increase to a permanent 25,000.We should keep that number in the forefront of our planning; Bill will join us at the next meeting."

"Hells Bells," the mechanical engineer cried, "We do not have anything like the facilities for that many; where on earth are we going to put them all?"

"That's my job," Henry softly said. "That's what I'm paid for. Many of those people will be just starting out in life. A few will be from the upper levels of university graduates that have been recommended by their professors and lecturers to put all the knowledge they had acquired while at the university to practical use, and thereby gain the best of experience they will find that the Quo-Vadis complex offers. Chris has committed himself and had generously offered to top up the earnings of the professional people, such as doctors, dentists and pharmacists this type of professional, until such a time they get established. For a time, most of those younger people will be happy to live in an apartment complex, so a fifteen-story apartment block is planned. When the work force is established, those young graduates will start looking for permanent housing. As you all well know, once having lived here, it is difficult to even think of leaving. Fortunately, we have not touched that land on the other side of the river. There is much attractive space over available there. I have already had Chris survey the area and have commenced an overall draft plan. It will be integrated with our existing plans. I will be asking each and every one of you to look at those plans and bring to me, what you see, in your particular field, will be needed. I may be very good at drawing up overall plans; after all I am a Town Planner," Henry cheerfully added, "but be well assured I need your expertise , when it comes to the fine details."

"Have you given any thought to what we will need by way of town transport services?" Oscar the transport consultant asked.

"That is a leading question," Henry replied. "I have looked over our needs there also. Many of the residents now living in the existing town usually drive their own cars to and from the airport to be flown out to the various mining sites, or each day drive to the mines in the escarpment. Multiply that five or six times, and at times we could have chaotic congestion. This is a perfect example of where I need you to apply your expertise."

"I will give you my answer to that problem now, Henry," Oscar quickly said. "As you put your plans together, make allowance for a super-efficient, light rail complex serving everywhere: the airport, the local mines, the proposed hospital, existing and proposed schools, shops. Everything that people travel to and from daily."

"Good one, Oscar," Henry answered with a note of gratitude. "That is one problem I can tick off as being solved."

"My very efficient right-hand girl, Susie, has compiled some interesting statistics. Please comment as you feel fit. Be very confident that the activities of Quo-Vadis Holdings will exist in this area for a long time; these statistics will alter as the demographics of many of the inhabitant's change. For the time being, the majority of the inhabitants will be mostly young; their needs will not be so demanding as an older population. If you look at these statistics from non-suburban areas with a general population and the normal mix of young and old, numbering around the 25,000 persons level, we found that for every 1500 to 2000 persons, one GP was required, and similarly for every 5000 people one dentist was needed. As I have expressed our circumstances and composition of population varies from the usual statistics, I am thinking one doctor to every three to four thousand persons and one dentist for seven to eight thousand would suffice. As town consultants, we would need to keep a close watch on those figures. I believe all of those who provide professional services will monitor their own needs and expand their practices as they see fit. That's enough for statistics for the moment—let's get back to the more practical things. Two of the major banks have sought approval to open and staff branches here. I cannot envisage they will need to create a very large book of loans; however, businesses and private people do all have banking needs and the service these two banks can offer will be appreciated. I think it's time for a break. Susie and I will grab some lunch and be back in one hour. That will give you a little time to amass those million-and-one questions that I know are out there."

The meeting resumed on time, and Henry resolutely asked, "Okay, Roads, you are number one of that million. I hope we can keep these questions short and to the point; otherwise we will never be able to attend to everything."

"Roads" stood and loudly said, "I heartily agree with Henry—let's keep it short and sweet. I want to ask about "Coppers," damn it all, I know we need them."

"Unfortunately, our need will be ascertained by the police administration, with there being no unemployment, with everybody fully employed and earning good money, I can see there will be very little need for police," Henry commented. Perhaps someone keeping an eye on lead foots (speedsters) and with a police presence it will give the community a sense of security."

"Traffic surveillance out on the main road is badly needed," the road gang counsellor commented. "They could haul in a few of those bloody tourists who do not know how to drive on a country road. Would you believe only yesterday I saw a guy in one of those foreign sports cars trying to overtake one of our six trailer cattle trucks on the curves? You know that twenty-kilometre section of the main road that winds in an out a fair bit. The blokes driving those cattle transports know how to drive and usually sit on 110 to 120 K. That stupid tourist nearly got himself killed. Those cattle trucks do go a bit fast, perhaps we can ask them to slow down a bit."

A heated argument ensured, stopping abruptly when Henry angrily snapped, "This is a useless argument; it is out of our hands. Policing traffic is what the police are here for. Let's move on to something more constructive."

Henry opened another large file saying, "We should discuss the hospital. As I have said, Chris has given us the perfect site. Soon I can see he will be asking, 'Have we taken time to discuss it.' Susan has been visiting some regional hospitals and has accumulated quite a bit of information for us. We presently have a nursing post; any person needing care beyond what the nursing post can provide is sent to the city. We must consider: do we need something more than that nursing post. In my opinion the answer is a most definite, yes. With a population of 25,000, there is no doubt, we will need a 'full on' hospital. I hope you chaps all realise that the decisions you make here and now will set the foundation for many things in the future. I am most grateful and acknowledge the wealth of knowledge and common sense you bring to these meetings. Look at the implications of the needs of a hospital; in some distant point in the future, the community may be asked to support it. For the present, we are most fortunate. Most communities I know of would kill to have a patron of the like of Quo-Vadis Holdings. Chris has once again most generously committed his company to the total cost of that hospital, from the ground up. Things like architectural design, the actual building, and that very expensive fitting out. Before we start Chris has suggested we invite a few of the best medical minds to come here and tell us exactly what we need. In his typical fashion, Chris has offered to use his influence to bring a good number of those specialists who lecture at the University. Typical of Chris he again emphasised; nothing but the best of the best, and the most modern and best-known equipment is to be installed; even if it necessitates sending some of those specialists overseas to see that specialised equipment in operation. Chris did say he would be most annoyed if he ever found we avoided purchasing something because of its cost. He expects our hospital must be able care for all but the most complex of conditions. The design should incorporate not just a ward but a whole a children's wing. Kids will always need some good medical attention. One of Susan's reports covers addictive conditions. These conditions require highly-specialised treatment—perhaps beyond normal hospital care. Dr Jason Mayo, the State's top drug and alcohol specialist has for some time been agitating Chris to set up a recovery clinic out here. Chris has not embraced the idea in the past. He is now suggesting we should consider it. There is an ideal site for such a place about fifteen K down the river from the resort. This project does not really embrace the direct needs of our community. I appreciate it is something far above us here, and we would be well served to invite some very learned people in that field to address us before we make a decision. I will invite Dr Mayo to come and talk with us. He will hate me for that! His wife insists on accompanying him on any visits he makes a visit to Quo-Vadis. She spends a small fortune on Penny's paintings and in the accessories shop.

"Thank goodness, this is the last matter on this week's agenda," Henry laughed, "but it is the most important. I need to discuss my own staff. Delays for service in the council offices are intolerable and are bad form. I urgently need at least twenty more people, and many more as we grow. To install and maintain all our proposed parks and gardens, there will be a need for a large outdoor staff—town maintenance staff, street cleaners, rubbish truck drivers—the list goes on and on. We will eventually become a genuine country town, not a company town. I need your approval to first of all recruit my own staff, and next to approach the local government minister to be gazetted as a new country Shire, and to seek that funding, which is generally granted to country Shires. We will have to separate our Shire from the ties of the existing mob. They do not do one positive thing for us except to procrastinate if ever we needed to talk about essential services. We do rely substantially on the good graces of Quo-Vadis

Holdings. Chris thinks he is responsible for the creation of this monster and is more than happy to continue with that total support. I believe as a community we should support ourselves. All the businesses operating here are privately owned and are making sound profits. It will not be popular but they should be required to make a contribution. They in themselves do employ many people—the cost of employing them is all a tax deduction to them, so a small levy of say a minimum of $100, increasing in proportion to the size of the business would be appropriate; and would be a further tax-deduction for them. Those houses which are now privately owned could be asked to pay an annual levy. Knowing Chris, he will not object to paying the levy on all those houses they own and rent out. Our position as nominated community leaders will be severely questioned because of this, but I am sure you can clearly see that if we continue to rely on Chris, through Quo-Vadis Holdings, to supply all those wonderful facilities, we will never become self-dependent. Chris likes the expense of supporting the community—it is a worthwhile tax deduction, and he would be most unhappy to lose it. Rex had more than a word or two to say on that particular subject.

"I have waffled on for long enough. Thanks for listening to me folks; I have given you much to think over. Susan has copies of everything we have covered today—you can take them with you. It may be that you find some things in those notes you feel require further discussion. Bring those matters up at the next meeting next Friday. By the way, Chris has told me he will support our decisions regardless of how we vote. He said he believes all you consultants are very solid and sensible fellows who are very sensitive to the community needs. I have to agree. Time for a cuppa and cake.

# Chapter 21

Chris had had a very large temporary office set up for Henry—a big tin shed!

"It is only temporary, until you get around to building something better for yourself," Chris assured him. Despite his rustic environment, after many long hours, Henry, ably assisted by Susan, had completed the master plan and building program. It had taken six months from that counsellors meeting. He had continued to meet with those advisors, tying up any loose ends. The advisors had all been sworn to secrecy, and all were very pleased and most enthusiastic about the final product. Susan had copied Chris's way of advising the community by distributing pamphlets to advise all of the community of the meeting; this time there was no hidden agenda. The pamphlet simply said that the meeting had been called so all could see the result of the amalgamation of the best of all those suggestions they and their nominated experts had put forth.

Once again, that small community school hall was packed to bursting point. Chris and Jackie had arrived relatively early; even then, they found it necessary to quickly grab seats towards the back of the hall.

Exactly at the nominated start time of 7 pm, Henry had not hesitated and stood on the teacher's desk so all could see and hear him. "Most of you here know me," he announced loudly. "For those who do not, I am Henry Grimes. I have been engaged to plan your new township. I have listened to, and taken into account, all those things you and the men you have nominated have suggested would make this community even better. I have taken each and every one of those suggestions and have integrated them with all my knowledge and experience into our final plan. You have been very patient, and I have finally been able to produce plans of what I propose to build. The plans are for your inspection and comment.

Do not hesitate to tell me if you see anything you would like to have included or changed. It is most necessary before I proceed too much further to have your approval. Susan, this lovely young lady, sitting here on my right has copies of all these plans. So that I can get a measure of your response to those plans, please take a copy and return them to her by Monday. You will note on the final page there is space for you to make comment or simply say yes or no to my plans. Do not hesitate to add any suggestions or enquire about a particular matter. This will ensure your interests are kept paramount and hopefully will avoid having to call these meetings. I have welcomed much guidance from the committee selected by you. Those twenty men who you considered the best in their particular field have given much time and effort to this massive project, without exception they have contributed much. I do humbly suggest you consider nominating each and every one of them to continue in some role of managing the community. I can only say each one has proven to me he is a man of integrity and ability and have all shown they each have your interests at heart.

This is what we have come up with," then stepping down from the teacher's desk to an adjacent table, with flamboyant showmanship, Henry ripped the cover from a ten-foot square, beautifully coloured graphic of his proposal. The graphic had been meticulously moulded in plaster; with hills, roads, the river, existing and proposed buildings, even the proposed light rail, everything thing the committee had discussed was there in accurate scale and detail. Penny and Anne had had great pleasure in painting colour detail to that masterpiece.

Henry had had many coloured copies printed and loudly announced, "No questions at the moment please. Look, consider and advise is all I ask. What happens from now on in is up to you all."

There was quite a crush around the coloured plan, and Susan was hard pushed to keep up with the request for the copies.

Chris and Jackie had deliberately kept out of most of Henry's planning and they too stood and inspected the coloured board.

"He is as you said, Jackie girl," Chris whispered. "He is very good; in fact, I would go so far as to say he is brilliant."

Very few suggestions for changes were forthcoming. The one from Jamie and Vanessa to have hire canoes and some picnic spots on the river was instantly added.

The proposed site for the town centre became a turmoil of activity. Despite having the appearance of an ant hill gone insane, Henry's capacity for planning ensured little conflict. The twenty previously nominated committee men were re-elected and became known as The Town Council; Henry was unanimously elected town mayor. The tin shed disappeared, and in its place a somewhat expanded, very attractive Giuseppe-built Township Administration Centre replaced it. The building had been architecturally designed and did comfortably accommodate all those extra staff Henry had requested to assist him to run the town. Giuseppe had not once complained with this project. He could see that that building was to be something special, enhancing his reputation even further. Henry's request to have the escarpment and much of the area surrounding the Quo-Vadis township declared a separate shire had been met with some resistance and was still sitting in abeyance.

Henry and Susan had joined Chris and Jackie for dinner at that silver service restaurant at the resort. Much of the conversation revolved around how well Henry's plans were coming together.

"I suppose you reckon you're worth more money, Henry," Chris said, and before Henry could answer, Chris quickly said, "I think you have earned a pay rise; do you think you are worth $500,000 per annum, and, one B class share in Quo-Vadis Holdings?"

"That sounds very generous," Henry softly replied. "What's this bit about shares?"

"Explain to him, please, Susie," Chris laughed.

"Well! Mr Town Planner," Susie very seriously said, having a great deal of difficulty in hiding the smirk on her face, "Daddy gave me two of those B class shares some years back; last September, the company paid $1,000,000 per share as an annual dividend."

"Did you say $1, 000 per annum, Susan?" Henry asked.

"No, silly Billy, I said $1,000,000," Susie replied with a little more than conversational tone in her voice.

"That's good money," Henry laughed, and looking softly at Susie said, "A man could get married on that."

Construction of the mall and the town centre went ahead almost according to plan. The only hiccup was the barney (fight) between the three supermarkets over a site. Henry settled it when he called the three together and in no uncertain words laid out the terms of their tenancy. "You have all given me details of what you require and the size of the space you need. What you must bear in mind here and now, if you do not use the space to the extent you have asked for you will lose the lot."

The intended managers of those supermarkets gave their requirements further consideration and submitted the revised requirements to Henry. The most conservative request, by the smaller of the three, was given priority. All three were most satisfied with the outcome.

While construction of the township proceeded, many of Chris's plans were proceeding most favourably: the duplication of the pegmatites mine and processing plant; the completion of the railway line to interconnected the iron ore mine and the pegmatites plant; two more quartz reefs in separate caves in the escarpment, having been bought into production, producing an increasing volume of gold ingots. These were only a few of the rapidly growing Quo-Vadis empire. With the buildings in the town centre nearing completion with only a little fitting out to the specifications of the intended tenants, to be completed; Giuseppe now turned to his first love—building homes—and for a while he was able to keep up to the demand.

Henry had resided in one of the suites in the workmen's quarters. One of the very early matters the newly-elected town council put on the agenda was the matter of better accommodation for their very important and popular mayor. For him to be residing in workmen's quarters, was not at all in keeping with the position, and as others had been provided with very nice homes they considered it appropriate for the mayor to be provided with something more in keeping with his position. There was an absolutely delightful spot about 200 metres down-stream from the town centre. The new river ran through a nearby healthy stand of trees.

"There must be some water near the surface there for those trees to be growing so well," Bill had said. Two fifteen-foot-high boulders, separated the river flow by about ten feet. They appeared to stand guard over the river outlet. Those boulders had caused the river to backup and form a good-sized pool. The newly-elected town council had relentlessly declined to even listen to any argument Henry put fourth that there are other homes which are more important, and they unanimously voted that the delightful place was most suitable for a very ostentatious residence to be built there for their very popular mayor. Giuseppe's architect was again commissioned to design something special.

It is perhaps needless to say, Henry reacted, and cried, "What the hell does a bachelor need with a five bedroom, five salubrious ensuites, a game's room, library and all that other stuff?

I only need a roof over my head and a place to lay my weary body down."

The house was built for him despite his protests. The interior decorator, who in those past years had fitted out Chris's apartment in the city, and all the houses in the sinkhole; had been bought to Quo-Vadis to once again do her thing.

At first, she wouldn't believe Chris when she had been told, "Spend as much as it takes—do not omit anything, regardless of cost."

Jackie had worked with her in the selection of furniture and fittings. The decorator finally got the message and let loose with a vengeance.

Even the very stoic Bill did comment, "That's mighty nice," as he walked through the house.

Very pretty garden beds, strategically placed in the landscaped lawns that ran down to the river and pool, enhanced the setting.

Giuseppe stood with Chris and Jackie out the front of the completed house; pride showed in his very posture. He growled, with a voice full of regret, "This is getting to be a very bad habit: first your home, then Bill's, and now this is one. If I had any one of the three in the city I would be asked to build hundreds."

Susan was having more than a little trouble to keep her feelings under control. She and Jackie had sat quietly beside the lake in the sinkhole indulging in some "girlie talk" when she confessed that things had come to a head three week earlier. She softly told Jackie, "Henry and I were at the office looking over some plans of the children's playground; he had been asked to add to the list of things to do. It was a large plan and he had had to come around to my side of the table to look at something I wanted to bring to his notice. As he reached across my shoulder to get a better look at what I was saying his head came very close to my neck, and as he stood back he ever so lightly kissed my neck. Oh

Mummy, it was like an electric shock that ran all through me. It didn't appear to affect him; he had only kept on examining the plan as he was doing before. I was speechless and couldn't talk for half an hour and I have not been able to get his touch out of my mind since."

"Well, young lady," Jackie lightly scolded, "What are you going to do about it?"

"What can I do?" Susan cried. "Henry only acts as if nothing has happened. I am a mess! Since Alan died I have never given a thought to being with somebody else; in fact, I think I am frightened of the prospect of a man touching me. I may be very naughty, Mummy, but I dream of being with Henry."

"We cannot allow this to continue," Jackie growled. "Come on, we are going shopping for something that may take Henry's mind away from those plans of his and make him focus on you for a while."

The next morning Susan arrived at the office, looking rather delightful, tight skirt that accentuated her slim shapely body and an open neck shirt that showed all her better points to their greatest advantage. Two top buttons of that shirt had not been buttoned up and at times allowed a flash of white lace trimmed bra to appear. Henry did compliment her on her appearance and much to her disappointment just took his normal seat on the opposite side of that drafting table apparently studiously applying himself fully to whatever task was at hand. No, that was not quite correct; more than once Susan caught him surreptitiously watching her. Things must've got the better of him and he stood and came to her side of that large drafting table to stand behind her.

"You have a piece of fluff on your shoulder, Susie," he softly said. "Allow me to brush it off for you." He pretended to remove a non-existent piece of fluff then continued to slide his hand down the open shirt collar and under her bra.

Susie was petrified, she didn't know what to do. Emotions and sensations ran rampant through her.

Henry quickly removed his hand and stammered. "Sorry Susie, I have wanted to do that for a long time. Can we talk for a bit?"

"I think we should, Mr Grimes," Susan replied. From appearances, she looked to be totally in control; that was not so: she could barely breathe and because her head was spinning and her stomach churned with thousands of butterflies she was afraid to attempt to stand for fear that her week knees would give way; so, she stayed fixed in her chair to keep from fainting.

Henry had quickly regained his composure was back to being Henry and when he very firmly said, "I have much to say to you; let's grab a coffee from the coffee shop and sit by the river; where it is quiet and we can talk."

They had sat by the river for over two hours, a little hesitantly at first then quite strongly Henry had confessed he had fallen for her almost from the first time they had met. Susie in return, had confessed she too had harboured strong feelings for him for a long time, and explained to him all that had happened to her. She expressed her fear of ever again being with a man.

Henry had listened to her story and quietly said, "Susie, I do understand and if you will give me a chance, even if it takes a long time, I am sure together we will overcome your fears. Please kiss me now and we will go back to work."

It was not just a simple kiss; it was the release of the passion they both had held contained for so long. Susie had wandered aimlessly back to work; she achieved very little for the rest of the day. Her talk with Jackie that night after dinner ranged from tears to moments of absolute happiness.

"I cannot help you any further," Jackie softly said to her. "Until it actually happens, you will never know."

"I am too scared to even consider trying, Mummy," Susan wailed.

For the next six months, Henry and Susie spent many happy hours together, either at the office during office hours, or in their own time. Now holding two prominent positions, being both the town planner, and the mayor, Henry was kept very busy.

Vanessa and Jamie had often brought up the subject of short-term accommodation. Chris took it on board and did extensive investigation, culminating in him selecting a well-positioned site that had suitable foundation, and appointing an architect to produce appropriate plans for another hotel. Henry and the architect did have many spirited discussions about traffic flow and parking and the hooking in of that building into existing infrastructure. Henry had found it necessary to redirect the planned light rail to service the hotel. He had envisaged the hotel would be patronised mainly by overseas visitors who would require many modes of transport—mainly hire vehicles they could use to explore all that adjacent fabulous Outback. He did see those visitors would enjoy exploring all those areas the light rail serviced. This project was only one of many activities that absorbed much of Henry's time.

Henry and Susie's courtship was a gentle thing; each being most sensitive to the other's needs. What did happen was most unexpected. This particular warm evening, after sharing a quiet meal at one of smaller cafes, they returned to Henry's beautiful home with the intention of sitting beside the river, to enjoy the peacefulness of that spot. It had been a hard day for both of them, and the opportunity to relax was greatly appreciated. Henry had bought a couple of cushions. As he arranged one for her head he had lent over and kissed her gently; they had kissed often; but this time the kiss was much deeper and without warning their bodies demanded more, and they shared a passionate session of lovemaking. As they lay on the riverbank afterwards, Henry softly whispered, "Susie, my Susie, I love you so much! Would you marry me? I think we have overcome that one obstacle that prevented our love being perfect. It is now a beautiful, wonderful thing."

She was on a high and full of mischief, and languidly replied, "Oh, sir, this is so sudden. You'll have to ask my father," then most seriously added, "If he says no, I will run away with you. It's not late—let's go and tell my parents now."

Chris and Jackie took one look at the pair and knew what had happened. As was typical with Henry he did not muck about, and without even saying hello, almost shouted, "Susie says I have to ask you can I marry her?"

Poor Chris and Jackie near exploded laughing. Chris was finally able to say, "I suppose I had better say yes, or you will . . ." he hesitated looking for the right thing to say.

Jackie helped by offering, "They will run away together."

"Have you been spying on us?" Henry asked with a voice full of humour— he was feeling good. "That is what Susie said not an hour ago."

They were married two weeks later. What was planned to be a very private beautiful ceremony, turned out to be a major community event, as all and sundry joined together to offer the very popular couple many good wishes and blessings. Chris was more or less required to open up the large mess hall in the small cavern in the sinkhole, to accommodate the celebration that ensued. Every woman who attended the celebration, and that was the majority of the women who lived at Quo-Vadis, had voluntarily bought with them their favourite culinary delight. It turned out to be a wonderful celebration. In all those days that followed, that beautiful Mayoral Lodge became a place of complete happiness for Henry and Susie.

# Chapter 22

Penny and Anne often sat with the native women as they painted their intricate murals. The women would explain much of the symbolic meaning of their works. Those women in turn would sit for hours watching Penny as she painted. Penny's subjects varied greatly from broad beautiful paintings of the Outback, or pictures of the native children or even the adults, to animals, flowers, even colourful insects. Her paintings were superb and sold rapidly. Many had short-term sojourns hung in various museums throughout the world.

This fateful day, Penny had almost finished a delightful landscape which included part of the multi-coloured escarpment.

"Is very beautiful," one of the native women commented. "When do you add its spirit? I cannot feel it."

"Spirit?" Penny questioned. "What are you saying?"

"Missy Penny," the woman replied. "Look at our painting—it is not beautiful like yours; look closely with your heart. Do you not feel the living vibrating thing in it?"

Penny looked long at that mural and closed her eyes as if thinking. "Yes," she whispered, "I can feel the story you are telling."

"You did find that spirit when you drew it from the paper bark and the pigments. The spirit poured outwards from the faces and bodies of the family. It told of the many sufferings of our people. Your painting was so good, the spirit you captured went even deeper and revealed the pride of being part of our wonderful native population. You even had the spirit there in their eyes of the children as they looked upwards seeing hope and happiness. You appear to have lost the way to bring the spirits to your work."

Penny knew well what they were saying; she had never recaptured that thing, that feeling that had flowed through her as she created that painting.

"Thank you, ladies, I know what you are saying, today you have told me something most important. I must think on it." Penny did think deeply on it; so deeply the thought played on her mind constantly. She revisited a number of those great masters that hung in the museums and galleries throughout the world. She sat for hours before them; looking deeply at each and every brush stroke; feeling the passion the artist felt as the brush touched the canvas. "Yes! They did have that something extra; even when the artist had chosen to only paint an elderly man, the wisdom and at times the suffering or even the unbounded joy, is there."

She revisited her own masterpiece in the National Art Gallery. That "spirit" the native woman had spoken of was there. What she had felt as she had painted that family had flowed through her and onto that paperbark. "When did I lose it?" she silently questioned. "Did I really have it or was it only a one-time thing." On reflection, she could not recall ever regaining the intensity that had been upon her as she painted that family. Penny knew Yindi had something special. "Perhaps I will ask her."

Yindi was most sensitive to Penny's problem. She had listened closely to Penny and taking her hand said, "Come with me." That beautiful daughter of Chris and Jackie led her to the Mia-Mia of the native witch doctor.

He too listened intently to Penny, and when she had finished her story, quietly said, "Missy Penny. What you seek is out there," and waved his arm in the general direction of the Outback, and continuing to speak ever so softly added, "If it is to be found, it will not be a matter of you finding it, it will find you."

"I would prefer not to do this; every time I ventured out there," Penny told Yindi, "I had very bad experiences. I am very frightened of the prospect of getting lost again. Your father did save me both times; it was only by the grace of God he ever found me. Still I know, that I will never be happy not knowing and for the sake of my art, I must go."

Penny did contain her fears and a few days later had loaded her mini Goliath to the maximum. She had made sure all the water tanks were full and had loaded eight twenty-litre drums of extra fuel. All the cupboards were stacked to their capacity with nutritious food, be it in tins or dry packets that only required a small amount of liquid to be added, Without telling another person she set out on her search.

On the tenth night out there, she sat and quietly discussed with herself what had she achieved. The answer was simple: she had achieved nothing!

"Am I looking too hard?" she cried in her mind. "The witch doctor had said, what I seek will find me if it is to be found. I guess I will never know. It is so frustrating. I know what I am seeking is there, somehow it stays just beyond my reach. I recall old Marlee the native elder telling me some time in the past; it is only if you come to love and truly feel this wonderful land, it will then reveal its secrets to you. Maybe I should spend more time with him and try and find exactly what he meant, by coming to love this land. I am getting low on fuel and tomorrow I will turn back," she dejectedly admitted defeat.

That night as she tossed and turned in her sleep, horrific images assailed her mind. She awoke screaming; images of her past ventures boiled through her, even though she was now awake. "I am going insane," she cried. Still those images persisted. In fear she burrowed deeper into her blankets, yet they were still there, churning through her mind, screaming at her, poking her with imaginary sticks. All night long she suffered, gaining a little relief as the sun rose and the images and anguish disappeared. "That's definitely it," she screamed out aloud. "I'm going back right now. I cannot stand another night like that." With no thought of packing in an orderly fashion she simply threw her camp gear haphazardly into the back of her mini Goliath, filled the fuel tanks from her reserve fuel drums, all the while thinking to herself, "I hope this is enough." With that, she virtually jumped into the driver's seat, and thumped the start button. That mini Goliath started immediately. "Thank goodness for Ed's expertise," she gratefully thought, then with a sense of relief said to herself, "Home, here I come." It then struck her: "I have not got a clue which way is home. I have been wandering about out here for days. I think north is that way so if I go in the opposite direction I should strike that new road Chris was making to get out to the pegmatites mine."

Her interpretation of north and south was a bit astray, and she actually drove away from home. She had driven about fifteen kilometres, but her mind was refusing to coordinate, and she carelessly ploughed into a deep patch of very loose sand. For the remainder of that day she tried to get her vehicle free. Despite her best efforts, all she succeeded in doing was to bog him deeper. At night she did not sleep for fear those nightmarish images would come again. Still sleep did overcome her and she was once again beset and tormented with those dreadful images and woke screaming: "Nobody knows where I am, and I fear this time they will have me, and I will die right here."

By sheer willpower she managed to stay awake for about a further two hours; then exhaustion both physical and mental overcame her and she collapsed into a deep sleep. Almost instantly those dreadful images rose in her mind. Something within her reacted; that which made her Penny, rose up in rebellion. "Leave me alone," she screamed at the top of her voice, "You are not going to have me; go away and crawl into the filthy hole you slithered from. You had three chances to get me and have failed every time; now go back to the hell where you belong."

The pestilence hesitated for a moment then faded into nothing to be replaced by a feeling of peace and contentment. Penny only collapsed where she had previously stood screaming and lay there in a deep uninterrupted sleep until the morning sun gently touched her cheeks. As she awoke, she realised that dreadful thing had not been there all night. "Am I free?" she cried. "I cannot believe it has gone. Right now, I feel so wonderful," she laughed. "This wonderful land has shown me there is nothing to fear and it will always be here for me. All I have to do now is to get this vehicle out of the bog and find my way home."

Unbeknown to Penny, when her mini Goliath had been taken to Ed's workshop for the most recent service and check over, as was usual Ed had updated everything and had added a few extras. One of those extras was one of those high-powered vehicle location devices which of recent times had become so popular with insurance companies. Anybody who fitted one of those devices were given a small reduction in their premiums. That small piece of electronic geniuses had been instrumental in enabling the location of many stolen vehicles.

Every morning, Ed had made a habit of fixing Penny's whereabouts. This morning he noticed she was still there—she had not moved from the same spot for five days—and thought to himself, "Foolish girl. She is either hopelessly bogged, or out of juice. I had best go and fetch her."

He bludged a lift to Quo-Vadis on the returning morning mail plane, walked into Chris's office, and demanded the use of Goliath for a few days. With full water and fuel tanks, and a load of extra fuel drums, and after hooking up his tracking device, he set off without explaining where he was going to, except to mention to Chris, "He was going out to fetch Penny." He left the bemused Chris standing, hands on hips at his office door, when he unhesitatingly drove Goliath on to the hoist, and all but disappeared.

Even with the tracking device it took him two and a half days to reach her. "Damn woman," he angrily thought. "She has been going the wrong way."

"Oh, how disappointing," Penny had laughed as he drove up and crawled from Goliath. "I was expecting a knight in shining armour, mounted on a white charger. Come to think of it, Mr Ed, you are much better than any fancy knight."

"I was only worried about my wagon," Ed answered. "What's wrong with it?"

Penny softly and humbly replied, "There is nothing wrong with your beautiful wagon, Mr Ed. I simply got it bogged."

"Is that all?" a rather relieved Ed said. "I will soon have you out of there and you can follow me back home. You were going the wrong way; if you hadn't got bogged you probably be halfway to China by now," Ed, who was in a much better frame of mind now his vehicle was undamaged lightly chided her.

Penny watched Ed as he worked and admired his simple efficiency. With her vehicle now free, he walked up and stood beside her and said, you will be okay now little lady."

"What do I owe you, sir?" Penny innocently asked.

Ed had chuckled, "Cash is no use out here; perhaps a little kiss will pay your bill."

"Easy done," Penny laughed, as she wrapped her arms around him and drew him close.

That little kiss turned into something more than little! Some hours later, as they rolled up those blankets hastily thrown on the ground beside Goliath, Penny softly whispered, "Mr Ed I think I owe you much more; let's just call that a small part of what I wish to pay you."

Driving both vehicles they did find their way back to Quo-Vadis six days later having been delayed while Penny repaid some more of her bill. Penny was obviously completely at peace, and Ed had a smirk of contentment written all over his face. She did find a multitude of excuses to spend a lot more time in the big smoke, predominantly in Ed's company.

While she had been hopefully awaiting rescue, Penny had completed a few small paintings, ranging from heaps of rocks to insects and even the odd lizard.

When the native woman had looked at those innocuous paintings, with great approval in her voice she had softly commented, "You have found it again, Missy Penny."

Conversely; when Anne had seen those paintings, she was rather surprised at the content, and very firmly said. "At first glance, these are not like you, but now I see they have something. I can't put my finger on it; they seem to have a life force captured within them. It is very good," then rather inquisitively asked, "Why are you and Ed spending so much time together? Are you a 'unit'?" Penny only laughed as she softly replied; "I have found much more than that I had set out to search for. Yes, Anne. Ed and I are very happy," Penny answered her. "Does it show that much.

# Chapter 23

Once again, as it tends to do, Christmas and New Year Eve's was approaching. Chris and Jackie really enjoyed it when the total family got together. This year was a little different; it appeared that it was going to be a much larger occasion. Jack was in his final year of his veterinary studies at the University. At twenty years of age, he was most popular with students and staff alike. He would return to Quo-Vadis, three out of four weekends, and holidays. Six weeks before Christmas he had approached Chris and Jackie with the request "Could he bring a number of his friends out to Quo-Vadis over the Christmas/New Year break, as they were from overseas, and had nowhere to go in that time; he thought it would be very good for them to share in the "Kennedy" Christmas celebrations. Many of those friends had never experienced a real Aussie family Christmas."

"How many, Jack?" Jackie immediately enquired. "Not that many really Mum—it may be only twenty or twenty-five."

"OH HELL!" Jackie shouted in alarm. "We could never fit that many in the dining room."

"I thought of that, Mum," Jack quickly responded; it was rather obvious that he had anticipated that reaction, and without taking another breath, and before Jackie could ask another question, very confidently said, "Dad and Uncle Bill have paved that terrific area around the house all the way down to the lake edge. The paving does extend even as far as the caves in the sinkhole cliff face. The trees Uncle Bill planted create a fantastic canopy over a big section adjacent to the house."

Bill had planted the trees in the early days when Quo-Vadis mining had commenced, and with his tender care and attention, and because the nearby cliffs protected those trees from the searing winds and the heat of the Outback, and the fact those trees were well watered with a comprehensive irrigation system they had grown, to shade that paved area keeping it cool and turning it into a very pleasant place. Before Jackie could say another word, Jack quickly said, "We could have Christmas dinner, out on the paved area, under the trees."

"And just who do you think is going to cook for all that mob," Jackie quizzically asked. "Last year we had to look after nearly thirty. All the ladies had 'kicked in' to help me. The kitchen had been chock-a-block full of girls tripping over each other—it was really great fun; now knowing this year with all the extras it will possibly be around sixty to sixty-five bodies. That's a lot of cooking!" Jackie was speaking almost as if she was already trying to wrap her mind around cooking Christmas dinner.

"You will not have to worry about that, Mum," Jack said. It was obvious his enthusiasm was rising. "Andre, the Head Chef from the Lithium camp has said he would be happy to look after all the catering. His camp is almost empty over Christmas anyway, but he has had to keep a small crew on to look after the few blokes who are still there. That catering crew is not that busy and would be available to help. He is thinking to cook 'bush style'—you know, barbecues over an open fire and veggies and stuff like that cooked the Hangi way. He said immediately I give him the nod he will set about preparing Christmas puddings. Remember how Grandma made her puds—they were great. She used to put silver coins in them. I remember having six extra servings just to collect the coins. Andre has dobbed Uncle Bill in. He told me Uncle Bill had given him a couple of handfuls of pea-sized gold nuggets to put in the puds instead of silver coins. Andre had nearly choked himself laughing, especially when he told me Uncle Bill had included an acorn-sized nugget as a special."

"Did you know about this, Chris?" Jackie asked.

"From what I am hearing, this has been being organised for some time." Chris was laughing as he replied, "No, Jackie love, this is the first time I have heard anything about. It sounds like Jack has it all organised without us even knowing. It does sound to be a great idea. Okay Jack, you have given a lot of thought to it, and now your mother will be able to sit back and really enjoy Christmas. And Jack my boy," Chris was almost chuckling as he said in a most jovial manner, "just to keep you and your mates out of the house, you can all bunk in the tradies' suites—they are empty at this time of year. I will expect you lot to do all the setting up, and cleaning up afterwards,"

"Thanks, Dad," Jack cried as he gave his parents each a mighty hug, adding, "Oh, there is one other small thing I forgot to mention. Would it be okay to set up for a New Year's Eve party too?"

"Here it comes," Yindi, who had joined in the conversation, laughed. "All the kids at high school have already been talking about the coming New Year party in the Quo-Vadis sinkhole."

Chris and Jackie could do little to stop from laughing. "You are nothing but a conniving little bugger, Jack Kennedy; you have caught some very bad habits from your father," Jackie cried. "But a New Year's party would be fun."

"Don't blame me for this kid, and his wicked ways," Chris happily laughed. "Remember, he is your kid, too."

Jack and his guests had arrived at the sinkhole fourteen days before Christmas. "By private jet nonetheless," one had quipped.

Bill had grumbled a bit when he had to grant his production staff early Christmas leave so the tradies' suites would be vacant. "Do you really need all 170 suites?" Bill questioned.

"Best be prepared, Uncle Bill," Jack had replied, obviously not telling exactly why he needed all 170 suites.

"I guess I should mind my own business," Bill had thought, "But 170 suites, each suite designed for three people—that's over

500 beds. What is that kid up to? Jackie will have a fit if that many turn up."

Jack revelled in the pleasure of showing his thirty-eight guests, over the many features of Quo-Vadis. Jackie had been so right when she had thought it will be more than twenty-five. They had all been chaperoned by Bill through the whole goldmining process, from that bumpy ride in an ore cart into the mine face in the Animal Cave, now one hundred meters long, so that they could view a gold-bearing quartz reef, to where the mined quartz was dumped down that shaft and fed to the first crusher, then on to the second crusher and smelter where they watched in awe the pouring of that very hot liquid gold into very accurately calibrated ingot moulds. Chris had supervised their visits to "the vault." The sight of the final product in the vault where the last month production was stacked row on row on the shelves left them spellbound.

"How much is all this worth?" one of the bemused guest's asked, whispering almost reverently.

"On today's market, about eight hundred million dollars," Chris chuckled.

"Now I really have something to tell my father, when I go home," the young fellow stuttered. "I keep telling him this country has some amazing things. This tops the best of them."

In the evenings they would sit around one of Andre's barbecue pits talking excitedly over what they had seen that day. Chris, Jackie, Bill, Ellie and Yindi, would often join them. It was a most pleasant time.

All the "rellies" (relatives) started to arrive in the three days just prior to Christmas.

Chris's mother, was aghast when she saw the number of people milling about in or around the sinkhole. "Dear me, look at all these people. How are *we* going to look after them for Christmas dinner?"

Jack had overheard, and quickly said, "That has all been taken care of, Grandma. This year you can sit back and enjoy yourself."

Jackie had to answer many questions about what Jack meant, before Grandma relaxed and said, "That sounds all very good to me."

Jack had known of an area where a cock-a-biddy (a severe type of whirl-wind,) had some years previously knocked down a grove of giant trees. The downed trees had dried out as they lay there. After commandeering a large loader and an equally large truck and with the assistance of several experienced road workers, armed with chainsaws, those logs were converted into twenty-foot-long, rustic seats and benches, to be transported to the sinkhole and set up for use at both Christmas dinner, and later for the New Year's party.

The children of the in-laws, mainly teenagers now, were delighted when told they were to be accommodated in the tradies' suites. The idea of being away from the watchful eyes of their parents appealed to them greatly. Almost everybody, including Grandma and Grandpa and all the parents joined in to string a multitude of coloured lights and decorations in the trees, and over the whole of the paved area.

Although it was completely spontaneous, Christmas Eve had been most pleasant. They had all, Jack's overseas guests included, sat around that large barbecue pit singing Christmas carols, to the accompaniment of that very expensive piano, that had hastily been carried out by many willing hands, being played by Grandma. A couple of Jack's guests had produced musical instruments, a couple of guitars, a flute and clarinet, and now accompanied Grandma on that piano. She knew all the tunes; Jack's friends just played along as best they could. Everybody sung along, regardless of their vocal capacity to carry a tune. Time was taken to exchange presents. Jack's guests, despite Jack's insistence it was not necessary, when they had learned of the tradition, had made a visit to the mall and had acquired small gifts that they too could hand out. Jackie had recognised these young people were going to be part of their Christmas and had Jamie at the resort gift shop prepare thirty-five golden mementos to be given to them.

Jamie laughed as he told her, "I had to prepare twice that number Jackie; because as the resort guests saw them they wanted one also."

As they lay in each other's arms later that night, Jackie softly whispered to Chris, "That was one of the best Christmas evenings we have ever had."

Dawn on Christmas Day. Andre and his staff—who at Jack's cost had stayed at the hotel overnight—arrived at the sinkhole. In very short time the catering staff soon had those rustic trestles converted to very beautifully decorated tables. Jack had hired a large crate of high-quality eating utensils, table cloths and crockery settings and had them transported in.

"Could have used all that sort of stuff from the lithium mine's mess hall," Andre had grumbled.

He shut up about that when Jack had snapped back, "Not good enough, mate."

Peter had butchered two prime steers a week before, and had hung them in the station cool room, alongside three good sized pigs.

"Good tucker!" one of the station stockmen had commented. Those steers and pigs now revolved slowly over the red coals of last night's fires. Six large turkeys, six ducks, and a dozen chooks sat cooking in those bush ovens especially built by Bill for the occasion. Vegetables and a variety of fruits were wrapped in foil and buried down under the sand of the base of one of the barbecues. Andre's special sauces sat on hot rocks, and the Christmas puddings were being heated so very slowly. The catering staff girls kept constant watch on the refrigerators in the tradies' mess to ensure the pre-cooked seafood and a large variety of soft drink were keeping cold. The aroma of the cooking made many a mouth water.

Grandma viewed the setting and expressed her great approval. "I must have many photographs for the family photo album!" she exclaimed, as she handed her camera to Andre with the instruction to take many photographs as Christmas dinner is served. Barons of beef, the pigs their skin crisp and brown, all those plates of poultry and vegetables adorned the tables. Jack had warned his guests not to eat a thing until his dad had offered a prayer of thanksgiving. Catering staff all armed with large knives and forks stood guard over this delicious fare and after a discrete nod from Jack served each and every person with generous helpings of whatever the person chose. The Christmas puddings, containing those small gold nuggets and served with cream or one of Andre special custards, went over very well, especially with Rex's ten-year-old son who found that acorn-sized nugget in his pudding.

By 4 pm, the area was strangely deserted apart from catering staff who moved quietly about cleaning up. The majority of those Christmas revellers had retired to many and varied places to sleep off their overindulgence.

"There is a great amount of tucker leftover, Jack," a rather concerned Andre said. "What do you wish me to do with it?"

"Please put it in all those big refrigerators and cool rooms in the kitchen in the tradies' mess. You can put it out on New Year's Eve." Jack advised him.

"How many should I prepare for, Jack boy?" Andre thought, it was a simple question.

"Not a word to my father or my mother; I am expecting five or six hundred. They will have a fit when they find out," Jack whispered, with a voice loaded with guilt.

Andre took the answer without showing any reaction, simply answering, "I think we will need a little more to feed that many than what we have in the cool rooms."

"Uncle Peter has another three steers prepared for me and the bakery in town is doing a special bake of burger buns. The veggie shop is sending over six crates of salad vegetables. Most of the kids will be more than happy just eating delicious steak burgers especially if they are slathered with one of your special sauces. Put out the cold stuff early and be prepared to be serving up burgers later. If there is any Christmas pudding left, please put that out later in the evening, and perhaps have a good supply of coffee on hand."

"All too easy," Andre replied. "My biggest problem will be to keep my staff working and not joining in the festivities."

Jack could only laugh at that, "I will not be surprised if I see you out there dancing too, Andre."

"Not bloody likely," Andre quickly replied. "Too old and unfit for that sort of caper. With what you have organised I can't see too many going hungry."

On the morning of Boxing Day, Chris, Jackie and Yindi left Quo-Vadis to visit the native camp to distribute a few presents and go on to say hello to the folk at the iron ore mine. They advised Jack they expected to be back about mid-morning of New Year's Eve.

What a sight greeted them. The first thing that struck Chris, was the twenty buses from the tourist park parked lined up in regimental order above the sinkhole cliff face. And because he could not drive into the Animal Cave to access the elevator, he Jackie and Yindi were forced to walk to the edge of the sinkhole. As they looked down into the sinkhole they were struck speechless. That paved area churned with young people, and the adjacent lake front was filled with laughing and noisy bodies. The noise was horrific.

"I tried to warn you," Yindi laughed. "Let's go down and join them. I see Jack over there on the right by that large platform."

"Platform?" Chris questioned.

Jack answered that question quickly as they accosted him. "There are actually two platforms, Dad. They are for the rock bands. I want the music to go on non-stop."

Chris just shook his head in wonder, then with a very concerned voice asked, "Where are your grandparents?"

"They are over there in the shade of the trees, just sitting there watching, with their mouths open. Please don't be mad at me, Dad; I am paying for all this myself. I have never spent much of all that money from my dividends and have plenty to cover everything."

Chris and Jackie just burst out laughing. "I said it before," the laughing Jackie said, "you are a sneaky little bugger. Have fun, we will catch up with you later. As a matter of interest is there enough room for all them in the tradies' suites; if there is not enough room in there, send some up to the hotel."

"Thanks, Mum," Jack answered. "It's a bit crowded up there—they love it."

Chris asked innocently, "Are the girls separate from the boys?"

Yindi quickly pushed in and answered for Jack, "Dad, that's a silly question," and left it at that.

Chris only rolled his eyes, took Jackie's hand and said, "We are out of here; let's go and sit with Mum and Dad. I am hungry. I think we should grab something from those tables now—I have a feeling all this food will disappear shortly. Look at Andre over there; he appears to be enjoying himself. Is that more steers cooking on that barbecue? Jack is certainly not going to let this mob go hungry."

His parents were pleased to see them and picked choice tiny bits from the laden plates.

"We have been sitting here watching all those young people," Chris's mother said. "They are beautiful children; there are even some of the young ones from the native camp in there somewhere. Jack told us they are going to university and he had especially asked them to come to the party. They went to school here with Jack, so he already knew them. The native boys said Marlee, the witch doctor, and some of the elders were going to come over later."

To try and describe the way that night unfolded is impossible, except to say it did grow, from a reasonably sedate beginning for a short while to move gradually on to become an eardrum shattering mass of gyrating, singing, shouting young people, dancing ('dancing'?) to that unending, for want of a better name, music.

Marlee, the witch doctor, and the tribal elders had managed to work their way to where Chris and Jackie and his parents sat, not without one or two of the elders being grabbed and swung into the dancing cauldron. The whole group had eventually managed to reach to where Chris and Jackie sat laughing at the groups endeavours to negotiate that treacherous path to them.

"This is some sort of massive Corroboree," old Marlee laughed.

"Did you hear that scream," the witch doctor whispered with reverence and awe. "It was the Eulooway, the evil spirits of the night; who had lived in the sinkhole for many, many years, screaming as they were driven from their home by this corroboree of your young ones. They may never return to here and will now sulk away to find another place to haunt. We can now come here without fear; the Eulooway have gone."

Jackie grabbed Chris by the arm and dragged him into the melee, crying loudly over all the noise "dance with me Mister Miner; the music has got my toes tinkling." They soon became engulfed in that happy crowd.

Jack rushed up and very correctly took his grandmother's hand and very politely asked, "May I have this dance?"

"I do not know the steps," his grandmother defensively said.

"It's easy," Jack shouted over the uproar, "just let your mind and toes absorb the sound and let your body move, as they say."

In five minutes, Jack's grandma was gyrating with the best of them.

A laughing Yindi stepped up and grabbed her grandfather's hand. "Your turn now, Grandpa," she shouted. Grandpa did his best effort to join in and in a way, did give in to that racket called music. The grandparents were deserted by the grandchildren when they swapped partners. In moments they were surrounded by happy young ones who took turns swapping their young partners to dance with them. After half an hour of this dancing, swapping partners, and more dancing, the elder lady looked about and shouted to her young partner at the time, "Can you see my husband?"

"He has piked out," the laughing young man shouted. "He is sitting over there sipping a large drink." She started to head in his direction only to be grabbed and swung back into the action. Chris and Jackie had lost track of one another and finally accidentally met for a moment. Chris almost had to wrestle her hand from that young fellow who was not going to give up this doll easily.

As they pushed their way to the drinks table, Jackie laughed, "Thank you for saving me, my hero. Another minute out there and I would have collapsed into a messy heap. Let's go over and sit with Dad; where is Mum?"

Her father-in-law answered her question by simply saying, "She's out there somewhere having a ball. I don't know where she gets all the energy from. It's one hell of a night, son. That grandson of mine sure knows how to organise a good knees-up."

His wife appeared from the crowded dance floor, took his drink from him and emptied the glass. "I needed that," she laughed. "I could not have stayed on my feet for another minute. These young people are remarkable, so much energy, so much joy and goodwill. It makes one know the future is in good hands."

"Ask them in the morning," Chris chuckled. "There will be many sore bodies tomorrow, especially the old one I am looking at now." He quickly ducked to avoid getting cuffed on the ear by his mother. "I'm glad Jack did follow my request, of no hard liquor," he said. "The security boys mixing in told me they had found not one instance of anybody using drugs of any kind. Apparently, Jack had warned everyone, anybody found with anything, even in their possession, would be booted out immediately and told to start walking; it is a long way back to the city."

Yindi was having a wonderful time; she had danced with so many boys and girls—it was such fun. Ralph Sitzika was the known lady killer from University. He had spotted Yindi earlier on in the evening and was taken by her beauty and grace as she danced, obviously enjoying herself. He had finally manoeuvred himself close enough to claim her from her present dance partner.

They danced well together for a while, then he politely asked her, "Do you want a drink? I am as dry as a bone. Let's grab something wet and cold and sit by the lake for five minutes."

Yindi was thirsty and without hesitation agreed that was a good idea. A couple of the boys saw Ralph and Yindi leave the crowd.

"Trust Ralph to cut out the best-looking chick here," one boy commented to his friend. "Five will get you ten (a two to one bet) he wins her before the night is out."

Ralph and Yindi stood at the lake edge and sipped their disposable mugs of cold soft drink. With much expert experience, Ralph slipped his free hand around her waist and whispered, "We could make our own beautiful music here and now, you beautiful creature."

It took half a second before Yindi delivered a very painful kick into his right shin and pushed him backward into the lake. "This girl is not for you, sir," she vehemently said, and walked back to the crowd to once again join in the dancing. The two boys saw her return, followed a few minutes later by a limping, very wet Ralph.

"That's a first," one boy laughed.

Chris had awoken just before 6 am on New Year's Day. Fresh from his morning shower, and because it was such a beautiful morning, he decided a brisk walk along the river and lake had great appeal.

Jackie had only rolled over and grunted, "No," to his invitation for her to join him. "I am going to sleep all day. I am stiff and sore and tired," she bitterly complained.

"Catch you later, my love," he called as he bounded down the stairs and out onto the patio, the scene of the previous night's revelry. The place looked like a disaster area. "Jack has a job when he gets up," Chris chuckled to himself. Surprisingly, there were at least thirty young people enjoying a morning dip in the lake and the delicious breakfast Andre was serving for them. The plate he had picked up was quickly loaded with scrambled eggs and slices of toast.

"Would you want tea or coffee, sir?" the catering girl who was looking bright and chipper asked.

"Tea sounds good," Chris replied, and with breakfast in hand he joined a table of young people who were all enthusiastically discussing the party last night.

"Aren't you Jack's dad?" a student across the table asked. All conversation at the table ceased in an instant. "This is the fabled Chris Kennedy—the true miner," one of the students whispered. "He's the guy all the Uni lecturers talk about."

"Yes, I am Jack's dad," Chris quietly said. "The rest of your statement is a bit of a beat up to enthuse you guys with what can be achieved with conscientious attention to your studies. I'm a very ordinary bloke who likes scrambled eggs and toast just like you."

That made them all laugh and the conversations continued; many questions were directed at Chris.

"That was one hell of a hoot last night, Mr Kennedy—half the mob are still asleep," one lad said.

Another asked the whole table, "What happened to lover-boy Ralph?"

"He has caught a rotten chill and is limping like he's been kicked by something pretty vicious," another lad answered.

Ralph was a real mess. Physical pain was there, but the mental agony was much more. "I am a full-on drongo," he admonished himself. "I should have known that the beauty that shone from her was not just skin deep; she really is a very beautiful person. I'm going to find her and apologise."

Yindi, like her dad, had also risen early and had jogged the full circle of the lake then had dived fully clothed into the cold water. Still dripping wet she had collected a hearty breakfast and joined her dad at the table. "Hi," everybody she greeted. "How are we feeling this morning?"

"There should be a law against girls looking as beautiful as you look this morning, Miss Yindi," one appreciative wag wailed.

Ralph had seen her arrive and had slipped quietly in to sit beside her. "I have to agree with him," Ralph quietly said, then quickly added, "Yindi, please do not think badly of me for what happened last night. I did deserve all I got. I am truly sorry. Please forgive me?"

"Forgive you," Yindi softly said. "Why? You did pay me a great compliment really; it is only natural for a young man to desire the attention of a girl."

"You have that wrong," Ralph chipped in, "A very beautiful girl is more correct. Am I to believe you're not mad at me," he said; suddenly his day had brightened up considerably.

"Not in the least," Yindi had graciously said.

Chris had already left, and she quickly finished her breakfast and said to Ralph, "Wait here. I will just duck inside and get out of these wet clothes; when I come back we can have a talk for a while. Jack tells me you have taken the course in palaeontology—that must be terribly interesting."

"Most people think it is dull and boring. I find it exciting," with enthusiasm Ralph replied. "Hurry back—I will wait."

He watched her as she walked into that beautiful house. "Into that 'house'", his mind spun. "That's the Kennedy house, she must be visiting." Yindi did hurry a little and quickly slipped into that rather becoming outfit she and her mum had purchased together. Ralph stood as she returned and because he could not continue having that question unanswered simply blurted out, "Are you a friend of the Kennedys?"

Yindi had a quizzical look on her face and softly replied, "I am a Kennedy."

Ralph had simply plonked back down, and cried, "You're joking, aren't you? Are you truly telling me you are the daughter of Mr Christopher Kennedy, the Miner?"

Yindi was quite amused with all this, and quietly said, "He's my Dad, and that lady who has just come out of the house and is over there talking with him is my Mum."

Ralph's mind was in a whirl. "Good grief," he whispered. "I had a dash at the topmost shelf— no wonder I got kicked," he humbly thought.

"What's the matter, Ralph?" Yindi asked, her voice full of concern. "You suddenly look quite sick."

Ralph did not know what to say or do, and could only stammer, "I should have been more respectful," He felt thoroughly chastened.

"That's all gone and done with," Yindi laughed. "You can start making amends for your bad behaviour right now by getting me a cup of coffee with milk, no sugar; get one for yourself, then come and sit with me for a while and tell me about palaeontology."

# Chapter 24

It was a beautiful morning and Chris and Jackie sat at the breakfast bar by themselves. With Jack back at university, using what was left of the Christmas and New Year break to endeavour to complete his last year of the veterinary course, and Yindi off with four of her girlfriends to Spain for a few weeks, apart from the household staff, that big house was all but deserted.

"There is not much happening at the moment," Chris said. "There is no reason for us to hang about here. Feel like going walkabout for a few weeks?"

"Yes, please," Jackie enthusiastically answered. "I do love it out in the Outback, especially when I have you to myself and we share every minute together. You remember how Yindi got started last time. It's a pity that will not happen again; still, we can practice a bit."

"Wicked, wanton woman," Chris laughed. "They do say practice makes perfect. If it is okay with you we can be off tomorrow morning. I will call Peter and warn him we will be pinching four of his best riding horses and four very strong pack nags."

In those long-passed portals of time, those times so far distant and of such magnitude that even the imagination of man could not even touch them, great galaxies were formed. How they came about is a question not even the most brilliant of scholars is prepared to give an answer to. Some of those galaxies were devoured by immense black holes. Those black holes grew and their density increased even beyond the bounds of the puny minds of highly intelligent men who despite their great intelligence could never grasp the magnitude of what has, or is happening, out there even to this day. There were many, many studies; some of those studies did answer some of the questions, but what was found was a "nothing" when taken in context of what there is to learn.

Perhaps; it could be thought that one monstrous black hole became so dense, the heat or something within it; caused it to explode hurling debris out into the vacuum of space to form that which we now see as the universe. Maybe the Big-Bang theory has something. What was formed by the debris is beyond the imagination of humankind. Galaxies of an uncountable number of suns with their attendant solar systems; some galaxies so large they were immeasurable in human terms. Other galaxies were perhaps smaller—the Milky Way galaxy was perhaps one of those smaller conglomerations of debris. Our own insignificant planet perhaps came into being about then. Humankind, through all the centuries, has looked at the night skies and endeavoured to put together those pieces of the immense jigsaw. Some of those pieces of debris slowly cooled to become planets. Here again time is irrelevant. When? Where? How? These are some of those many questions yet to be answered. We could take liberty and say that although the molten surface cooled and hardened with the empty coldness of space, the core remained as a molten mass of extreme temperature. This core was subject to extreme pressures which in some instances became so intense that, the fledgling planet exploded again hurling debris out into space. Those debris in part cooled rapidly and became meteorites. Some of those meteorites contained a vast amount of diamonds. From time to time, again exactly for how long one cannot even hazard to guess, some of those meteorites peppered that stable planet we know as the Earth. One large meteorite ploughed into the Earth in that desolate place now known to humankind as the Outback. It was a monstrous piece of rock. The impact as it hit the earth was so severe it is possible to give thought, only thought mind you, that it could have disrupted the orbit of the earth as it circled its attendant sun. It ploughed deep into the granite surface—at times small fragments broke off. Where it hit, mountains of broken granite were thrust up to form a small mountain range around the periphery of the crater. Time, location and weather, were perhaps a few of the reasons that contributed to make this place inhabitable to humankind, and it became a place of dark secrets.

One intrepid foolish explorer, had set out to explore this forbidden place. He returned as a tongue chewing gibberish shouting idiot.

"He always was a bit odd," was the general comment from the blokes in the bar of the local pub, "but now is completely off his nut; keeps raving about spooks and things like that."

That small mountain range did form the northernmost boundary of the Quo-Vadis grazing lease that Chris had acquired from the Simpsons. Chris had flown over those mountains from time to time thinking to himself, "I must have a closer look at this place sometime." That time had not happened until now, as he and Jackie rode nonchalantly toward that mountain range. Sometime in the past, Chris had talked with the native elder, Marlee, about that small mountain range.

"That is a bad, bad place Abdiel Boss Chris; it is a place of many terrible spirits. I fear that even your great power would not be enough to protect you. It would be wise not to even think of venturing in there."

Because it was some time ago Chris had been given that advice, he had conveniently; forgotten it and had omitted to mention old Marlee's warning to Jackie. They had set up camp, had a fine meal, and now lay looking up at that star-studded sky, stargazing. Only peace and contentment surrounded them as they lay on their blanket.

"It makes one realise just how small and insignificant we really are," Jackie whispered; she was feeling just so good. As she lay there, she unbuttoned her shirt and allowed the cool evening breeze to flood across her; oh, so beautiful breasts, and reached across to take both Chris's hands and place them firmly on those breasts, whispering, "No practice this time, Mister; make me pregnant."

"Is this wise? You know what the doctors said, you may be offering me your very life."

"Then it may well be; if I die I will die a very contented girl." For a good part of the rest of the night stargazing was forgotten.

As the morning sun lifted its head above the horizon, Jackie opened one eye and sighed; "Tell that sun to go back to bed; I don't feel like moving,"

"We will never get to look at that mountain range if this continues," Chris laughed. "Come on now, you delicious bundle of desire—up you get, and let's get underway, before I weaken and spend the rest of the day wrestling with you. Did you notice we have been following an animal track for the last couple of days; there must be a waterhole hereabouts. Perhaps we will find it later today."

"You and your animal tracks," Jackie laughed. "The last time you followed animal tracks you found gold; what are you looking for this time, my Mister Miner?"

"Oh, whatever," Chris replied without really making a commitment.

Late morning found them riding Indian file slowly along that narrow animal track. "We look to be going downhill, rather than going up the mountain," Chris called over his shoulder. The animal track now wended its way between rather spectacular cliffs. The cliff faces that gradually increased in height, were spaced about twenty to twenty-five metres apart and composed of a spectacular array of different layers of colourful minerals.

"How beautiful they look," Jackie called to her man, who was riding about ten metres ahead. She was not sure he had heard her as he did not reply, so engrossed was he in what he was seeing.

He must have heard her as he simply grunted, "Yeah."

It was nearing lunchtime and pangs of hunger beset Jackie. "Time for a cuppa and a bite to eat, Mister Miner," she called.

"I'm for that," Chris replied, as he slowed to a stop and dismounted. "I will get a fire going to boil a billy; you can see to the lunch. What have you got?" Halfway through his reply he hesitated and said, "Hold a moment, Jackie girl, a little flow of water has broken through from the bottom of the cliff on the right and a small creek is flowing down the track ahead. Hold lunch for a bit." He was already climbing back onto his horse and called, "I want to have a look at where this creek goes to."

The now excited pair of explorers slowly walked the horses alongside that small creek for a further half an hour. Chris who was in the lead suddenly stopped. "Holy Cow, look at this Honey Girl!" he cried. He had a multitude of names for Jackie, mostly complimentary or endearing. 'Honey Girl,' pushed-up alongside his horse to see what it was.

"Oh Goodness Gracious!" she exclaimed.

The creek had bounded over a short drop to form a pretty little waterfall and into a perfectly clear pond.

"This is what the animals were seeking," Mister Know-it-all, Chris told her.

"That's obvious, even to a dumb broad like me, Mister," Jackie laughed. "Just look at those trees—they are a beautiful verdant green—and all those birds, Chris. I have never seen so many different birds and colours in the one place ever before. I have counted at least eight different types of animals here already. The grass is just so green and lush, and over there," she pointed, "there is a good size flat spot where we can set up our tent." She reached across the space between the horses and gently laid her hand on Chris's arm. "Please say we can stay here for a while, Chris; it is so peaceful and beautiful."

452

Chris replied instantly, "I would like that."

The brightly coloured four-man tent appeared out of place when they set it up in that natural setting. The delayed billy had been set to boil, lunch prepared, horses unloaded and set loose to graze.

"Chores all done," Chris cried. "Now where's my cuppa and lunch?"

As the intrepid pair of wanderers sat sipping tea and munching their lunch, they watched as if hypnotised, as a large male kookaburra dived down to seize a small snake in his beak and fluttered upwards into the cloudless sky. The snake was about thirty inches long and the bird and its burden had climbed to about 100 feet when the bird dropped the snake. It plummeted down to be smashed against a large rock; immediately the kookaburra's mate dived in and seized the inert reptile just behind its head, and repeated the process of fluttering upward, this time to about fifty feet where it too dropped its burden. Once again, the snake crashed onto the rock, this time only to writhe feebly, its back broken and half its innards hanging out. Both birds glided in to land on that rock and began to dance around the helpless reptile. Sharp beaks snapped at it and in short time more wounds appeared. The snake finally ceased all movement and the birds commenced to attack it with a vengeance. The female bird ripped away a section of flesh and quickly flew to a hollow in a branch high in the gum tree from which the attack on the reptile had begun. She disappeared into the hollow branch.

"I believe she will have a couple of chicks in there," Chris rather reverently whispered. "I have read the kookaburras are known to take snakes that way. I feel we have been most privileged to actually see it happen."

Night had appeared quickly and darkness flooded their little camp. "Ready for bed?" Chris enquired with a rather hopeful tone in his voice.

"Ready and willing," Jackie laughed as she divested herself of all her clothes. Sleep came quickly after all their extra-curricular activities were over. Chris was awakened suddenly by Jackie screaming and pushing away at some unseen horror. He gently shook her awake and she collapsed onto his shoulder.

"We must go from this place," she hysterically cried. "Those dreadful horrible things that tried to take Yindi as she was coming into the world are here; can't you see them, feel them?" She was panic stricken.

Chris enfolded her in his arms and softly said, "Hush, my love, together we will fight them and chase them away and free you from them forever." He still held her tightly as he lifted his head and shouted, "I; ABDIEL, THE FAITHFUL CHILD OF MY GOD, CHALLENGE YOU SCION OF EVIL TO SHOW YOURSELVES, AND I WILL FIGHT YOU WITH ALL THE POWER THAT HAS BEEN GIVEN TO ME. I WILL DESTROY YOU ALL IN THIS VERY PLACE AND IT WILL BECOME A PLACE OF PEACE AND BEAUTY FOREVER. COME NOW ,MY VERY BEING IS RESTLESS TO SEND YOU BACK TO THAT DREADFUL PLACE FROM WHENCE YOU CAME.

Chris's powerful voice echoed around that waterhole; even the insects of the night ceased their chorus, and animals of the night paused in their prowling. Absolute stillness prevailed, only to be broken by screams full of pain and anguish, as something disappeared into the darkness of the night.

Chris held the shaking body of his wife a little tighter. "They are gone my little one," he softly said. "They are gone and will not return to bother you ever again."

Jackie pulled even closer in Chris's protective arms and burst into tears—tears of relief and the knowledge she has nothing to fear, and that this man will always protect her. "Please hold me, and never let me go," she blubbered through her tears.

He held her close until the tears ceased and she dropped off into a deep sleep. He continued to hold her for a while longer then gently eased her back onto their sleeping mat. She did not stir but slept that deep sleep until the sunbeams played gently across a beautiful relaxed face.

She came a little more awake as a cheery voice called, "Want a cup of tea, Beautiful? Come on, it's a beautiful day and this place is crying out to be explored."

"I hate you, Mister; how dare you be so bright and chipper this morning. Go away, I want to sleep a bit longer."

"Sleep all you like," Chris answered, his voice full of good humour. "In half an hour I'm off exploring."

That woke her up, and she cried, "Not without me, you rotten beast. Do you think it's okay to have a dip in the pond?"

"Sure is," Chris answered. "I had a splash earlier—the water was a bit chilly but it was really fresh and invigorating."

It truly was a beautiful, bright sunny morning. Chris had earlier done a little exploring and found a track of sorts leading up the cliff face. He had followed it a short distance and found another small watercourse.. "It is only run-off from the recent rain; it will possibly dry up later in the season," he told her. By the time they had worked their way up that steep practically non existing winding track, they were both hot and thirsty, and did drink deeply from that small stream. Jackie even slipped off her strong boots to dabble her burning feet in that cool water. After a further fifteen minutes of hiking upward they found themselves at the highest point of the mountain range. The view was amazing. From where they stood they could see the mountain range circumvented a basin of, by Chris's estimation, about twenty kilometres in diameter.

"The whole place looks like the pictures you see of giant craters made by huge meteorites," Jackie slowly said.

"I think you have hit it right on the button, Jackie you smart little critter," Chris quickly replied. "I am willing to wager this is one very old crater, I couldn't even hazard a guess how old. I think these mountains were made by the impact of that meteorite. It must have been some sort of impact; it would have been so severe it pushed all that rock, the mountains are composed of, out and up. The basin has been slowly filling for all that time with material eroded from these mountains by wind and weather. There is quite a fair bit of vegetation in that basin now. Let's go down into it—I think I can see a lake or a pool down there."

The sides of the crater were quite steep and it took over an hour to reach the basin floor. "I think that pool I saw is over there," Chris shouted, and pointed, then strode off in the direction he had indicated.

He was obviously very excited; when Jackie did catch up to him he was standing at the edge of the pool peering intently at something he held in his hand.

"Look at this," Chris almost shouted, as he thrust a yellow encrusted stone into her hand.

"What am I looking at Chris?" Jackie innocently asked.

"That, my love, is a large diamond!" Chris exclaimed. "Let me clean the mud off so we can get a better look at it." Cleaned up, the chestnut-sized stone was a beautiful clear diamond.

"What's it worth, my very clever Mister Miner?" Jackie very excitedly asked.

"I haven't got a clue," Chris softly said as he experimentally weighed the stone in his hands. "I'd say it's about three to four carats. I saw something recently where some Hollywood bloke had bought his girlfriend a diamond about that size, it was reported to have cost him," he hesitated trying to recall exactly what he had read, then continued, "I think it said he had paid about $750,000."

"WOW!" Jackie excitedly exclaimed. "Can I have it Chris?"

"Only if you have it made into a pendant and wear it alongside your nugget, just over your heart to remind you how much I love you," Chris gallantly said.

"That's not exactly what I had in mind," Jackie laughed. "I'm going to look for another one and have the pair made into earrings. No! On second thoughts, it is too heavy for an earring; I think your idea of a pendant sounds better."

While Jackie searched for more of those "stones" along the edge of the pool, Chris was off examining the rock structure of the area. She finally caught up with him excitedly carrying four more stones.

"Not a bad morning's work, eh, Mister Miner? Three million dollars for an hour's pleasant strolling. What have you to show for your absence?" she asked.

"I have to tell you, Mrs very-very-rich-Kennedy, I have found much more than four stones," Chris said. "It was a very large meteorite that made this basin. It contained, or was made up of, call it what you like, but it was nearly a complete space diamond that shattered into thousands of fragments when it hit. I think a very large piece of it may be buried deep down, maybe 1000 feet or thereabouts. There will be tens of thousands of fragments scattered along its path, some smaller, many larger than those four you are holding. There are buckets and buckets of diamond crystals in pockets. Before we do one more thing—no! after we collect a few more 'stones' from around here—I can show you where to find lots—only for your jewellery box, mind you. We will then climb back to our camp as if nothing has happened and spend a very pleasant time together for a week or two."

Those weeks were more than very pleasant for them. They slept comfortably entwined, ate much of the bush tucker offered by the area, talked excitedly about the diamond find and hiked all around those mountains that surrounded the basin. It is not appropriate to call them mountains—that is not a good description. They were nothing but a 400-foot-high pile of a big variety of rocks.

Chris was constantly excited as he investigated all those rocks. Jackie had walked along with him, continually asking questions. She revelled with great unspoken pride, as she watched an expert in his field apply his talent. Time passed all too quickly, and Chris with a voice full of regret, finally said, "I could spend the rest of my life here and never unearth all its secrets. We must leave and get back to reality soon, before I become completely captivated and actually stay."

"I'll stay too," Jackie enthusiastically added. "I do agree we should go soon; I do have a small problem which I should have looked at."

Chris was instantly concerned, and demanded, "What is it, are you in pain?" he cried.

"It is nothing serious at the moment," Jackie whispered, "but it will grow. I will have no pain for a while, so do not worry, my wonderful full of life man, I have only 'missed.'"

Chris did not immediately understand what she was saying. "Missed?" He questioned.

"Missed my period—I am overdue," Jackie softly answered, adding, "Chris, my dearest Chris, I think we have done it again. I think I might be pregnant."

"No!" he cried in anguish. "The doctors all said that was almost impossible and if it should happen you could die. We must get you back quickly and have the world's best gynaecologist examine you."

"Oh, do settle down you ninny. I feel fine; in fact, I feel great," a very happy Jackie laughed.

They did pack up their camp the next morning. Jackie protested at the haste—she wanted to go back up to the basin and collect a few more stones. Despite having hiked all over the mountains in the recent weeks, they had never once returned to the basin.

"There is no way you are going to attempt to climb up there in your condition," Chris had very sternly said.

"Do I look unwell, and fragile? You wonderful caring dope—the exercise will do me and the baby good," was her reply as she turned and walked towards the track that led up the mountain.

"I'm going. Are you coming?" Needless to say, their departure was delayed another day while they collected stones from the pool edge. It had taken a little time as Jackie had been most selective as she picked and chose from the many stones on offer.

Jackie was finally satisfied and loudly called, "I've got twenty good stones. I think that's one for everybody. The bag is getting heavy so you will have to carry it back, Mister Muscle Man," she happily said.

"So now I'm only a blinking packhorse," Chris grumbled humorously. "Let's go, this horse needs feeding, and the minute we get back to camp you can pay the horse hiring fee, and you can make mad passionate love to me for the rest of the afternoon. If you cannot wear me out using me as a packhorse you will have to find some other way," he chuckled.

"Be warned, you foolish man, I feel so good, I might just do that," Jackie cried as she headed up the track out of the basin.

Chris resolutely followed along, muttering to himself, "Wanton woman."

Two weeks later, both "rested" and glowing with good health they rode into the loading yards at Quo-Vadis Station. Peter was supervising the loading of two of those monstrous six-trailer cattle trucks. He was alerted to their presence by one of the stockmen calling loudly over the racket of bellowing cattle. "Hey, Boss Peter, Boss Chris and his missus are here."

"Where?" Peter excitedly shouted back.

"Over by the big gate; all the horses have returned with them this time—they must have had a plurry good time, they look top-notch."

Peter yelled again loudly to the stockman, "Take over here, Jacky; keep them moving. I'll be back soon," then raced unperturbed through the milling cattle.

The reunion was most enthusiastic. "Come on down to the house, Izzy will want to see you. You have been away for over a month," he admonished them adding, "You both look so well, it must be great to get out there and live without a care."

Izzy was equally pleased to see them and demanded that they stay for a couple of nights.

"We cannot stay," Jackie had replied. "We must get to the city. I have a small problem that should be looked at before Chris dies from over-concern." She hesitated for a moment, then quietly added, "I think I may be pregnant again."

"Oh no!" Izzy exclaimed in anguish; didn't the doctor tell you another pregnancy would kill you."

Jackie interrupted her cries and softly said, "That's why Chris wants to get me back quickly."

"Take my jet and fly straight to the city," Peter offered. "Thanks mate," Chris replied, "but I want to go to Quo-Vadis, make a few phone calls, and not rush around like a chook with its head cut off. I have been keeping an eye on her; she is really very fit and well and something tells me not to worry so much. But like Jackie said, my over-concern will kill me. I do want to keep Mum and Dad informed—you know what they are like if they are advised later rather than sooner. Do you know if Jack and Yindi are about?"

"Yindi is back. I think she is out at the native camp," Peter replied, then continued almost as if it was an afterthought, adding, "Jack came out a couple of days ago. He was wondering had we heard from you. You had better give him a call too."

"Thanks Peter," Chris said, then added, "That's a big mob you are loading. Have you got a buyer for all of them?"

"Yes," Peter replied. "We sure have; them and many more. It appears the Japanese like our beef and send special buyers to take all we can supply. I have agreed to supply on the condition that four of our stockmen travel with the cattle to ensure they are handed over in only prime condition. The buyers didn't mind this arrangement; they said that's four less they will need to find for crew on the ship. They did hesitate a little when I told them the wages of those stockmen and the costs of the business class return airfare for the stockmen, would be added to the cost of the cattle."

Five days later, after having attended to all those phone calls and having answered all the inevitable questions thrown at them, Chris and Jackie arrived at the city apartment. Chris had kept it all these years, and it was now being used by Jack as he attended the university. They had arrived, at the apartment, unannounced in the early evening, and had sprung Jack in the midst of entertaining a young lady. After several rather embarrassing moments, Jack cried, "Mum and Dad, what are you doing here?"

"Not as much as you," Chris chuckled. "Hi son, looks like we should have let you know we were on the way. Regrettably things came up a bit quickly, and I overlooked doing that."

Jackie had hesitated for a moment, while the girl swiftly snatched up her discarded clothing and rushed to the bathroom. It was only then that Jackie threw her arms about her son, and firmly but fondly said, "Jack Kennedy, I thought you were a good boy; now I find you are equally as bad as your father. It must be this apartment." Despite the admonishment she hugged him tight and proceeded to assail him with dozens of questions of the like, "How are you?"; "How's Uni?"; "Do you see the professors?" and many more, then finally, "Who is she?"

"Her name is Tamastry—Tammy for short. She's only a friend, she comes over sometimes and we study together. She is going to be a vet also."

"Looks like study is going well, Jack boy," Chris was laughing. "We have an appointment at 7.30, so we are only here for a moment to drop off our bags, so you do not need to interrupt your," he hesitated for a second or two, "studies." Chris's eyes glinted with merriment.

Jackie punched him gently in the stomach and growled, "You men are dreadful."

The gynaecologist had delayed departing from his rooms so that he could especially attend to Jackie. He had been her consultant during her pregnancy with Yindi and knew only too well her medical history. "Okay young lady, what have you pair done?" he very gruffly said. "You were warned no more children. I am more than surprised to hear it has happened; all my scans showed your organs were incapable of conceiving again. Janice," the specialist called to his nurse, "Janice please set up the ultrasound, I think at this first stage it would be wise to avoid the x-rays. I may need a CT scan. Are the radiologists still waiting?"

"Yes, Doctor," the nurse replied. "They agreed to wait— only if I promised to buy them dinner after we finish and that you send their girls a very big bunch of roses each tomorrow, confounded conniving men," Janice laughed.

"Okay Chris," the Specialist quickly said, "all that will be on your account. Now, buzz off and grab a cup of coffee. Come back in one hour."

It was the most tasteless coffee Chris had ever had. It was not because the coffee had anything wrong with it, it was simply because Chris's mouth was just not working properly, and his tastebuds seemed to have closed down. The hour seemed to drag on and on, and he actually returned to the specialist rooms five minutes early. The examination room door was still closed.

The nurse poked her head out for a couple of seconds, and quickly said, "You are early, Mr Kennedy, we will be a while yet, the doctor is having a few problems."

"Oh Hell," his mind screamed, "I have killed her," and in a state of complete desolation he sat blank faced and unmoving for another half-hour.

Finally, first the nurse, followed by a laughing Jackie, then the specialist, filed out. The specialist saw him sitting there, and lightly said, "Good, you are here; I have a fair bit to talk to you about." He turned to his nurse and said, "Thank you for staying, Janice; we have finished here. You might as well go home. Come into my office you pair—we need to talk this over. I still do not believe my own eyes and find it difficult to believe what I have seen."

Chris's heart ended up somewhere down near his large feet. "Please do not muck about Doc," Chris cried. "Tell us all the news."

"No news," the specialist laughed. "Everything is okay—I still do not believe it. All our scans after Jackie had her last child showed irreparable damage. Now I see every one of those organs have repaired themselves and the pregnancy will be perfectly normal."

He spread a series of CT scans across his desk and using his pen to indicate what he was saying said, "This is the scan from the earlier birth. Look at the damage, here, here, here and here. Now compare that with the scans we did today. Look as carefully as you like, you will find no sign of that damage. Jackie can keep on having children for a while yet."

Jackie interrupted him by saying, "I'd like to get through this one first and see. It is alright for you blokes: once you have done your bit, you only have to sit back and watch while we women get fat and awkward. Still the rewards in the end make up for all that." She had turned to face Chris, and with tears running down her cheeks she softly said, "I am so happy, you wonderful man; you have given me another baby." Then laughing joyously said, "I think we will have to give serious consideration before we head off on walkabout again. I appear to end up pregnant every time. You may now take me out to dinner at the best restaurant in the city and buy me a bottle of my favourite red."

The specialist declined their invitation to call his wife and for them to join the happy couple for dinner. "Another time, folks; this is your night, and I think it would be best for you two to have it to yourselves."

It was well after midnight when they arrived back at the apartment. There was no sign of Jack. "Tammy must have her own place," Chris laughed.

They had showered and sat wrapped in warm dressing gowns sipping a cup of tea, discussing the day. "Okay my beautiful mother-to-be, I think it is time to get back to some serious work. Tomorrow we will have to spend some time with Rex and fill him in about the diamonds. I will use his equipment and try and find out about the leases that exist out there. All the data we collected will make it quite easy to locate those mountains; the difficulty will be to sort out the leases."

"I will come with you only for a while, my dearest one; once you and Rex get down to detailed work, I get left behind and lose interest. Your sisters and I are going shopping. I want to see a jeweller to see if I can get that first stone you found for me and some of the others, mounted on chains. I only want to learn the outcome of what you and Rex find, and if we can get the mining lease."

"Diamonds," Rex threw his arms into the air in anguish. "What next? When are you going to stop, brother of mine? Any time you get out into that Outback of yours you come back with a problem for me. I do have to say, they are usually nice problems, but this one is a doozy. The first problem I see we must overcome is Native Title. Do you recall the name Matthew Blackstone, the native lawyer? He has joined Kennedy and Dixon and is a junior partner. It is a very good arrangement. With all his knowledge of native title law and the clout of the firm as strong as Kennedy and Dixon, he sees, and we do agree with him, there is much mutual  befit. Already his department is engaged in several red-hot litigations."

"As soon as I can identify the leases and find out if in fact the leases have been issued to cover the area, and perhaps if those leases are subject to native title I will definitely spend some time with him." Chris said. "What I do need at the moment is the use of a really good computer and one of your best research blokes with the brains to drive that computer. If he is good enough we will be able to sort out what titles exist and who they have been issued to."

"What are you looking for?" Rex rather nonchalantly asked.

"Only a small mountain range," Chris hesitated.

"Well? Don't stop there," Rex snapped. "A small mountain range of what?" he growled.

Chris answered in one word: "Diamonds," he whispered, "Enough diamonds if we put only the smallest portion of them on the market, at present prices we could buy Quo-Vadis Holdings in total at least 100 times over."

"No!" Rex cried and thumped his head down several times on the desk in front of him. "That much," he whispered. "Did you have to do that," he cried out as if he was in pain.

"Sorry bro, I did not plan to do that. Jackie and I only went walkabout; she got pregnant and I got a diamond mine."

That comment made Rex sit up straight, and immediately said with a voice full of concern, "I thought another pregnancy was a no-no."

"It's another story, bro. I will tell you about it some other time. Jackie is perfectly okay, and there is nothing to worry about," Chris replied.

Chris and the research expert worked for two hours. It hypnotised Chris to watch him dance his fingers over that keyboard as he hacked into records old and new. He finally pushed his chair back saying, "I think all that which you are looking for, Mr Kennedy is here; I will now send it to the printer. There is quite a lot so it may take some time to print out."

They sat back and waited while that printer spat out sheet after sheet of diagrams and dates giving all the details of titles that had been granted, the currency, and to whom. Chris collected up all the sheets, then sat and wrote a short note addressed to Jamie and Vanessa at Quo-Vadis tours. The handwritten note simply said, "Bearer of this note has provided me with a great service. He and whoever he chooses to accompany him are to be accommodated free of any charges including meals, tours and whatever. He is also to be provided with the best of transport from his home to Quo-Vadis Resort where he may stay for a maximum period of two weeks. Kindly arrange his itinerary to meet his needs."

Chris handed the letter to the computer expert, saying, "Ring that number on the envelope—tell them you have a letter I have given you as a token of gratitude for a job well done, then just sit back; they will organise the rest."

As a matter of interest, Chris did receive a letter from the computer expert about five weeks later. The letter did say thank you, and that he, his wife and five children had had a wonderful time at Quo-Vadis.

Carrying that bundle of printouts, Chris headed back towards Rex's office. Halfway down the corridor a soft female voice called, "go no further Mister; Rex has had you all morning. I want you for the rest of the day. Your sisters have deserted me and I need a nice lunch." Jackie strode purposefully down the corridor relieved him of his burden of printouts, which she handed to a bemused secretary passing by, instructing her to, "Please deliver these to Mr Rex," firmly grabbed Chris's arms and dragged him toward the elevators, laughing and saying, "Come with me; I have much to tell you."

Chris did not get back to see Rex that day. They had dined well and now walked nonchalantly through that beautiful public park, laughing often as Jackie related details of her morning.

"The girls and I walked into that very upmarket jewellery store. I asked to talk to the jeweller. I had a battle to get past the ladies at the counter who had become almost rude, and when I said we were not there to buy anything only to contract the jeweller to mount some stones I had found, the lady serving us had all but turned up her nose and had become most offhand. She got up my nose at bit, and I guess I did raise my voice. That attracted the security guard, and he politely offered to escort us from the shop. Your eldest sister is great—she went for that poor fellow like a fox terrier with a rat. With all the noise we were making the jeweller poked his nose out and asked, quiet politely mind you, 'What was the problem?' So, I showed him the stones and had quickly asked, could he mount them without altering them. He took one look at the stones and collapsed onto the floor in a messy heap. All hell broke loose then; we were accused of knocking him down or threatening to rob the store or something untoward. The poor fellow had managed to get up and had all but dragged us all into a very nice office. He had sat down very quickly,

I was glad of that because he looked like he would fall down again at any minute. I had to laugh; he took a few deep breaths, got out a large handkerchief, and mopped his brow, all the time he was muttering to himself. He had finally picked up the phone of his desk, pushed a few buttons, said something to somebody about getting three other blokes and two more security fellows to his office immediately, and have the girls bring four good strong coffees. After he had done all that he had reached over to me; I noticed his hand was shaking, but he managed to say, 'May I see those pieces, pieces now, not stones. He had kept whispering 'goodness gracious,' over and over. Three other blokes, evidently jewellers from his workshop, and two big security guys had knocked and bowled in. The oldest guy appeared most concerned, and had very loudly asked, 'Is something the matter, sir?' The jeweller, did reply to him, and rather sharply said, 'Please, all of you find a seat; I want you to look at these four pieces. You may never see the likes of them ever again in your lifetime.' Those three blokes got a little bit agitated—I think one of them actually wet himself. Another one asked, 'Are they genuine, sir?' By that time, the jeweller was looking a little bit better and quickly said, 'That's why I called you three.' He had passed my stones across his desk to his workshop boys who had each whipped out one of those funny little glasses—you know what they look like and fitted them to one eye. They had all spent a couple of minutes very carefully turning the stones over and over peering at them all the time. 'This piece is remarkable, sir!' one bloke had whispered. The other chaps all quickly said, 'So are these.' The older chap did quietly ask, 'Are we to cut and mount them for you, madam?' Your rotten sisters ribbed me mercilessly for the rest of the morning about that; any time I said anything they would answer and always added, yes, Madam Jackie, or no Madam Jackie. I did tell those jewellers I did not want them cut—only mounted on a gold chain—and that I would provide all the gold they would need. I did ask the jeweller what he thought they would be worth. He stumbled around giving me an answer, and had those stones— sorry, pieces—cleaned and weighed. They shone like stars. Your youngest sister lost patience with him and had shouted, 'For goodness sake, tell us how much? Jackie will not hold you to any price—she only wants to give them away as gifts.' One of those workshop guys darn near had a heart attack, and was almost crying when he said, is she really going to give away a diamond worth around one million dollars?' The boss jeweller managed to get a word in and had interrupted everybody by saying, 'Miss Jackie'—I did correct him— 'It's Mrs Jackie'—that set him off on a different track—and he asked, 'Mrs, Mrs who?' I did apologise for being rude and not introducing myself properly, so I told him, 'I'm Mrs Christopher Kennedy.' It took a moment for that to sink in—I thought he was going to collapse again. He finally stuttered, 'You are the wife of Chris Kennedy, the miner?' Once he got that out he looked a little more comfortable and had said, 'Thank you, madam; that explains much.' He finally got around to saying that the pieces did weigh an average of 3.4 carats; cut and mounted each piece would retail at around 1.2 to \$1.3 million, and he would be happy to take them on consignment as he could not afford over \$4 million to buy them from me. I told him they really were gifts and left them with him. Oh yes, before I forget, would you quickly send him about five or six kilograms of eighteen-carat gold, that he could have made up into very attractive chains. He did say the 0.9999% stuff you send to the mint would be too soft for a chain. I did do some shopping and have bought another nice nighty; want to see it?"

"Not unless you are in it," Chris had replied quite seriously, but he still had that twinkle in his eyes.

All Jackie then said was, "Later," and quickly added, "All this talking has made me thirsty; buy me a drink and take me home. The jeweller will have security people bring the pendants out to Quo-Vadis when they are finished. I hope it is okay; I did tell him to make sure those security guys go out to the tourist park and tell Vanessa I told them they were to see her and she would arrange for an aeroplane to bring them out to Quo-Vadis. Well, my man, you have heard of my day; what have you been up to? Working hard I hope and earning lots and lots of money."

"Didn't earn a cracker. I have spent a fair bit of my day working with a very good computer research guy. He was amazing to watch. Before we go home to Quo-Vadis, I wish to go back to Rex's office to collect that bundle of printouts you so unceremoniously took from me, and you, young-lady, are going to help me sort out all those leases. I wish to tie up that loose end as quickly as possible. Unless we get hold of those leases, any plans we make will be a complete waste of time."

Jack was at the apartment when they called in to collect their bags. He apologised for not coming home last night, using the excuse that Tammy was so embarrassed she could not face you again, so he stopped at her place for the night.

"I hope you finished your . . . studies?" Chris quipped with a large wink at his son.

"Don't encourage him," Jackie snapped. "His grandmother and I will have a bit to say about all this when you come home next weekend."

"That's an order," Chris laughed. "Ignore it at your own peril."

The printouts had revealed the whole of the mountain range was completely devoid of any native title. Notes referring to the mountain range had simply said, "Forbidden land." Native title was recorded for a small parcel of land bordering the hinterland of the northern reaches of that mountain range. Chris did discuss the matter with old Marlee, the native elder, who had explained to Chris the holders of the claim were not good people.

"I will leave it for the time being," Chris said. "Later on, I will get Matthew, the native lawyer, to have a look at it. I would prefer not to have 'not good people' as close neighbours." He was able to show Jackie that the boundaries of their grazing leases run right through the centre of the basin. No other grazing leases had been issued for that area, notes attached which applied to that area, said. Do not issue grazing leases, area unsuitable for grazing, no water. "I will ignore that and make application to extend our grazing lease right up to the edge of that native title. It is obvious to me nobody has gone to the trouble to explore those mountains or examine closely any of the aerial surveys and had never discovered the water in the basin. It is fortuitous that that mountain range was never comprehensively surveyed, and the deposit we found was very obviously never discovered."

The mining leases were a different thing. Mining leases had been granted to three different companies. They had been granted twelve years ago. Chris told her, "The mining leases would predate our grazing lease application, so I will have to take Bill and hotfoot it back there and peg out anything that has not already been claimed, and then approach those three companies and try and purchase their claims. I didn't see any mining activity while we were out there, so maybe, and hopefully, they have lost interest in those claims."

Jackie had watched Chris wade through all those sheets of printouts. She had sorted the discarded sheets into files, which did enable Chris to revisit them easily.

"I am amazed you can glean all this information from these printouts," she admiringly commented to Chris, to which Chris nonchalantly replied, "Is not a lot of trouble; it is really all part of my training to be a miner."

The first two companies who held the mining leases asked a few relevant questions, to which Chris answered telling them quite correctly, overlooking the true reason, he was wanting to round off his grazing lease. Demand for beef from his station had grown and he needed as much space as he could get. He told them he appreciated it was not good grazing land and fodder in there is only available after those occasional unseasonal rains hit that area. The first two mining lease holders did ask $100,000 and $80,000 respectively.

"Far too much!" Chris had exclaimed, "It would take forever for me to recover that amount of money from grazing in there," and counter offered $10,000 each. His offer was readily accepted.

The third and smallest mining lease holder was proving most difficult. Chris was hesitant to offer a large premium and negotiations reached a stalemate. He thinks it may have been Yindi's doing that old Marlee and the elders of the tribe heard of Chris's plight. Since Jack's New Year party, they had no fear of now entering the sinkhole, and this morning six of them called on Chris at his office.

As is usual they came straight to the point. "You say you have chased the evil ones from the mountains, Abdiel Boss Chris. You are very powerful and we believe you. We have heard of your problem, and because you are such a good friend of our people we will help you."

"Tell me how you can help me, wise ones?" Chris respectfully questioned.

"As we believe it is now not forbidden land, we will register a claim to extend the people's land to include those mountains. They really are part of our land, and it is only that we were fearful even to be associated with it; is why it had never been claimed earlier. Once our claim is registered we will have Matari (Mathew) write to say we allow you to use the mountains in whatever manner you wish. Should you make any money from those mountains, we do not wish to share it, as we still retain a little fear. You may have driven the spirits away, but it is possible, because they had lived there for so long, some small portion of their wickedness may be still in the stones.

"Thank you. I am honoured that you are my friends and are willingly to help me in this way," Chris very earnestly said as he shook the hands of each of them.

Matthew only laughed long and loud when told of the elder's plan. "They know that once granted, native title overrules all other claims."

"I do now," Chris laughed with him. "They are a canny lot; in my wildest dreams I would never have thought to do that."

The holdout leaseholder did come to Chris after the judiciary hearing of this new native title claim, saw there was no reason not to grant the claim. The leaseholder was very angry—he had only held out hoping to squeeze many dollars out of Chris.

"The bloody lease is now useless to anybody, even as the grazing lease you wanted it for. Those confounded natives," (that was not what he called them) for which Chris had him thrown out of the office, which Rex had allocated to him. Solicitors acting for that lease holder called on Chris the next day with an offer to sell the mining lease to him at a much-reduced price. Those solicitors were straight forward only after Chris had handed them a cheque for $2000. They quickly said you realise of course Mr Kennedy, that the area is now under the jurisdiction of the native peoples.

Chris was not inclined to waste a moment with these people, and simply answered, "Yes," as he showed them the door.

On his return to Quo-Vadis, Chris held Jackie very tightly and shouted, "All done, Jackie girl. My next problem is, how the hell do I mine for diamonds. This was not covered in the lectures at university. I think I remember Professor Strahan saying that was another course. Looks like I have to bring Bill, Riley, and the professors in on our little secret."

"Do you really have to start another mine?" Jackie softly said. "All we have to do is go up there sometime and collect a few pieces to keep my jewellery box topped up."

Riley and Strahan once again were totally intrigued with what they called, "a miner's dream come true." Chris had almost talked himself dry explaining his latest discovery, and his very strong desire to keep it all most secret.

"Not interested in that part of your problem, son," Strahan had flippantly said. "We only want to glean from your discovery as much knowledge as we can of space diamonds and meteorites."

Bill's response was somewhat different. "Mine diamonds! How the hell do we do that?"

"I don't know, either," Chris had reluctantly admitted, then continued saying, "I suppose we had better find out. While the professors are doing their thing, you and I—and Jackie, of course—are off to South Africa to have a look at a fair dinkum diamond mine and processing plant."

"A trip to Africa," Jackie shouted excitedly when she was told of their plans. "Will there be lions and tigers and elephants?" she exclaimed with delight.

"I doubt the tigers," Chris had laughed, "but you will probably see many more animals that will grab you and eat you if you're not careful."

"Oh" Jackie had shuddered, "how exciting."

The big mining company were most reluctant to share much information. Bill did dress as a mining engineer and carrying a folder of technical looking documents; had managed to wheedle his way past the security boys by saying, he had been asked to look over the possible replacement of a particular machine.

After a short delay and several phone calls to the office, a rather reluctant guard did let Bill through. The guard did remain beside Bill all morning, while Bill examined much of the processing machinery making numerous notes of what he was seen. "The machinery is very old and needs to be updated," he told the guard who very sharply answered, "They won't spend a cracker unless it is absolutely necessary."

Chris in the interim had spent several hours with the head of the finance department of the mine. He learned of just how tightly held the marketing of diamonds had become. With the market for artificial man-made diamond crystals growing, the producers of natural diamonds were finding the market for the natural product had become very tight and difficult. Chris learned the gem market was still very strong and that there was still a buoyant demand for good quality pieces.

"What you are saying is all very interesting," and in an innocent-sounding voice quietly asked, "What's a kilogram of industrial material cost these days?"

"Prices vary a bit," the senior finance executive replied. "Competition in that area is very aggressive. We used to be able to control that market; nowadays $100 US will get you a kilogram of top-quality clear crystals." The executive was becoming a little hesitant to discuss prices further.

Chris did not let that worry him. "What about gemstones?" he quickly enquired.

Regardless of his previous reluctance, the finance executive produced a large volume which Chris perceived to contain details of gem stone sales, and quickly said, "That's not easy to answer, it does depend on quality and weight."

"Perhaps you could tell me, without commitment of course, what this is worth?" Chris asked, as he fossicked in his pocket and produced one of those chestnut-sized stones he and

Jackie had collected. "I bought it from a native fellow some time ago when we were on, what do you call it?"

"Safari," the executive quickly offered. "Yes, that's it, we were on Safari way out there, only Heaven knows, exactly where we were," before saying to himself "I bet I will have a monstrous pimple on my tongue for telling that fib."

The finance executive reached into a side draw and produce a jeweller's glass. He examined the stone for a couple minutes, then without looking up quietly said, "This is a very good piece, sir. It is clear quality without a flaw; exactly where and when did you meet that native?"

Chris thought for a moment, then thinking again to himself, "looks like I have to cultivate another pimple, and tell him a bit more bulldust," replied, "Sorry Mister, I was with a guide, I do not have a clue where I was. I could have been in another country for all I know."

The executive placed the gem on a small electronic scale he kept on his desk, mainly for decoration. "Um," he growled, "3.2 carat, clear quality, uncut, wholesale, say $5000."

Chris appeared to be very excited with that and cried, "Wow, my wife will be rapt."

The executive nonchalantly returned his jeweller's glass into the draw, and said, "I'll take it off your hands right now, Mr Kennedy. You will be hard pushed to get a better price."

"This bloke is a bloody thief," Chris again thought to himself. "I know it's worth at least 10 times what he is offering," then without so much as blinking an eye said, "Thank you for your offer, sir; my wife wants to make it into a ring for herself. She would kill me if I sold it."

Chris left soon after that—he had learned enough. He caught up with Bill; Jackie was out at a nearby animal reserve looking at lions and "tigers."

"What have you learned?" Chris asked.

"I have learned enough to know we have a hell of a lot to do," Bill replied. "I now have a fair idea of what is required and a heap of photographs. The machinery I saw is very old and does not look to be suitable for our purpose. I think we will have to rely on the Professors and see what they have to say."

They all flew out the next day. Jackie was happy to go— she didn't like the place and the animals were not very nice, and she did not see one tiger!

They had to wait for the Professors to return to Quo-Vadis. It was two weeks later before the weary learned men returned—they were obviously elated with what they had found. They dumped a small sack on to Chris's desk, "We think these must be yours, son," they were laughing heartily. "You may have dropped them when you were out there." Bill examined the contents of that sac. His only comment was a loud – "HOLY COW.".

That small sack contained no less than fifty stones, large and small; one stone was the size of a small hen egg. "You must take care not to dump what you mine on the market, in no time you would cause an upheaval and possibly destroy the whole diamond industry," they advised him. "We have found that the place is, as you say, one giant crater caused by a meteorite we estimate around 150 metres in diameter. It was a conglomeration mainly of diamonds from the core of some long-exploded planet. There was a proportion of iron and many other minerals, some of which we have yet to identify. The whole crater that meteorite caused is a mineralogist's conundrum. The meteorite had dug into the earth's surface for about ten metres before it hit solid granite and started to shatter into thousands of diamond fragments. We were able to investigate its path to a depth of around fifteen feet with some very hard digging." Riley displayed his blistered hands to confirm that statement. "We gave up digging; we could see that at that depth the meteorite had reduced to about fifteen to twenty metres and was keeping on its downward trajectory to possibly stop about 1000 to 1200 metres down. The actual depth would depend on what inhabiting material it hit. You are correct in your assumption the impact did form those mountains. We would like to come back at some later date and try and establish how old those mountains really are."

"Thank you, gentlemen," Chris quickly said. "Before you leave, we do require some assistance with another thing; to quote Bill, how the hell do we mine this stuff?"

"Open cut, of course," Strahan quickly replied.

"I have considered that; that is not really the problem. The methods used overseas do not suit our purpose," Chris sighed.

Both the Professors laughed simultaneously. Through his laughter Riley managed to say; sometimes Mr Christopher Kennedy, the celebrated miner, when you have a problem that appears impossible to solve, like any good student you must pursue the answer by trial and error."

"No room for error," Bill grumbled. "We do not tolerate error or failure in this club; we will just have to work it out. The present method is very labour intensive. Even if we shift the processing to Quo-Vadis we could never have enough staff. I saw at least twenty to twenty-five girls stationed along a conveyor belt picking out pieces that had been illuminated by an x-ray machine. Those girls were changed every two hours with a new team. No team was required to do more than three terms a day. That's a lot of girls. You blokes," looking very intently at the two professors, "have access to most of the departments at the university. Perhaps there is someone, possibly even one of the lecturers in the area that discusses electronics. There is something on my mind that those pretty smart electronic blokes could build a machine that would recognise those x-rays activated stones and collect them. If they can do that, it would do away with the need for all those girls. Chris and I have been discussing various levels of crushing. We can only settle on five different levels. We could pass each level of crushing through a collecting machine. The machines at each level would pick up only gemstones of a pre-set size. The final level of crushed material would then contain only industrial diamonds. There will be gems collected still attached to rocks; those rocks would be fed into the next stage crusher."

Both the professors were struck speechless with Bill's suggestion.

Finally, Riley spoke out, "There is no such machine in existence; but I see no reason why we cannot experiment with that thought for a while. And you, Mr Bailey, have you ever given any thought to lecturing at the university on the subject, which you appear to be most conversant with, crushing and processing?"

"Take it easy, Professor Riley," Chris cried. "Don't give him a bigger swelled head than that which he already has."

Irrespective of Bill's earlier comment, trial and error was not entertained; it was only after much trial and error that the collecting machine was perfected.

Exactly where the diamond processing plant should be constructed had been the subject of much discussion. To build it in the mountains was going to be an excessively expensive project. The cost and time of transporting all those, in some cases, delicate machines, and the need to install another 380 kilometres of underground cable and connect all those machines to the power network, staffing, and the absence of sufficient constant supply of water were but a few of the strong negatives that had to be considered.

To top all that off, Chris's security chief very strongly expressed his concern when first told of the project. "How could he possibly provide satisfactory security cover for what he could see would be one of the juiciest targets he had ever heard of," he cried in dismay.

Strahan and Riley solved one of the problems for them. Whilst exploring the network of caves in the escarpment, they had found a very large cavern only about eight kilometres south of the Animal Cave. They had not found an external outlet, and access was limited to one, five-metre diameter tunnel running from the underground river. They had deduced that there must have been a good outlet at some time in the past for the river to have eroded out a cavern that size. A strong flow of water was still continuing to flow down that tunnel. The professors had discovered all this purely by chance, when Riley accidentally dropped his miner's helmet into that flow. The light on the helmet continued to operate, and the professors had watched the helmet disappear down the tunnel. The water flow was not deep and the curious professors had followed that helmet to discover the cavern. In the limited time available, they had not established where the present water flow exited.

Guided by the professors' directions Chris and Bill did embark on their own exploratory exercise. The upshot of all this was that they declared the site was perfect and did outweigh all of those negative aspects of installing the plant in the mountains. The cavern only required a good amount of foundation work and the construction of a further tunnel to run four kilometres from the cavern to the external face of the escarpment to open up an external access.

It was a complex, highly-efficient processing plant that was put into action two years later. The small river that had led the professors to the cave was now contained in a three-meter diameter pipe. Chris had found that that water flow did escape down a large hole in the cavern floor. As he had a practical use for the water in the processing plant he had captured the flow. Now, after leaving the plant, the constrained river flowed down a pipe, and out that new tunnel he had constructed, then poured from the escapement face to join the outflow from the Animal Cave and on to that ancient river bed and into the lake at the resort.

The actual location of the diamond mine was known to only twenty-two very trusted people. That paranoid security chief had gone to great lengths to investigate those people's bona fides. Chris sent two large camouflaged multi-wheeled loaders to the basin with strict instructions those loaders had to be stored well out of sight when not in use. Once a month, those twenty-two men drove a convoy of six strange looking trucks out to the mountains. A very rough discrete track had been cut through the side of the basin to give the trucks access. Those trucks were another example of Ed's expertise—forty-tonne carrying capacity bins, on sealed trays, the roof of those bins would slide back to enable loading. The loaded trucks were then driven back to Quo-Vadis, and on to the diamond processing plant. Unloading the trucks was accomplished by the trucks driving over an unloading chute and when the tray of that truck yawned open the load poured down the chute. Very few actually saw what those trucks had been carrying.

The electronic collecting machines worked a treat. "Oh hell!" Chris exclaimed as he viewed the gems from the first week's processing. "I cannot just sell this lot; we will have to extend the vault and store it."

The mine and the plant operated only one week per month, mainly to collect industrial "gravel."

From time to time, Jackie did put in an order for one or two new accessories!

Rex had smiled broadly as the invoices to pay for all that cost of setting up came in. "That helps this year's tax problems," he thought. "I hate to think what happens to my beautiful accounts if he ever starts selling all that he is producing."

Ralph Stirzika was a changed man. No longer did he chase every bit of skirt he laid his eyes on. He had no time for that. His application to his studies absorbed most moments of his day and often his nights. Upon his return from the party at Quo-Vadis, his devotion to his studies surprised his parents and tutors alike. That girl, no, that beautiful creature, Yindi Kennedy, plagued his mind constantly. He thought about her at least two to three times a day. He had always been friendly with Jack, and when Ralph learned from Jack that Yindi was staying at the apartment with Jack for a few weeks, Ralph did interrupt his studies to make rather frequent social calls. On the third visit he was rewarded with finding both Jack and Yindi were in. They were discussing where to go for an evening meal. Without hesitation Ralph had offered to take them both to a particularly nice little restaurant he knew. Most generously he did say it was his shout. Jack was taken with the idea of eating out of place he had previously not known about but did strongly stipulate he would wear the bill. It was a most pleasant evening. Ralph learned quickly that these were two highly intelligent people who could discourse comprehensively on many subjects, even his favourite subject, fossils. Yindi was quietly impressed when Ralph was able to identify for her those bones she had made up into that very decorative necklace of small bones she was wearing, made from some bones she and the witch doctor had found in the dark recesses of a hitherto unknown cave.

Ralph's palaeontologist's mind was stimulated, and he had immediately said, "You must have coffee with me one morning; those caves sound most exciting. You say very few know of them."

They did enjoy morning coffee breaks at least twice a week over the remainder of Yindi's three-week city visit. Yindi was to leave the next day. As they sat at the window of their favourite coffee house, she had quite innocently suggested, "Why don't you come out to Quo-Vadis over your next semester break? I am sure my friend the witch doctor will be pleased to show you around, especially if you can tell him all about those old bones, and perhaps spend some time with him discussing many of the rock paintings—not many people have seen them. Don't push him into allowing you access into the sacred caves. That may come later."

Ralph had responded in an instant: "That would really be something special. I may be able to use what I find in my final paper. I am pleased to have to tell you that I finish my ten years of study this year. Before I can call myself a graduate palaeontologist, I have to do twelve months of fieldwork and submit a satisfactory summary."

Ralph did spend five weeks at Quo-Vadis. Chris and Jackie found his presence most pleasant, and often engaged in spirited debate with him. His knowledge of rock age went beyond the level Chris had reached to obtain his miner's degree. Chris's knowledge had increased considerably with all his hands-on experience; still, he did readily accept and respect this young man's capacity. It pleased Chris that this young man readily accepted and sought to unravel that extensive trove of ancient knowledge stored in this land called the Outback.

Upon his return to university, Ralph had set to his studies with a vengeance; a new determination to definitely complete his course this year had set upon him. These days he was often interrupted by Miss Yindi Kennedy who had found an increasing number of excuses to have to go to the city.

"Getting a bit serious do you think?" Chris commented to Jackie.

"He really is very nice," Jackie replied. "They are a good match. She lets him get away with nothing. Just the other day Ralph went out to visit the witch doctor without her. When he got back, Oh Boy!" Jackie exclaimed, "You should have heard her chew him up. He is no coward, he didn't wear her problem. I heard him say back at her, 'If I want to see the witch doctor I will, with or without you. Your kitchen girl had told me you were still asleep when I left just before dawn. I didn't feel like putting up with you in a bad mood; you are not really such a nice person first thing in the morning, and I wasn't going to risk copping a blast for waking you.' Yindi had come to me after that argument," Jackie laughed ; "she was most contrite when she asked, 'Am I that bad in the mornings, Mummy?" "I had to laugh," and told her, "Until the sunbeam kisses you each morning, you are impossible" She had walked away saying, "Ralph is right; I must go and find him and apologise" I saw them together later on that morning; they were chatting and laughing and seemed to have patched things up."

Chris laughed heartily at Jackie's discourse, and with a voice full of humour chuckled, "I am most grateful that you are an absolute joy to be with, be it first thing in the morning or at any time during the day, or night; Jackie girl."

Moses Stirzicka, Ralph's father, was from a long line of Jewish diamond merchants. He ran a highly respected diamond distribution business, and had been long married to Ralph's mother, Avril. Apart from Ralph, they had two daughters, both married, and another son, Joseph, who was six years older than Ralph. Joseph had worked all his working life alongside Moses in the diamond distribution business. Of late, they were finding things were becoming more and more difficult as the big diamond cartels made it almost impossible for Moses to obtain a regular supply of the good quality gems that he was reputed to always supply. Moses was highly respected in the industry and knew much more about diamond's than most jewellers.

From time to time, Ralph would bring Yindi to dinner in the family home. Both Moses and Avril were pleased about this— they did like Yindi; she was far above any of the others Ralph had bought home and Avril did enjoy sitting chatting with that very interesting young lady.

This evening, Yindi casually had said to her, "You both must come out to Quo-Vadis to meet my parents."

Moses and Avril had heard so much about Yindi's parents and Quo-Vadis from Ralph they readily agreed, "That would be nice."

Yindi had not hesitated and quickly said, "I am going home tomorrow, perhaps you could come with me." As was the norm, - everybody else always asked, Moses quickly said, "when Ralph kept talking about this fabulous place called Quo-Vadis, and we had heard so much about your parents I tried to find Quo-Vadis on the maps, I could not find any record of it anywhere."

"It is way out in the Outback," Yindi lightly replied. "It is best to fly there."

"If that's the case, I will try and get tickets online now; would you kindly assist me, Yindi?" Moses asked. "You would know much more readily what airline to search, and the best times to fly," to which she replied, "No need for you to do that, I will look after all that stuff for you."

"Then there is little excuse not to go," Moses laughed. "Will your parents mind having guests sprung on them without warning?"

"I will call them later on this evening," Yindi replied. "Mum and Dad will be pleased to meet you. May I pick you up at 11:30 am?" and quickly added, "Do not pack much—it is hot out there at this time of year, and a bathing outfit is almost mandatory."

"This is all most exciting," Avril cried. "How long will we be away, Yindi?"

"As long as you please," the young girl answered. She had a very big smile on her face. "By the time Dad has shown you all over Quo-Vadis you may be there for a year or two."

Moses was most alarmed at that and quickly said, "I hope you are jesting, young lady. I cannot be away that long."

"Yes, Mr S. I am joking; however, I do have to warn you, there is much to see, and much more to enjoy," Yindi laughed.

Yindi, called for them at exactly 11.30 next morning in her Dad's chauffeur-driven town limousine.

"Where to, Miss Kennedy?" the chauffeur asked.

"Regular airport, thanks Mike," she replied.

Moses watched out the car window as the city rolled by. He became somewhat alarmed and cried, "Sir, this is not the way to the airport; do you know the way? you are heading in the wrong direction."

Yindi was seated with her back towards the chauffeur and had reached across and took Moses' hand. "Don't be alarmed Mr S," and quietly said, "He knows the way."

The very alarmed and almost panic-stricken Moses cried "Won't we miss our flight going this way?"

"No, sir," Yindi replied, "They will not leave without me."

"You talk as if you own the aircraft," the jeweller almost angrily snapped.

"I do," Yindi laughed. "Dad gave it to me for Christmas."

"You own an aircraft? A young snip of a girl like you actually owns an aircraft?" Moses stuttered.

"Sure do," Yindi quietly said, as the limousine swung into a parking lot. "We are here. Mike will look after the bags and we can all get on board and be away quickly."

Moses whispered softly as if endeavouring not to waken somebody, "Isn't this a very exclusive private airfield, Yindi?"

She had quietly replied, "Yes Mr S, my Dad owns it, and allows a few special people to use it."

Moses sat back heavily into the soft seat of the limousine and whispered to his wife, "She picks us up in a limousine; owns an aeroplane—not just any old aeroplane; look at it Avril, it is the latest model CL300 private jet, and now she tells us, her dad owns a private airfield on the outskirts of the city."

Yindi had overheard Moses and had softly and very respectfully said, "Please do not let all this disturb you; it is best if

486

you find out about us now rather than later when it is too late," and ushered them on board her ostentatious aeroplane.

Three hours later the CL300 circled Quo-Vadis airfield. "Don't tell me your father owns this airfield also?" Moses sighed.

"It's our home airfield," Yindi replied. She was watching out a window as they came into land. "Good, my mother and father are waiting. I see they have brought Goliath; that's very good—he has lots of space."

"Goliath!" Moses exclaimed.

"Oh, he is Dad's bush-basher; he is beautiful," Yindi explained.

Moses was feeling much better. It had been a very pleasant flight during which he had partaken of a delightful snack and now with half a bottle of good red wine under his belt, he had resolved to take things as they came, but when Yindi pointed to that large very ugly huge twelve-wheeled-monster sitting there waiting, his resolve all but melted away. He watched as Yindi raced ahead to embrace the fine-looking couple that stood beside that monster.

Chris stepped forward, hand extended, and enthusiastically said, "Welcome to Quo-Vadis folks. I am Christopher Kennedy—Chris to all except this beautiful creature, who has a lot of other names for me when she is mad at me; please meet Jacqueline Kennedy, Jackie to all."

Moses stepped forward and boldly said, "Thank you for your welcome," he hesitated, "Chris," then quickly said, "I am Moses Stirzicka—please call me Moses—and this is Avril, my long-suffering wife—Chris, sir," he continued, "since quite early this morning my world has been turned upside down." As he spoke he had turned to Jackie and with a glint in his eye softly said, "And now it is spinning even faster; I see where Yindi gets her beauty from. Are you sure you are not her sister?"

Jackie only laughed and replied. "Thank you Mister Super-smooth, I can see where that son of yours stole his devilment from. You'll do as an alternate grandfather."

"Mum!" Yindi shouted in alarm. Not another word was said, although Moses and Avril smiled quietly to themselves. The group walked to Goliath; the three women were already chatting amiably. Chris pointed out a few features of the nearby Outback. Seven shiny jets, along with several other aircraft sat parked on the tarmac.

"Are all these yours?" Moses asked in awe, to which Chris replied, "There are a few others out on scheduled runs; these are some of the workhorses of Quo-Vadis Holdings. That made Moses feel a little better. "All these aeroplanes belong to a company," Moses quickly said.

"Yes," Chris nonchalantly replied, "My company."

That did not help Moses one little bit. "Are you folks up to a short tour?" Chris cheerfully asked.

"I am," Avril replied. "Moses is a little overwhelmed at the moment; don't worry about him, he will be alright shortly."

Chris took Goliath up a recently constructed road that had been blasted up the escarpment face. As they climbed higher and higher, the Outback for miles opened up before their eyes.

"So, this is the Outback," Moses quietly said. "It is far different from what I had envisaged."

Chris had pulled Goliath precariously close to the edge of the road to allow a monster ore truck pass.

"You do things in a big way, Chris," Moses commented as a ten-foot-high wheel rumbled only inches from his window. "What's that truck carrying?" he enquired.

"Quartz," Chris quickly replied, "About thirty cubic metres of quartz; each meter of that ore would contain ten to twelve percent pure gold."

"No more," Moses laughed, "I am still trying to get my mind to settle on the first surprise of Yindi owning her own aircraft. All these other things will have to get in line and wait for this brain of mine to catch up. Apart from a magnificent view, what else is up here, Chris?" he asked.

"Thought I would give you a look at a working goldmine. It will not take long—the reef here is only twenty metres down," Chris replied.

Moses and Avril stood with their mouths agape as Chris pointed out the gold vein in the quartz reef on both sides of that mine. "This is one of the five gold mines, the company is presently operating," Chris rather humbly said. "It is the only one on the actual surface of the escarpment; the others are all located in tunnels within the escarpment itself. We can have a look at one of those later."

Moses was quiet for some time after that. It was as if he was trying to get his brain into some sort of order.

As they drove Goliath onto the elevator in the Animal Cave, Chris explained, "This is one of those mines within the escarpment I was talking about earlier. In fact, it was my first mine here. We started the tunnel about eighteen years ago. It has progressed over five hundred metres into the escarpment. We have another mine coming toward it; the two mines are still a fair distance apart. After these two hook up we will start on the other side of that cave that houses the second mine. That mine will then still have over three hundred and eighty kilometres to go."

Moses appeared to have regained his composure, and quickly asked, "Is this reef part of the reef you showed us earlier? Is that reef that long?"

"Sure is," Chris replied. "We have only recently proven it to be so. What I showed you earlier is a second reef running parallel to this one. We have not opened any serious mines in that second reef as we have more than enough on our hands at the moment."

Moses appeared to be in a state of total confusion, and cried plaintively, "Chris! Chris, can you please stop all this sightseeing, and find me a strong brandy. It is getting to be a bit much."

Yindi, who was sitting alongside him took his arm and hugged it tightly, and, chuckling brightly, said. "Get used to it Mr S. He has not got anywhere close to the really good stuff yet."

"If that is how it's going to be, you better make that two-extra strong brandies Chris," Moses laughed. "I can see this is going to be one hell of a few good days." Then without stopping for a breath, cried "You actually own all this, Chris?"

"Yep," Chris replied.

"That is positively indecent," Moses laughed. He was feeling a little better and he did like Yindi holding his arm.

By the end of two weeks, after having been shown the Quo-Vadis township, the resort, Quo-Vadis Lithium, Quo-Vadis Iron Ore, those massive hydro generators of Quo-Vadis Power, spending a couple of very pleasant days at Quo-Vadis Station, meeting with the native people, and after being taught by the expert, Bill, the art of wetting a line, Moses was a totally different man. Now having discarded his business suits, clad in tattered miner's shorts and shirt, dug up by Bill from goodness knows where, with feet enclosed in strong miner's boots, he bowled into the kitchen of that beautiful house, and flung four large trout onto the kitchen bench. "I caught them myself Avril," he shouted to his smiling wife. "Bill is putting away the fishing gear; he is going to show me how to clean them and to cook them."

"Fish are cleaned in the laundry, thank you, sir," Jackie very sternly said, and laughing added, "Is Bill going to barbecue them? 'Yum' I love the way he does fish. Chris told me to let you know he will wait for you in his office in the small cave. I think he has something to show you; better have a brandy before you go. No, on second thoughts, I think you should take a whole bottle."

Moses left Bill to clean the fish, and strode quickly and confidently, glass of brandy in one hand, half a bottle of brandy in the other, to Chris's Cave office.

"Come in Moses," Chris called. "Please shut the door after you."

The strong room door was open and Moses could see into the vault. "Is that all gold?" he stuttered as he saw the ingot-lined shelves.

"Yes," Chris quietly replied. "That is the last month's smelt from the mines; the mint people, in a special armoured car, are on the way to collect it."

Moses had given up being astounded with these "little" surprises Chris came up with, and respectfully softly said "That is a lot of gold, *young fella*."

"That is not what I would like you to look at Moses," Chris said without hesitation. "I do need some professional advice."

"There is little I can tell you, son," Moses laughed. "However, I will be happy to help you if I can."

"Thank you, Moses," Chris said. "If you would kindly follow me, there is another strong room on the right-hand side; it's a bit bigger than this one. We have lined it, floor, walls and the roof with fifty-millimetre-thick special steel. It does have some special security features. Entry can only be gained by one of the very few people who know the security code. Should any other person attempt to open the door, a silent alarm is activated in the security team's office." Chris punched a series of numbers into the keyboard of his computer, walked quickly to that very large strongroom door and swung it open, and stepped inside. "Come in to Chris's conundrum," he laughed.

Moses stepped in and instantly dropped his glass and the bottle of brandy and grabbed Chris's shoulder for support. Shelf after shelf, row after row of trays lined the walls. "They are diamonds," Moses gasped.

"You see my problem, Moses," Chris very softly said. "We have collected this lot over the last six months. If I put it all onto the market place, it will really stuff up prices, and possibly bugger up the world's diamond market. Can you tell me, is there something, anything, I can do with them? I have stopped mining, and I have run out of space to store them. And even if I build a strongroom twice the size of this strongroom, it too would soon become chockers." (full up).

Moses had managed to regain his decorum, and with a most professional voice said, "Sorry Chris, this is out of my, or anybody I know, league. You are stuck with it. When I look at what you have here I can only think, even the most affluent of men do not have anything of the like of the magnitude of your problem. It is remarkable: those pieces are worth untold millions, but because there are so many they are worthless. Like I have just said, it is some sort of a problem to be stuck with."

"You are a diamond distributor, Moses," Chris wailed. "Could you not drift it slowly onto the market?"

"No, I do not know of anybody who could help you; there is far too much," Moses very strongly replied. "Perhaps I could help you a very little and at the same time help myself. Of recent times I have found it most difficult to continue trading. My usual sources have dried up, as the big boys will not supply the trading houses. They say competition from the producers of the artificial industrial material is killing them. At a glance, I can see that the majority of those pieces are indeed rare gems, exceptionally white and plus D clarity. The retail jewellers who usually buy from me would love them. I am a businessman Chris; my business is on the verge of being forced to close. I can see you offer me a lifeline. It would be good if I could purchase small amounts from time to time and on sell to the jewellery shops. Those shops sell engagement stone pieces for 5 to $600 a carat, increasing in price progressively the bigger the pieces get. What I can offer you will make little impact on your hoard. I do tell you it will save me, not only financially; it will mean we will continue to be people of the highest reputation. I have been paying the big boys more than $400 a carat for small stones. They really rip into me if I want something in the form of a two to three carat gem."

Chris hesitated before strongly saying, "Moses, I believe both you and I can see, and I know Jackie hopes, that in time our families will become one. To keep all this as a business deal would you consider taking all the gems you want, be they small or large or whatever, at $200 a carat; you keep the margin you get above that."

"Even large gems?" Moses questioned. "That's not realistic, Chris."

"Do you have to be so bluntly honest," Chris growled. "To get anything at all on a regular basis for those diamonds, even at a reduced price, is far better than getting almost nothing. If I don't sell to you, who can I sell to? I have no wish to spend my time out there shopping to every Tom, Dick and Harry, and pre-empting things a bit, I would much rather keep it in the family. You know Yindi would spit chips if she heard you and I discussing her future as we are, but you would have to be totally blind to miss the signals that pair are sending."

"You do not compromise, do you Chris," Moses respectfully said. "Very well, so that I can maintain some dignity let's consider, $200 a carat, and 50-50 for any sales I have above $1000."

"I would agree to that," Chris resolutely said. "What about these?" Chris punched some numbers in a keypad that enabled him to pull out a sealed tray. He flicked open the lid and placed the tray on a conveniently nearby table so as to enable Moses to get a good look at the contents of that tray.

"They are black!" Moses exclaimed. "Perfect black diamonds. Chris in my many years of dealing in diamonds I have never once seen one, let alone a whole tray full of them. I can never sell even the smallest of them." He almost reverently picked up a large stone, about the size of a golf ball, and quietly said, "This bauble alone could buy Buckingham Palace, and have pocket money left over. Please put them away, I could never dream of putting them on the market."

Chris responded quickly, and almost snarled, "It looks like I have no alternative; I will have to have them made up into accessories and give them away."

Moses could not believe what he was hearing and was almost weeping. "If you do that, lad," he cried, "make sure whoever you give them to is aware of their value and should they ever wear them in public they should have a large contingent of security men close at hand. I do not think there is one insurance company who would be prepared to cover the risk. Where did all this come from, Chris?" Moses asked. "You said you have stopped mining for diamonds; is there many more?"

"Many," Chris very slowly answered. "I think rather than try and explain it to you, tomorrow morning we will fly out to the mine, and you can see for yourself the enormity of my problem." Then, with a great deal of merriment in his voice, said, "You had better come armed with a full bottle of brandy."

Poor Moses—he did need that brandy before the day was over.

# Chapter 25

About eighteen months before the Stirzicka's visit and in due course, Samuel had arrived. It was while Chris had been involved in setting up the diamond mine and the diamond processing plant. Chris was taking no chances this time. The gynaecologist and his team had been warned that they had been put on notice to be available instantly the birth was imminent. The team, consisting of eight trained nurses, and one certified maternity nurse, much to their delight, had been billeted at Quo-Vadis Resort, in the two weeks prior to Jackie's due date.

Jackie, true to her obstreperous disposition— "Just being darn difficult," Chris called it—had flatly refused to await her time in a city hospital. As far as she was concerned, she was going to have it that her baby would be born in her own home at Quo-Vadis. Jackie's contractions had begun in earnest in the early hours of Sunday morning. The gynaecologist who had been dragged grumbling from his bed, and flown in, and with the bleary-eyed nurses tripping over one another buzzing about a perfectly relaxed, but rather uncomfortable Jackie, the large bedroom took on the appearance of an out of control riot.

The melee all ceased entirely, and quietness prevailed as four native women, accompanied by old Marlee and Chris, walked in.

Chris took one look, and very loudly and firmly shouted, "Everybody, except you doctors, OUT! Take a break, go downstairs to the kitchen make yourselves a cuppa. It is a very pleasant morning so you may find out on the patio looking out over the lake very much to your liking. You will be called immediately should we need your assistance."

The two doctors looked questionably at each other, as the four native women, as before, took station, one at each corner of the large bed and commenced that soft chant. Jackie appeared to relax and lay back a little deeper into the softness of the bed. Chris and Marlee sat quietly un-speaking out of the way.

One hour passed, then old Marlee stood and cried, "BURNUM comes."

Jackie strained a little, took a deep breath, and bored down hard. Burnum slipped quickly into the world—very quickly—and most gently he was picked up and wrapped in a cloth decorated with native symbols.

Old Marlee appeared to have drifted into a trance. As he recovered, he softly said, "The child has been given the name of one of our greatest warriors, for, as he was, this child will be a great warrior." With that Marlee left the room.

The baby was placed on Jackie's shoulder; he fussed for a moment then started to wail. She eased him up so she could get a better look at him, then gently said. "Hello my beautiful son. Cry long and strong so the whole world hears you and takes notice."

The nurses had sat on the patio, ears tuned, and at that first wail, rushed up the stairs and took over. Jackie signalled for the native women to come to her; she said nothing but for each woman she touched her own heart then placed her hand on the heart of the native woman. Each acknowledged the touch with a nod and a smile, then turned and left the room.

The perplexed doctors, who had stood back and watched all this, pushed their way through the nurses, who quickly stepped away. The doctors did a brief examination of Jackie, took a look at the after birth, examined the baby, turned and left, saying one to the other, "That was remarkable; if only all births could be accomplished with so little trouble and as uncomplicated as that!"

Chris had pushed in and tried to get to Jackie's side; he was unceremoniously shoved aside and told, "You will have your turn shortly, Mr Kennedy. In the meantime, please get from under our feet while we attend to your wife and son."

"I have another son!" Chris exclaimed.

"Yes," the nurse replied, "A fine little boy."

"Is Jackie all right?" Chris shouted.

"She is perfectly okay, so please stop shouting and go and sit out of the way," the nurse snapped, becoming weary with this noisy man.

"Confounded bossy woman," Chris grumbled. "A man deserves better treatment than this." Never the less he plonked himself onto the corner chair recently vacated by old Marlee.

He did not have to wait long before one of the nurse softly said to him, "They are ready now, Mr Kennedy. Come and meet your son."

Jackie reluctantly passed the baby to Chris, who was hard-pushed to restrain the tears that welled up within him. "Marlee has given him a very powerful native name; now I will give him a name. He will be called Samuel—Samuel Joshua Kennedy."

Yindi had grown to be a beautiful young lady. A few months passed her seventeenth birthday, tall, slim and like her mother, she had soft honey blonde hair and deep blue eyes, she was coveted by many a young man. Much to their dismay she showed no interest with getting involved with any of them. That Ralph Stirzicka had plagued her mind from time to time. She doted on her little brother and would play with him for hours. The Stirzickas—Moses and Avril—had been visiting at Quo-Vadis for the recent four weeks, and it was with much reluctance they decided to return to the city, and for Moses to continue to manage his now very successful diamond distribution business. They had used the visit to enable Moses to select a good number of pieces from Chris's troublesome horde.

"My workshop will cut and mount these and within the month we will have them in the jewellery shops," Moses told Chris. He also told Chris that his son, Joseph, during a recent telephone conversation, had told him many of his long-standing customers were patiently awaiting fulfilment of many orders.

The day previous to their intended departure they had walked past the open double doors of the family room. Yindi and Samuel were sitting comfortably on cushions on the floor with the sunshine streaming in over them, through the large windows. They were playing catch—Samuel's favourite game. For an eighteen-month-old, his coordination was remarkable and each clean catch was rewarded with a little applause from Yindi and a deep chuckle from Sam. Moses and Avril had paused as they walked passed the open double doors to watch the game. They smiled broadly when Sam threw the soft ball a little high and it bounced off Yindi's pert nose. She instantly grabbed him and the laughing pair rolled around the floor.

Avril had squeezed Moses arm and whispered, "She will be a wonderful mother."

Moses had hesitated for a moment, then softly asked, "Has Ralph said something to you I should know about?" to which Avril quickly replied. "No, he has not said anything yet. I think he is waiting for her eighteenth birthday, and for him to finish his studies. After that it will only be a matter of time I do hope. She is perfect for him."

Ralph and Yindi had spent many hours with the native elders and the witch doctor along with many of the peoples of the tribe, who from time to time bought him many priceless fossils, be it plants preserved within some rock, or bones of some animal from the distant past. They did enjoy hearing Ralph tell them what they were; all agreed he was, "some plurry smart cookie."

Ralph's final year's thesis on the nature of the flora and fauna that existed in the Outback in the past millennium was applauded by his lecturers and his co-students alike. His research had been greatly assisted by crawling through long-forgotten and never-before explored caves, which the witchdoctor showed him.

His big regret was he was unable to include any photographs. The natives would not allow him, under any circumstance, to photograph those hundreds of previously unseen and unknown sacred cave paintings. As his mother had surmised, he had resolved on her eighteenth birthday he would ask Yindi to marry him. Yindi did receive his proposal most enthusiastically and during bouts of laughing, crying, giggling and of course kissing and hugging she whispered her acceptance.

Ralph had procured a very fine diamond ring and attempted to slip it on her finger.

Yindi had withdrawn her hand, shouting, "NO"!

"I only wish to show the world how much I love you," Ralph cried.

"Did you make that ring Ralph?" Yindi cried. "And as you made it, did you put your love into the making of it?"

Ralph was greatly perplexed, and replied, "No, Yindi, I did not make it. I bought it from one of Dad's jeweller friends."

She was unmoving and quickly snapped, "That is not good enough; I can have 100 like that and 1000 better. I do love you deeply Ralph, and I will marry you one day, but not before you show the whole world that you truly love me. That ring may be enough for many, but I need something I can see and feel your love bursting from it."

A very nonplussed Ralph discussed the problem with his parents. Avril was particularly perspective, and did say, "She is very wise, is our Yindi; she sees that love does not necessarily flood from a ring unless that ring itself has been made with love and pride and made with such care she can feel that your caring is always with her. For your father's and my sake do not tarry to find the solution, so we can announce the engagement to the world."

That had caused Ralph to think deeply. He took the problem to the elders and the witch doctor, who had quietly said,

"If you seek the answer with honesty and even pain, that answer will come to you in its own time."

The question remained unresolved for over six months and was only partially answered on that day when he and the witch doctor were crawling down a very narrow cave. He was hot and thirsty and had more than once whacked a knee or an elbow on a sharp rock. The witch doctor was slightly ahead had crawled into a small cavern. On the floor of that cavern were several almost perfect fossils of several animals.

"This makes all the effort of getting here well worthwhile. I can see, even at first glance, I have never seen the likes of some of those fossils before," Ralph had excitedly exclaimed.

He examined the fossils for the next half an hour. The witch doctor watched him with great interest as Ralph endeavoured to disturb the fossils as little as possible. There were two fossils that somewhat resembled smaller versions of the Tyrannosaurus Rex. "They are too large to have come down from that cave we just crawled down; there must have been a larger entrance and these two had got themselves trapped by a rock fall that had closed off the other entrance. That merits some further investigation," Ralph thought to himself.

The Witch doctor had picked up what looked to be the forearm of one of those large fossils and had separated a large finger-like piece, which he handed to Ralph. "Here is the answer to your problem," he nonchalantly said.

"What problem are you referring to, my very clever friend, and what exactly do I do with it? It is a fine fossil, but I cannot see what it has to do with any of my problems."

The Witch doctor only smiled and quietly said, "Think on it, Ralph, sir; in its own time it will share its secret with you."

That large finger bone rode in Ralph's collecting sack for some time. The evening had been quite pleasant, Yindi had dined with him and his parents, and he had enjoyed the after-dinner chatting. She had left to return to the apartment she shared with Jack then to go back to Quo-Vadis the following morning. Ralph had showered and prepared for bed when something urged him to take a quick look at the bone. He spent several minutes examining it and was returning it to his collecting sack mumbling discontentedly to the piece of fossil, "When are you going to give up your secret to me? You are nothing but a useless hollow piece of an old bone." It hit him like he had been smashed in the head with half a brick. "Hollow bone! Is that your secret?" he cried. He seized the fossil and examined it even more closely. "Yes," he whispered, "I can see there is one section about sixty millimetres long that appears to be hard and solid. I wonder, if I can use this," he said to himself as he squeezed the section of the bone to test its strength. It gave not one iota. He picked up his treasure and rushed out calling to his parents, "I am going to the workshop; don't wait up for me—I may be a while."

He drove quickly to the workshop and set to work. He cut off a five-millimetre slice from the centre of the firm area of the bone, tested it for strength, then set to shaping and polishing it. For three days and three nights without stopping, except when nature called, he did not eat or sleep in all that time. On the morning of the fourth day the head of the workshop placed a large sandwich and a hot cup of coffee beside Ralph; he acknowledged the action only by looking up at the headman and grunting "Thanks," barely interrupting what he was doing.

"What on earth are you doing?" the headman asked. "You've been at it for days; you look dreadful."

Ralph very carefully picked up the thing which had demanded his attention for all that time, and shouted triumphantly, "It is finished! It is a ring for Yindi; it is infused with my very being."

The workshop head looked at that rather insignificant piece of bone. He was totally confused and rather emphatically said, "That bit of bone has taken you all this . . ." He hesitated as he looked a little closer. "I see it," he softly said, "It almost speaks to me. Ralph! You have created a masterpiece."

Ralph returned home and used the remainder of his day sleeping and allowing his ravaged body to repair itself. Yindi had not heard from her man in the four days he worked on the ring , and fearful her rejection of the diamond ring—although it had happened a while back—had offended him had decided in an endeavour to make amends she would call on him to discuss the matter. "It must have been on his mind for some time," she had thought. "I wonder why it has come up just now. It is most unusual not to hear from him "

Avril, as was the "norm," answered Yindi's knock at the front door of the Stirzicka home and welcomed her warmly. "Ralph is in; he is sleeping," she very softly said. "He came home this morning. He looked dreadful; did you two have an argument?"

"No, not a real argument, Mother," Yindi whispered.

"Mother?" Avril questioned.

"I hope that is all right with you," Yindi replied. "Ralph has asked me to marry him, I have happily said yes, but he still has to show me he truly loves me."

"Ralph has told us of this," Avril almost sadly said. "I do hope he finds a way soon. You are such a beautiful person and are perfect for one another." She gave Yindi a gentle hug and led her into the family area where Moses sat reading.

Ralph had been awakened by Yindi's knock and now staggered into the room. He was unshaven, his tussled hair almost covered his face. He still was still wearing the clothes he had been wearing for the four days he worked in the workshop. As he saw her he shouted loudly, "Yindi, you are here!"

She had laughed, and quietly answered, "Of course I am here, you dill. Do I look like a ghost, and do you smell as bad as you look?"

Ignoring that comment, Ralph fumbled into his pocket and stepped up to her softly whispering, "Yindi, I must ask you again, would you marry me? Would you wear my ring?" He presented the glowing piece of bone to her.

Yindi looked at it for a moment, picked it up from his hand, and slipped it on her finger. She kissed it lightly, whispered oh so softly that Avril and Moses barely heard her as she said; "You have given me your love, from this moment and forever I am yours," and with tears streaming down her cheeks she reached to him, and despite the hair and the smell kissed him most passionately.

With the "loose end" tied up, the engagement was now the cause of much celebration in both the city and at Quo-Vadis. The happy couple returned to the Outback, Ralph to pursue his calling, Yindi to either work alongside him, or to gather more material for her next book on native culture.

One pleasant evening found them by that waterhole that Chris and Jackie had discovered in the mountains many years ago. Earlier that day, Ralph had unearthed a most interesting fossil and they had decided to remain overnight so he could get an early start with his exploration. They had swum in the waterhole, eaten well of the fruit from the trees, and were sitting quietly on their separate bed rolls preparing for sleep. Yindi had stood and walked around the fire to stoke it together. As she passed by Ralph she leaned in, lightly touched him on the shoulder, and kissed him good night. As their lips touched, the inexplicable happened, and the night became a par-excellence of love. As she finally, and rather languidly arose in the morning. Ralph saw a small stain of blood on the bed roll that had lay beneath them.

Yindi saw it too and almost reverently whispered, "You have given me proof of your love in this ring, I have given you proof of my love in that blood.

# Chapter 26

Jackie had kept in contact with several of the classmates she had studied the secretarial course at TAFE College with. She and six of the girls would from time to time meet and share lunch. These girls were closest to being friends she ever had. With her varied past she had never really had much opportunity to form any strong friendships, and on a social level would be considered a loner. Now with Chris and her three children she felt little need for other people in her life and in truth she did not have much spare time. She did find the relationship with Chris fulfilled her every need and she had little need for others. Much had happened in her life since moving in with Chris in the regional city, those many years ago and starting work at the tourist park, meeting Bill and Hector and Hector's daughters, then marrying Hector which was really only a marriage of convenience to give Chris's son Jack, legitimacy, and with the eunuch Hector dying, and her finally marrying Chris to become part of a very beautiful family, her need for others in her life never became an issue. Now with three beautiful children and sharing a very wonderful and satisfying relationship with her very successful miner husband, she did feel her life was complete.

The classmate girls all had stories to tell and would brag or gossip of much of what was going on in their lives, even to the extent of divulging some most risqué secrets. Jackie usually said very little, just maintaining what appeared to be amazed attention.

She and Chris had come to the big smoke at Chris's accountant brother Rex's request. With the complexity of Chris's empire, it was, without a doubt; most beneficial to have somebody with the expertise of Rex and his very large accountancy practice to attend to all Chris's accountancy needs. Rex had contacted Chris to let him know there were several important matters that needed Chris's attention. Normally Jackie would have accompanied Chris whenever he was required to visit Rex. On this occasion, and as those things were of little need for her to be present, she arranged a lunch with the classmate girls. She liked to dress up a bit for these occasions. Her attire this time could not be considered ostentatious although the whole outfit was of the highest quality. She very rarely went anywhere without wearing that nugget of gold—the first piece of gold—she had found in the sinkhole. It hung from her neck on eighteen-carat gold chain, and now was accompanied by that four-carat uncut diamond—the first diamond Chris had found in those mountains. She had nonchalantly slipped on a golden bracelet whose total circumference was studded with varying sized diamonds from Chris's diamond mine. Why he had to call that mine Quo-Vadis Gravel amused her.

She had listened only half attentively to her luncheon companions. One of the more vivacious girls was relating in detail an adulterous affair she was having.

"How could she," Jackie had thought. "I could never even think of being unfaithful to Chris."

It caught Jackie off guard for a moment when that girl had suddenly turned to her, and almost proudly asked, "What do you think of that, Jackie?" and quickly followed that question by saying, "With your looks, Jackie, I bet you have had some fun a few times."

Jackie was shocked and very firmly almost angrily, answered, "No, Stella, I love my husband deeply—he is a wonderful husband and father, also he fulfils my every need. He provides all I need whether I ask for it or not. At times he even anticipates it and provides the need I had only been thinking of."

"You have never told us much of yourself or your life, Jackie," another of the girls quietly said. "This is the first time you have mentioned you have children. Looking at you one would never guess you have children. You have not changed at all, you still look like the seventeen-year-old who graduated from TAFE. How many? Boys or girls? How old are they? You did say once your man had a small goldmine—is it successful? Come on, Jackie," she urged, "it is time you told us about what has happened in your life since college."

Jackie only thought for a moment before Stella interrupted her thoughts, demanding, "Come on Jackie, we are awaiting."

"Very well, but really there is little I can say," Jackie said. "Chris my husband is a very successful man. He has provided me with a beautiful home way out in the Outback."

"The Outback. Isn't that lonely for you?" another of the girls interrupted.

"No, not at all," Jackie replied. "My sister and her husband live nearby on our cattle station, and Bill—he is Chris's right-hand man—and his wife live next door. The children, Jack, Yindi, and even little Sam call them Auntie Ellie and Uncle Bill. Our adopted daughters live with us, and another good friend, Penny, the renowned artist, has her studio nearby. There is a constant stream of interesting people in an out of our tourist resort and any time I wish I can fly almost anywhere. I have my own aeroplane."

The girls were quiet for a full minute, then Stella sarcastically said, "You are telling us a big fat fib; you are just dreaming."

Jackie had become a little angry at that and indignantly snapped, "I do not lie, Stella, everything I have told you is the truth."

Not to be put down, Stella had become very aggressive and snapped, "Well I for one do not believe you."

Jackie had simply reached beneath the neck of the outfit and drew out the pendants of the gold nugget and the diamond. "These are two of my most precious accessories," she softly and quite convincingly whispered. "The gold nugget is the first piece of gold I found in the river that runs nearby to our home, and this is the first diamond Chris found in the basin where he has his diamond mine." She had not finished, and forcibly said as she thrust her wrist forward, "This bracelet is made from gold from one of his five gold mines, and all those stones are diamonds from his diamond mine. Do you believe me now?"

"I am so sorry Jackie," Stella apologised. "I worked in a jewellery shop for a while. Those stones are real; that bracelet must be worth a fortune but you wear it hidden as if it was a very unimportant accessory."

Jackie was still hot under the collar and with contained anger, gently said, "It's quite alright, Stella, so long as you and the girls know I tell the truth is all I ask." She was cooling down but still had something more to say. "As a matter of interest, I have a boxful of other accessories and some very beautiful necklaces all made of gold and diamonds that Chris likes me to wear when we entertain overseas visitors."

"What is the name of your husband's company," another of the girls asked. "I work in the company's office where the government register every company; and have never seen a record of Kennedy Mining."

"You will not find his companies registered under the name of Kennedy. Each of his many companies have the prefix, "Quo-Vadis." His main company is Quo-Vadis Holdings Proprietary Limited. Chris is the sole owner of the holding Company.

"My goodness," that girl almost choked as she said. "I shouldn't say this but that company is worth billions and looking at you more closely I can understand how you can afford an outfit like you have on."

"Thanks, Julie," Jackie responded. "It's one of my favourites. I have a seamstress who makes up my clothes for me."

"Well you can see who lunch is on girls," Stella quipped, "Miss, no, Mrs Moneybags can shout."

Jackie had a genuine tone of regret in her voice as she softly said, "I suppose this put paid to our little lunches; I am sorry for that as I did enjoy meeting with you all."

Another of the girls quickly responded, "No way, I want to hear much more of your life, Jackie Kennedy."

The luncheon ended a short time later and the girls separated to go their own ways but not before dragging a sincere promise from Jackie to keep coming.

Jackie told Chris of what had happened. He laughed long and loud, finally getting to say, "I would have given a bracelet or two just to see their faces. Why don't you send your plane for them and have the next lunch out at Quo-Vadis?"

"That will be too much like bragging," Jackie said.

"It's too late to worry about that now, my love," Chris chuckled. "You have let the cat out of the bag and now you will have to run with it."

Jackie thought for a while then softly said, "It would be nice to have them here. Very well, but keep an eye on Stella, by the sound of things she will have your pants off in a flash."

Chris didn't hesitate, and with a laugh in his voice said, "There is only one girl who will even get a button undone, and you know very well who that is," he wickedly said as he reached for her and started to unbutton her shirt.

Jackie's offer to have the next luncheon at Quo-Vadis was greeted most enthusiastically. The girls' enthusiasm was dampened a little when they were told it would not be the usual brief meeting, and that they would have to make arrangements to be staying at Quo-Vadis for at least a week. They brightened up considerably and their enthusiasm returned when Jackie told them they were expected to bring their partners and children with them, and every expense—travel, meals, their accommodation with even breakfast being delivered, in the very attractive lodges at the Quo-Vadis Resort, plus any other incidental expenses they may incur—were all "on" Jackie. Stella had spoken with the other girls, gleefully telling them that she was at a loose end at the moment and that she is dying to meet this Chris, Jackie so adored.

One of the girls had admonished Stella by saying, "You wouldn't, would you?" leaving it at that.

As it happened the six girls arrived at Quo-Vadis, without partners or children. They had all decided if they were going to have a holiday at a reputed very high-class resort, all expenses paid, they were going to enjoy it to the fullest.

Jackie did smile a little, when she saw them arrive, and very quickly said to Chris, "I am glad I arranged for them all to stay at the Resort; had they stayed in our home I could envisage Stella making some late-night sorties, hoping to find you by yourself."

Stella did seize the chance to get Chris by himself. She had kept a very watchful eye on Chris's comings and goings and when she saw him going alone to the office in the big cave, quickly followed along. Chris was working on the survey of a new rail line, when, without invitation she had just walked in. He had been collecting some pieces which Moses had requested and had left the doors to both vaults wide open. Stella got a good look of what was inside the vaults. "Good God!" she exclaimed, "I do not believe my own eyes. Jackie had told us you were a very successful miner, but she did not mention any of this."

Chris had stood and now was standing with a very aggressive pose before her. "Stella," Chris loudly growled, "I am most concerned you have entered in here without invitation; now I must have the security men take you into custody and I shall lay charges against you for trespass." Poor Stella didn't know what to do or say, and burst into tears, blubbering a plea asking him; "to forgive her indiscretion and promised to never, never ever, mention to anybody what she had seen."

Chris was unrelenting and snarled, "Your promises are worthless. I can see you live a life of deceit and cheating. A term of incarceration may help you come to terms with what you are, and upon your release you may hopefully be a better person."

Unknown to Stella, Jackie was in the diamond vault, selecting some very small gifts she intended to give to the girls before they left. She had stood very quietly listening to Chris admonish Stella and did feel a little sorry for her as she listened to the chastened Stella plead with Chris. Jackie knew very well that Chris was only bluffing; however, his performance was so convincing that she almost believed he would go through with his threats. She was rather surprised when the Chief of Security and two very large security men knocked and entered. With a very firm voice, the Chief enquired of Chris what the nature of his problem was. Chris, with a very angry voice, told the security men of Stella's misdemeanour. The Chief snapped a couple of orders and the two security men had stepped up to Stella and with one on each side, firmly seized an arm and escorted, the uncontrollably crying, Stella from the office.

Immediately they were out of hearing, Jackie turned to Chris and cried, "You won't put her in jail like you said you were going to, will you?"

Somehow all through the episode Chris had managed to keep a straight face. With the security men and Stella out of sight he flopped back into his chair and burst into uncontrollable laughter. "No, my love! You know me better than that," he managed to chortle as he gasped for breath. "I only want to put the fear of the devil into her. She will spend the night in the suite at the resort with those two large security men constantly on guard outside her front door. They would tell her she is in protective custody awaiting Mr Kennedy to formally press charges. Tomorrow morning, you and the other girls can go to her unit and tell her you have all appealed to me not to file charges, and because I'm such a nice man, I have reluctantly agreed to set her free. You will have to recruit the other girls to join you in your subterfuge and fill them in of all that has happened."

Jackie only smiled broadly and softly said, "You are one very rotten, rotten man Christopher Kennedy, but I still love you so very much. All the girls, apart from Stella of course, are going to love this."

Two days later Stella did come to Chris as he and Jackie sat on the patio of their home. "I have come to say thank you, Chris. While I sat in the unit with those two security men guarding me, I got a bit of an insight with what the future held. I came to realise that there was much in my life that was in fact based on cheating and deception. When I go back I will be endeavouring to make an honest attempt to lead a much more worthwhile life." She started to cry a little and turned and left them.

Jackie took Chris's hand and softly rather emotionally said, "Well done my man, I do believe she will try to be a better person."

For the remaining few days of their visit the girls including Stella had a wonderful time. Jackie did have the jewellers in the accessories shop mount those small diamonds she had selected and at a prearranged luncheon in the "Vadis"—the very upmarket restaurant at the Resort—she presented each of her friends with diamond earrings as a memento of their visit to Quo-Vadis.

# Chapter 27

Rex had called Chris and told him they needed to meet and discuss a very disturbing development. Chris and Jackie responded quickly to his request and this morning sat opposite him in his very tastefully decorated office.

"Well, Chris, my filthy-rich brother, who has made me filthy rich as he went on his way, the inconceivable has happened. Late yesterday afternoon we received a writ on your behalf. The writ has been issued in an overseas country by a consortium of very substantial investment companies, claiming that because of your intransigence to list Quo-Vadis Holdings Pty. Ltd, they have been precluded from sharing in the profits of that company for the benefit of their clients. They claim your action is paramount to monopoly trading. Our legal team have great doubt if the writ has any authority in an Aussie court. Somehow the blasted media have got hold of all this and as is the norm for them they will beat it up until something else comes along; in the interim, and to preserve our reputation, it is well worth defending the action. I did contact the news editor and asked him why he considered this newsworthy. He came up with that old well-worn comment. '*The public have a right to know!* He got quite nasty when I told him that after this is over we will sue him and his newspaper for creating a mischief to damage our reputation.

Our legal boys have lodged an intent to defend the case and have made a strong request the matter be heard in an Australian court, and because of the amount involved we have suggested it be heard before the full Bench of the High Court— that could be as many as six judges. A preliminary hearing is set for next week. The writ demands—demands mind you—that Quo-Vadis Holdings Pty. Ltd. list on the stock exchange and have shares available to the public. The corporate boys on our own staff have had a yarn with a couple of red-hot corporate lawyers and they all say it is totally unprecedented and does not have a hope of success. They base their advice on the fact that; "with Quo-Vadis Holdings Pty. Ltd, being a privately-owned company, there is, and never has been a matter anything of its like before in the courts.

"I did try to dampen the enthusiasm of those plaintive companies and have asked that before the matter is heard both the defendant and the plaintiff lodge $1 million with the court by way of security to meet any costs the court awards. I hear although they did balk at that, their security has been lodged. I have lodged ours."

The full bench of the High Court judges listened intently while the plaintiff's lawyers ran through a long list of claims. The legal team from Kennedy and Dixon—Rex's accountancy company—read through the list of claims, and announced to the court those claims were nothing but a mish-mash of nothing concrete, and often quoted non-existent rulings, and did question the demand that the court be advised the value of Quo-Vadis Holdings Pty. Ltd. "We do ask why?"

The learned judges smiled a little when they announced, "We do see knowing the value of the defendant's company at this stage of proceedings has little bearing on the case; however, for our own edification it would be beneficial for the court to know exactly what we are dealing with," and ordered that Quo-Vadis Holdings Pty. Ltd. advise the court of its value. Chris's legal team immediately launched an objection to this, which after three days of what, to Chris, was stupid argument, the judges, all now thoroughly unhappy, simply ordered the objection was not allowed, and ruled that a certified statement by accountants Kennedy and Dixon showing the value of Quo-Vadis Holdings Pty. Ltd. be submitted to the court within twenty-one days.

Rex quickly stood and interjected, "Gentlemen It is impossible to provide that figure as requested. Quo-Vadis Holdings Pty Ltd. is a private company and it is strongly requested that its privacy be respected. To provide that figure, does infringe on that privacy and any ask for any further proceedings be held in camera (behind closed doors)."

"Understood," the Chief Justice said, then addressing the court continued, "This matter will resume at 9.30 am in the morning. Members of the press and the public will not be admitted." That caused a rumble of dissent from the press boxes.

The court convened precisely at 9:30 am the next morning. Rex stood and loudly said, "Gentlemen of the court, I regret I cannot advise the court the true value of the plaintiff's company. There are too many un-assessable assets."

"Impossible," one judge snapped. "What assets cannot be valued?"

Rex produced a thick pile of pages, and confidently said, "I have here a list, and copies for all, of those assets that cannot be valued." He handed that pile of papers to the clerk of the court, who handed a copy to each judge. With spectacles in place, the judges perused the list for about fifteen minutes, often referring a particular item to a neighbour.

Finally, the Chief Justice folded his copy neatly and said, "Mr Kennedy, these lists cannot be believed. Does an un-measurable quantity of diamonds, an unproven reef of gold and pegmatites reef of extra ordinary dimension really exist?"

Rex took a deep breath and quickly replied. "Yes, sir, you can now perceive why we are unable to confirm for you any sort of valuation of Quo-Vadis Holdings. I have spoken with the plaintiff, my brother, who advises me he will be extremely pleased to provide, transport and accommodation at Quo-Vadis for you and your wives for as much time as you require to be able to see for yourselves that all we are saying is correct; and for you to come to an understanding of our conundrum."

The Chief Justice adjourned the case for one hour and the six judges rose to meet in the Chief Justice's rooms. They returned

514

to the courtroom, took their seats while the Chief Justice said, "We agree with what you are saying, Mr Kennedy; we will adjourn this case to reconvene at," he hesitated, "Quo-Vadis. Now tell us how we get to, Quo-Vadis, and how long do you envisage our assessment will take?"

Rex was smiling a little as he replied. "Again, I am at a loss. I cannot answer how long it will take; that is a matter for you honourable gentlemen. As to how to get there, I will leave that to Mr Christopher Kennedy." He was now smiling broadly, then continued with a voice bursting with humour. "He tells me those monster six-trailer cattle trucks are operating day and night and he can load some chairs on an extra trailer and hook it onto one of those units to transport you all out to Quo-Vadis." It will take two days to travel to Quo-Vadis. It is almost one thousand kilometres out into The Outback.

The Chief Justice hesitated for a moment then laughed loudly, "You better be jesting Kennedy."

Rex quickly and lightly replied, "I do jest. A private aircraft will be made available for your exclusive use as early as you wish. I humbly suggest you be prepared for an extended stay. To endeavour to get this matter dealt with quickly, that aircraft will be available to you tomorrow at any time you choose to nominate."

"You did say our women folk were included, sir?" the Chief Justice questioned.

"Yes," Rex quickly replied. "I do believe they will find a holiday at Quo-Vadis Resort will be much to their liking. I do take the liberty and warn you esteemed gentlemen there is much to interest them, and you may find they discover many interesting things they will wish to purchase. I should advise you that all expenses, other than the items your ladies desire to purchase, will be for the attention of Mr Kennedy.

It wasn't until one pm the following day that the judges and their respective, rather-harassed wives bordered the CL300 and were on their way to Quo-Vadis. The good ladies finally sat back to enjoy the ambience of the CL300 that was not before complaining to one another over the indecent haste.

"That husband of mine came home last night and told me to pack a couple of overnight bags as they were off on holidays. Not a word about where we were going and for how long," one of the ladies complained, and quickly added, "Wherever it is, it must be nice. I have never before travelled in such a luxurious and comfortable aeroplane." Her repine was further softened as a steward offered her a long, cold glass of champagne.

"It's a bit better than a chair in a trailer on the cattle truck," one of the judges commented.

The resort staff had been advised of the imminent arrival of these important people, and the moment the CL300 touched down, bags were snatched away by porters and the guests herded into a very comfortable bus to be taken the short distance to the resort. Jamie met them, introduced himself, then led each couple to individual luxury lodges advising them of a few of the features of the resort, and invited them to dine at either of the silver service restaurants. The group agreed to meet at The Vadis at 7 pm. Each couple did take the time to stroll through the manicured gardens and enjoyed the platitude of the resort. They laughed at the antics of several children searching the riverbed for nuggets and were particularly pleased when one small lad triumphantly announced, "I have found one."

The first week passed rather quickly, and it became a regular occurrence for the group to dine together at The Vadis. This evening they sat in the lounge sipping on after-dinner drinks of their choice.

"If this is a sample of the auspiciousness of Quo Vadis Holdings," one of the judges commented, "I am beginning to see Rex Kennedy's problem of trying to ascertain its value; how does one put a price on the contentment this resort alone produces. I may stay a little longer. It is quite obvious that he had spoken truthfully when he had said it was impossible to value the company. The single fact that, should they dump all those diamonds on the market, it would kill the industry, and makes those diamonds either invaluable or worthless. And all that gold in a quartz vein of indeterminable size, add to that acres of pegmatites and an iron ore mine, a cattle station and a massive power generating complex, where would one start or finish?" Their decision to the writ was more or less decided there and then.

While Chris and Bill had chaperoned the judges around Quo-Vadis, Jackie and Susan had walked with the ladies throughout the township and had spent several enjoyable hours happily poking through the shops in the shopping mall. Jackie introduced them to Penny and after confirming that this was the very celebrated Penny Carstairs with all those wonderful paintings displayed in the very best of buildings, those ladies were ecstatic when she invited them to her studio and allowed them to purchase some paintings that had yet to be made available through the regular outlets. A similar thing happened when Jackie took them to the accessories retail outlet. Chris had warned the jeweller that should any of those eminent ladies wish to purchase diamonds they were to be sold to them at the wholesale price of $200 a carat, plus the cost of the mounting. Of course, these ladies knew diamonds, and mayhem reigned.

"My husband bought me a diamond ring with a stone less than half this size. He will die when he sees this ring I have just purchased, at such a very attractive price."

It took a further two weeks before the thoroughly-relaxed group extricated themselves from Quo-Vadis. Chris and Jackie had been the perfect hosts, even to the extent of having them dine with them in their beautiful home. The judges' wives found Jackie to be very pleasant company and oohed and aahed when she took them upstairs to look through her collection of jewellery. Two black diamond pendants did cause much comment.

The court convened two days after the return of the judges. The Chief Justice did not hesitate, and quickly said, "This whole complaint over the Quo-Vadis Holdings Pty. Ltd shares is found to be nothing but a horrendous farce in an endeavour to besmirch the reputation of a very honourable company and panic them into an action which is unprecedented. This court unanimously finds in favour of the defendant Quo-Vadis Holdings Pty Ltd, with all costs of this court having the need to very inconveniently reside at Quo-Vadis Resort for three weeks are awarded to the defendant.

     The plaintiff's solicitor immediately rose and shouted "OBJECTION, we demand a further hearing be held in a court of our choice."

     The Chief Justice, became visibly angry, and very forcibly snapped, "Your objection is denied, and this court will now let it be recorded that any further complaints of this nature against Quo-Vadis Holdings Pty Ltd. all be thrown out even before they reach a court room."

     "Are we all done?" Chris whispered to Rex. "Yes, bro, all done, except you have to work out the cost of having that mob out at Quo-Vadis. Remember you only have $1 million to play with."

# Chapter 28

With that court case behind him, the dynasty of Christopher Kennedy, the miner, was able to continue on its merry way.

Although it has little relationship to mining, the story of Sam (Burnum) is but one part of the dynasty that is worthy of recording in this book. As a boy Sam, wandered unaccompanied throughout the Outback. He had no fear of its vastness and more than once did cause Jackie a level of concern when he went "missing" for days on end. He was a great favourite with the native people as was his sister Yindi and her now husband Ralph. Their wedding had been an enormous affair attended by many people from the University and from Ralph's parent's extensive connections throughout the jewellery industry. Almost without exception, people living in the township of Quo-Vadis all attended. It had been an exercise in logistics, to get all those people from the city to Quo-Vadis and somehow with expertise Vanessa and Jamie had been able to find accommodation for them. The unconventional wedding ceremony and reception was held at the native village and conducted by the pastors from the three churches at Quo-Vadis, with the Witch doctor adding a native flavour to the whole occasion. All those who had attended agreed wholeheartedly it was a marvellous wedding.

It was some weeks later that the ten-year-old Sam walked nonchalantly through the bush. Tracks were for other people. He almost stood on a small black ball of fur that wobbled up to stand defiantly in his way.

"Hello mate," Sam said. "What are you doing here? You look pretty beat. Want a drink?" Sam quickly filled a shallow plate with water and placed it before the pup, who sniffed it for a moment then licked the plate dry. Sam had topped up that plate three times before the pup stopped licking and sat back no longer growling. "Had a rough time, have you young fellow?" Sam asked the pup, not really expecting an answer. At the sound of Sam's voice, the pup appeared to relax a little and Sam softly said, "I bet you are hungry. See if you can eat this?" He had some slices of dried beef in his small sack, and he placed one strip down in front of the pup, who had again sniffed the offering then snatched it up and attempted to chew it. "Too hard for those baby teeth I see, Mister," Sam laughed, so he took out another strip and using that razor-sharp knife he always carried in a sheath on his hip, cut the strip into small pieces that he placed onto the plate and added some water then offered that to the pup who was still battling with that first offering. Again, the pup cautiously sniffed the softened meat then, as if experimenting, licked up one small piece and chewed it to pulp. It must've pleased him for he set to and licked the plate clean. "That's all I have, you have eaten a lot you hungry little buggar." He had heard Uncle Bill use that word often; Mum yelled at him if she ever heard him use it. Sam reached down to attempt to pick the small animal up, thinking to carry it to the native village. "The people there could look after it." The pup seized his outstretched hand and bit hard, drawing blood. "Okay Mister, if that's the way you want it you can have it," Sam snarled as he stood and walked away. The pup gave a little whimper and tried to follow. Sam's long stride soon left the pup far behind.

Early next morning Sam had completed his visit to the native camp and was intending to return home. He was using the same route he had come by. There was no actual track—he only pushed his way through the dry Outback scrub. "Well I'll be a monkey's uncle," he had heard Uncle Bill say that also—he wasn't sure exactly what it meant. The pup, nose to the ground, staggering more or less in his footsteps of yesterday. "I find it hard to believe," he whispered to himself, and asked the pup, not expecting an answer of course, "Are you trying to find me?" Sam again poured some water into his plate which the obviously thirsty animal lapped up quickly. "I do not have any tucker for you mate,"

Sam softly apologised, then still talking softly said, "If you will let me carry you I will take you home and feed you properly." He reached down to pick the pup up, anticipating another nip. Not this time; the pup simply allowed Sam to lift him up and stuff him into his thick shirt. The pup squirmed a little, and appearing to like the warmth of Sam's closeness, settled and in the matter of moments went to sleep. "Poor little bloke he must be completely wacked," Sam thought to himself, then as an afterthought asked himself, "I wonder how Mum and Dad will take it. Dad does not like the wild dogs—he reckons they kill too many calves."

Chris was rather nonplussed when Sam lifted the emancipated bundle from his shirt as he walked into the kitchen. "Whatchya got there, son? Is that a dog?"

Sam quickly and rather defensively replied, "It's only a pup, Dad. He tried to follow me," and related the whole unlikely story, and without taking a breath, asked, "If I promise to look after him and train him, can I keep him?"

Jackie came to Sam's rescue—she knew well his habit of bringing small things home, like that small goanna with a broken leg which his very clever vet brother Jack had splinted and bound. That blasted goanna, now over three-feet long, often scared the daylights out of her, when she unexpectedly came across it sunning itself out on the patio. "You know the deal Sam," she very firmly said, "No animals in the house. You feed it, clean it and clean up after it."

"I can do that," Sam answered enthusiastically.

After three months the pair became inseparable. The pup would lay outside the kitchen door and when Sam appeared he would stand and take station at Sam's left side as he had been trained to do.

One afternoon, the pup without hesitation, dived in and seized a large snake Jackie had not seen as she reached under a bush to retrieve a small empty box that had blown there. The pup had made short work of the reptile as he snatched it up and killed it by biting its head off, before it struck her. Jackie had screamed loudly, which bought Chris running.

When he saw the remains of the reptile on the ground before the pup, all he could say was, "Did the pup kill it?"

Jackie was still in the state of mild shock, and only blurted out, "He killed it even before I saw it. It was rearing up and was about to bite me."

Chris was obviously quite disturbed and only whispered, "That's a King Brown. If that had bitten you it would have easily killed you. Where's Sam?"

Jackie had still not come to terms with what had happened, she had been so frightened; it took a moment for her to answer. "He's inside, he had to go to the toilet. Before he left he had told the dog 'on guard'. His dog thankfully knew exactly what he meant."

Sam had appeared when he perceived what the uproar was all about. He gently patted the pup affectionately and said, "Good boy," and quickly followed that, saying, "I taught him to do that, Dad. I used a piece of old rope and put a knot at one end to train him where to grab a snake. This is the fifth one he has killed; it is by far the biggest."

Chris grabbed the dog by the scruff of the neck and ruffled it affectionately. "You have trained him well, son," he proudly said.

From that day on the pup was allowed in the house. At night he would lay on his mat alongside Sam's bed. He was a perfect gentleman, and the house staff adored him. They had all been very sternly warned, "Do not feed him titbits." Sam suspected from time to time the girls relented. That confounded pup would sit on the floor at the end of the kitchen bench giving them the full benefit of that pitiful doe-eyed, imploring look until a selected slice of something delicious was "accidentally" dropped in front of him. It disappeared in an instant.

Sam often visited the native camp; the dogs there soon learned not to confront the pup, although by now a little over half grown he was much larger than the biggest of them. It was during one of those visits to the Witch doctor, that a rather belligerent young native youth, much older than Sam attempted to intimidate him. The pup instantly stood between the two protagonists, growling a warning to the youth. It was more than I growl—it started deep inside the pup's chest and burst from those bared teeth. The growl sounded much like the rolling thunder from one of those many dry thunderstorms that happened in the Outback.

The Witch doctor had watched the interlude and quietly called to Sam, "Calm your dog, Sam, and bring him here." The witch doctor fearlessly took the pup's head in both hands, looked deep into its eyes and blew softly into its flaring nostrils. "He is called Thunder, Sam boy; his voice says it all."

Thunder accompanied Sam all through his schooling years. Like Sam, he grew to be a giant specimen of his species. Sam, now eighteen years old had grown to a strapping six-foot-seven-inch-tall youth, very good-looking, with Jackie's blonde hair and blue eyes.

Chris's rather colourful description of his son was, "He's built like a bloody Sherman Tank. I think he is a throwback from an earlier generation; his great uncle Troy was built like that."

That black-as-midnight dog Thunder stood on four large feet and measured near three-feet high at the broad shoulders; when he rose up on those powerful hind legs, his massive jaws nearly reached up as tall as Sam.

With his very high academic achievement, Sam's application to enrol at the military academy had readily been accepted. Thunder had had to undergo a very intense military training program before he was enlisted into that special dog squad. Sam excelled in the military academy and soon became highly respected for his leadership and decision-making qualities;

consequently, he progressed rapidly up the ranks. His squad had been appointed to conduct many rather clandestine sorties. This year Captain Samuel Joshua Kennedy and dog recruit Thunder led the special commemorative parade at the National capital. Sam's parents where near to bursting with pride as both man and dog were awarded those special medals for Valour Under Fire. Many of their exploits were recorded in those limited access files, and many men owed their lives to that dog and his master. One particular file had recorded how the man and his dog had led his squad around a carefully placed ambush by a contingent of insurgents. It is not known how many of the enemy died swiftly and quietly from that knife Sam carried or from the slashing teeth of Thunder. Sam and Thunder were sent many times, often unaccompanied, on those special missions, the records of which were kept in Top Secret files. Sam declined any further promotion, saying the level of Captain was far enough up the ladder for him.

Sam wore a good-sized black diamond pendant. The first time he wore it to the native village, it caused an uproar. The witch doctor had stood some thirty feet away and shouted, "You must not wear that, son; within it are the many souls of our forefathers."

After much, at times, heated discussion and because of his immense popularity with the whole tribe, the witch doctor and elders agreed that because that pendant had a special meaning to Sam they would help him. Sam had worn that pendant into battle many times, and his squad believed that that bauble protected them. As a consequence, the squad was called the Black Diamond Squad. The Witch doctor and elders gathered together over 100 like-minded native men and women and for three days and nights they danced chanting around Sam and Thunder. Thunder's thick steel spiked leather collar did have a chip from the same stone that made Sam's pendant fixed in its buckle. On the fourth morning of all that dancing and chanting, that once brilliant black diamond was nothing but a black stone.

"Our forefathers have moved on," the Witchdoctor quietly said, then in no more than a whisper added "You are to be a great warrior, Burnum, but be warned, that as you kill, the souls of those you kill will again gather in that stone and it will once again begin to glow."

Over the years that stone, along with the chip in Thunder's collar, did again begin to glow.

There were many instances in the illustrious career of Captain Sam Kennedy worthy of report. One of those instances was that what occurred at that small country town's Annual Agricultural Show where locals from near and far gathered together to enjoy a couple of days displaying their prize animals, and to watch various amateur sporting events, such as wood chopping, boxing, horseracing and a multitude of others. The interschool sporting competition was extremely popular, and proud parents stood on the sidelines shouting encouragement to their progeny. Women folk would have innumerable items of the like of knitted garments, crocheted throw overs and many more, diligently sewn over the previous year for sale. The home-made cakes stalls were very popular. Many people wandered through the dog and cat pavilions. It was a time of wonderful community.

Sam with Thunder at his side would contentedly wander through these shows, as did, at times, several thousand people. This year a news-seeking television station, who had heard that this annual event in this country town had a very special atmosphere and had sent a crew to collect a short news clip that could be used as a fill-in if and when they had the need to add something of a pleasant interest to their evening news.

Sam had attended this show in two previous years, and as he had a few days leave available, he had decided to again spend them at that show. All was proceeding as normal. Sam had just acquired a large cream cake, which he was endeavouring to consume without getting too much cream all over his face. Thunder had managed to cadge a slice of chocolate cake from one of the stall holder ladies by allowing her young child to ride briefly on his broad back.

Without warning, four battered utilities ploughed into the crowd, injuring many. As the utilities roared to a stop, men with faces covered and loose robes flying about them bounded out and started blasting indiscriminately into the crowd with automatic rifles. In an instant, what had been that quiet young gentleman, and his fine-looking dog, flew into action. Thunder moved like lightning and in less than a minute one of those men lay dying, his throat ripped away. Sam's hard flashing hand had smashed open the skull of another. Moving so very quickly, Sam swept up the dropped automatic weapon and with great accuracy blasted accurately into the milling assassins. Four of them died with that first burst. The others seeing the fate of their companions turned on Sam and poured round after round at him. Sam moved like shaken silk, and several bullets only nicked his arms and shoulders. Thunder was in their midst; he wreaked havoc amongst them. They could not fire on him for fear of hitting one of their companions. Now five assassins lay dead or dying in Thunder's wake. Those ugly assailants had had enough. Of the twenty who had attacked, only three remained standing. They threw down their weapons and in panic raced toward one of the abandoned utilities, only to have their way barred by that shining black very angry dog. They fell to the ground screaming "Mercy, Mercy!" That was ignored as man and dog continued to complete their carnage.

Sam placed an arm over the growling dog to calm him. Thunder calmed and only licked Sam's cheek as if to say, "I'm okay now," then lay at his master's side.

Sam realised he had taken a slug in his right shoulder and was bleeding profusely. Two policemen, with their revolvers waving rushed up shouting, "Down on the ground you bastard, hands on your head, and don't move."

"Wake up, you silly beggars, I'm on your side," Sam snapped. "I need a doc. Is there one about?"

The doctor, one of three who had been attending the show, came to him about five minutes later. The three doctors were very busy. Thirty-two innocent people had died, and at least 100 others were injured to some degree. The doctor apologised to Sam saying, "I should have attended to you first, I saw it all—your incredible action saved many; we owe you and your dog much." A TV cameraman moved in and started to film. With a discrete movement of Sam's hand, the camera was ripped from the cameraman's arms by that black mountain of muscle. The cameraman attempted to wrestle his camera from that dog, only to give up when he saw there was little to retrieve. It had been smashed beyond recognition by those massive bloodstained jaws. The news reports that night commenced with a breaking news story of how hundreds were killed, and over 500 people attending the show had been critically injured in a raid of terror on a peaceful country town, and how one man and his dog had prevented many more victims by stopping the raid and killing over 100 terrorists.

"It was only about twenty," Sam defensively said to the nurse who attended him as he lay in a hospital. "I didn't think there were that many people killed and injured; the whole story is a gross exaggeration."

There was some long-distance film of Sam and Thunder at work, nothing close enough to enable identification. The news report had continued, "The man who had courageously fought to prevent further slaughter has not been identified; it is believed he and his dog gave their lives to save many."

"That suits me fine," Sam laughed. He wanted no kudos, and actually believed he should have acted earlier. The hospital staff attempted to restrain Thunder from Sam's bedside but had given up after Thunder, who had been locked outside the front door, simply chewed a hole large enough to enable him to simply walk in, leaving that front door in shambles.

When it became known Sam was in hospital recovering, news reporters hovered about the hospital precinct like sea gulls around a potato chip, seeking to be the first to interview that hero. Their wait was in vain, as Sam and Thunder slipped past them like wisps of smoke.

One thing that did come out of all this, was that Sam had met that very tall, registered nurse, Nancy. Nancy was a real country girl. Born and reared on a small dairy farm about five kilometres outside the country town. She was most attractive, her tall slimness—she was near six-foot-three tall—accentuated her well put together attributes. Because of her being so tall she lacked committed suitors.

Sam was strongly attracted to her. Now at the age of twenty-five, Nancy had more or less accepted that she would most probably end up a crabby old spinster. The attention she received from this hero had flattered her and she found herself gathered up into the whirlwind existence of the Kennedy's and the life of being an army wife.

Sam and Nancy had married eight months after the initial meeting. Nancy quickly became a part of the family, loved and respected by all. Sam of course had many long absences on military service. Nancy used those absences to take a nursing position at the new Quo-Vadis hospital. Her experience proved invaluable. One of her greatest joys was to visit the native village where in early course she set up a nursing post. Even the Witch doctor became a regular visitor, most often just to have a chat.

That major devastation in her life and the life of all at Quo-Vadis occurred two years after their marriage.

A military jet landed at the Quo-Vadis airport. Four high-ranking military officers disembarked and asked of the whereabouts of Mr Christopher Kennedy. They were taken to the elevator in the Animal Cave and given entry into the sinkhole. Chris was working in his office in the house. Jackie answered the door-knock. She had a sense of apprehension as she opened the door, and when asked, "Mrs Kennedy?" only answered, "Yes," then remembering her manners, invited them in, and asked, "What can I do for you?" Before they could answer, Jackie said, "I will get my husband," and ushered them into the large lounge room. She immediately sent one of the girls to get Chris.

"You have a beautiful home, Mrs Kennedy. One does not expect to see homes like this out here," one officer commented. Chris arrived, and the officers all introduced themselves. He was very concerned, and quietly said, "By your rank, gentleman, I do not think this is a social visit. What is the reason for your call?"

The officer, bearing the insignia of Field Marshal, took a deep breath, and reverently said, "Mr and Mrs Kennedy, we regret to have to advise you that Captain Samuel Kennedy and his dog Thunder have both died in the service of their country. We are not at liberty to divulge where and when this occurred. We can tell you that they died saving a large number of our soldiers. The death of both him and his dog was an act of extreme bravery and a display of unequalled courage."

"Oh no", Jackie cried. "This surely cannot be right."

The Field Marshal gently took both her hands and said, "It is so; he was the bravest of men and his death is a great loss to not only us personally but to the whole country."

Jackie let out a soft sob and collapsed onto Chris's shoulder.

"How did he die?" Chris softly asked. "Did he die painfully?"

The Field Marshal glanced quickly at the other officers, then rather hesitantly said, "Regretfully I cannot answer that; he was leading a very special secret mission. It was recorded it was his wish that should he ever be killed in service that his remains were to be bought to Quo-Vadis, his home. We would desire to have him interred with full military honours. We have been unable to contact his wife; do you know where we may find her?"

Chris thought for a moment, as if trying to get his brain to focus, then answered, "She is out in the Outback with Sam's sister, Yindi, and her husband Ralph. I will send a man for her."

The subsequent funeral was, regardless of the wishes of the military, only a small family affair. There was only a gentle breeze blowing that day as Sam's ashes were cast into that breeze to be spread across the Outback. Thunder's ashes followed immediately. The whole native tribe had softly chanted as Sam's and Thunder's spirits were cast into the care of the Dreamtime.
It was many months before laughter was again heard at Quo-Vadis.

Nancy had been devastated by Sam's passing. She had come to Jackie one sunny afternoon, to softly tell her, "Mother Jackie, I am slowly coming to terms with his passing. It is not fair!" She exclaimed, "I had not even had a chance to tell him he was to be a father."

Jackie had reached to her and hugged her tightly, saying, "You are family, Nancy. You and your child must always remember that, and that there is a special place in our hearts for both of you. We will rejoice with you as we share Sam's child."

# Chapter 29

Jack had come home. He was restless at being at such a loose end. He had had enough of Uni, having completed a mining engineer's degree, with honours, graduated from the political science course, practised for a short while as a veterinary surgeon in the provincial city and studied business administration under the guidance of his uncle Rex; he now longed to be home, not so much from homesickness but he was like his father, drawn to the earth of the Outback, and what was hidden in its secrets. His greatest pleasure was to work alongside Chris and Bill as they went about their daily activities of supervising and administrating all the activities of the group. When Chris ventured out on an exploratory mission, Jack's questions were never-ending. He had to be edified exactly why and how Chris had identified that exact spot where the next hole should be drilled to investigate what was down there, be it they were searching for the continuation of the quartz reef, the depth and quality of the pegmatites deposit, or for water to satisfy the needs of the ever-growing herds of cattle from the station. It gave him great satisfaction when the majority of those holes confirmed exactly what Chris had sought. Chris was without peer and his identification of the presence of whatever they sought was generally successful. Jack absorbed everything Chris said, and had the greatest of satisfaction when the drill cores revealed from the holes he had selected; and he had been right with his selection of drill hole positions. It was with the greatest confidence Chris did put him to work to re-establish the deserted mine of his stepsister and her deceased husband Allan. Chris had eventually bought the lease and mine from Susie.

The price he had offered had been refused by Susie. "It is far too much," she had said. "I would not know what to do with all that money." Chris had finally got her to agree to settle by transferring two B-class shares in Quo-Vadis Holdings to her.

Those shares returned her around $2 million per annum. Using all his expertise, and replacing much of the equipment at the mine, Jack soon had that mine operational and contributing to the profits of the Holding Company.

"More money to find a home for," Rex had wailed. "As if the problems your old man created for me were not enough," he laughed, "now the son is getting in on the act."

To Chris's delight, Jack took an avid interest in the administration activities of the group and was insistent that Chris involved him with the renegotiation of various contracts when they came up for review. Jack had a sharp mind, and the renewed contracts were always successfully negotiated to the satisfaction of all parties. Chris had sat in on these meetings at first; as time progressed, he would have Jack go it alone.

This was the case when the spodumene contract with that Japanese consortium came up for renewal. Both Chris and Bill had been pre-occupied with the installation of some new equipment at the iron ore mines and had "suggested" to Jack, it would be most helpful if he would travel to Japan and renegotiate that contract with the Japan Lithium Corporation. Jack had studied the file in depth and had become most conversant with what was involved. While at University he had made friends with several of the Japanese students. He had found it most amusing his attempt to teach them some English; now the shoe was on the other foot and he asked them to help him with the Japanese language. There were a few months before the contract was actually due for renegotiation, and Jack set about, with great diligence, to learn that difficult language. He achieved a good level of competence and could conduct a reasonable conversation with his Japanese friends in their own language. He now felt he could approach the renegotiation of the contract with good confidence. Chris had suggested Jack take a Japanese interpreter with him, as Chris had needed to do in the past as he negotiated the original contract.

Jack's friends had disagreed with this, and had advised Jack, "It was much better form to be seen as being one who understood the Japanese people and their language." Jack declined Chris's suggestion. The shipping manifests all showed Jack that every delivery to Japan Lithium had been on schedule and the shipments had increased over the past year. Quo-Vadis Lithium were presently shipping 400,000 tonnes of spodumene concentrate per annum to them. There were several requests by Japan Lithium on file to increase the size of those shipments. This was to be the main thrust of the renegotiation.

Bill had laughed when he was made aware of those requests. "Who do we look after first, fellas? The British Company has made the same request." Bill had heard on the grapevine that the quality of the concentrate Quo-Vadis Lithium produced was superior in quality, and the yield of Lithium by volume was most attractive.

Jack found he had to travel to Japan by an international airline, as the private aircraft of the Quo-Vadis group could not fly that distance without refuelling. Rather than go through the hassle of having to organise refuelling points, Jack did decide to use the international commercial carrier. As was natural, he was seated in the first-class section of that aircraft. Much to his delight, the co-traveller seated alongside him was a most attractive Japanese lass. His attempt to open any conversation with her was met with obvious reluctance and he gave up. He had the impression she would have liked to have been a little friendlier but was inhibited by Japanese old-fashioned protocol. She was obviously a girl from a family of high status, and it was not the done thing to befriend strangers on aeroplane flights.

She did appear to take a little more interest and did try not to be seen to be rude as she surreptitiously took more than one peek at the file Jack had opened and was studying. It was the file that contained the correct names and pronunciation of the senior executives of Japan Lithium.

As they disembarked, he quietly and politely asked could she tell him where the private limousines could be found awaiting? She had squashed any chance of friendship by replying in excellent English, "There are stewards in the airport who are there to assist people like you."

At twenty- four-years of age, Jack was a very fine figure of a man, having all the features of his father: tall, untidy mop of black hair, clear brown eyes, very well built, and softly spoken. He had never found it difficult to attract the attention of the opposite sex, and thought to himself, "She must be coming straight from Antarctica."

He didn't have any commitment for the rest of the day and decided to look up the family of one of his University friends. It was a good decision and he had a most pleasant evening after being invited to their home. They had heard a great deal from their son about this Jack Kennedy and it pleased them immensely to meet him in person and to hear first-hand, news of the life their son experienced at University.

Next morning, he walked into the offices of Japan Lithium at exactly 10 am as had been arranged and was, without delay, ushered into the office of the owner of the company, Takeda Hiedo who welcomed him most congenially, saying, "It is most refreshing to have a visitor from a Western country who is so punctual. I have asked some of my people who you will be talking with to join us; they will be here shortly," then without taking a breath, he enquired after the health and well-being of Chris and Bill.

"They are both well," Jack politely replied. "They must have great confidence in you to allow one so young to negotiate the company's contracts," Takeda commented.

"This is the first time I have been sent to negotiate the renewal of a contract, of such major importance sir." Jack replied, "Both Bill and my dad are heavily involved in the installation of new machinery in one of our new mines. They did ask me to convey their apologies for not being available."

Takeda had immediately thought to himself, "This is an excellent development, this young man is very inexperienced with matters such as we have to discuss today. I must take maximum advantage of his lack of knowledge. I would like to have him to commit to an increase in the tonnage they supply and to have him agree with that increased tonnage, their profits will be greater and they will have a margin where they could reduce their material cost to us. The price we are presently paying them is 15% lower than what we have to pay our other suppliers and with their product being of substantially better quality these terms will be definitely to our advantage."

Over the ensuing two days, Jack and Takeda's assistants covered most of the points of the contract. Takeda had sat in on all those discussions and in the course of that short time had developed a strong liking for this forthright and honest lad, to such a point that he invited Jack to dine with him and his family that night in his home. His friends at University had told him to be invited into a man's home was a great honour and did show he who was invited was greatly respected.

Surprisingly to Jack, Takeda did commence to talk about his family. "I only have one child," he told Jack, "A daughter, much to my regret. I will have to wait for a grandson to carry on my business. Are you the first son of Mr Chris?"

Jack was very surprised that Takeda was being so forthright but didn't hesitate to answer. "Yes, sir, I am the first son. I do have a younger sister who writes books on native culture. She and her husband, who is a graduate palaeontologist, spend much time with the natives exploring the Outback where we live, searching for ancient relics. I have a brother who is a highly decorated senior officer in the Army.

"You sound a most interesting family," Takeda commented. "I would like to hear much more. I will send a car for you at seven. It is a short drive—my home is in the country."

Jack did make an urgent telephone call to one of his Japanese friends at the University. He had to try and learn the protocol surrounding dining in a very traditional Japanese home. After a one-hour conversation, Jack's only thought was, "I hope I do not make too many blunders." He was further surprised when the car that had been provided for him drove through several acres of manicured gardens and halted in front of a very beautiful Western-style home. His surprise continued as a butler met him at the door and escorted him into the house. As they passed what was obviously the dining room he quickly looked in expecting to see the Japanese dining mats and cushions his friends had told him of. Instead the dining room was set up Western-style with a precisely laid formal dining setting.

The butler led him into what was more or less the family area. Takeda sat talking to a fine-looking Japanese lady and a young girl. Takeda welcomed him and introduced him to his wife, Yaka, and had turned to the girl saying, "Daughter, please meet Mr Jack Kennedy. Jack this is Yushiko, the joy of my life."

The girl stood and turned to Jack, she recognised him instantly. "You," she whispered in a very confused voice.

"You have met?" Takeda asked in an equally confused voice. "We have, sir," Jack answered, "We sat together on the flight coming here." Then most gallantly added, "How pleasant it is to meet you again, Miss Takeda. I do hope I did not offend you at the time of our previous meeting."

Yoshiko only gently laughed. To Jack her laughter was like the sound of a bubbling creek, as she answered. "No, Mr Kennedy, you did not offend me. In truth, it was I who could be accused of being rude. In that instant, Jack was smitten. For the first time he got a good look at her. Tall, much taller than the average Japanese girl, with hair as black as midnight that shone so beautifully it appeared to reflect the light from the many ceiling lights, and two black orbs that look steadily at him from a face of perfect proportions and a soft creamy complexion.

What had he been taught? Look, but do not touch, the greatest compliment he could pay a girl was to admire her with his eyes and respectful actions.

Yaka recognised the silent signals flashing between the two- young people and promptly said, "Perhaps we can all take a walk in the garden. Jack, you would have to forgive me if I exhibit a great pride in it."

Jack remembered little of the walk in the garden, and dinner afterwards; all he could remember were those two large soft eyes that never seemed to leave his face. He did manage to carry a good share of the dinner conversation, telling the Takeda family a little of himself, and his academic achievements, and discussing a multitude of subjects.

As Takeda and his wife prepared to retire that night, Heido (that was his first name, Takeda was the equivalent to a surname in Western culture) had said to her, "Young Jack is a fine stamp of a young man."

Yaka had smiled to herself and only answered, "Yes."

Jack met with Takeda the next morning; he was intending to windup negotiations quickly and to return to Quo-Vadis, without delay, where he believed he could shake off this feeling of hopelessness, happiness, elation, call it what you like—that girl had taken over his mind.

In a most surreptitious way, Takeda introduced those controversial points he believed were to his company's benefit, that, because of Jack's inexperience were going to be relatively easy to have Jack to agree to. To his great surprise, Takeda found that quietly spoken impressive young gentleman to be a formidable negotiator and had to concede not only those matters he had thought were a foregone conclusion, but several other points the previous contract and not covered that were not exactly to the benefit of Japan Lithium Corporation.

A further surprise came when the meeting had concluded and only Takeda and Jack remained in the office. Jack, boldly, before he had a chance to chicken out, said, "With your permission, sir, I wish to court Yoshiko, if she will agree to my courtship."

For the first time in his life that very successful businessman was struck for words, but after a slight hesitation, he softly said, "You are certainly full of surprises, young fellow: first of all, you run circles around me at the negotiating table, and now you tell me you want to steal my daughter from me too." He had managed to recover himself, and in his normal very powerful way continued. "Jack, it is good you adhere to the old ways and have asked for her. Generally, these days, young ones only move in together, without regard of the parents or their wishes. Since you have very correctly asked, I must reply in a like fashion. I have no objection to you courting Yoshiko. All I have to say is, be well warned: she is a headstrong young lady and will make up her own mind whether or not she agrees to your courtship."

Jack was much relieved, and quickly said. "Thank you, sir, I will take my chances with that. She will find I am not one to be deterred or turned aside lightly. Do you have her mobile telephone number?"

Takeda burst out laughing, and loudly chuckled, "By the great dragon, you are really something else, Jack Kennedy. Not only have you given me a good beating this morning, now you are going to draw me into the conspiracy. No!" he exclaimed. "Find out her number yourself; then laughed a little as he said, I will assist you a little; she works at that solicitor's office three blocks down and finishes work at 3 pm. If you hurry you may catch her before she leaves for the day. It will be most interesting to see her reaction and if she accepts your request to be allowed to court her, and she gives you her telephone number."

Jack did manage to waylay Yoshiko as she walked from the solicitor's office, and she did accept his invitation to join him to grab a quick cup of coffee at a nearby coffee shop. She did not hesitate to accede to his request to give him her telephone number or agree to having dinner with him that evening. In the ensuing months, both Jack and Yoshiko did accumulate a big number of frequent flyer points before Jack took matters in hand and organised a refuelling point for his private aeroplane.

Both sets of parents watched with humorous interest as the Jack and Yoshiko's relationship developed. Yoshiko had been warmly welcomed into the Kennedy clan. The Takeda family, was small and   the family interaction was generally only on formal occasions; other than a few friends from the solicitor's office, she had a very insulated life. To have an extended family as complete as the Kennedys and close associates who were all treated as family, gave her a sense of wonderful pleasure.

One evening as fifteen of the "mob" sat at the dinner table, Chris had laughed heartily and more or less addressing Yoshiko had laughed, "I sent him," indicating who he meant as he pointed to Jack, "on a simple errand to renegotiate a contract, and what does he do? He comes back not only with an improved contract and the real bonus of this beautiful young woman. As head of the Kennedy clan I say, Welcome Yoshiko."

Yoshiko humbly and quietly replied, "Thank you, Mr Kennedy."

Jackie, who was seated next to Yoshiko, gently took her hand and said softly, "I too offer my heartfelt welcome, Yoshiko. Did you know in the language of our native friends, you are a sister to Yindi? She is known as the Daughter of the Sunbeam, and in your own language your name means Child of the Sun."

It was over five months into the courtship before Jack kissed Yoshiko. As she regained her shattered composure, she whispered softly "It's about time! Now get to work, you have much to catch up on."

Arrangements were made for Takeda Hiedo and Takeda Yaka, Yoshiko's parents, to visit Quo-Vadis. The Japanese businessman was gobsmacked by all that was Quo-Vadis. His first real statement was, "I thought he was only a son of a successful spodumene miner, now I see I am only a poor lithium producer compared to what he is."

They had stayed with Chris and Jackie for over a month and had become strong friends. Hiedo, ever the businessman, recognised a marvellous business opportunity, and sat with Chris and Moses, discussing the possibility of extending Moses's diamond distributing activities into Japan. He could see that the partnership with Chris supplying high-quality pieces, Moses, with his great knowledge of diamonds, and his own knowledge of the Japanese market it would be a most beneficial venture for them. The whole idea appealed greatly Chris, and in very short time, Moses was sending prepared diamond pieces to Japan. Their needs barely made a dent in Chris's hoard.

It took a relatively short time before the jewellery retailers were purchasing a volume of "stones" from Hiedo. Chris had asked Moses to cut and mount a couple of good-sized black stones and send them to Hiedo. The stones when mounted were a matched pair. They were 1.7 and 1.71 carats respectively. Hiedo had a large order to deliver to a jewellery retailer who controlled many jewellery outlets. After completing the usual delivery formalities, which were always conducted in a very secure out of the way office, Hiedo had produced the two black diamond pieces and nonchalantly asked, "Do you think you could sell these?"

The store owner, who always conducted the delivery formalities, had stood perplexed for about thirty seconds then whispered, "Black diamonds, how much?"

Chris and Moses had given Hiedo a mutually agreed upon price of AUS $1 million each. The price did not appear to shock the jeweller one bit as he quickly said, "Settlement in fourteen days." Hiedo knew the jeweller very well as a most honest man and agreed, adding several stringent conditions all relating to security and insurance.

Hiedo had only been back into his office less than ten minutes when the jeweller telephoned him. There was none of the usual greeting or small talk only an excited jeweller saying, "Hiedo, do you have any more of those black pieces? I have sold those two within half an hour of putting them out in our secure display cabinet. They sold for $1.8 million each. I have already received calls from four of the friends of those people who had purchased those pieces, asking do I have any more of those black diamonds for sale."

"We must take care here, Hiedo," Chris counselled. "We must not flood the market. I suggest we make only two or three small pieces available and perhaps take orders from anyone who wishes to purchase a black stone and advise them that availability is very limited. In this way, we will maintain the value of black stones."

Hiedo only laughed and said, "HA! I see where young Jack got his negotiating skills from."

The jewellery distribution business of that intrepid trio was most successful. As mining the stones cost him virtually nothing, Chris was happy to supply uncut pieces to their little consortium at a wholesale price of $200 per carat. Moses doubled the price after adding cutting and mounting costs, and Hiedo doubled the price to the retailers who were now able to retail pieces at very attractive prices.

Those two black diamond pieces did return the group a nice little profit of $1.2 million per stone or $400,000 each.

"Struth," Rex had cried, "Please stop bro, my office has only managed recently to place last year's profit, and now you do this to me. How much per annum can you envisage your little game will return? By the sound of things, I will have to increase the annual dividend. Your B-class share-holders have all been complaining about their tax liability; this will not help one little bit.

It was one of those evenings when the Outback sunset was at its spectacular best. Yoshiko was visiting Quo-Vadis and Jack had arranged for them to dine at *The Vadis;* that silver service restaurant situated on the shore of the lake at the resort. He had parked the car and they were strolling casually through the beautiful garden on their way to the restaurant, when Jack softly suggested, with it being such a beautiful evening and the sunset as it reflected from the waters of the lake was just so special they should take a few minutes and sit by the lake and enjoy that magnificent display nature provided. As they sat there the reflection of the setting sun off the lake shone onto Yoshiko's beautiful face. Jack knew the moment was perfect and knelt down before her and so very softly whispered: Yoshiko, Yoshiko; you are so beautiful and I love you so very much—Will you marry me.
Yoshiko only took a deep breath, she said nothing for about fifteen seconds, then knelt beside him and softly said—Yes Jack; I will marry you. I have been wanting to tell you this for such a long time, then   gently reached to him and enfolded him in her arms and kissed his lips.
The sun had set before the glowing, very happy couple made their way to the restaurant.

Both sets of parents were ecstatic when Jack told them Yoshiko had readily accepted his proposal. The actual wedding did take place twice. The first was at Quo-Vadis, under those beautiful shady trees on the patio in the sinkhole. It was an elaborate affair with over 1000 guests attending. Chris had laughed as he said to Jackie, "These things are getting bigger and bigger, I suppose Yindi will be next.

The second ceremony was in Yoshiko's hometown, a small village set in the mountains some 150 kilometres from the city. It too was a large affair conducted in the very traditional Japanese way. Jackie and Chris, of course, had travelled to Japan for that wedding.

Jackie had quietly spoken to Chris at the end of the ceremony saying, "That was very beautiful, and full of wonderful meaning."

Heido was not at all pleased when told by Jack, the couple will be living at Quo-Vadis. Jack explained the reason for this decision was that he had become more and more responsible for much of the operation of Quo-Vadis Holdings and needed to spend much of his time with Bill, uncle Rex and his Dad being instructed and learning the intricacies of operating an enterprise of the size of that vast and complex mining empire.

Another very beautiful Giuseppe-built house was added to the homes in the sinkhole. The house did have a beautiful wing attached, which was reserved exclusively for her parents use. Chris did make the latest model private jet available for their use if and when they chose to visit. The frequency of those visits increased after the happy couple took the greatest of pleasure in advising Hiedo, Yaka, Chris, and Jackie four months after the wedding that they could confidently tell them, that ultrasound scans had confirmed that their grandson was on the way. These days, Jack was totally involved in the running of Quo-Vadis Holdings with Chris and Bill, and Yoshiko was finding great pleasure with being gainfully engaged in assisting Vanessa and Jamie in the operation of the tourist park and the resort, particularly since there had been a big influx of Japanese tourists who had been influenced by Hiedo talking enthusiastically to his many business contacts about Quo-Vadis Resort and the Outback. Both Five Star hotels enjoyed substantial occupancy. Even business people in the regional city were enraptured with the numbers of Japanese visitors passing through and staying overnight or sometimes for several days as they enjoyed much of the entertainment and learning the history of that regional city. The fact that those visitors spent quite liberally added to the business people's approval.

Peter, the husband of Jackie's sister, Isobel (Izzy), had shown himself to be more than just a very good station manager. His knowledge of cattle, although the majority of the immense herds of Quo-Vadis Station in the early days of its development, since being purchased by Chris, were in the main, thousands of those unending numbers of scrub cattle driven from the National Park, at the request, and with the blessing of the Park Rangers. Peter had used his unique experience to husband those beasts, and with Chris's ability to drill for, and find much water, Peter had created many thousands of acres of lush pasture. Those, once emaciated, vermin-riddled animals, rejected by the cattle buyers, had become prime specimens and were highly sought after.

Peter had become intrigued with Chris's connection and access to all that wonderful information either known or being researched into by the University. He did invite twenty-two students enrolled in their final year of their studies to obtain a degree as Bachelor of Science; to Quo-Vadis Station. Several of those students were pursuing studies that they may add, BSC in Agriculture to their degree. They were impressed with how and what Peter was doing and asked him many questions. From his years of experience, he was able to answer their questions to their satisfaction. Once again, the evening campfire discussions were a highlight and the interaction was most edifying to all.

One of the students, a rather quiet and less outspoken lad, had approached Peter and humbly said, "Mr Peter, I have found this to be a special place, laugh if you must, but I feel the land has spoken to me." He hesitated, "I feel strongly it wants to share its secrets with me."

Peter had been watching this lad and had been very impressed with his approach to his studies and replied to him. "I will not laugh, I know just how you feel. All you have seen here has been bought about by people who love this wonderful land, most of all by Mr Kennedy, who loves this land with a passion and in return the land loves him and reveals to him so very much."

The young man had listened carefully to what Peter was saying, then said, rather softly but with strong conviction, "Do you think when I finish my studies, you would have a permanent position for me here. I have been given a vision of what this place can be made into, and with that knowledge I have acquired at University, coupled with your great experience, and with that unique power of Mr Kennedy, we could bring forth that vision. It will require much time and patience, and probably much money, but I promise you in the years ahead the rewards will be immeasurable. I will not ask for a huge salary, only enough to keep body and soul together."

Peter had not hesitated to employ the lad who graduated that year as a Bachelor of Science in Agriculture and Forestry.

That student, Mr Graham Aldridge, became part of the crew at Quo-Vadis Station. The native stockmen gave him great respect, for they knew he loved the land and it spoke to him. Over the ensuing years and with the productive use of his time and access, to his amazement, to what appeared to be limitless money, he and Peter turned the Outback acres of the station into a highly productive beautiful land.

At first, Graham did have his failures. With much perseverance and application of his scientific knowledge; it was some time and after many of his experiments, using seed that had been found to be suitable for planting in dry soils, that he had used his knowledge to modify; before he did produce a grain most suitable, only as stock feed. His efforts to produce a grain, suitable for milling, had not been at all successful; still he persisted.

Peter had travelled with him every inch of the road he took and applauded his successes and failures. The erstwhile compatriots in these activities, Chris, Graham, and Peter would often sit on the edge of an undeveloped section of the grazing lease, discussing just what could be done with it, after which Chris and Bill would walk all over that land. The priority was to find water and if it was there, they soon located it. They were never deterred should their investigation be fruitless, and Chris would very quickly run water from some adjacent water source, and Graham soon had that once desolate area green and lush.

Peter had acquired some prize bulls, the cost of those animals, surprised all.

Rex had laughed when shown the invoices, saying, "I can always rely on that mob out there to find a new way to spend money." That very clever cattleman had now bred a breed of cattle the meat of which was almost fought over by the cattle buyers. "Oh well," Rex sighed, "You win some, you lose some."

Needless to say, the Quo-Vadis Station had become a unique oasis in the vastness of the Outback and a rolling green jewel in the empire known as Quo-Vadis. The Kennedy family often came together on formal or even impromptu occasions. Peter and his family more so than others were regular visitors to Quo-Vadis. On the most recent occasion, Izzy, Peter's wife, had told Jackie she was going to need some help to accommodate the whole of Peter's American family who were travelling to Quo-Vadis for a long overdue visit.

"How many?" Jackie asked. "We can have some here at Quo-Vadis, if it would help."

"There are many more than you think," Izzy had replied with a note of desperation in her voice. There's Peter's parents, five brothers and their wives, and goodness knows how many children. Then I hear there are several of his cousins and their families coming too."

"Send the whole lot to town, and book them into the hotel. I'll shout, so they will not have to pay a thing for their accommodation," Chris generously offered. "Perhaps Peter's mum and dad, could stay at the station with you."

Izzy hadn't quite finished, and added, "There may be more than we first thought. I think there are a couple of Peter's aunts and uncles talking of coming also. Peter has been talking to his mother using Skype; I know, over the years he sent her many pictures of scenes of places about the station and the Outback. I think his mother has sent copies to everybody." Izzy laughed as she poked Peter in the ribs, and said, good-heartedly, "It's all his fault."

"When are they coming?" Jackie asked.

"I think they want to be here for Christmas," Izzy replied. "How wonderful," Jackie jubilantly shouted. "The whole Kennedy family are coming here for Christmas dinner; now we can make it a real big Christmas occasion."

"I am not going to have you girls burdened down with all this," Chris in his indomitable way told them. "I'll get the mess hall in the cavern set up; that hall can easily accommodate a lot. There is a very good caterer in town; if I book him now we can have him bring his whole operation out here for a few days. That will relieve you girls of most of the work and be free to enjoy yourselves. Everybody can pitch in, even all the kids can have fun decorating the mess hall to make it a jolly Christmas spot. We could even run a few fancy lights out on the patio, and into the trees; like Jack did for last year's New Year's party; just to make it extra nice."

Both Jackie and Izzy didn't hesitate and said, "That's a brilliant idea."

"I do love our big family gatherings," and looking remorseful at Izzy said, "It is something we never had at Christmas."

"I am sure everybody will really remember this Christmas," Izzy chuckled. "For a lot of them it will be so very different, no snow, and hot," then quickly said, "If I remember correctly, that mess hall is air conditioned."

Everybody agreed it had been a wonderful occasion. One hundred and six casually dressed people had sat at the beautifully set tables for Christmas dinner.  With the offer of generous bonuses, the catering staff had applied themselves with gusto, and the chefs in that very up-to-date mess hall kitchen did produce a magnificent   traditional Aussie Christmas dinner. Bill's trick with those small gold nuggets in the Christmas pudding did receive great applause from the American visitors, parents and kids alike.

The one common complaint the next morning, was several adults crying, "Why, oh why did I overindulge?"

Peter's aunt Sylvia was a journalist for a daily newspaper with an extensive distribution. She of all people had a wonderful time in the six weeks they had all stayed at Quo-Vadis. Bill took it upon himself to show her almost everything, even, with Chris's permission he had shown her through those vaults in the office in the Animal Cave. Chris had suggested a nice gift may have been appreciated. That gift was a 4.5 carat diamond cut and mounted on a gold chain by Moses. She had tried to refuse it at first, but when Bill told her Chris would be most offended should she refuse the gift. It was only then she reluctantly, tongue in cheek, accepted the present. The ever-wise Bill had suggested she wear that pendant on her return flight to America. With it then being personal jewellery, it would not attract tax. Being an inquisitive female upon her return she immediately had that pendant valued. The jeweller was a little overwhelmed and did finally value it at US$540,240. While she had been at Quo-Vadis she had actually written three articles which she had sent to the editor to be included in the travel pages of the newspaper each Friday.

The edition that contained the first article, was sold out and newsagents lodged so many orders for the following week's publication the editor was required to ask the printers to make two extra runs to supply the demand. He berated her severely for not warning him prior to the first issue containing her articles, about the Outback. "I would have maximised interest by having advertisements telling of the special feature that was coming," he wailed.

The whole episode did cause some problems at the tourist park. Jamie and Vanessa had to employ two additional staff just to take the bookings that were flooding in from all over America. Jamie had a similar problem with the influx of Japanese tourists and American tourists coinciding. Thankfully Yoshiko had taken care of all those Japanese tourists. That confounded editor from Sylvia's newspaper, compounded their problem when he had taken a three-week break and had been accommodated in one of the luxury units at the resort. He had written a rather complimentary editorial in the issue of the paper printed on the day of his return. For three weeks after that the telephones at the tourist park ran hot.

Chris and Rex were most unsympathetic and had laughed loudly when Peter complained, that many of the native Stockman who should have been out herding cattle were fully occupied with tourist campouts.

Rex responded by saying, "Hark back, Mister Yank, you and your mob started this."

# Chapter 30

Ed had always been available, sitting quietly in the background. Since meeting Chris and over the ensuing years, he had been called upon by the Quo-Vadis group to produce many and a variety of things. The Quo-Vadis group, right from those early days, had become regular customers. Regardless of other pressures, Ed always ensured Quo-Vadis orders received priority attention. He had become rather successful. The demand for mini Goliaths, those ugly vehicles, not as large or as comprehensively fitted out as the original Goliath, had reached such proportions he had to install a production line and subsequently moved his operation to a much larger site, out of town. After Penny had joined him they had moved into that new house he had had Giuseppe build for them. Ed was now a very contented man.

He and Chris often met to discuss the intricacies of one of Chris's new projects, or just to talk over the complexity of running a large business. It was only today Ed had asked Chris, "Do you have many confounded problems with workers?" he complained. "I only get a man trained just right and some bastard pirates him away, by either promising him better pay or conditions. Damn it all! I pay top money and the new factory has every mod-con; it darn near sent me broke building it. When I asked them why they are leaving they usually say they feel they think a change would be good. Strangely enough, a lot of them do come back asking, is there a job available for them."

Chris was most sympathetic and offered several suggestions as to why this would happen. "The most obvious problem I think exists, Ed, is opportunity," Chris said. "I do not have the problem of staff being pirated. Being out in the Outback there is little in the way of exposure to alternatives like there is here in the city. I counsel all my supervisors to try to be aware of the needs of every man in their department. Any problem they cannot handle quickly should be bought to the notice of management. Sometimes the source of the problem is best moved on even if he, or be it she, are considered a valued worker. Rex, my brother, would tell you any negative agitator in a department is a cancer—cut it out, even if it causes some pain. In the long run, this is usually proven to be for the betterment of the whole department. With the growth you are experiencing there must be opportunities to split some larger departments. Try to install the leaders of the new areas from outside the department. Promotions to supervisor level from within the department will often cause much dissent with those not promoted, as there could easily be much talk or thinking that some individual had been overlooked for the position. Conversely, promote good people from outside the area. It's a complex situation; fortunately, I have had Rex to help me. He has much experience in this sort of thing. He is your accountant too, have a yarn to him—I'm sure he can help you."

Penny did continue painting. Ed had included a studio in their new house. She explained it was different. She didn't get the same degree of inspiration as she did when painting in the studio in the sinkhole at Quo-Vadis. As a consequence, she would often spend a week or two residing and painting in the studio back there. Annie still lived at Quo-Vadis, and they would often work together on the same painting. Some of those paintings they produced either in conjunction, or independently, continued to receive great acclaim, and invariably most paintings were sold even before they left Quo-Vadis.

The magnetite smelter had proven to be a major challenge for Chris and Bill. Before they had embarked with even giving it too much consideration, Mr Christopher Kennedy, The Miner, had almost driven the long-suffering drilling contractor, Tom, insane with his very forceful requests to put down exploration holes, here, there and everywhere. Chris had wanted to ascertain the extent of that magnetite deposit before committing what was going to be a good deal of money.

Tom's progress was very slow. In final desperation after having the drill bit break off again, deep down in the drill hole; he shouted at Chris, "This bloody magnetite stuffs up my bits two or three times a day. It is not the cost of those bits that pisses me off—you have to pay for all that—it is how much strife it is to recover the broken drill; this magnetite stuff is a fair bitch." Tom was very obviously quite cross.

The two professors, from the mining seat at the University had been "just poking about" the magnetite deposit and had heard Tom complaining. On their next visit, later in the week, they presented Tom with a drill bit made in the metallurgy laboratory at the University. It had been made from the purest of high quality magnetite that had been infused with some other elements. What those elements were they would not disclose, saying, "We would like to see the outcome of this experiment first."

Tom thanked the professors, saying, as he fitted this new bit to replace that bit which had only just broken off. "I am a desperate man I will try anything."

Later that day he was tentatively asked by Professor Strahan, "Any better, Tom?"

"Keep your fingers crossed, Prof," Tom replied. "So far so good. I do have to say with this new bit we are drilling deeper, much quicker. Do you have some more?"

He was quite disappointed when the professor told him that was a one off and he would have to learn to make his own in future.

As a result of the accelerated drilling Chris was able to establish that the magnetite deposit embraced a huge area, all within the mining lease owned by Quo-Vadis Iron.

The professors introduced Chris to a young man who was about to complete his mining degree. They had a very high regard for the lad, and considered he had a bright future in the mining industry. They had told him, "There was no better place to gain experience than with the Quo-Vadis group." Chris had not hesitated and had quickly set this young engineer to work out there on the magnetite deposit. His engagement proved to Chris. Together he and Mervyn James, that newest recruit, were able to set up a most efficient magnetite mining operation.

The magnetite smelter was a different matter. "Smelter Master Bill" had to spend a couple of months at an existing iron ore smelter before he was confident he could produce the quality magnetite product Chris required. Construction of the smelter did take some time. The professors were constantly in attendance as construction progressed and did suggest some alterations now and again. Those alterations along with the machinery being installed being the most modern and proven machines known, ensured there was no magnetite smelter in the country to its equal .

At first the smelter was used primarily to produce ingots of high quality steel. As his confidence grew and with much advice from the metallurgists from the University, who enjoyed the hands-on experience they obtained while working with that smelter, Bill commenced to add other elements to the smelting operation. Consequently, Bill produced a good range of very high-quality steels. Ranging from a variety of steels that could be used in the building industry right up to weapon grade steel for the military.

Mervyn James did not hesitate, when Chris asked him to accept the position of Magnetite Mine/Smelter Manager.

A short spur line now ran from the iron ore mine out to the magnetite smelter, and rail wagons loaded with those high-quality ingots were added to the increasing volume of rail traffic in and out of the iron ore mine.

Much to Chris's concern, many of trains were being subject to extensive delays. The major factor that caused those delays was the increasing need for line maintenance. The line had been built many years back, at the time the original iron ore mine had commenced operation.

"We do need an additional line," Chris had told Jackie, one evening as they sat together for their daily ritual of discussing the day's activities.

"What's stopping you?" she innocently asked.

"That, my love," Chris replied, "is a very good question. I'm glad you asked. I have wanted to talk to somebody for a while, and because you see things that aren't clouded by technicalities there is no-one better to bounce my problems off."

"What's the biggest problem? What do you see is the main cause for the delays?" she asked.

"It's the continual need for track replacement," Chris quickly answered. "The rail lines are not coping with the many very heavy ore trains, and the timber sleepers are subject to all sorts of problems, like rot, and, in some places, confounded termites."

Jackie only laughed as she said, "Do what you normally do: get rid of the problem. Put in better steel rails and use those concrete sleepers they use on the interstate railways."

"You are brilliant, Jackie girl," Chris enthusiastically cried. "You are right. All I have to do is to get hold of about 4000 kilometres of special steel railway line and tens of thousands of concrete sleepers. Getting that stuff will not be easy. If I can't get it, I will just have to make it."

Bill and Rex listened to the suggestion however they were rather sceptical about embarking on a project of that magnitude. The main problem ,to their minds was that; "there were no companies we know of  who could handle orders as big as that," Bill growled, only to be cut short by Chris interrupting and saying,

"Like I said to Jackie, if we cannot find anyone who can make those rails and sleepers, we will have to make them ourselves."

"I was enjoying a little peace and quiet and now as it always happens my dear brother raises his ugly head and shatters it," Rex cried, throwing his arms up in apparent exasperation and pretended to be weeping. "How much, and what is the expected return, and when do you expect to start spending all this money?"

"I have given all this much thought," Chris sighed, as if he was speaking his thoughts out aloud. "We have our own steel for the rails; that steel that comes out of the magnetite smelter is a top product and using a little imagination can be made to be absolutely perfect for the rails. We have run out of roads to build and all those tailings from the goldmines and the pegmatites mine are crying out for use. A crusher can be set to produce a volume of gravel. There is a big deposit of dolomite on the backside of the escarpment; we can add the dolomite to the gravel and produce a perfect base for the rail line. There is any amount of granite about. We do have crushers that are not operating at full capacity. One of them can be taken off-line and used to produce that very fine gravel that when added to cement, can be used to make the sleepers." He interrupted his discourse for a moment while he was thinking, then continued saying, "We will have to buy heaps of cement, and quick drying elements, build a pretty fancy batching plant and sleeper producing factory near the crusher. We could build a substantial conveyor belt and the wet mixture produced in the batching plant could be poured into sleeper moulds on that belt. The professors may be able to get the people from the civil engineering department at the Uni interested. Perhaps they will be able to offer us some advice?"

The project went ahead without a hitch. The lecturers from the civil engineering department did make a few suggestions and after being advised the research would not be constrained for want of financial support, they developed a formula that enabled the manufacture of sleepers with a sound inhibiting capacity.

Production of the rails was a different proposition. It was all very well to produce a steady flow of magnetite steel ingots. They did have a ready market for those ingots but were at a loss with what to do from there. The metallurgy department at the University had said they could help by providing a formula that could be used to produce a steel most suitable to be used for railway lines; however, they were most sceptical as they believed that the production of the amount of steel rail by the known foundries could only be done over a number of years.

Chris did never know why or how the answer appeared. Call it chance, good luck, or whatever. Chris preferred to call it providence!

The four friends—Chris, Jackie, Ed, and Penny—were sharing a very pleasant social evening dining at a very nice little restaurant in the provincial city. They were dallying over their last drinks when Chris nonchalantly mentioned the rail problem. Ed had thought for a while, then quietly asked, "Are you guys staying in town tonight? If you are about in the morning I have someone I would like you to meet."

"Jackie and I want to spend an hour or two out at the tourist park tomorrow afternoon," Chris replied. "Vanessa and Jamie only want to talk about building bigger reception facilities to handle the increased volume of business from all those overseas visitors. Tomorrow morning would be good; make it early, say seven."

"There goes my sleep in," Jackie laughed, and said, "I want to come too; something tells me this is important."

From time to time over the years, Ed had had need of a few special castings. A school friend had a small foundry—it had never amounted to much and his friend had struggled. He had never pursued his education beyond high school. He was a very intelligent man and his level of experience in the founding of metals was without peer. There was no casting, be it iron, steel, brass, aluminium, the list was endless, that eluded his ability. Unfortunately, all that experience amounted to nothing. Because of his lack of management skills and he had always struggled to keep his head above water.

Jackie and Chris were waiting in Ed's office the next morning when Fredrick (Freddie, to all,) J. Lowan entered. He acknowledged Jackie and Chris with only a nod, and promptly took a seat in the corner. Ed conducted all the traditional introductions and after the handshakes and small talk, rather bluntly said, "Freddie is in a bit of financial strife, and for what it is worth so am I. Your brother Rex has told us both we need a substantial injection of capital. Could you help us out?"

Chris had delayed his answer for a moment, then, in a very businesslike manner said, "That's what I like about you, Ed. With you there is no mucking about—you come straight to the point." Then after taking a deep breath continued, "Anybody but you Ed, I would promptly tell, 'Go jump in the lake', but since it's you Ed, I will listen. What's the proposition? How do you envisage repayment? And what security is available?"

Ed answered all this rather weakly as he replied saying, "All I have for security is my new factory. It is the reason I am so tight—I spent too much building it. Freddie only leases his factory; other than his machinery he owns nothing. He has to move the whole foundry. Residential development has crept close, and the town council have served him a notice to move."

"Not good," Chris slowly said. "I could help you, Ed, but you, Freddie, are not a good proposition."

"Chris," Jackie quickly intervened. "Can I ask Freddie a few things?"

"If you think it would be helpful, yes, please, go right ahead," Chris gently answered.

With a very firm business like voice; Jackie quickly said ; "Freddie; Ed tells us you have much foundry experience; have you ever been required to do your thing with very high-quality steel, magnetite steel?"

"Not a lot," Freddie replied. "One of the mines up north had me make some crusher jaws using special magnetite. From all reports those crusher jaws I produced were great; regrettably they told me, the price of them precluded any further orders."

Chris had seen where Jackie was heading, and quickly said, "If I asked you to produce 4000 kilometres, maybe more, of special magnetite steel rails plus fixings and a few other bits and pieces, could you?" and as an afterthought added, "I may also need a few of those special steel crusher jaws."

"Technically, that would present little problem, Mr Kennedy," Freddie answered. "Regrettably I do not have the facilities to even think of doing that."

Chris was becoming rather excited, and said very quietly to Jackie, "Jackie girl, you have really earned your keep this day." He looked very hard at Freddie, and quite loudly said, "If you had the facilities, by facilities I mean a brand-new very large foundry, fitted out with the most modern equipment, would you be interested?"

"No point in daydreaming, Mr Kennedy," Freddie ruefully answered. "That could never happen."

Ed had a grin on his ugly dial that would have put a Cheshire cat to shame as he laughed. "Shut up Freddie, take a deep breath and listen closely to Chris."

"Thanks Ed," Chris said, and without even hesitating moved his chair a little closer to Freddie, ensuring that Freddie could clearly hear what he was about to say. "Freddie! I am in need of your services. I will build you the most modern foundry in the whole country. In return, you will sell me your business, and agree to come and work with me for a minimum period of five years, after which you will be welcome to continue working with me should you wish. In that time, you will produce my railway lines, and perhaps many other things. I can envisage there will be a further commercial demand for our product. We will talk about that if and when it happens, and you Ed, you can stop laughing. I have some special projects in mind and are offering to buy your business too. We can work out details of those propositions later. I'll leave that to Rex and his boys to sort out. All I can add is that neither of you will ever regret joining me."

Rex almost had a heart attack when Chris told him what he had done. "I do respect your ability to make good decisions, brother," Rex bleated. "This one tops them all. It is your problem if you are prepared to risk your capital to bail those pair out of their troubles. Good grief! Have you any idea what's involved in setting up a foundry? That can only be done in a gazetted heavy industry subdivision. And staff?" Rex stomped around his office, waving his hands in the air, "Where the hell are you going to find them? What a challenge!"

"We already have the staff in Freddie's foundry," Chris interrupted his ravings, "and the modern equipment being so efficient, I cannot see the need arising for too many more staff."

From then on it all happened. Chris had purchased a 500-acre block about sixty kilometres from the provincial city boundary. The city's town planner, although it had little to do with him, had laughed at Chris's application to have that block rezoned as heavy industrial. Chris received similar treatment from the Crown Lands Department. Their laughter had turned to sneer when Chris submitted a further application for Quo-Vadis Holdings Pty. Ltd. to purchase all the land embraced by his grazing and mining leases.

"Forget it, Mr Kennedy, to grant freehold over grazing and mining leases is very rare, and because of the extent of your leases you have no hope of approval."

They quickly reversed their attitude when Jack bought his Political Science Training to the fore, possibly "aided" by the pressure brought to bear by some of Jack's friends from the Political Science classes he had shared with them, who had gone on to become elected parliamentarians. The pressure on the Crown Lands Department was further increased when the people from the higher echelon of the Treasury Department intervened further. Chris finally received a letter from the Crown Land Department, which said sale of the nominated land had been approved, and officers from the Department will be travelling to Quo-Vadis to ascertain the value of those improvements he had made to the leases, and requested he reply to the letter advising them of his estimate of the value of those improvements. Chris's reply was very short; it simply said, "We conservatively value those improvements at a minimum of $15 billion." Those four officers from the Lands Department, stayed at the Quo-Vadis resort for three weeks. Chris did not show them more than one goldmine and somehow the diamond mine was overlooked in their scrutiny. The four men did become rather pleasant about his request and at the completion of their assessment and their visit and agreed unanimously the value of the improvements could be set at $15 billion.

The whole settlement then became a very complex affair. "Thank goodness for Rex and his office," Chris had told Jackie. "They simply took over and very efficiently completed the whole transaction."

It was required by law that sale of those blocks be advertised. Several hopeful applicants quickly withdrew their applications when advised purchase price was $15 billion plus $50 and much of the land was subject to native title. It was agreed with a lot of humour, that the $15 billion the Crown lands Department was to pay Chris for the improvements could be offset with the $15 billion Chris was to pay for the land. Rex had made a special visit to the Lands Department and several of the officers laughed with him as he handed over that $50 note by way of settlement. All this had taken over six months; although the outcome had been completely satisfactory, the delay had annoyed Chris. "I must be getting old and cranky," he laughed as he explained all that had happened to Jackie.

In the interim, Freddie, Bill and Freddie had not been idle and had researched, ordered, and now awaited delivery of much of the plant to set up the new foundry. That huge empty shell of a building, with all the modifications included, sat patiently awaiting the new machinery.

Freddie was ecstatic. He told Bill, "I used to read those mining magazines that came out every month, and almost drooled over some of the machines advertised. Now they are coming here. I can hardly wait."

The batching plant (the concrete mixing plant) had been fully operational for one month and stocks of those special sleepers lay in the marshalling yard awaiting dispatch. The sleepers all had fixing bolts positioned as the cement was poured into the moulds. The batching plant overseer was a pedantic type. He watched each and every one of those sleepers as they emerged from the plant on that four-kilometre long conveyor belt. The cement mix did include quick drying additives and by the time those moulds had travelled the slow four-kilometre trip the cement had hardened sufficiently allowing those moulds to be moved off the conveyor belt so they could be stored for a further two days. They were then inverted and the finished sleeper extracted and quickly loaded onto flat-bed trolleys to be taken to the dispatch yard.

Several track-laying machines sat on rails all ready for use. Eighteen months from that meeting in Ed's office, the first beautiful special steel magnetite rails made their appearance. That rail line site became an organised "melee."

Chris had surveyed the route the new line was to take. With the advantage of satellite views, his new line was able to avoid the need of those tight curves which the ore trains could only negotiate by slowing down to a little more than walking pace. He did incorporate several short tunnels. Now all those crushed tailings were being laid to form a very dense track ballast. The installation of that ballast had already travelled over fifty kilometres before the sleepers and the rails had commenced to follow along behind the ballast crew. A good-natured competition developed between the ballast laying crew, and the rail laying crews, to see who could complete the greatest distance each week. Chris had encouraged that competition by awarding the winning crew a twelve-litre keg. He had engaged a highly experienced track laying contractor. The contractor was a little perplexed when Chris required that a 1.75 metre access tunnel had to be placed adjacent to the rail line. He was further confused when another contractor arrived, and commenced laying that very expensive electrical cable and attendant equipment, along with water pipes in that tunnel, and asked further questions of Chris: "What are these very solid concrete block foundations we have to install, all equidistant apart on both sides of the track to be used for?"

Chris had only smiled and answered, "That's for me to know, and you to guess." All the contractors had been warned; on completion of the first line, they were to immediately commence the construction of a second line adjacent to this first line.

The first seventy-two wagon ore train was sent down that new track and completed the trip in two hours less than the fastest time previously achieved. The train driver engineers were particularly impressed with those long sweeping curves the train could negotiate without having to slow down. "The whole trip is now so quiet, because of those sound inhibiting sleepers; we can even listen to music as we travelled," one of the drivers enthusiastically replied when asked "How was the trip?" by another train crew who had yet to travel the new line.

Rex was very pleased with, "This track maintenance cost." He had told Chris. By calling the cost of those two tracks, "track maintenance," he was able to halve the tax burden of the holding company for the next three years, and, tongue in cheek, said, "Keep it up bro. Do you have any more tricks in mind?"

"Good question, my pencil pushing brother," Chris happily replied. "Since you ask, I will tell you, I do have a thought or two of things yet to be done."

The recruitment of people to build up the staff level required to operate the foundry, surprisingly enough proved little problem. Every applicant was made very aware they would be required to travel that sixty kilometres from their homes in the regional city. Most of them organised and joined very effective carpooling schemes. The very attractive salaries and the most modern of conditions offered did offset this negative aspect.

Chris was unhappy with the carpooling need, and with the permission of the city fathers, and the transport department, Chris was allowed to install an electrified rail line to the heavy industrial subdivision. Now fast, very comfortable, Ed designed electric trains, operated a scheduled service, from a specified platform in the provincial city to the subdivision.

Ed had watched the growth of that subdivision, and because he was part of that octopus, "Quo-Vadis Holdings" Chris quickly agreed for Ed to have his operation moved to be adjacent to the foundry. Other private heavy industries had also looked upon the site and had considered it had many appealing facets, and in short time a small satellite industrial community developed.

As was their ilk, property developers recognised the potential and residential sub-divisions appeared along the way. The rail line patronage did increase to such a level that Chris found it necessary to install three additional lines to enable the scheduling of express trains.

It was mandatory for all the heads of all at Quo-Vadis companies to meet on the first Monday of each month. Comprehensive reports were required and all were given an opportunity to air anything that had occurred with them during the past month, be it negative or positive. One matter that had been raised at the last meeting was the ageing of the transport fleet and the increased cost of fuel to operate it. It was accepted by all that the cost of fuel would always be ongoing and the cost to replace the fleet did amount to many dollars. The matter was not really resolved that meeting, and each officer was invited to think about it and bring any thoughts to the next meeting.

Chris had only winked broadly at Rex. "Uh oh," Rex thought to himself. "What's he up to now?"

Rex and his wife had stayed overnight at Quo-Vadis. As they shared dinner that evening, Chris rather enthusiastically said to Rex, "That matter about the transport fleet Jeff raised this morning fits into one of my ideas. What do you think of an idea to hook up the line that already exists between the pegmatites mine and the iron ore mine and on to the coastal town and to run the line through to Quo-Vadis? We could even run a short spur line out to Peter's cattle yards. From Quo-Vadis we could run an 850-kilometre line to the heavy-duty subdivision. As you know, we already have a very good electrified line from there to the regional city. I would not want to run rail tracks to the resort. A rail line out there would only intrude on that beautiful ambience that exists out there.

I would need your thoughts on this bit, Rex! Presently we have surplus power from our power station in the sinkhole. By the way, I'm thinking of installing two more generators not to service any particular need, at present, as we already have 900 MW available. The two generators I am looking at have quite a bit larger output capacity. Each generator will produce one GW; that's equal to one thousand MW. We have the water flow to drive those brutes. I will be surprised if we ever have to put them both "on line" at the same time. They will cost a shilling or two; we could offset some of that cost by selling our excess power to the government.

The power station operators had laughed when they told me that the day we switched on all the crushers and smelters and hooked in all the new equipment at the magnetite mines the meters recording the power consumption only kicked up to 31%, which included all the existing power of being consumed in the gold mines, the resort and the whole of the township. They were really impressed when the valve on the penstock opened automatically and an extra generator kicked in."

"It is just as well Jackie and Ellie were not cooking that day; those two may have just overloaded the system," Rex laughed.

"Regardless of how much power that pair used," Chris chuckled, "it would not have made any difference to the power network; all the houses, and all gear in the caves in the sinkhole, are serviced by the first generators we installed in the caves. How's the 'bickie' barrel holding, Rex?" Chris joked.

"Doing alright at present," Rex replied. "When you start planning it does scare me a little. Your own personal account is my biggest problem. With you still holding 68% of the B-class shares your personal dividend we are about to pay, will be around $65 million; add that to the dividends you have received over past years, much of which is unspent, it is quite a worry. Better send Jackie shopping again," he laughed.

"Leave me about twenty-five million in the account, just for pocket money," Chris said trying to be funny. "Transfer the rest to Holdings as director's loans; by the time I have finished I may need it there."

"This sounds interesting, and I do hesitate, but I must ask why?" Rex said, not without a little panic in his voice.

"It's like this, brother of mine," Chris replied, "now that we have replaced all the old line from that iron ore mine to the provincial city, with a dual rail line, and have that existing dual line from the iron ore mine to Quo Vadis Lithium, I'm going to extend that line from there all the way to Quo-Vadis, then 840 kilometres to the Provincial City, via the industrial subdivision. That will give us a very good rail link all the way from the Coastal Port to the Provincial City. I want to electrify the whole network, all 4000-plus kilometres of it, and replace the existing fuel-driven locomotives with new electric locos. Foundations for the stanchions to support the overhead wires that the locos draw their power from, are already in place in that section of line we have just finished building. The high-tension power cable and appropriate substations have already been installed in that section also. One attractive aspect of all this will be the major fuel saving, and because maintenance on those electric locos is nothing like maintaining the existing diesel locos, there will be a further saving there."

Chris's plan was enthusiastically received at the next monthly meeting. Bill made everyone laugh when he very solemnly said, "This bloke, this madman, Chris Kennedy forgot to mention that everybody will be on dry bread and water while he does this."

Everybody at that meeting had a comment or two to add. Peter was obviously pleased when Chris agreed a short spur line from that mainline to the cattle yards at Quo-Vadis Station was of good merit after Peter had explained, "that moving stock to market by rail would ensure, since the stock would not be subject to the rock 'n' roll of the road trip, they would arrive at the market in much better condition."

Bill had also contributed to the discussion by saying, "The mint people would be very happy when we offer to deliver all the gold bullion from the mines in a special armoured rail wagons. It will alleviate their present need of having to send a special crew and armoured car out to Quo-Vadis each month."

Suggestions came thick and fast; all were strongly in support of the plan. Vanessa had waited to the very last before she offered her suggestion and did warn Chris what had come to her mind, would take a little time to explain. "Go right ahead Vanessa girl," Chris answered her, and continued saying, "That's what these meetings are for, we expect everyone, even a dumb broad like you, to have their say," as he ducked to avoid the pens and pencils she threw at him.

"I'll dumb broad you, smart arse; you can apologise after you hear what I have to say." She was laughing good-heartedly as she said this and continued. "Our tourist trade can gain greatly with what you are thinking of doing. Think on this. We can offer tourists three to four week fully air-conditioned train trips through the Outback. We could even go much further than that. We are aware that cruise ships are operating up and down the coast all the time these days. We can offer cruise operators a package they could add to their itinerary. Make those trains into something special, private compartments with their own mini ensuites, community carriages, really top-class dining carriages, evening entertainment, the list goes on and on. What I am trying to say is make that train the most luxurious train in the world. I think you should consider running a spur line up and along the escarpment. The views from up there are truly spectacular—ask Penny and Annie, they will tell you they never stop finding new vistas to paint. You could even incorporate a visit to one of the working goldmines. When I come to give it a little more consideration, there is much more. I have not had a chance to discuss this with Jamie—he usually has a few bright ideas."

Rex just threw his hands into the air, and wailed in a hopeless voice, "I was hoping to run those trains at a loss. With your idea, Vanessa, I can see those trains may not make that much of a profit but the overall value to the group is very real."

Chris stood and addressed the meeting. "I thank you one and all, for your opinions; we will now embark on this massive project."

The construction of the rail lines and the electrification of the network was finally completed after three years. At times the contractors had over 20,000 men working over various portions of those four thousand kilometres.

Bill and Chris would sit at some advantageous point and watch; they were totally hypnotised with what had the appearance of a very angry ants nest. It did cause Bill to comment, laughing as he said, "I am glad we contracted all this out; it makes me dizzy just watching."

Ed's staff these days included several highly qualified engineers. Those engineers were called upon to design and supervise the building of those very special electric locomotives, built to Chris's specifications. They found the challenge stimulating and enjoyable.

Ed's factory even built all the carriages. The carriages were extremely comfortable and did contained large spacious compartments as had been suggested by Vanessa. Ed had added a few  extra touches to her suggestion and had fitted the compartments out with king-size beds, lounge chairs, as well as the mini ensuite and a small kitchen. They were serviced daily by competent staff. The dining car had been modified and a second level added. This level was set up as a complete night club.

The Outback tour included in the cruise operator's itineraries were most popular. At times, those beautiful trains contained up to fifty passenger carriages and with all the extras, like beautiful dining carriages, community carriages, etc. etc. the trains did reach up to seventy carriages long. Those silver trains were a most impressive sight as they streaked almost silently across the Outback.

Chris, Jackie, Rex and his wife, Bill and Ellie, did do the "tourist thing," and as a group, took the whole package. At the completion of the trip they sat in the lounge of Chris and Jackie's home and talked over the plusses and minuses of the trip.

"I have one major complaint," Jackie very seriously offered, and then endeavouring not to laugh, exclaimed, "It was far too short. When can we do it again?"

Isobel, Rex's wife simply said; "she had loved the trip and being a Townie (a person who lived their life in the city.) Although she had been living on the Quo-Vadis station for a few years; she had never experienced the enchantment and beauty of the Outback. Before taking this trip, she knew little about this beautiful place. One thing I could suggest is that it would be really good is to have an old rugged bushman type set up in one of the entertainment carriages for say half an hour each morning to tell those travellers who were interested, a little of the history of The Outback and a few of the tales, be they fact or fiction and perhaps highlight their relativity to the area they were to travel through that day. That land is ever changing as one travels through it. One day it is flat and parched, the next day it may be rugged with colourful cliffs and plateaus or changing to vast swamp like land. An air of mystery and intrigue seems to prevail all the time.

The Quo-Vadis Foundry, now managed by Freddie and guided financially by those very talented accountants from Kennedy and Dixon, had changed from a small firm on the verge of bankruptcy, to a very successful vibrant business. Many of the heavy industry businesses that had opened in this estate had found the rail connection to their doorstep was most useful, in particular Ed, who had moved his manufacturing business to be adjacent to the foundry.

The prime product of the foundry, in this initial stage, were those steel rails. Magnetite ingots from the smelters were able to be railed directly to the foundry from the smelters at the magnetite mine for processing. The quality of those rails received international recognition, and Freddie had a substantial backlog of orders awaiting completion. That very modern production line requiring a minimum number of staff was most efficient and the foundry was able to complete not only Chris's rail requirements but those international orders also. Once again the rail network proved its value. Those orders were loaded onto flat-bed wagons and left the foundry by rail, either destined for locations out in the Outback or ports all over the country to be loaded onto ships from far distant lands.

# Chapter 31

Rex was having all sorts of problems keeping up with Chris. "Good grief, bro," he cried, "I only just set up in a new building and before I know it, BANG, you find us another company to add to the list of those we already look after. The time is long past for me to move the business into premises that have the potential for expansion if necessary. Kennedy and Dixon have always been located in the city's business centre and many of our very good clients operate from premises in and about there, so it is prudent for us to remain in the CBD."

Rex, Chris, and Jackie had an appointment with an owner of what appeared to be a suitable site. Rex was called away at the last minute and asked Chris to go ahead with the appointment saying, "I will catch up." They had plenty of time, so Chris had decided to walk to the meeting. The walk took them past the new redevelopment of the inner-city railway station and adjacent bus complex.

"I used to catch my bus from here," he nostalgically told Jackie. "I wonder if Mrs Mac still has the news agency." The news agency was still there, and Mrs Mac buzzed from customer to customer ensuring their needs were well attended to. As she approached Chris and Jackie she quietly said, "What can I do for you fine looking pair?"

Chris had only smiled broadly and said, "I would like a system nine in the next lotto please."

Mrs Mac hesitated at that, and after looking a little closer she exclaimed, "Chris! You know when you walked in I thought to myself, I think I know him. How are you? You look very well. You have not changed much, and who is this lovely creature?"

"You haven't changed one little bit Mrs Mac," Chris quickly replied. "You are still able to talk at 1000 words a minute.

This is my wife Jackie. I have told her how you sold me that winning ticket."

Jackie gently took Mrs Mac's hand and softly said, laughing all the time, "So it was you that started the mess this man has made of his life."

"What?! What?!" Mrs Mac cried in alarm. "I have not spoken to him in years; if he is in a mess it is his own doing!"

Jackie only squeezed her hand a little firmer and chuckled, "I am joking Mrs Mac; this beautiful husband of mine has done so much in his short life."

"You have me all confused," Mrs Mac sighed. "You have aroused my curiosity. I would like to hear the whole story. There is a nice little coffee shop next door. You can buy me a coffee and explain all this to me," and called over her shoulder to a man behind the counter, "Take over, Jake, I'm going for a coffee."

Over two cups of coffee Jackie had explained much and Mrs Mac had a twinkle in her eyes when she said, "He has made one hell of a mess; it is a nice mess, I must say," then added, "You are lucky to have caught me still here. By the end of the month I will have moved out, everybody on the block has been given the boot, you know kicked out."

"Kicked out?" Chris questioned.

"Yeah," Mrs Mac replied, "Some investment mob from India has bought the whole block and is going to pull it down and I hear they are going to set up a huge outdoor market selling all sorts of cheap stuff."

"That's a shame," Chris growled. "It is a superb site. It's perfect for all you little businesses, opposite the bus station and I hear the underground railway has been diverted to have a central city station underground over the road from it. That would have fed many passers-by to your shops."

"We have heard about all that too, Chris," Mrs Mac sharply said, "but because none of us are landlords the Council tell us nothing."

"OUCH!" Chris suddenly cried.

"What's up?" Mrs Mac concernedly asked.

"I kicked him in the shin to wake him up, Mrs Mac," Jackie chuckled. "Are you with me, Mister?"

"I better say yes, otherwise I'll get kicked again," Chris laughed.

"Look at it, Chris," cried Jackie. "It is the perfect site just crying out to be developed properly."

Chris thought for a few moments then softly said, "You have done it again, you beautiful creature; you come up with the right answer every time. We need to look not one-inch further." "Mrs Mac," he addressed his old friend, "You will not have to move for too long. I will buy the site from your oppressors. Yes! I will rip everything out and, in its place, build a forty to fifty-storey building. There will be provision for shops on the lower two levels, and even a few apartments on a couple of upper floors. The majority of those floors remaining will be tenanted offices. Mrs Mac, if you would be good enough to arrange a meeting with all the shopkeepers, say Monday next week, I will bring my brother Rex, and I will talk it over with you all."

For quite a while the project did turn out to be a little bit messy. Jack again used his influence, and after Rex had met with the city planner and the Council, the permit for the outdoor market was withdrawn and approval given for the construction of that very up-to-date modern office block.

Those overseas developers did make an obnoxiously large profit when they sold the land to that octopus Quo-Vadis Holdings.

"I thought octopi only had eight tentacles, but this beast has many more," Rex complained as he was in the midst of organising yet another department to administer the affairs of Quo-Vadis City No.1 Pty. Ltd.

In his typical fashion, Chris ensured the quality building was completed quickly. Those shop holders who had had premises on the site had been temporarily relocated on adjacent land and were most enthusiastic with what they saw as they watched the building as it progressed. It was a fine example of imaginative architecture, built U-shaped embracing a small manicured park and walking paths that wound through attractive flower beds. Seats and a few rustic tables were placed beneath mature trees specially procured to provide a little shade. At night the park was lit up by "farie" lights strung throughout the trees, that attracted shoppers to the area   All the new shops faced out onto the park. The shopkeepers were unanimous in their approval. The gentleman's hairdresser did comment, "Bit better than the old premises, and the good part is rental is less than 25% we used to pay." Mrs Mac's newsagency held a prime position.

Chris did receive a small subsidy toward the total cost of having an underground concourse installed under the street. The city planner enthusiastically agreed the proposed commercial block was a far better use for the land and that the under-road concourse alleviated the potential pedestrian problem caused by the rail and bus stations. It was most advantageous to the proprietors to those shops; that access to that concourse was placed in the middle of that small park and that bus and train travellers were almost fed into their laps.

Kennedy and Dixon were situated in the twenty top levels, and other office areas were soon absorbed by many businesses. That very good law firm Chris used so often was also one of the early tenants.

This little project all happened while Chris was building his new rail network. "It's true," Rex lightly laughed to Jackie, "That thing on that man's shoulders is not really a head; it is one very big can of worms. How he keeps track of everything amazes me."

"Me too," Jackie was smiling as she said, "I used to worry his brain would explode; now I can only believe he does not have a brain but does have a very big something that's very scary in there. Whenever I do get a chance to 'see it,' I can never work out where it starts or where it ends, so nowadays I just hang on and hope for the best."

# Chapter 32

Rex and Jackie had cornered Chris. "My wonderful man, my wonderful husband and father, my wonderful provider, and most of all my wonderful lover," she started and continued on saying, "your brother who truly admires you, and I, who truly love you, have decided – Enough is Enough. Rex tells me that the information board he is required to have displayed at his office entrance that informs people that these are the registered officers of all your Quo-Vadis companies is so large it takes over three quarters of the walls in the reception room. You have so much! In fact, so much I do not know half of it; it is time for you to sit back and watch Jack and all those very talented men and women you have employed run the ship. Perhaps, you could take some time for yourself and even take up that offer from the University to give a lecture or two now and again; most of all, you could spend much time with me. I am sure there are many beds that require fixing."

That last bit went clear over Rex's head. "I am not going to ask what Jackie means by that," Rex laughed as he said, "Listen to what she is saying; Bro. it is time to leave a bit for others."

There is another thing, Mister," Jackie very firmly said, "There is so much of the Outback out there crying for you to come and explore it. I want to take some of Peter's best horses and spend much time with you out there. Not to discover more minerals, OR," she could hardly keep from laughing, "or to get pregnant again! It would be so you and I together could get in touch with this wonderful land again."


The story of the dynasty of Christopher Kennedy the Miner as it proceeded down the years, is perhaps worthy of being told at some later time.

www.ingramcontent.com/pod-product-compliance
Lightning Source LLC
Chambersburg PA
CBHW051929020726
47501CB00001B/37